I0736078

BRANDED *by a song*

LJ EVANS

This book is a work of fiction. While reference might be made to actual historical events or existing people and locations, the events, names, characters, places and incidents are either the product of the author's imagination or are used fictitiously, and any resemblance to actual persons, living or dead, business establishments, events, or locales is entirely coincidental.

Published by LJ Evans Books
www.ljevansbooks.com

Cover Design: © LJ Evans Books
Cover Images: © Unsplash kiwihug and Deposit Photos ninanaina / MaslovaLarisa / Olga_Bonitas / kateja
Developmental and Line Editing: Evans Editing
Copy Editor: Jenn Lockwood Editing Services
Sensitivity Editors: Griot Editing Services and Hong Kobzeff
Proofing: Karen Hrdlicka

Library of Congress Cataloging-in-Publications in process.
ISBN: 978-1-962499-06-4

Printed in the United States

BRANDED
by a song

LJ EVANS

War of Art by Tim McGraw
The Ones That Didn't Make It Back
Home by Justin Moore
Hard Days by Brantley Gilbert
When You're Gone by The Cranberries
Forever's Gotta Start Somewhere by Chard Brownlee
Holding Out For a Hero by Elise Lieberth
It Goes Like This by Thomas Rhett
Just a Fool by Christina Aguilera w/ Blake Shelton
Take Your Time by Sam Hunt
Meant to Be by Bebe Rexha w/ Florida Georgia Line
Look What God Gave her by Thomas Rhett
Let It Be by The Beatles
Somebody Like You by Keith Urban
I Wonder What You Kiss Like by
Natalie Pearson & Brooks Chivell
Last Habit by Matt Stell
I Have a Dream by ABBA
Prayed for You by Matt Stell
Don't Stop by Fleetwood Mac
What Ifs by Kane Brown w/ Lauren Alaina
God Whispered Your Name by Keith Urban
Here Tonight by Brett Young
Somebody Like That by Tenille Arts
Nobody But You by Blake Shelton w/ Gwen Stefani
The Good Ones by Gabby Barrettt
In Case You Didn't Know by Brett Young
Dreams by The Cranberries
Got What I Got by Jason Aldean
Chiquitita by ABBA
Someone You Loved by Mitchell Tenpenny
Why We Try by Matthew Mayfield w/ Chelsea Lanske
Done by Chris Janson
But I Do Love You by LeAnn Rimes
Has Anyone Ever Written Anything For You by Stevie Nicks
Be a Light by Thomas Rhett

Dedication

To Kelly, my beautiful sister, who loves rock stars more than the world, who introduced me to the hair bands of the '80s up close and personal, and who is so talented it hurts.

To Megan, for being on this book journey with me from almost the beginning, for never holding back your punches, and for being the gift you are to me and the world.

Chapter one

Brady

WAR OF ART
Performed by Tim McGraw

The jet landing on the runway in Albany jerked me out of a fitful sleep. I dragged a hand through my sandy hair and rubbed the sleep from my eyes as I fought against the exhaustion trying to pull me back under. It felt like I could sleep for a month straight and never rid myself of the bone-weary feeling gathered deep inside my soul.

It was due to much more than the long days of the world tour I'd just wrapped up. This tiredness was tangled with the twisting doubts circling through me that the critics might be right. My music *was* stale and repetitive.

My songwriting partner, Ava, would rant and rave at me if she heard my silent agreement with the naysayers. The lyrics, hers and mine joined together, weren't exactly the same, but the rhythms and chords blended so precariously close to all the other songs I'd released that it was hard to tell the difference between my first album and my third. There was no growth. No hint of change.

The reviewers had heard the truth I was trying to hide from myself and the world. There was a hole in my world—in my soul—and it reflected in my music. A gaping emptiness that begged to be filled. Knowing it only made me more of a cliché than ever before.

I needed a break from it all to try and find the heart that usually drove me.

As the jet doors opened, I wondered if staying with my family for the holidays was really the smart choice. I was pretty sure it would take the utter fatigue I felt and amp it up by about a hundred watts until every single part of me ached. But I hadn't missed a Christmas with my family yet, and I wasn't going to start now. It was bad enough we'd all left Cassidy alone for Thanksgiving. Oddly enough, my little sister had seemed relieved we wouldn't be there to cut the soy alternative turkey with her.

As my bodyguard, Marco, and I walked down the stairs, high-pitched screaming exploded into the chilly air. My head jerked toward the private airline terminal where a crowd was being held back by rope and security personnel I didn't know. There seemed to be a revolving door of them these days with Garner's company. It made me even more grateful for the man at my side, who'd been through the fires of hell and back with me.

A black SUV with tinted windows pulled onto the runway in front of us, blocking me from the crowd at the terminal.

"Your parents are in the SUV and ready to go," Marco said, his deep voice matching his muscular frame. His black hair and dark eyes almost matched the black he always wore. He was so dark from head to toe, he could almost be a shadow if his skin wasn't the shade of cut oak instead of deep night.

The crowd grew frenzied as we hit the tarmac. My name squealing out of hundreds of fans echoed around the space. I wasn't sure I had much to give them today.

"How'd they find out we were even here?" I asked.

Marco didn't respond, as unsure as I was of how the press and the fans found things out. He just stood there, waiting for my move.

The crew of the private jet set our luggage down, and we moved toward the SUV in tandem. As Marco threw the cases in the back, the only other long-term member of my security team emerged from the driver's seat. Trevor was as opposite to Marco as you could get. Light hair. Light eyes. Lean instead of Marco's mean. But they were both smart, savvy, and had proved themselves over and over again, even when there had been gunfire and loss of life. I didn't know what I'd do if they weren't watching my back.

"Hey, Trev, enjoy your holidays," I said, pulling him into a brief hug.

"You too, man," he said, slapping my back before pushing me away with a fist to the shoulder. He exchanged greetings with Marco before heading off toward the main terminal and the flight he was catching home.

The back door of the SUV opened, and my dad stepped out followed by my mom. Her face lit up at the sight of me, and my heart lurched with regret at my earlier thoughts of not wanting to be with them for Christmas. My parents loved me. I loved them. Love was never a limited commodity in our household—

only understanding.

Mom looked older than when I'd seen her in August, but she was as carefully put together as she always was in her tailored jeans and fitted jacket. She was in good shape for a woman closer to sixty than fifty. Her hair had once been the same dirty-blonde color as mine but was now littered with white, making it seem like she'd spent hours getting highlights in a fancy salon.

"*Mo leanbh*," she said as she enveloped me in a hug. No matter how old I was, I was still her baby. It was reassuring and disconcerting.

"Hey, Mom," I said, hugging her back tightly.

Mom let me go, and Dad took her place, wrapping me in a hug of his own. His clipped gray hair and beard made him look a bit like the Grissom character on *CSI*, the Basque heritage showing in his square face and square body that I'd inherited.

He patted me on the back and stepped away. "It's good to see you."

"Marco!" Mom greeted my bodyguard with almost as much enthusiasm as she'd greeted me.

Dad pounded him on the back.

The crowd grew frantic, screams blaring through the cold air that filled the Albany skies with clouds and pending storms.

My mom startled at the screams, glancing toward the group gathered.

"Why are they here?" Mom asked.

I wanted to laugh but kept it to myself. Mom would never get what my life was like since becoming famous. I'd tried to include my parents in it so they could see it for themselves, but they'd only been to a couple of the smaller concerts early on. They'd never seen me in front of tens of thousands of fans.

"I'll be right back," I said, heading toward the crowd.

"What are you doing? I thought we were leaving?" Mom called.

I ignored her, almost running to the fans who were smiling and happy to see me. They were already snapping pictures and shooting videos with their phones. Marco was at my side, straight-faced and in mission mode while he scanned the throng.

"Y'all showed up for little ol' me?" I said to the group, and they were screaming my name in return, shoving out papers and phones.

The first person I reached was a plus-sized woman with auburn hair and brilliant green eyes. Pretty in a way I was sure got overlooked by many of the people in her life. I took the paper from her hand.

"Who should I make it out to, babe?" I asked and wanted to smack myself in the head at the word 'babe.' It proved just how tired I was, because it only slipped out of me when my brain and my body were beyond tired these days.

"Deena. D-e-e-n-a. Oh my God. I can't believe you're actually here," she breathed out, eyes awestruck.

"Deena, your gorgeous smile and candy-apple green eyes are gonna be stuck in my head for days," I told her, giving her back the paper and then grabbing her phone from her other hand.

I stuck my arm out as far as I could, then turned so I was placing a kiss on her cheek while taking the selfie. When I turned back, she was ten shades of red.

"You have a beautiful holiday, Deena," I said and then moved to the next person along the rope.

I spent about fifteen minutes signing everything, including arms, papers, and CDs. Taking selfies while smiling, flirting, and reminding myself that these were the people who'd made everything happen for me. These were the people who bought my songs, not some stuffy critic, sitting behind a desk, using his words like a knife to my gut.

My phone pinged out my manager's ringtone. It was my "Ghost" single that had rocketed up the charts off my second album—right before everything had gone to hell with Fiona, the stalker. Right before we'd upped the security details with Garner's men and they'd given me the code name based on the song title. I'd laughed at the time and said if I was Ghost then Lee was the leader. I'd changed his name on my phone and never changed it back.

> *GHOST TEAM LEADER: Trevor says there's a crowd there. Stop signing autographs and go spend time with your family.*

Lee was right. I was using the crowd to delay the inevitable—sitting in a car with my parents for an hour while we drove home to Grand Orchard. Pretending for them. Wearing the cheerful face they knew as their son, Cormac, rather than the country singer, Brady O'Neil.

I handed back the paper I was signing and then smiled at the rest of the throng. "Sorry, darlin's, that's all I have time for today. I hope you all have a beautiful holiday, whichever ones you're celebrating."

I blew the mob a kiss while people continued to clamor my name, disappointment curling through their voices and me. I hated letting them down. But if I didn't stop at some point, I'd be there for hours, and the longer I stayed in one place, the more people would show up.

On the way back to the SUV, my phone buzzed again.

GHOST TEAM LEADER: Remember they love you.

We both knew he wasn't talking about the mob. More than just my business manager, Lee was the person who kept me on track whenever I started to derail.

ME: I've never questioned it.

GHOST TEAM LEADER: Remember you actually have a family to spend the holidays with.

ME: I'm one of the lucky ones.

GHOST TEAM LEADER: Damn straight.

ME: Hug your parents for me.

Like the rest of my team, Lee was going home to his family for a much-needed break.

GHOST TEAM LEADER: Mom will say you do it better.

ME: She'd be right.

GHOST TEAM LEADER: Smart-ass.

I climbed into the SUV, glancing into the back at my parents. Mom looked frustrated, and Dad looked like he'd been pacifying her—both familiar actions and reactions. Ones that went back decades and had nothing to do with the fact that I'd just made them wait fifteen minutes, although I was pretty sure it was what had started the conversation.

I did the one thing I didn't want to do. I smiled and asked them how classes were going. It was worth it when Mom's face changed from an almost scowl to pleasure. She dove into a discussion about the prestigious college in Ireland they were guest professors at for the year. They talked about the differences between the students and the faculty there versus the one at Wilson-Jacobs College here in the States, where they'd taught my entire life.

It was never a surprise to me that my parents were well-liked by their students. They were dynamic, attractive, and impassioned. Mom energized the undergraduates with various Gaelic and Celtic stories and legends, while Dad bestowed the gift of languages and cultures to them.

While they'd been hip-deep in the world of academia, I'd been traveling the world, wrapping up the tour. We'd coordinated our arrival back in the States so we could drive home together.

"How was Japan?" Dad asked.

"It was Paris." Dad seemed embarrassed by my correction, and I softened it with a smile, adding on, "It was good."

It had been good—until the critics had started tearing at me.

"When do you leave again?" Mom asked.

"I have to be in New York for the New Year's Eve show. Then, I'll be in L.A. for a few weeks, wrapping up the live episodes of *Fighting for the Stars* and attending a couple of award shows. After that, I'll have a break."

"I wish you'd been able to come home more over the last few months," Mom said, her worry for Cassidy showing as it always did.

When they'd first told Cass and me about the guest professor positions in Ireland, I'd promised to come home more often. I'd promised because Cass had made me. She hadn't wanted to be the reason they passed up a once-in-a-lifetime opportunity, and it had felt like a fair compromise at the time. A lie to my parents to give my sister what she craved: time to be an adult.

In my mother's book, I'd smashed all my promises to hell when I'd extended the international tour for five more stops. It wasn't anything new to our relationship. Mom expected me to drop the ball when it came to Cassidy. The trust she gave me was always tissue-paper thin and easily punctured.

My only solace was that Cassidy had insisted she was doing fine. As if she could hear my thoughts, my phone buzzed with a text from her.

CASS: Where are you?

ME: Just leaving the terminal. We should be home in about an hour. Miss me that much?

CASS: I'm freaking out.

Cassidy wasn't really a freak-out kind of person. She was a buckle-down-and-get-things-done kind of person. She'd gone from graduating at the top of her class at college to spearheading a campaign on nutrition for the local clinic, all at twenty-three.

> *ME: Why? What's up?*

> *CASS: Promise you won't take their side.*

> *ME: Cass, now you're freaking me out. What the hell?*

> *CASS: I shouldn't have said anything. Forget it.*

> *ME: Not likely. Did you destroy the house?*

> *CASS: God no, nothing like that.*

> *ME: What could angelic you possibly have done that would upset them?*

> *CASS: I'm hardly an angel, big brother.*

Like it or not, our mother would always see her that way.

> *ME: Tell me what's going on.*

> *CASS: I'm just nervous. It'll be fine. I'll see you soon.*

Cass was never nervous. Calm. Driven. But not

the anxious type. So, for her to be jittery meant something big was up. But even after multiple prompts, she stayed silent. I stared out the window, wondering what the heck was going on with her. Mom and Dad were chatting in the background, oblivious to my inner turmoil, but Marco looked over at me a couple of times with a raised eyebrow.

I just shook my head. There was nothing I could do about any of it until we arrived.

My phone buzzed again, this time with a message from my friend and PR manager.

> *DANI: The idiot from The Reporter doesn't know what he's talking about.*

Dani had taken a flight direct from Paris to Georgia, to the waiting arms of the man she loved, a retired Navy SEAL who'd helped with our security for a while. Together, they were carving a life for themselves on an estate that had been in his family since before the Revolutionary War. I could feel her slipping away from me as they made plans for their family-owned business's new charity. I'd told Lee to expect her resignation any day. We had a bet going on how soon it was going to happen.

> *ME: Nash actually let you out of the bedroom already?*

> *DANI: Har har. I don't want you to obsess over the article.*

> *ME: I have plenty of time to prove him wrong.*

> *DANI: You have nothing to prove. You*

*just won two more AMAs in November
and are up for two more Grammys.*

*ME: Go make mad, passionate love
with your husband so he continues to
let you come play with me and let me
worry about myself.*

*DANI: "Let me come play." You know
how bad that sounds, right?*

I smiled as I typed my response, knowing it
would not only change the subject, but get a reaction
out of her.

ME: Babe.

*DANI: *** slapping head GIF ****

*DANI: I owe you at least one when I
see you again.*

ME: Merry Christmas, Dani.

DANI: You too. Don't obsess.

ME: I won't.

*DANI: You will. But try not to. Just be
with your family.*

ME: That's the plan.

"Does your phone ever stop?" Mom asked.

I laughed. "When I'm with the team, there's no
one else to text me, so that's when it's the quietest."

"Leave him be, Arlene," Dad said. "He's a big

rock star now. We're lucky we get time with him at all."

"Come on," I said with a smile and shrug. "I've never missed a holiday."

It was the truth. I'd also never missed a birthday or an anniversary without a call and a present. They were important to me, and I tried to show it the best I could amongst the nonstop life I led.

I rolled my neck and went back to staring out the tinted glass.

We were almost to Grand Orchard. The rows and rows of apple trees with their bare branches were the proof. I'd loved escaping into the orchards with my friends growing up. We'd spent many a Friday night partying with the smudge pots as a background. I smiled at the memories of me on the tailgate of William's truck, playing my guitar, making people swoon, and ending the night with kisses. I hadn't thought of my one-time best friend or those secret parties in years.

The orchards gave way to the college grounds, which were almost as old as the land itself. Old ivy and brick that had been modernized on the inside. The college gave way to the town, which looked like it should be cast in either a horror movie or a movie from the 1950s. Quaint and cute. Almost too perfect. A stereotypical college and tourist town rolled into one.

Marco turned down the first street past the college and was soon parked in front of the Craftsman-style home I'd grown up in. The single-story house had floors slanting in the kitchen that almost matched the angled roofline of my childhood bedroom. The room had been added on to the house a century ago, and I'd barely been able to stand up straight in it once I'd turned sixteen. No matter how old and beat-up the house was, it was still home.

The wheels had hardly come to a stop before the front door opened, and Cassidy emerged onto the porch. I'd hardly had a chance to look at her before Mom was barreling out of the back and jogging up the stairs. Mom froze on the top step, her mouth falling open, and my body stilled, taking in my sister.

Cassidy shared my tawny, thick mane of hair, and she was almost as tall as me, but whereas I had bulk, she was long limbs and no meat. Now, she looked like she was barely able to keep her center of gravity because her belly was sticking straight out from her almost too-thin frame.

Holy fuck. She was pregnant. My twenty-three-year-old sister with no boyfriend—that I knew of—was pregnant. Far-along pregnant. Pregnant enough to be showing a belly. Pregnant enough to have told us when she obviously hadn't.

No wonder she'd been freaking out. I was freaking out seeing her like this. I had no idea how off the edge Mom and Dad were going to dive. Dad had joined Mom on the step, and they were both staring at Cassidy as if they were seeing a mirage.

I left the SUV and the bags to join them.

"Cassidy Marie. What on earth?" Mom's voice was full of unshed tears. I didn't know who they were for, but it wasn't what Cassidy wanted, because her chin raised in defiance.

"Surprise. You're going to be grandparents." Cassidy tried to make light of it, but her voice was tight and missing the lightness it normally had.

"Who? What? Jesus…" Dad was blustering.

"Who doesn't matter," Cassidy said. "I chose to have the baby, and that's all there is to it."

"How could you?" Mom asked, hand to her heart. And again, I wasn't sure what she meant. How could Cassidy get pregnant? How could she do it without having a partner in her life? Or how could she keep it from my mother?

"Can I suggest we go inside?" I asked.

Mom whipped around. "You knew? You knew and didn't tell me?"

"No—"

"No one knew," Cassidy said over me.

"The whole town obviously knows," Mom thundered out.

"Since when have you cared about that kind of propriety, Mom?" I asked. Mom was not exactly a flower child, but she definitely wasn't one to buy in to some nineteenth-century rhetoric about babies out of wedlock.

I pushed past both my parents and wrapped my sister in a hug. "Congratulations, Sis! I'm so happy for you. What a great Christmas present."

That seemed to unlock my parents. They came forward, and we were suddenly tangled in a group hug that wasn't our norm. All arms and legs and limbs, with a sniffling Cassidy in the middle of it all.

Chapter Two

Tristan

THE ONES THAT DIDN'T MAKE IT BACK HOME
Performed by Justin Moore

Laughter wafted from the kitchen as I came down the stairs. Hannah's tiny voice and my grandmother's sweet one. Both lyrical and smooth, blending together. I wasn't sure what they were chatting about, but—by the way things were banging—I was pretty sure they were already in the middle of baking.

Grams wanted to bring several dozen cookies to the Holiday Open House at the music store later. I'd promised I'd help, but for the first time in what felt like centuries, I'd actually slept in—if you could call six o'clock sleeping in. Grams hadn't knocked on the door because she knew what it was like to barely sleep at night.

It was just one of the many ways she and I were alike. It comforted me to know she understood rather than admonished it as my mother did. Grams had lost her husband, too. She may have lost him to a stroke instead of an IED, but it was the same kind of loss. Unexpected. Unplanned.

Except, I couldn't really say Darren's death had been unexpected. Every time he'd been sent out on a mission as a Navy SEAL, my heart had seized up until I knew he was back safe. Now, my soul was permanently locked into a collapsed state that would never let go because he'd never walk through the door again.

Molly heard me before they did, and her nails scrabbled on the wooden floors as she came bounding out of the kitchen and jumped her furry brown-and-white body into my arms. My wiry-haired fox terrier was a bundle of energy, and no matter how well my friend Nash had trained her, we hadn't been able to break Molly of jumping into the arms of the people she loved.

I'd barely put Molly down when a whiff of baby shampoo and a spin of a beaded shawl warned me Hannah was taking her turn. I pretended to fall to the floor with a groan as if the weight of her had caused me to collapse.

She was already giggling as my fingers found her stomach, increasing the laughter until it filled the sugar-scented air. My four-and-a-half-year-old barely weighed more than a couple of sacks of potatoes, but she still loved to pretend she was the size of the Hulk.

"Got you!" she shouted, planting a kiss on my cheek.

"You certainly did, *Chiquita*," I said, sitting up to wrap my arms around her.

I picked her up, and her legs went around me like a little monkey's. We entered the kitchen to find Grams smiling our way. Her hair, which had once been as golden as Hannah's and mine, was now white, and her eyes that had also been our same honey color were now just a pale reflection.

Even with the faded hair and wrinkled skin, it was hard to believe she'd just turned ninety-three. She didn't act like she was that old. She was spry and full of energy, even when she had to take shots and heavy doses of pain medication to help curb her arthritis.

"You should have woken me before you started," I told her.

"Morning, *cariño*. I would never wake you when you were out cold."

I stared at the disaster they'd made. Flour, sugar, rolled-out dough, cookie cutters, and more ingredients littered almost every available surface. It looked like a bakery had exploded in the kitchen Grams had renovated just a few years before I'd joined her permanently in Grand Orchard.

"You two have quite the head start," I said.

Hannah squirmed, and I set her down. She ran over to the wooden steps Grams had commissioned just for her so they could cook together. Hannah climbed up and picked up a Christmas tree cookie cutter.

"Mommy, come see all the trees I've made," Hannah said.

I gave Grams a sideways hug, and her peppermint scent washed over me before I turned to join my daughter at the counter. There were at least thirty trees in all sizes spread amongst the dough. "Wow, why just trees?"

"They're the most fun to decorate," she said with a shrug.

Her shawl filled with purple geometric shapes and black beads was covered with flour and dough. It was keeping the bright-fuchsia silk pajamas underneath it clean, but it was an expensive, irreplaceable garment to use as an apron.

As if reading my mind, Grams whispered in my ear, "It's just material."

The shawl had been one of hers before Hannah had borrowed it from her closet a few months ago. It was my grandmother's fault that Hannah was shawl obsessed. She'd been the one to introduce Hannah to Fleetwood Mac and Stevie Nicks. These days, it was hard to get Hannah out of the house without a shawl draped around her just like her musical idol.

Hannah had even insisted on getting her bangs chopped in a fringe and her long hair shagged so that she was like a little mini-me of the '70s version of the superstar.

We spent a couple more hours cooking and decorating. Grams looked tired before we'd even left to open the music store at ten, but she hid it behind a grin that matched Hannah's. When we got to the store Grams had owned for over half a century, we turned on all the lights and the three trees she'd insisted we put up before we set out the treats and drinks.

The day before Christmas Eve, all the shops on Main Street held a Holiday Open House. It was harder and harder to attract people to the shops these days as they opted for the box stores, malls, and now the online giants. Grand Orchard drew enough tourism during apple season for the boutiques and antique shops to stay in business, but by the holidays, the crowds had trickled away again. The stores would go through a dry spell that would last until the orchards were in full bloom and people returned to take pictures of the beautiful flowers.

Once the college kids from Wilson-Jacobs went home for the summer, the town would shrink back up again, and the stores would have to survive on what they'd made during the better parts of the year. At least my grandma's Bi-Annual Apple Jam Music Fest would give them a little kick of extra cash this May.

Helping my grandmother with the planning for the festival for the first time, I'd realized how much work it was. I'd realized how much she'd done for so many years on her own. It was almost ludicrous. I wasn't sure who I was more frustrated with: me for being so caught up in my own world for so long, my parents for letting Grams handle it without their support for decades, or Grams herself for not asking for help.

With the lights on and holiday music filling the space, people started filtering into the store. Hannah stood on another stool behind the counter, greeting them all by name. My heart tugged at the sight of it. We'd become embedded into this small town in a way I'd never been in any other town, not even the one in Delaware I'd grown up in.

In the early afternoon, my grandmother disappeared for a while to go visit the other stores and chat with the owners who'd been her friends since my grandparents had moved to Grand Orchard in the '60s. When Grams came back, she had a wrapped package in her hand. She gave it to Hannah.

"Merry Christmas, *Chiquita*," she said.

Hannah's eyes grew big. "But it's not Christmas yet."

"Close enough. When Irma saw this come in, she

put it behind the counter for me. She knew you'd want it."

Irma was the owner of the antique store across the street. She was one of Gram's line dancing pals. It was hilarious and fun to watch the group of gray-haired women breaking out their cowboy boots and keeping up with the younger crowd at Mick's bar on country night.

Hannah hugged Grams without even opening the present. "Thank you."

Grams laughed.

I smiled at the image they made. I loved that my daughter was a hugger. She was better at giving them out than I was on most occasions. I'd had to have several talks with her about asking people for permission first, because she would routinely hug other kids she'd just met, which sometimes upset their parents. It was sad, but at the same time I understood it. I wouldn't want people touching Hannah if she didn't want it, but it was just a damn hug—from a four-year-old.

Hannah opened the paper to reveal a top hat in almost pristine condition, and I couldn't help the chuckle that escaped as Hannah's eyes grew to the size of galaxies. She took in the hat reverently.

"Is it hers?" Her voice was breathy and shocked.

Grams chortled. She had a beautiful singing voice, and somehow it came through when she laughed. Like a melody you knew by heart.

"No, *Chiquita*, it didn't belong to Stevie, but it looks a lot like hers," Grams said, referring to the picture behind the counter. The one with my grandparents and the entire Fleetwood Mac crew at one of the very first Jam Fests they'd ever thrown.

Hannah put the hat on, and my throat closed up. She looked stunning. A smiling, happy child with her father's eyebrows and chin but with my eyes, hair, and smile. Darren had missed it all. He'd barely seen her as a tiny six-month-old baby crying as she teethed. He'd never gotten to see her larger-than-life personality or the pure joy radiating through her whenever she was at a piano.

And he was missing another Christmas just like he'd missed her very first one.

Some days, the pain inside me was as large and sharp as the very first moment when they'd told me he was gone. The knock on the door and the sad eyes of his unit commander still haunted me. I'd lost my legs at his words. I'd collapsed on the floor, holding my gut, crying. But I'd also been filled with anger. Anger directed at Darren for leaving me. Leaving us.

Most of the time now, the pain was just a constant ache inside me. A hole that couldn't be filled. Until moments like these. When Hannah did something that took my breath away, and I couldn't share it with him. Reminding me that my soulmate was gone.

As if sensing the pain filling me, Gram's eyes met mine. She made her way over to me and wrapped me in a hug so strong you would doubt she was in her nineties. "Let it wash over you. It's okay."

I nodded.

Four years later, there was barely anyone in my life who could handle the fact that I still grieved. Almost everyone I knew expected me to somehow have moved on, to have put it behind me. And no one seemed to understand I never would.

Grams was the exception. She got it.

"Better?" Grams asked.

I nodded. I was. I just had to let it flow over me before I came back to the present—to Hannah, with a top hat on her head and a blue, gauzy shawl wrapped around her jeans and sweater. She picked up one of the mics Grams had behind the counter, pulled herself onto the scratched wooden counter, and started singing Aly and AJ's upbeat song, "The Greatest Time of Year," filled the store.

Love and admiration replaced the heartache. I pulled Hannah off the counter, and the three of us danced and sang and laughed as the holiday music streamed through the room, my strangled-cat voice mixing with their two beautiful ones. I let the joy of it settle in my bones because Darren had shown me one thing: these moments were supposed to be lived and felt and remembered.

♫ ♫ ♫

It was seven thirty when Grams sent me packing with a drooping Hannah. Grams herself seemed to have caught a second wind somehow. Maybe it was the coffee from the bakery three doors down or the energy she gathered just by being a happy extrovert. Whatever it was, she didn't look tired. It wasn't uncommon for her to stay until the store shut at nine o'clock as she scraped every last nickel from the holiday.

Hannah and I bundled up in our snow gear and left the store to walk the small distance from Main Street to Gram's house a few blocks over. Hannah refused to take the top hat off, and it began collecting flakes of snow as they drifted to the ground, shimmering in the holiday lights strewn across the store windows.

By the time we got to the house, the hat wasn't the only thing with a small layer of snow. We were almost covered, but I wasn't ready to go in yet. Instead, I grabbed Hannah's hand and twirled with her for a minute, sticking out my tongue and catching the first flakes, loving the idea that we would have a white Christmas. Hannah copied me, the soft fluff melting as fast as it landed in our mouths.

"It looks like sugar, but it tastes like water," Hannah said with a hint of disappointment.

"There's a pretty famous quote that goes something like, 'The simplest things are often the most beautiful,'" I told her.

She looked doubtful and shivered as the cold finally set in to both of us.

We walked up the steps and removed our wet gear in the entryway. I sent her upstairs to put her pajamas on while I started the fire and let Molly out of the laundry room. The dog hated the snow and barely made it off the back steps before returning to me to wipe her tiny paws. She settled down next to Hannah's top hat by the fireplace.

I banged out a quick text to Grams.

> *ME: Will Irma and Floyd bring you home? It's snowing, and I don't want you to slip.*

> *GRAMS: They already rang to insist.*

At least I wouldn't have to worry about her trying to traipse home over icy ground.

When Hannah came down, she was in a pair of fuzzy footie pajamas, making her look like the little girl she was rather than the mini-adult she often acted like. We curled up together on the armchair with a pile of books as the flicker of the fire and the lights of the Christmas tree sparkled over us.

Tomorrow, the rest of my family would arrive, and the house would be chaotic, filled with my parents, my sister, her husband, and the triplets who had recently turned three. But for tonight, it was peaceful. And I let the pleasure of it settle over me so it would be another moment of joy I had stacking up against the wall of pain. Someday, the wall would be completely hidden behind the better memories, and my body would release itself from its seized position. Maybe then, I would truly feel like part of the world again.

Chapter Three

Brady

HARD DAYS
Performed by Brantley Gilbert

We were putting the last remaining ornaments on the tree, but the moment wasn't the serene one it should have been. Instead, my stomach was lurching, and I was fighting to keep my cool.

"I don't understand why you won't tell us who he is, *cailín deas*," Mom said, frustration leaking from every pore regardless of the "sweet girl" endearment she used.

"You've been home for barely a day, and I'm already sick and tired of this question," Cassidy said. Her tone was neutral, but her eyes were flashing.

"Why does it matter, Mom?" I asked.

She turned to me with eyes narrowed. "Don't start. If you'd been here this fall, we would have been able—"

"To do what, Mom? What exactly could I have done?"

Dad jumped into the fray. "Cassidy, we just want to make sure the man takes responsibility for his actions."

"I don't want his money, Dad. He offered to pay for the abortion. I told him no. End of story," Cass said.

The man wanting her to have an abortion was new information. I could never see Cass going that route. As a little girl, she used to cry when we killed a bug, her heart so tortured by the loss of any living thing that she couldn't stand it. It was the same reason she'd become a vegetarian once she found out where meat came from.

I put the last ornament on the tree and decided I needed an escape from the drama. If I felt that way, I was sure Cassidy was even more ready to fly the coop.

"I was thinking of heading downtown to the Holiday Open House. Want to come, Cass?"

"Yes!" she all but screamed.

"It's going to snow," Mom said.

"Okay?" I said with a frown. It wasn't like snow was an unknown commodity for us, having grown up in upstate New York.

"It'll be slippery."

Cassidy rolled her eyes. "I'm not going to fall."

"She'll be with me," I told Mom, but she looked at me doubtfully.

"Let me go get my snow boots," Cassidy said and went down the hall to her room.

"I'm going out to the apartment to grab my gear," I hollered after her, heading in the opposite direction.

Our house was so old that nothing connected. Rooms were cut off from each other by walls. The hallway to the bedrooms required a U-turn through the living room and dining room before you could get to the kitchen. It made me feel claustrophobic these days. The house needed a remodel. It needed walls torn down so that everything could be open and breathable, but my parents wouldn't hear of it, even when the kitchen was barely serviceable with its antiquated appliances and chipped laminate countertops.

I'd offered the renovation as a gift, but Dad had been insulted, and Mom had cried. They wouldn't take a penny from me, even when I told them how much money I'd made off the last album, without even considering the tour. I hadn't been bragging. I'd just wanted to show them I could afford it. Instead, it had backfired on me as if I was rubbing my money in their faces.

The back door squeaked when I opened it—more work needing to be done that would be denied if I brought it up. The cold hit me so hard I shivered right down to my bones. I hurried from the house, leaving my parents and their pride behind as I mounted the steps to the apartment above the garage.

I'd abandoned my tiny, sloped room in the house for the apartment ever since I'd made my first album. Growing up, it had been rented out to college students, but once I'd "made it," I'd taken over the lease so I could keep it as my private getaway. It was the one and only way I was able to infuse any of my income into my parents' pockets.

The lights in the apartment were all on, and Marco sat on the pull-out couch in front of the TV. He'd declined our request to join us for dinner and tree decorating, saying he had calls to make, but I wondered if he just felt like he was invading our privacy. I didn't want him to feel that way. He was almost more family to me than the people in the house.

"Cass and I are heading downtown to the Holiday Open House," I told him, as I pulled on a thick winter jacket and a pair of snow boots I had sitting by the door.

He gave a curt nod, joining me at the door and donning his own gear.

"You don't have to come with us," I told him.

"Don't start," he said.

"I'm in Grand Orchard during winter break. Even the college kids who might have asked for an autograph are gone," I said with a smile. The permanent residents of the town all knew who I was and weren't impressed. None of them were going to come screaming down the street at the sight of me or break into my house to steal my underwear. Coming home had been an easy way to keep my ego in check over the years. Winning music awards or having an album go platinum wasn't going to get you a gold star in the locals' books. Now, if you happened to win the apple pie contest at the county fair, that was something to write home about.

Marco didn't reply. Instead, he just followed me out of the apartment and down the steps to where Cassidy was waiting. She had on a white coat so puffy she could have been the Pillsbury Doughboy. But her eyes were shining, and her cheeks were already turning pink in the chill. She looked pretty, the white beanie on her head only making the wild waves that were her long hair stand out more.

She looked up at Marco and smiled. "Knew we could get you to come out and play somehow."

He grunted, but his lips twitched.

She looped her arm with mine, and we headed down the tree-lined block to Main Street. The entire street was lit up with holiday lights. The scent of hot apple cider was wafting from all the shops. People were laughing and talking as they passed from one store to the next. It felt like the entire town had come out to celebrate, which was probably the case.

This was Grand Orchard. The core of it. The people whose families had been here for generations mixed with those who'd moved here for the small-town lifestyle. It was quaint and appealing in a postcard kind of way.

My phone buzzed.

> *GHOST TEAM LEADER: Tell me you haven't killed anyone yet.*

> *ME: The night is young, and I am now in the center of Quaintsville, so no promises.*

> *GHOST TEAM LEADER: Do I have to tell Marco to put you on a leash?*

> *ME: Marco looks completely uncomfortable.*

Which he did. He was dressed in black military gear as if he was ready to scale down the side of a cliff or up a wall with an incendiary device. His growly face and hooded eyes made him stand out like a sore thumb. He looked like some superhero or Egyptian god, but he had none of the ego to go with it. Just a humble man from nowhere, who was ready to step in front of a bullet for me.

GHOST TEAM LEADER: Don't taunt him.

ME: Why am I always the one who everyone assumes is doing the taunting?

*GHOST TEAM LEADER: *** Eye roll emoji ****

I snorted because, before Dani had become part of the team, Lee had never used an emoji or a GIF in his life. Now, they were a regular part of his written language.

As I put my phone back into my pocket, Cass stumbled on the curb. I caught her with my arms, steadying her, a moment of panic flowing through me.

"You okay?" I asked.

"Yes, Mom," she threw back at me.

I knew better than to take it personally.

I'd been six years old when Cassidy was born. Old enough to have a sense of displacement, but young enough to love the idea of being a big brother. I hadn't been able to fulfill that role for much of my life. Cassidy's developmental delays had become apparent early on in her language and mobility, and it had sent my parents into a tailspin.

Since being diagnosed with Triple X, they'd hovered over her. Sure, it had all been done out of love and a desire to see her become the best possible version of herself she could be, but it meant a whole range of tutors, individual education plans, and physical therapy to counter the mental and physical manifestations of her syndrome. By the time she hit high school, there was really no reason for anyone to ever suspect Cass had experienced early delays, as long as you didn't ask her to participate in sports.

Cass pretty much led as normal of a life as any of us these days. Her hypotonia was the only aspect of her Triple X diagnosis that reared its ugly head now and then. With the weight of the baby changing her center of gravity, she had to have some balance issues that her decreased muscle tone couldn't counteract, but she wasn't giving in to it. That was Cass. Always the fighter.

The first store we entered was Sugar Lips Bakery. The owner, Helen, had been behind the counter my entire life. She was my parents' age but had softened into a ball of sweetness over the years versus the taut energy that was my mother.

She saw Cass and came charging over, wrapping her in a hug. "Cassidy! I was thinking of you today when I was making my gluten-free cinnamon balls dipped in dark chocolate from that new cacao supplier you sent my way."

"Wait, since when do you have a gluten allergy?" I asked Cass.

Helen and Cass both stared at me. "Since I was in high school." Cass smirked.

I flushed a red that I rarely did.

How did I not know this about my sister?

While Cass convinced Marco to try the gluten-free products, I bought ten huge boxes of treats to be overnighted to my support team and bandmates. I filled out shipping labels as Cass visited with Helen and Helen's daughter, laughter abundant throughout their conversation. As other people came in and out of the store, they also greeted Cass with warmth and cheerfulness. One thing was clear: my sister got more attention than I did.

My lips curled up at that thought. Cassidy the Nutritionist was known by children and grownups alike. Listening in, I learned more about my sister than I had in months. She'd obviously spent time at the schools to teach healthy eating, helped people with dietary restrictions, and held weekly group discussions at the clinic down the street.

By the time we left the store, Cass was practically glowing. Dressed in white with the holiday lights shining on her, she looked almost ethereal. Angelic. If it wasn't some kind of blasphemous sin, I'd say her baby had been created by divine intervention. It was easier than thinking of some jerk screwing my sister and then leaving her to handle the change in her world all on her own.

As we neared the music store, my heart sped up, and all thoughts of Cass and her life flew out of my head. Instead, images of a wrinkled, gray-haired woman took over.

Elana.

It had been too long since I'd last seen her.

When I entered, she was in a heated discussion with a tall, black-haired man with pale skin whose lips were flashing a smile. "You're lucky *Chiquita* isn't here, or your slander of Stevie Nicks would have you banned from the shop, Jin."

He laughed and was joined by a beautiful brown-skinned woman whose full, smiling lips were tilted up as much as his. She tucked herself up against him, and when they did, it was apparent they fit. In the same way Dani fit with Nash and my friend Georgie fit with her husband, Mac. An ache hit me in the pit of my belly. A strange longing to have that. Somebody I fit with. Someone to fill the heart beating erratically inside my chest.

Elana turned her ancient eyes and met mine. The smile on her face widened so much the wrinkles on her face almost made her light-hazel eyes disappear. She was moving toward me at the same time I was moving toward her, and it was like one of those stupid romance movies where we joined in the middle with me wrapping her in a hug and swinging her around. Except, romance was the last thing that joined us.

Love, however, did. Love for music. Love for each other.

"Cormac!" She squeezed me so tightly I was afraid those skinny, ancient arms of hers would break off.

"Merry Christmas!" I told her.

"The acoustic version of 'Ghost' you played live in Paris was incredibly moving!" she said with a smile as she stepped out of my arms and patted my face, taking me in. "You look exhausted."

Not only had she known where I was, but she'd also listened to the slower version of my song, registering the changes in it. I was surprised when I shouldn't have been. Just like I shouldn't have been surprised that she saw the fatigue written over my skin.

"Just got back to the States yesterday. It'll wear off," I told her.

She turned to Cassidy and Marco who'd trailed into the store after me. She hugged Cass and winked at Marco, which caused him to cough and move away to the aisle of vinyl records and CDs that took up the bulk of the space on the main floor of the store.

The store's normal smell of vinyl and instrument

oil was covered tonight by the smell of spiced cider and holiday cookies. The treats completely covered the top of a cheerily decorated table blocking the staircase to the practice rooms and storage space. I'd spent years of my life going up and down those steps with instruments and boxes in hand. Elana had been my teacher, my employer, and my friend. The store had been my second home. Sometimes, it had felt like my real one.

"How's the baby?" Elana asked, squinting at the enormous, puffy jacket hiding any sign of Cass's baby tummy.

"Moving a lot, just like you said."

"A boy. I know it's a boy." Elana grinned.

The couple at the counter came forward, greeting Cassidy before wishing Elana Merry Christmas and heading out into the snow that had started to fall again.

"You just missed *Cari* and my great grandbaby," Elana said.

I laughed. "Isn't that the way it's always been?"

Because it was true. I'd always been off to music camp in the summers when Elana's granddaughter had come up to spend weeks at a time with her. It was as if the universe had decided the two of us could never be in the same space at the same time. For many years, I'd doubted the existence of the girl at all while simultaneously being jealous that she got to call Elana hers.

"Are your parents home?" Elana asked.

I nodded, and Cass winced.

Elana laughed. "You should have told them."

"They would have rushed home."

She was right. Cassidy had kept the secret from

all of us because she'd known the truth. Mom would have given up her position in Ireland and come running home to save Cass from something she didn't need saving from.

It was a baby. Millions of women a year had them.

"I'm going to head across to Irma's. Catch up to me in a few?" Cass asked. It was her way of giving me a few minutes alone with my mentor.

"Sure."

She headed out, and I turned to Marco, but he was already nodding at me and following her.

Elana moved toward the wooden counter at the rear of the store with its antique register and art deco lights, and I followed. She sat on the stool behind it. The same position she'd sat in for years while we discussed bands and songs and lyrics. Others who'd come into the store—college kids and adults alike—would often join our debates, taking sides and spurring us on. Whether we were for or against each other, it had never ended in hard feelings because the respect and acceptance we felt always outweighed our difference of opinion.

"The ass from *The Reporter* knows nothing," Elana said, and I laughed because it was almost verbatim Dani's words the day before.

"We both know there's a truth to his words."

She shook her head. "Just because your music is consistent does *not* mean it is stale."

I groaned. "See. Consistent. Tell me the truth. You were arguing about Fleetwood Mac when we came in. Would you call their music consistent?"

"They made music over three decades. It isn't the

same. You've released three albums," she said.

"I can't help but agree with him," I told her. "My fourth album should have a new sound."

She stared at me before getting up and heading down one of the rows of albums. She came back with a Johnny Mathias album. She handed it to me. "Merry Christmas."

I looked down at it. "Blues? You know that isn't my vibe."

She smacked me gently on the cheek. "Didn't you just say you were looking for something new? You just need to be inspired again. Remember some of the classics I taught you when you were first starting to play piano and that damn saxophone."

"Damn saxophone! You liked it when I played the sax."

"Maybe you need to play it again."

Maybe.

The door swung open, and Marco emerged, carrying Cass in his arms. The sight had my heart hammering.

"What happened?"

"I just twisted my ankle. Normal stuff," Cass said. "But this behemoth won't let me walk on it."

Relief took the place of the panic that had filled my chest.

I turned back to Elana. "Looks like I gotta run."

"Looks like you do," she said with a smile, pulling me into a hug. "Don't let them force you into something that isn't you. Consistent is better than stupid."

I laughed, squeezed her back, and whispered into

her white hair, "Merry Christmas."

She squeezed me a little harder again and then let me go.

When I looked back at the door, she'd already turned back to the vinyl records, flipping through them as if in search of something else. I wished I'd had more time with her. I was going to come back soon. After *Fighting for the Stars* and the award shows, I'd come back and sit for a few hours at her feet and have her tell me everything I was doing wrong. I'd let her rid me of my newly found insecurities as she'd once rid me of my anger.

I turned back to Marco and Cass. As we left the store, I asked, "What happened?"

"She fell down the two steps outside the antique store," he said.

"I'm fine. Don't talk like I'm not here," Cass stormed.

"Is the baby okay?" I asked her.

"Yes. The baby is kicking and twirling as we speak. It wasn't even a real fall. My ankle gave out, and I hit my hands. My palms are more messed up than anything else."

We walked in silence as the light snowflakes turned into a heavy flurry. By the time we got to the house, we were all covered. Mom must have been watching for us from the window, because she opened the door as we approached.

"*Cailín Deas*!" Mom called out.

"She's okay," I replied.

Marco bundled her inside, setting her down on the couch, and Mom was there in an instant, pushing my bodyguard aside to get to my sister.

"Where are you hurt?"

Cass held up her hands, which were red from the cold and scraped from the sidewalk. "Seriously, everyone has to stop overreacting. I just need a Band-Aid, some ice, and a brace. It'll be fine."

Mom turned to me with her face full of fury. "Where were you?"

I swallowed as her scold turned me from the grown-ass man I was into the head-in-the-clouds kid I'd once been.

"Marco was there," I reassured her.

"Where were *you*?" she repeated.

I took off my beanie and ran a hand over my hair. "At Elana's."

Mom snorted. "Of course you were."

"Mom!" Cassidy's voice, full of an anger we normally didn't hear from her, halted my retort. "You can't blame Brady for my clumsiness. What do you think has been happening while you've been gone? Do you honestly think I haven't fallen, or bungled my toes, or slammed fingers into cabinets? I'm not a child. I can take care of myself."

"You've done a great job of it. You're pregnant, alone, and hurt. This is why I should never have gone to Ireland. It's why I'm not going back. Your father can go and handle things for both of us."

We all stared at Mom like she had four heads, even Dad. There was no way he could teach her Gaelic study classes. Not ever.

"If you don't go back to Ireland, I'll move out," Cass tossed back at her.

"Don't be ridiculous. With what money?"

"I have a job, Mom. It's not like I don't have an

income. Between the grant the city gave the clinic and my normal salary, I'm making more than enough money to get my own place."

The threat of her leaving the fold had our mom swallowing hard. It was a threat my mother couldn't have her follow through on. What would my mom do if Cassidy left the nest? She lived to protect her. The fact that they'd taken the assignment in Ireland had been a huge leap of faith that none of us had been sure she'd do until the very last moment. In truth, the tension between her and Dad over the topic had probably been the only thing that had gotten her to set foot on the plane.

"We can talk about all of this later. For now, Cormac, get the ice. I'll get the bandages." Mom headed toward the hallway and the single bathroom the four of us had shared during my childhood. She stopped to take in Marco and said quietly, "Thank you for being there for her."

It stabbed at every wound inside me from a childhood where I'd always been the one to screw up the one job I had: make sure Cassidy was safe. I'd screwed it up so many times it had become a familiar refrain. I'd screwed it up even more by moving away to Juilliard and never coming home again, because it meant I wasn't there at all.

I grabbed one of the ice packs from the stack of them in the freezer, handed it to Dad, and then left. I made my way up to the apartment, placed the record Elana had given me onto the kitchenette's counter, and then went into the tiny bedroom, sinking on the bed with my head in my hands.

How easily Mom could reduce me to my twelve-year-old self. As if she'd just come home and realized

Cassidy was nowhere to be found. Realized I'd been so lost in my guitar that I hadn't responded to Cass's request to walk the dog, and she'd left the house without me. In that moment, I felt very far from the twenty-nine-year-old man with three platinum albums, over a dozen awards, and several hundred million dollars in the bank that I truly was.

This was the one place in my life I could never seem to get things right.

It had to change.

I had to be better than this.

I was determined to do just that.

Chapter Four

Tristan

WHEN YOU'RE GONE
Performed by The Cranberries

Molly woofed, staring at the dog treat canister that read *Three Dog Night* with a picture of three dogs holding guitars under a night sky.

"No more treats. Grams will give you more than enough when she comes down," I told the dog as I set the oatmeal pan in the sink to soak it.

"She's late," Hannah said as she took a spoonful of the oatmeal barely drizzled with honey. Bland. Boring. Healthy. Ever since Grams' heart attack shortly after the new year, Hannah had put herself and the rest of us on a strict health food diet.

In a matter of weeks, Hannah had gone from the Christmas-treat-indulging child to an oatmeal-loving grown-up. The hearty grain had become her favorite breakfast food. I thought she might eat it for every meal if I let her. I should have refused when she'd begged to be a part of the meetings with the nutritionist the hospital had recommended, because

Hannah had taken everything Cassidy O'Neil had said to heart. Now, she scolded both Grams and me any time we deviated from the list of approved items stuck to the refrigerator door with a Dave Matthews Band magnet.

The clock over the mantel in the living room chimed eight o'clock, and worry flew through me. Grams was definitely late, but just like she let me sleep in on the rare occasions I could accomplish it, I usually did the same for her. I'd take Hannah over to the preschool at Stacy's and then come back and check on her.

I put the snack we'd made for the preschool— homemade granola bars with nothing fun in them—in a Tupperware container and then placed them in Hannah's backpack.

"You almost ready?" I asked.

Hannah nodded, took the bowl to the sink, and used the wooden step to rinse it and put it in the dishwasher. It hurt me a little that she was so grown-up when, really, she was so little. Her fifth birthday was barely weeks away, and yet, she was acting like a ten-year-old.

Molly scampered to the door with us, wagging her tail.

"No, girl. Stay. There's too much snow on the ground," I said.

Hannah wrapped the maroon shawl Grams had given her at Christmas around her throat like a scarf before stuffing her arms into the thick snow coat she was growing out of faster than I could blink. While I pulled on my winter wear, she put her backpack on, kissed Molly on the head, and then placed her top hat over the two braids I'd put in her hair that morning.

Hannah looked up the stairs, her eyes serious. "Can I kiss her goodbye?"

I shook my head. "Let her sleep, *Chiquita*. I'll give her a kiss for you."

We made our way down the street and over a block to my friend Stacy's house. Hannah rang the doorbell. The house was similar to Grams', a two-story Craftsman in a town of Craftsmans, but Stacy and her husband, Jin-Kang, had gutted and redone theirs when they first moved to Grand Orchard two years ago. Jin worked in the app world and could do his job from anywhere, and Stacy had given up her teaching job in Albany to make the move. Now, she was running a tiny preschool out of their home while she concentrated on getting approvals for a charter school.

I hadn't known Stacy when I'd signed Hannah up for her preschool classes, but now she was the best female friend I'd ever had. We practically lived in each other's houses. My sister was in Florida, my parents and Darren's parents were in Delaware, and Nash and Dani were in Georgia. That was the extent of my friendships. Grams, at ninety-three, had more friends than I did.

"Well, don't you look spiffy," Stacy said, looking down at Hannah. Stacy's beautiful spirals of black hair danced around her chin as she smiled at my daughter. The smile reached all the way to her brown eyes, making them sparkle.

"Thanks. I'm putting the granola bars in the kitchen," Hannah said, pulling off her snow boots and coat before heading for the kitchen where Stacy's six-year-old son and three-year-old daughter were at the table, finishing breakfast.

"Hey, *Chiquita*, aren't you forgetting something?" I called after her.

She ran back, hugged me, and then took off again. "See you after school, Mommy."

My heart left my body and went with her, as it always did.

When I looked at Stacy, she gave me a soft smile, knowing exactly how I felt about my girl. She felt the same about her two.

"She didn't get to say good morning to Grams, so she may be a little off," I told her.

"I'll keep an eye on her mood."

"Thanks. Have you heard anything after the presentation last night?" I asked.

Stacy and Jin had given an update on their charter school to the County Board of Education the night before. The approvals were a breath away, and the building they'd leased was set for renovations in the spring. I'd wanted to strangle some of the board members on her behalf as they'd asked her the same question twenty different ways, but Stacy had been calm and collected.

"It's so close it almost feels real now," she said.

"It'll be here before you know it," I responded.

We chatted for a few more minutes before the noise of the kids took her away, and I headed back to the house. I fully expected to find Grams in the kitchen with the half a cup of coffee Hannah had reduced her to per Cassidy's instructions, but the house was silent.

That was when my heart started to thud an anxious tune.

I dropped my coat and headed up the stairs. I

knocked on her door, but she didn't answer. When I opened it, the scent of peppermint filled the air. Grams always had the red-and-white candies or the peppermint oils from Nash's company with her. She said it soothed her nerves as much as her stomach.

As I entered, she didn't budge, and it hit me how still she was lying. Her back was to the door, and she was buried under a bundle of blankets. Layers of them. Ever since the heart attack, she couldn't seem to stay warm even when we turned the thermostat up.

My hands were shaking as I moved around the bed to her—not just my hands, my entire body. But it was my heart that was shaking the most.

"Grams?" I called softly, not wanting to startle her.

When I got to her side of the bed, her face was smoother than I'd seen it in years. Almost as if some of the wrinkles had been absorbed back into her skin. Her eyes were shut, and her mouth was slightly parted. She was on her side, arms curled up in front of her beneath the blanket.

"Grams?" I reached out to tap her shoulder.

Nothing.

"Grams!"

Panic. Pure panic. I reached for her wrist to find her heartbeat. She was stiff and cold.

Oh God.

No.

Please, no.

"Grams!"

Her body was rigid as I tried to move it again.

She was gone.

She'd been gone for hours, and I hadn't known.

Thank God I hadn't let Hannah come in.

My brain traveled through all those thoughts and then back to my grandmother whom I loved with a huge chunk of my heart. The heart that had already lost so much. How could the universe take her from me too?

The heart attack had been scary enough.

This.

This was unbearable.

I sank to the floor, forehead to the bed, and the tears started. I knew they wouldn't stop for hours. I knew that, no matter how much I fought them, my body would demand their release.

"Grams. What the hell am I going to do now?" I sobbed.

I sat there for a long time. Minutes. Days. Hours. It all blended. Then, I pulled my phone from my pocket and called 9-1-1. The sirens from the fire station down the street came almost immediately. We were so close to downtown that their sound echoed through the house.

My brain whirled. She'd died in her sleep, and I hadn't known.

Guilt mixed in with the pain swirling through me as I walked down the stairs to open the door for the emergency responders.

On the porch, I dialed my mom.

"Morning, baby," Mom said.

"Grams is dead," I told her. I didn't have the energy to filter it. I didn't have the energy to soften the blow. It hadn't been softened for me. My grandmother had left us. Left me.

"What?" she gasped.

"She's gone. She died in her sleep. I…I just found her."

The tears came harder, choking me. Mom's strangled sobs on the other end only increased my own. I watched from within a layer of fog as the fire truck parked in front of the house, and two firefighters jumped out, coming toward me with their medical kits.

"The firemen are here," I told her.

"What? Why? Is the house burning?" she cried.

"No, they're EMTs," I said.

She didn't reply. I heard my father's voice in the background, heard her telling my dad. I hung up. I didn't know what else to do.

"Ma'am," the fireman said, one of the few locals in this small town who I didn't know.

"She's upstairs. She's already dead," I told them through the tears.

His eyes were full of pity as were the man's behind him. They went in, and I didn't follow. I couldn't go back in there yet. I sank onto the porch steps, arms crossed over myself, hugging myself tightly, rocking.

I picked up the phone again.

"Hey," Stacy said with the laughter of the kids in the background filling the space. Hannah with her best friends Kiran and Jalissa. Joy. Joy that had been ripped out of my heart. That would be ripped from my daughter once she knew.

"Gra—" I couldn't get it out, just croaked anguish into the phone.

"Tristan?"

"Grams…"

"Oh, honey," Stacy said. "Jay's here with the kids. I'm on my way."

I let the phone fall to the ground. It was ringing. My mom's ringtone. Her face on the screen. I couldn't pick it up.

The firemen came down the stairs with somber faces.

"We've called the coroner," the first one said. "We're so sorry."

"Do you have someone we can call?" the second one asked.

Stacy was running into the yard. She was at the steps and pulling me against her, and I was crying. Tears for me. Tears for my daughter who'd already lost so much. Tears for the worse moments that I knew would come later. After. When there was no one coming to hold you up. When the night was dark and long and the ache for the missing person filled every part of you.

♩ ♩ ♩

The rain was driving down in almost torrential waves. It felt like it hadn't stopped in three days. I stood, leaning against the porch rail, staring out at it and wondering if—like all the books and songs said—raindrops were tears from heaven.

Grams wouldn't want tears. She'd want laughter. There was plenty of it in the house right now. I could hear it through the windows and doors. The crowd at the house was smaller than the one at the church had been. The entire town had come out to say goodbye to Grams, but only the family and closest friends had followed us back here.

The door opened, and Nash came out, dressed in a black suit instead of his Navy uniform. The last time we'd buried someone, he'd been in dress blues. Medals on his chest. Hand raw from pounding the trident into my husband's coffin.

Today, he looked like someone else. Not the Nash from Darren's funeral who'd been full of guilt. This Nash was just full of sadness. For me.

He put his arms around me, and I let him. A comfort I'd rarely allowed him to give me in the past. Not when I was fighting anger at him for coming home with Darren's body in pieces—so many pieces that they hadn't allowed me to see him.

I rested my head on his shoulder.

"What can I do for you?" he asked, and there was the anguish I'd heard from him before. It was in the depth of his voice, twisted with emotions he didn't let show.

Once upon a time, I'd let Nash take care of Hannah, Molly, and me for too long. I wouldn't do it again. Not when he had his own family now. He'd been married to my friend Dani for over two years. They had a dog, and a house, and a life that was exactly what Darren would have wished for him.

"Thank you for coming. That's enough," I told him.

"You didn't deserve this," he said quietly.

I was so tired. Tired of the war of emotions that had been going through me over the last week. The anger. The heartache. The reflections back to when I'd first been told Darren had died.

"She was ninety-three," I told him. "It hardly

made sense to think she'd outlive me, but that's what I wanted. That's what I needed."

The damn tears leaked from the corners of my eyes again.

Waterworks. I was good at them.

We stood there for a long time, the rain the only sound between us as I fought for control. I was ready for everyone to be gone so Hannah and I could grieve in peace. My daughter was almost as tired as I was of people asking how she was.

She wasn't even five yet, and she'd lost the two most important people in her life. She didn't know how to feel. She couldn't even process it, and yet, people insisted on asking her.

I looked in the huge front window and found her sitting on Dani's lap with the dog at their feet. Hannah was wrapped in her maroon shawl, holding her top hat with clenched fingers. She'd barely taken either of them off in a week. They were both gifts from Grams.

She'd been so mad at me when I told her.

She'd asked me why I hadn't gone to wake Grams sooner.

I'd tried to explain that it wouldn't have mattered. She'd been dead for hours, but hours meant nothing to little kids. It was a vague, unknown notion.

My mom had explained it better. "You know how long *Mama Mia* is?" It was Hannah's favorite movie of all time, and Hannah had nodded. "Grams had been gone for as long as it would take to watch that show twice before your mom found her."

She'd been dead at least four hours they said.

But I still couldn't quite forgive myself for not checking on her sooner.

I wasn't sure I ever would.

After Hannah had thought about what my mom had said, she'd asked who was going to continue to teach her to play piano, which had me sobbing right along with her, because I didn't know. Piano and music had been one of the many things they'd done together.

As Nash held me, I let myself cry again. But I promised myself it would be one of the last times. Hannah needed to see me get through this with strength, not fading away. She would be watching me to know what to do, unlike when Darren had died.

This week had been bad enough for her to witness, with everyone falling apart in rounds. My mom, my dad, my sister, the triplets—who didn't even know what they were crying about—and Grams' friends who'd come to the house once the news had spread through Grand Orchard.

Gram's lawyer had even cried as she read the will to us. My sister, Bailey, had gotten angry and stormed out because she and her babies had barely gotten a mention. Mom had clearly been confused as to why Grams would leave me everything, including the house and the store.

My family was unhappy with the inequity. I couldn't blame them. Bailey had said some pretty hurtful things about how I'd purposefully weaseled up to our grandmother, and now she was barely speaking to me, which was just one more hurt piled on top of the pile of hurts.

Money screwed people up.

It was true that I'd built a relationship with our grandmother that my sister hadn't, but it wasn't because of some grand ulterior motive on my part.

Bailey had never wanted to give up her cheerleading team and dance competitions in order to come to Grand Orchard with me in the summers. I hadn't had Bailey's hobbies and interests back then. I'd loved painting, and I'd loved my time with Grams. I'd adored listening to her passionate voice as she discussed music, the past, and her life. She'd spent her childhood traveling all over the Iberian Peninsula with my great-grandfather who'd been a famous flamenco singer. The stories of how they'd brought the music and dance to America, and how it had led her to my grandfather had filled me with a sense of belonging when I'd needed it.

Everything was all messed up now. Not just without Grams, but with my family. I'd take having my grandmother back over any of the money she'd left me. But she must have known I wouldn't want to leave Grand Orchard when she was gone, and this was her way of making sure I could stay. She was right. I didn't want to leave, because I didn't want Hannah to lose her friends on top of losing Grams. Grams had given me everything she owned so I could remain here. She'd trusted me with the things she'd loved most, not just for me, but also for my music-loving daughter.

Of all the things floating through my brain, only one was certain: I had to keep it all together. For Grams. For Hannah. For me.

Chapter Five

Brady

FOREVER'S GOTTA START SOMEWHERE
Performed by Chad Brownlee

When Marco and I had arrived back in Grand Orchard late last night, the apartment had smelled stale with disuse. I'd left after Christmas with a promise to come back and stay once my last round of obligations were behind me. Now, almost eight weeks later, *Fighting for the Stars* was done, the award shows were over, and my performance at Dani's From the Ashes charity gala marked the end of any appearances on my schedule until the fall.

It wasn't soon enough, according to my mom. She would have preferred I'd been back weeks ago. She'd almost quit her guest position in Ireland mid-year because she'd been terrified of leaving Cass alone. She'd prolonged going back until the very last moment. One slip on the snow and all of Mom's fears had sprung to life. Fears about Cassidy and fears that I wouldn't be there when my sister needed me the most.

I had the same fears, but I was there now and not

planning on going anywhere.

While I made a pot of coffee in the tiny kitchenette, I looked out the window and caught a glimpse of the apple trees that lined the edge of the campus. They had green buds on their branches. They'd be in full bloom before too long, bursting to life in the span of a day, as if from nothing.

The front door opened to admit my sister, and the breeze caught a stack of notes on the counter, sending them sailing to the floor. I picked them up, showing them to my sister before setting them back down.

"Looks like Mom has a whole host of things she needed to tell me," I said.

Cass grimaced. "It's like I'm seven all over again."

"Can I get you anything?" I asked. The kitchen was pretty bare from my absence, but in truth, it never held much. When I was home, I normally ate with my family.

"Where's Marco?" she asked, eyeing his military duffel on the floor by the pullout couch.

"Went downtown to Waterton's," I said. Waterton was a local guy with an alarm company slash private security firm who my actual security team used when I wanted to keep things low-key at home. "Why?"

"Just making sure you didn't do something dumb like send him to the college," she said.

During one of the many late-night conversations I'd initiated since Christmas, Cass had finally revealed to me that the father of her baby was one of the professors at the school. When I'd looked him up, I'd been surprised to find a young law professor whose picture reeked of pompousness. I couldn't picture Cass dating him. She was all environment, health, and butterfly wings, and he was obviously about money, corporations, and prestige.

"Tell me why you even dated the man," I said. My hunch was it had been a rebellious reaction to Mom's smothering attention.

"It really isn't any of your business," she said flippantly. "I'm off to work but wanted to make sure you were going to be home for dinner before I made too much."

I wanted to push her, but it wasn't the time. I'd talk to the douchebag himself first and see what happened from there.

"What are you making?" I asked, and even though I tried to keep it out of my voice, she heard the wariness because Cass liked to experiment in the kitchen with things that shouldn't be put together.

"It's just lasagna, you big baby."

"Will it have eggplant, dairy-free cheese, and gluten-free noodles?" I teased.

"Duh," she said, flipping her hair over her shoulder.

"Then, I'll need to go to the store to buy the largest cheesecake I can find to counteract all the healthiness."

She punched me in the shoulder, and I flicked her earlobe before scrunching my ear to my shoulder to escape her long fingers tickling my neck. I put the counter between us, but she was already heading for the door.

"I'll see you after work," she said.

"Don't get hurt, or Mom will never forgive me!"

But the door had already slammed shut behind

her. Thoughts of Mom had me pulling the sticky notes toward me. They were mostly reminders of Cassidy's doctor's appointments, Mom's schedule, and what felt like a hundred different emergency phone numbers. About halfway through the stack, my hand froze, and my heart clenched. "Lawyer for the estate of Elana Johnson called. See the music store for a box she left you."

Estate? Left me?

My heart seemed to stop dead before it broke into a pattern of deep thuds that were wild and out of control. Elana was gone? It was impossible! I'd just seen her at Christmas. I had plans to spend more time with her, revisiting our debates on jazz and blues.

There was no way she'd died and no one in my family had called me.

No fucking way.

I opened the search browser on my phone. The first link that came up with her name was the bi-annual Apple Jam Music Fest website. The second announced she'd died in her sleep in January. In fucking January! It was the end of February.

Guilt and nausea twisted through my stomach along with the pain and anger.

Anger that Mom wrote the words on a sticky note instead of calling me. Harsh black and white ink that she knew would wound me when she knew Elana had been the most important influence in my life. I could almost taste the bitterness filling me. Goddamn it.

I hadn't gotten to go to her funeral. I hadn't been allowed to say goodbye.

Heat blossomed through me as the rage consumed me. Anger that Elana would have been the first one to force out of me. I'd been full of it as a teen, fuming over every perceived slight: my parents missing a recital, their lack of acknowledgment when I made lead chair, their nonchalance at my mastering my fourth instrument. Elana had told me to let go of the rage before it infused itself into my soul and turned my music to rotgut.

And now she was gone.

And no one had told me one damn thing.

I wasn't sure I could forgive them for that. I couldn't turn a blind eye, look the other way, and ignore the fury inside me.

I took off for the bathroom, splashing my face and catching sight of my reflection in the mirror. I looked like Brady O'Neil, famous country singer, and very little like the scrawny Cormac O'Neil who'd learned everything he knew about music and forgiveness from a woman who was now dead.

I had to do things today that would require me to be both Brady and Cormac.

The scruff on my face was starting to shape itself into a beard much darker than my hair coloring and could help with a disguise, but I still very much looked like the man on the cover of my third album. My floppy blond hair was a signature Brady look that my stylist would growl at me for touching. I suddenly didn't care. I needed to uncover the me who'd given everything up for a dream.

I found a pair of scissors in the drawer and started hacking at the long waves. It was a disaster by the time it was done, uneven and badly angled, but it was shorter and off my face, bringing the focus back to my plain brown eyes.

In my room, I abandoned my normal Brady wardrobe for something Cormac would have worn to attend a lesson with Elana. Chucks, torn jeans, and a worn Soundgarden T-shirt. No flannel. No cowboy boots or cowboy hat.

I grabbed a beanie and shoved it on over the bad haircut. The advantage of the cut was that it allowed me to pull the knit fabric all the way to my eyebrows. Looking in the mirror one more time, I realized it was one of my better disguises. With my sunglasses, I was pretty sure no one would ever mistake me for the man whose face was on a bulletin board in Times Square, advertising the next season of *Fighting for the Stars*.

I grabbed my keys and wallet and headed out. The sky was a deep gray, fitting my mood but not my need for the sunglasses I slid on. I crossed the tree-lined street to the college that had been named after two black women authors, Harriet E. Wilson and Harriet Jacobs, from the 1800s. Two women who'd fought for their family and humanity.

All I could see when I looked at the school were my parents and the disappointments that filled the space between us. My telling them that I didn't want to go to Wilson-Jacobs had just been one of the many I'd handed them. While the college did have a music program, it wasn't at the level I'd wanted. I'd wanted the best. I'd wanted Juilliard. They'd wanted the free education I would have received as their son.

We loved each other but couldn't stop letting each other down.

This was one of the worst things they'd done to me. Elana was dead, and they hadn't told me.

In the mood I was in, I wasn't sure I should have been going to the university. I probably should have postponed it, but the anger was fueling me enough to continue. I found the asshat's name in the directory and walked up the stairs of the business building to his office. Professor Clayton Harding was sitting at his desk, typing on a laptop. He had brown hair and brown eyes that would put him in the running for a young Harrison Ford look-alike contest.

He glanced up as I appeared in the doorway but then went right back to his computer.

"Office hours aren't until three today," he said.

"Not here for your office hours," I said, taking a seat in the chair across from him. His walls were lined with awards displaying his name. A huge crystal prize that was bigger than my Grammy stood on a shelf behind him.

He looked up at me with a glare. "I don't recognize you from any of my classes. Who are you, and what do you want? I'm in the middle of something important."

"More important than your child?"

His eyes narrowed, taking in my beanie and the sunglasses sitting on top of my head.

"I don't know what you're talking about," he said quietly, with a warning in his tone.

"You know, the one my sister, Cassidy, is about to have," I continued, keeping my tone casual.

He got up and shut the door before coming back to sit on the edge of the desk. "Look. I told Cassidy I'd help her out with that. I offered to pay for the abortion, which was more than I needed to when I didn't even know if the baby was mine."

I stood, closing the space between us, anger surging back through me. "I hope you aren't insinuating Cassidy would lie about something like this."

He didn't back down. "No. I'm saying she and I had stopped sleeping together weeks before she told me she was pregnant. I don't know who was in her bed after me or if I was even the only one she was sleeping with. We weren't dating. It was casual fucking."

I grabbed his shirt, twisting it so I was right in his face. "That's my sister you're talking about, asshole."

"Sister or not, she agreed to the terms," he said without a hint of remorse, not even upset that I was in his face and five seconds from hitting him.

"And exactly what terms were those?" My voice was deep with the raw emotions the entire morning's shitstorm of news had hit me with.

"Just what I said. Sex. When I needed it or she needed it. We took precautions, so if she ended up pregnant, it wasn't because I was irresponsible."

"Sleeping with a student is one-hundred-percent irresponsible."

"She wasn't my student. In fact, she wasn't a student at all. She'd already graduated the night she approached me at the bar. She initiated it, and I was clear about what I could and could not offer. This little college has just been a résumé builder. After this semester, I move on to Harvard, and that means more to me than a baby I don't want."

His lack of emotion spiked the wrath building in me. He truly didn't give a rat's ass about my sister or her baby. He didn't care about anyone but himself. I didn't understand Cassidy at all if she had walked into a bar and picked up this prick.

I shoved him away from me and took several steps back before I lost control and pounded him in the face a few times. Before I lost my cool and did something that ended with me in the headlines with a prison cell as my backdrop. Dani would kill me. Then, I remembered she'd turned in her resignation. I no longer had a PR manager until we replaced her.

More loss. Piles of it.

"You truly don't care that you're going to have a kid? That there will be a piece of you out in the world?" I said gruffly.

"Quite the opposite. I do care. I care that she's having the baby when I would prefer it didn't exist at all. It was why I told her I'd pay for the abortion, regardless of whether it was mine or not."

I just stared at him.

"You're a fucking asshole," I said quietly.

"It isn't the first or last time I'll be told that. Now, if you'll excuse me, I have an important paper to finish writing."

He straightened his clothing and took a seat behind his desk. He started typing and ignored me while I continued to glare. He was a complete and utter waste of life—a completely selfish human being.

As I turned to leave, my fury at him turned inward because it was obvious I knew nothing about my sister. I'd made assumptions about her based on the little girl I used to know before I'd left for Juilliard. I may not have been hovering around her like my parents, but I was refusing to let her grow up just like they were.

I stormed out of the building, shaking.

I knew nothing about my family, and they knew nothing about me. Love wasn't knowledge. It needed to change.

My feet crossed the campus and headed in the

direction of downtown. The dark clouds finally broke, sending down a stream of water that had me jogging toward the overhang of the buildings along Main Street. As I stalked toward the music store, I barely registered any of the other businesses that had been a permanent fixture of my youth.

The bell above the door jingled as I walked into the shop. The smell hit me first: vinyl, old instruments, and the oils for cleaning them. My heart clenched. God, I'd loved this place. It no longer looked like the happening spot to get music it had once been when I was growing up. Even then, the push to digital had been casting the CDs to the side. Now, with the resurrection of interest in records and Elana's volume of them, I would have expected the store to have the same number of customers as the antique shop on the other side of the road.

Just being in the store eased my heart a little as I tried to shrug off the rolling depths of emotions surging through. But being in there also amplified the loss I was feeling as my fury receded. It felt like someone had grabbed my heart and sliced it with crisscross cuts. Not deep enough to bleed out, but deep enough to leave multiple scars.

"I'll be down in a sec," a female voice hollered from the stairs at the back leading to the practice rooms and a dusty storage area.

I pulled my beanie down lower, almost covering my eyes, and scratched at the beard. I slid the sunglasses to the top of my head and eased down the A row. I flipped through a stack and came up with a *Back in Black* AC/DC album that would fit right in with my collection back in New York City.

A clatter on the stairs drew my head around, and

my entire body froze as a woman came into view. Streaks of mahogany mixed in with a golden mane pulled back into some sort of knot at the top of her head, barely holding itself together with curls spiraling everywhere. I blinked twice to make sure I wasn't seeing things, but no, the bun was secured with paintbrushes—two large, one small—as if this person was using the mound of hair like a seamstress used a pincushion.

She had a smudge of what I assumed was paint on her cheek, and she was wiping her hands on a cloth. She was delightfully curvy, but it was partially hidden under an enormous sweater that landed almost at her knees where a pair of black leggings trailed down the rest of her. She wasn't tall or short. She was somewhere in between, and I found my body traveling to her before I'd even considered it.

When I got closer, her hazel eyes looked almost golden in the stream of the stained-glass lights that had hung over the counter for as long as I could remember. This woman had a hint of Elana in her. Something about the eyes or the mouth. And maybe that was why I had an odd sense of déjà vu when she squinted at me. Like I'd met her but not. I met a lot of people each year. Thousands. I didn't remember them all, but if I'd met and forgotten this woman, I was going to bonk my head into the side of the wall a few hundred times.

"Is that all you need?" she asked, referring to the AC/DC album stuck in my hand.

No. It wasn't why I'd come at all.

I'd come because of a damn sticky note saying one of the most influential people in my life had died and no one had told me. I'd come because I was not only angry, but also hurt and sad, but now I wasn't sure what I felt because this woman was looking at me as if I needed something else. Something more. Something I couldn't name. And hell, hadn't I had those same thoughts myself? The gaping hole in my soul was growing wider and wider.

"Who are you?" I finally asked.

She looked completely taken aback by the question. As if no one had ever asked her that before.

I was losing it.

"Did you want that or not?" she asked, her eyes dropping to the record again. She was shifting from foot to foot as if it was hard for her to stand still, impatient. Ready for me to be gone. She confirmed it by adding on, "I'm about to close up."

It was noon on a Monday. Since when did the music store close at noon on a weekday? When school let out for the day, the kids would be streaming in here for lessons. Eventually, the college kids escaping their dorms would come hang out, trying to be hip while they argued music and instruments, and Elana would laugh at them like some royal princess in a salon in Paris in the twenties.

Then I remembered Elana wasn't there anymore. Maybe they didn't have anyone to teach the lessons either. Maybe this woman, with her honey-colored eyes, didn't even know how to play an instrument. The hints of Elana in her may not have rubbed off in staves and clefs and keys. Still, she had enough of Elana's Spanish heritage for it to hit me that she must be Elana's granddaughter. The one who'd spent weeks of her summers here while I'd been away at camp. The one Elana called *Cari* or *Cariño*. The one I'd never met and, yet, been more jealous of than anyone else in my life.

"Are you *Cari*?" I found my voice finally.

She stilled, the restless energy flowing through her all but leaving her body. Her squint deepened as if trying to figure out why I looked familiar, and I fought the urge to pull my sunglasses back on. Wearing them indoors was even more ludicrous than wearing them in the rain.

After staring for so long I thought she'd figured it out, she cast her eyes to the ground and moved behind the counter as if putting the old wooden surface between us would somehow block out the words I'd thrown at her.

"Only my grandmother called me that," she said, emotion filling her voice, and I immediately felt like a jerk. Elana was gone, and I'd just shoved it in her face.

"My name's..." My voice disappeared as I realized not only did I not want to say my name to this person if she hadn't yet identified me, but that Elana wouldn't have left the box to me under anything but the name I'd first been introduced to her as. My given—very Irish—name from a mother who spoke every form of Gaelic out there. Elana had still called me it even after I'd asked her to stop. Not only had she refused, but she'd given me a two-hour lecture on heritage and family.

The woman in front of me smiled. It was a small smile, as if she wasn't used to giving her full one, because I had a sense that her full one would have lifted her cheeks right up into her eyes and made them shine with glitter and happy dust. Even so, it was still a smile, and it pulled me right back out of memories of Elana to the present.

"You forget your name?" she asked, and then she put her hand in front of her grin as if she was embarrassed she'd made a joke.

I shook my head, put the record down on the worn wooden countertop, and stuck out my hand. "I'm Cormac."

Her eyes widened slightly. "Oh."

She took my hand, and the moment our skin touched, I swear to God, a portal to another world opened somewhere behind her. It sucked me right in with an energy that only a transdimensional corridor or a black hole could create.

I didn't give a damn anymore about a box from Elana, or my sister who was ready to burst, or my parents who had long ago forgotten the things that were important to me. The only thing I cared about was following *Cari* into that black void and hoping I never came back.

Chapter Six

Tristan

HOLDING OUT FOR A HERO
Performed by Elise Lieberth

Cormac was holding my hand in a way that said he didn't want to let go, and that startled me almost as much as the energy zinging its way through my fingertips. It made me pull my hand back and wipe it again on the rag I'd brought down with me from the studio, frustrated at the interruption, and the lack of light, and the fact that I had to get back to the house before we were late for our appointment this afternoon.

The man in front of me looked familiar as if I should have known him. As if I'd met him in another lifetime. But I could have sworn Grams had told me I hadn't met him when she'd started a pile for "Cormac" after the heart attack had scared her into getting her things in order. She'd said his name with that mischievous grin she wore when she was keeping a secret she couldn't wait for you to figure out. Her twinkling eyes stabbed at my heart from the memory.

It wasn't fair.

I shouldn't have had to lose her too.

"Right. Cormac," I said. "I'd almost given up on you. I left a message with your parents several weeks ago."

He nodded. "I've been… out of town, and when I got back, it was at the bottom of a pile of messages they left."

Even with the twinge of familiarity surrounding him, I trusted Grams to know we hadn't met. In all the time I'd been living with her in Grand Orchard, she'd never once called out his name as we walked through the town. He hadn't greeted her at the shop, or any restaurant along Main Street, or church on Sundays. Not even during the summer, when the college kids all went home and the town shrank down to the size of a pie instead of the entire bakery, had we run into him.

"Let me go get it for you," I said and headed back up the stairs.

Instead of staying down in the store as any decent person would do, Cormac followed me up the rickety steps. They groaned under his weight even more than mine. He was tall and built, his T-shirt sticking to muscles in a way that clenched my heart even tighter than thoughts of Grandma had. That made me think of another muscled chest that had once been mine.

When we hit the top, Cormac sucked in a breath. The main room had once been used as storage until I'd moved to Grand Orchard. Grams had reinvented it once she'd decided I needed a spot of my own. She'd insisted on emptying the boxes, installing a skylight, and adding a sink in the corner. She said it was a necessity when we both knew it wasn't. She should have used the money to redo the practice rooms with their soundproofing so old and grungy they looked like Styrofoam stained with coffee.

"Wow. This looks different than when I used to haul the deliveries up here," he said.

I'd forgotten he'd worked for Grams. She'd told me that in the same breath she'd told me he'd been one of the best students she'd ever had the privilege of teaching. But like all of Gram's mysteries, she'd kept the rest of him sealed up inside a vault of things to figure out once she'd passed.

I shook my head and pulled the trunk from the top of the apothecary cabinet I'd recommissioned for all my paints. Then, I turned, holding it out to him.

"Here you go," I said.

His eyebrows lifted, a motion you could barely see because he had his beanie tucked so low.

"I thought it was a box. This is an antique trunk," he said.

I shrugged. "If you knew Grams, then you knew how much she loved her secrets."

"What's in it?"

"Mostly old records. She wouldn't let me see the rest and made me promise I wouldn't look. She said it was between the two of you," I told him, taking the old-fashioned key on a blue ribbon from the hook on the wall and handing it to him.

"Wait. You didn't look. Not even after…" His voice trailed away, and I swore those dark eyes shone with unshed tears. I hadn't expected someone who hadn't seen her in years to care so much that she was gone.

"No. She asked me not to, so I didn't," I told him, crossing my arms and backing away because he was exuding some kind of smell or energy or aura that was attacking me in a way I didn't like. Didn't want.

"Are you even human?" he asked with an entirely too wicked smile. Completely one-hundred-percent all wickedness.

I grabbed my coat and umbrella from the hooks.

"Is it still raining?" I asked.

He nodded, head tilted, assessing me.

I hated it.

I was tired of being tested. Would she crumble? Would she fall apart? How do we pick her up if she does? But more than all of that, I hated that I had fallen apart. Repeatedly. Over and over again. Four and a half years of falling apart.

I pointed the umbrella toward the stairs. "After you."

He looked like he'd object. Some macho-istic complaint of females leading the way. My heart gripped tighter. There'd once been someone who would have demanded it. That I go first. This man didn't. He just nodded, gripped the trunk which was surprisingly heavy, and headed down the stairs.

I followed, flipping off the lights as I went.

We ended up at the front door, and I opened it for him because he had his hands full. I turned the sign in the window to *closed*, set the alarm, and then walked out, locking the door behind me. Grams had only been broken into a handful of times, the love she grew in the people around her somehow keeping her safe. Maybe that was just Grand Orchard for you. Safe.

I'd felt safe here.

These last few weeks, though, I hadn't known what to feel.

We stood under the overhang as the rain continued to float down just beyond it, the drips from the roofline tumbling down and hitting my gray Chucks that used to be white. The ones splotched with paint drops.

"Would you like me to tell you what I find?" he asked, drawing me back to him, eyes twinkling just like Grams'. No wonder she'd had a lot of affection for him. It was surprising that we hadn't ever met when I'd spent so many weeks with her during the summers. It was as if the world had decided we couldn't live in the same universe.

And now we were.

We'd collided together, and I had no desire to collide again.

I shook my head. "Nah. Like I said, if she'd wanted me to know, she would have told me."

He smiled. "I don't know a single person who would be able to resist finding out the answers to the 'What's in the box?' question."

I didn't want to smile, but my lips twisted anyway. "You do know the story of Pandora, right?"

His smile increased, dimples appearing, and I had that weird sense of knowing him again, and I stared hard, absorbing the details of him, trying to place it. He suddenly seemed uncomfortable under my gaze. His smile dropped away as he juggled the trunk in order to bring his unnecessary sunglasses down onto his nose.

"Those should really help you with all this sunshine," I couldn't help teasing with a wave of a hand to the rain and dark clouds.

He nodded.

"They're magic. They protect me from more than mere sunlight. They protect me from demons and angels and weirdos."

I snorted. "Weirdos?"

His grin returned. "So, the demons and angels didn't even phase you, but the weirdos did?"

I opened my umbrella and turned away from the grin that was unsettling me, stepping down from the sidewalk, ready to head across before traveling the few streets to Stacy's house.

"Where are you going?" he called out behind me.

I turned to face him. He was still standing under the overhang with Grams' antique trunk in his hands. My heart pattered because it was one more thing of hers I was losing. The sign for the store was above him. I'd turned it off, but at that exact moment, the sun peeked through the rain and the clouds to hit it: *La Musica de Ensueños.*

The music of dreams. Grandma had believed in it. A pattern to our lives we danced to. Above the building, a rainbow suddenly appeared as the sun and rain and clouds mixed together.

It was all too much. A gorgeous man my grandmother had loved. The store she'd poured her heart and soul into. The dreams and rainbows.

I didn't believe in them anymore. I wanted to. Because I wanted them for my daughter. I wanted to give them to her on a silver platter.

I turned away, walking in the rain that still trickled down around me, not understanding why the man on the sidewalk watched me until I disappeared around the corner market. Not understanding any of it, but most certainly not understanding why Grams had wanted a man she hadn't seen in years to have her things.

My head was there, at the store with a square-chinned man with sparkling eyes, when I got to Stacy's house. I knocked and let myself in with my key. Stacy and I had exchanged keys ages ago because we always seemed to be running to get something for each other or taking each other's kids home. It was just easier this way.

"Hello!" I called out.

Stacy came flying from the room they'd converted into a classroom. Her face was completely lit up.

"We finally got the approvals from the state and county school boards!" she all but screamed, her smile taking over the entirety of her face.

"Congratulations!" I hollered back.

Then, we were hugging each other and jumping up and down and dancing. Good news. We needed it. She'd worked hard to make the charter school happen. She was starting small, pre-kindergarten through second grade, but it would be a start. As funding and income increased, she'd be able to grow it more.

"When are we celebrating?" I asked.

"Soon. We'll have to see what night Jay can watch the kids for us."

Jay not only worked part time for her, but he was also getting his teaching credential, so he had his hands full, especially as midterms and spring break neared. The best thing about Jay was that he was beloved by all of the kids that Stacy took care of, including my daughter.

I squeezed Stacy again before stepping away. "I really am happy for you!"

She was beaming, and I couldn't blame her.

My phone buzzed, an unknown number calling, and I sent it to voicemail. I caught sight of the time. The run-in with Cormac at the store had me behind schedule.

"I hate to run, but we'll be late for our appointment with Cassidy if we don't head out now."

"Hannah, your mom's here," Stacy hollered.

Hannah came skipping from the other room, her shawl swaying about her with a book clutched to her chest. She jumped into my arms. "Mom!"

I caught her and hugged her tightly.

"Guess what?" she asked.

"What?"

"We went to the library, and I got a heart-healthy cookbook," she told me, all proud.

Stacy and I exchanged a look over the top of her head. Once Grams had her heart attack, Hannah had taken the healthy food thing to the limit. She'd thought it would save my grandma, and now I was pretty sure she thought it would save me from leaving her as well. I wasn't going anywhere, but tell that to a child who never knew her father and had just lost her idol. I was lucky she wasn't throwing tantrums and refusing to step foot out of the house, but that wasn't my little's way. Nope. Not only was she too old for her years, but she was also too smart for her age as well. It wasn't like she was reading college textbooks or anything, but she was well past the beginner books. It was the reason I was so grateful Stacy would continue to be her teacher at the new school.

"Is that right? Anything in it you want to make?" I asked.

Hannah frowned. "I have to talk to Cassidy about it."

"Why is that?"

She lowered her voice to a whisper. "They have chocolate cake in here."

She said it like it was a huge sin, and my heart tugged.

"Well, they do say chocolate is an anti-inflammatory," I told her.

"What's anti-inflammastory?"

I resisted the urge to smile because my daughter did not like to be the butt of anyone's joke. "Not inflammastory, inflammatory. It means it reduces body parts that might be swollen."

"But it's chocolate," she said because she'd placed it in her "not good" category in her head.

"Well, remember what Cassidy said the last time about balance. I'm sure it is because of that, but let's go so we won't be late, and you can ask her yourself."

We gathered our things, hugged Stacy goodbye, and headed down the street to the clinic. Everything important to me in Grand Orchard was within walking distance of the house. There were strip malls on the far edge of town where the boundaries were being pushed and where the college kids could get their fix of all the fast-food chains, but I liked all the homegrown stores near the heart of the town.

I'd almost canceled our appointment at the clinic today because it was really a follow-up for Grams, but now I was glad I hadn't, because I needed my daughter to hear from someone else that eating a few treats wasn't going to put her in the hospital.

Cassidy greeted us in her office with a warm

smile.

Her pregnant belly was sticking out from her slender frame even more than when I'd seen her weeks ago at Grams' funeral. I vaguely remembered that stage of my own pregnancy. Where everything hurt as the baby pressed on every internal organ, but you were also full of bliss and expectation. Days away from being able to hold the baby and count its fingers and toes and kiss its cheeks and nose.

"You look good," I said.

"I'm tired and never stop having to pee, but I'm doing good otherwise," she said before tapping Hannah's top hat. "How are you, lady?"

Hannah hugged her and then shoved the cookbook at her.

"This book says we can have cake. Is it true?"

Cassidy laughed, and Hannah frowned, causing Cassidy to straighten her lips as much as she possibly could. "You know it is. We've already talked about how eating sweets is okay in moderation."

"But it has butter and sugar," Hannah pressed, flipping open the book and setting it down on Cassidy's desk with the chocolate cake recipe showing.

"Which are both allowed in moderation," Cassidy said. "Let's take a look at the recipe."

We chatted with Cassidy for about twenty minutes and ended with several weeks' worth of meal plans that included desserts. I was going to have to send her a whole basket of treats from Sweet Lips as a way of saying thank you for getting my obsessed girl eased into a milder plan.

As we stood, Cassidy grimaced, rubbing her

back.

"Are you okay?" I asked.

She nodded. "Just full of Braxton Hicks contractions all day."

"Warm bath," I suggested.

"For sure. I'm going to head out early and do just that."

Hannah hugged her goodbye, and we left, heading first to the store and then carrying our groceries home while Hannah chatted about Cassidy, the food, and the cookbook. When we finally reached home, she skipped over to the laundry room door keeping Molly at bay and released the hound. The dog spun around Hannah several times before the two of them took off for the kitchen at a run, the maroon shawl flying like a superhero cape. My daughter was a superhero. Resilient. Strong. Some days, I wasn't sure where she got it, because I rarely felt that way.

I felt weak all the time.

After dinner, I helped Hannah with her bath, we read through several of the recipes in the cookbook, and then I tucked her into bed with the latest *Ellray Jakes* book by Sally Warner. Because of Stacy, I was putting stories with people of color as the protagonists in front of my daughter. It was yet another reason Stacy was going to be an incredible teacher and administrator. She was going to change the world one life at a time.

My phone rang, and Hannah saw Nash's face on the screen before I did. She picked it up. "Hi, NaNa," she said with a smile. Her nickname for Nash from her baby days sent warmth through me as did his nickname for her.

"BoPeep! How the heck are you?"

"We're making chocolate cake tomorrow," she said, and Nash chuckled. I let them chat for a minute and then told Nash I'd call him back after putting Hannah down.

I kissed my daughter on the forehead and tucked the blankets around her like a phyllo roll before turning on the lava lamp on Hannah's side table. I'd leave it on until she fell asleep and I came up for bed. I brushed a hand over Molly's fur at Hannah's feet and then shut the lights off with the door cracked open.

I went back down the stairs, determined to tackle the mountain of paperwork and bills that I'd been ignoring ever since my mom had left. She'd been here for almost a month, helping do all the most important things after Grams' death, just like she'd helped me through it all after Darren had died. But after the will had been read and everything had pretty much been left to me, there had been a wall that had come up between me and the rest of my family.

Mom hadn't wanted to hear about anything related to the store or the house. So, I'd shoved it aside while waiting for the official death certificate and documents from the lawyers in order to switch everything over into my name.

Two hours later, I pushed a hand through all the papers spread out on the antique rug in frustration. I collapsed on my back next to the paperwork. How could Grams not have told me things were so bad? I'd been here for over three years, and she'd never once let on that she was a beat away from losing the store. Instead, she'd done the opposite. She'd gotten the loan for the small remodel and to fix the roof. She'd insisted that Hannah, Molly, and I live here rent-free. She'd barely let me buy groceries or pay for utilities.

Guilt ate at me.

Her love for it all was why I didn't understand how she could have allowed things to get so out of hand. She'd continued to give lessons even when people weren't paying, she'd still ordered new albums and CDs—even when she rarely sold the stock she did have—and she'd ordered a bunch of instruments to give to the public school. In the meantime, she hadn't paid her property taxes in over a year, and there was now a lien on the store.

It didn't seem like her at all, and yet, it did. My ever-optimistic grandmother had thought everything would come right again with the proceeds from the Apple Jam Music Fest. It was slated for the weekend before Memorial Day, and she and I had been working on it for over a year. But since she'd passed, I'd not opened one thing in regards to it. I hadn't answered any of the emails from people who were scheduled to play, those who'd purchased vendor tables, or even attendees asking if the three-day event was going to go ahead as planned without her.

I hadn't answered because I hadn't known.

The first year I'd moved in with her, she'd already had the plans for the festival well in hand when I'd arrived. I'd just helped after the fact. I'd basically been a gopher, going where she'd told me to go, making sure people knew where to set up their booths, ensuring the green-room catering arrived, and guiding the volunteers to their positions. She'd been ninety years old at the time and proved all the age-ists wrong. She was as whip-smart and firm in her old age as she'd been when she was younger. At least, that was what I'd thought. When she'd started planning for the event this time, I'd been glad I was there to help even when it hadn't seemed like she really needed me.

One thing was certain: I couldn't fill the shoes she'd left behind. Elana Johnson *was* the Apple Jam Music Fest, and now she was gone.

My phone buzzed with a text from Stacy, making me remember I hadn't called Nash back. They would both be a welcome relief from the pile in front of me.

> *STACY: Jay says he can watch the kids Friday night. You up for a PAR-TAY?*

> *ME: You mean a drink at Mickey's?*

> *STACY: There may or may not be karaoke involved.*

I was not a singer. I warbled and rarely knew all the words, but it was Stacy's night, and I'd do just about anything she wanted if it meant celebrating her.

> *ME: If that's what you want, then that's what we'll do.*

Jin wasn't a karaoke-lover either, but he would do anything for his wife.

> *STACY: You're a real friend.*

> *ME: Remember that when we have pretzels thrown at us because no one can stand my frog croak.*

> *STACY: We'll put Jin in front. He can deflect them for us.*

> *ME: You're lucky he loves you.*

> *STACY: Yep. I really, really am.*

I went to call Nash and saw the red dot reminding me of the missed call from earlier. The person had actually left a message. I hit the button and was greeted with a deep male voice. "Miss Morgan, this is William Chan from Platinum Bank and Trust. It's my understanding that Elana left the music store to you. I'd been in discussions with her about buying it. I'd like to continue those talks with you at your first opportunity."

I sat stunned for a moment. There was no way Grams would have sold the store. She would have cut off an arm and given it away before she signed it off to someone else. It was her entire life. But then I stared at the pile of bills, late notices, and bank statements, and I wondered if she hadn't been doing just that. Owning a music store in the digital age wasn't profitable. Selling instruments and lessons was barely breaking even. Still, Grams and her store had been a staple in the community for over sixty years.

I thought about calling my mom, but if I hadn't known Grams was thinking of selling, then my mother certainly wouldn't have either.

"Grams, what the heck were you doing?" I muttered.

I didn't realize I was crying until the first tear hit the papers on my lap.

I brushed at it and then at the ones on my face.

No. I wasn't going to cry. I was tired of crying. I was tired of feeling sad.

The thought of feeling anything at all brought back Cormac's visit to the store. To the casual touch of our fingers that had my body reacting in a way it hadn't since Darren. From our very first teenage bumbles to our days of passion whenever he came home, Darren and I'd had a connection that was much more than just physical. It hung in the air when we were together like the mist rising from a cool stream on a hazy morning.

I closed my eyes and let my thoughts drift back to those touches. The last time we'd made love before he'd lost his life. The tangle of our bodies in a house in Florida as we'd shed our clothes with speed before Hannah woke up from her nap. The slow touch of his hands over the stretch marks on my stomach I'd been upset about and that he'd kissed with tenderness. The kisses he'd placed on my breasts that had lost their firmness in the battle with nursing.

I'd felt old and used, and he'd brought me back to life with every touch.

Now, I just felt old and used, and I hadn't expected ever to be brought back to life again. I hadn't wanted to be brought back to life because that meant taking a risk on someone else, and I wasn't prepared to do that again. Regardless of the fleeting sense of awakening I'd felt at Cormac's touch, it was the last thing I was going to follow up on. The focus of my life was going to remain on my daughter, my art, and Grams' store. It was more than enough to fill my days. Besides, my girl was the one who deserved a bright and beautiful future, and I was determined to make sure she had one.

I deleted the message and hit Nash's phone number. As late as it was, if I didn't call back, he'd just worry. I was grateful for him. For Stacy. For the people in my life who were always there for me. I relied on them too much. This thing with Grams and the store…I could do this on my own.

Chapter Seven

Brady

IT GOES LIKE THIS
Performed by Thomas Rhett

The rain had soaked through all my layers by the time I got home from the music shop. My entire round of unsatisfying business that morning had resulted in one thing. I was full of chords and words acting like a montage to the vortex of feelings I was drowning in. Starting with the sticky note this morning all the way until the moment *Cari* had touched me. I set the antique chest down on the coffee table and dragged my guitar out of its case.

Music flowed through my head, and I poured it out. It was sweet and bitter and harsh and gentle. It was echoes of my past and glimpses of a future that would likely never be mine. It was a deeper tone than my last album. Not darker, but maybe richer. After starting over, with a tweak here and there, I set my phone down, hit record, and captured the bulk of it. It was raw and needed work, but it was a start.

I sent it to Ava, knowing she'd make sense of it. Knowing she'd find the truth in the words and the notes like she always did.

I was surprised when my phone rang.

"Who's the poor woman you've subjected to this latest round of casual flirtation?" she asked.

"Why does there have to be a woman?"

"Okay, who's the poor man you've subjected to this latest round of casual flirtation?" she said with a tease in her voice.

I chuckled, and some of the pain and longing eased inside my chest.

But the truth was, the feelings I'd had with *Cari* hadn't felt flirtatious at all. It wasn't anything I'd ever felt. Like I'd busted through the veil of this dimension to another one.

"Why does it have to be a person, was what I meant," I said.

Her turn to laugh, her husky voice soothing me. "Are you taking up with animals then?"

"Shh, don't even suggest it. Some tabloid will pick it up, and that will be the death of my career."

"I heard, back in the day, Richard Gere had his own battle with tabloids and animals, and people still love him."

"When was the last time you went to a Richard Gere movie?"

She laughed. "I get your point. Now, back to the song. What's up?"

For some reason, I didn't want to tell her. It was unusual. I wasn't one to keep secrets. I wasn't one to hide away parts of me from my friends.

"Just been a day," I told her.

"Well, whatever is fueling it, it's good," she said.

"I've already got some ideas on how to finish it."

"I knew you would."

"You're in Grand Orchard?" she asked.

"Yeah. Cass is about ready to burst. I want to be here for her."

"Babies…" she said with a sigh.

"Babies?" Eli's voice came through over the phone, followed by another sigh and his husky voice lowered to a murmur, saying, "Want to go to work on another one?"

Ava's former Coast Guard husband was deep and broody and her perfect match. I could almost see him with his arms around her waist and lips on her neck.

I'd always been happy she'd found someone who could love her the way she deserved to be loved, and yet, today it filled me with fire. Not because I wanted Ava, but because I wanted someone. Someone who got me the way Ava and Eli got each other. I wanted to wrap my arms around someone and kiss their neck and have them crumble at the knees. My vision filled with *Cari*.

"I'm going to leave you two at it then," I said with a hint of laughter.

"Talk later," Ava said and clicked off.

My sister's Prius pulled into the yard, and I headed out to the driveway in time to help her with the reusable grocery bags she was hauling from the trunk. In the kitchen, we put things away, and then she set to work putting together the lasagna she'd promised earlier that I knew would taste good, regardless of how much I'd harassed her about it.

"Do you want help?" I asked.

She shook her head. "No, I like doing it."

I watched as she moved around the kitchen like the expert she was. She'd been experimenting with food for as long as I could remember, replacing the meat in recipes with other ingredients, like her pulled pork sandwiches made from jackfruit, of all things.

"I looked through Mom's reminders today." I tried to keep the note of bitterness from my tone. "Weren't you supposed to be out on maternity leave starting this week?"

"I'm trying to save as much time as possible for after the baby is born. Plus, what would I do? Sit around with my feet up, eating bonbons or something?"

"What do you have against bonbons?"

She laughed. "Nothing if they're made with cocoa from child-labor-free farms."

"How did you become the flower child of our family?"

She hit me with a towel. "Caring about what we eat and our world hardly makes me a flower child."

"Speaking of people who are not flower children, what's the deal with Professor Asswipe Hardy?"

Her mixing hand froze. "What do you mean? Or rather should I ask, what did you do?"

"I just wanted to see the guy. Maybe intimidate him a little," I said with a shrug.

She laughed.

"What's so funny?" I asked.

"You, being intimidating."

I growled. "I can be intimidating."

"Did you have Marco with you?"

"No."

Cassidy laughed so hard she had to wipe her eyes, and while I wanted to be mad, I couldn't be with her peals of joy ringing through the air. It had always been this way with Cass. She was bright and happy and beautiful, even when she struggled.

After she calmed down, I asked, "Why aren't you upset with him?"

"I never wanted him for keeps."

"He isn't your type at all," I said.

She turned back to her work, forming layers and avoiding my gaze.

"Cass, really. What was the deal with you and him?" I asked.

"He didn't see me as someone who'd overcome anything. He just saw me as a pretty woman he could screw."

"A casual round of sex? That sounds more like me than you."

"Maybe we're more alike than you think," she said.

I watched her work again, wondering if it was true, and hating that I didn't know, just like I didn't know about her gluten allergy.

"I haven't spent much time getting to know the grown-up version of you. I'm sorry about that, and I want it to change. It's why I want to stay and help you with the baby."

"I don't need help. There are millions of single moms out there. I'm just one more."

"And I bet all of those single moms would tell you to accept help when it was offered. Why the sudden need to do everything solo?" I asked.

She blew out an air of frustration. "It isn't a

sudden need. I can accomplish whatever I want, and I don't need anyone to guide me along."

"So, this is you thumbing your nose at Mom and Dad for trying to keep you in cardboard and bubble wrap?"

"No." She shook her head but then stopped. "Maybe."

I let it go for now, determined to figure out a way to help her.

"What else did you do with your day besides try to torment Clayton?" she asked.

My good humor evaporated. "Did you know about Elana?"

She nodded, and a sense of betrayal hit me.

"Why didn't you tell me?"

Cassidy looked surprised. "Mom said she told you."

"She wrote a freakin' sticky note and pinned it to the middle of a stack of them on the fridge. She didn't actually tell me."

Her face fell further. "I'm so sorry. I should have known something was off when you didn't come home for her funeral. I just thought—"

"That I was an uncaring asshole?"

"God no. I just thought it was too hard for you to come back."

"I sing songs for a living. It's not like I'm on a 007 mission. Why does everyone think I can't come back for the important things?"

Cassidy's eyes grew wide, and she doubled over with a hand to her abdomen and a moan escaping her.

"Cass?" I jumped up and put an arm around her

shoulders.

"Contraction. Fake contraction. I've been having them all day," she said.

"All day? Did you call the doctor?" I asked.

"Oh, shit," Cass said, looking down, and I was surprised to see water trailing down her legs under her maternity dress.

"Right. Hospital." I grabbed my phone and dialed Marco. "We need to get to the hospital."

"Are you okay?" Marco's deep voice asked.

"I'm fine. It's Cassidy. She's having the baby."

"I'll be there in five," he said.

I had no idea what Marco had been up to all day, but I was glad he was here, because I wasn't sure I'd be able to drive the car straight enough to get it to the hospital with my sister groaning in the passenger seat.

♫ ♫ ♫

It was nearly midnight, and Cass had sent me out of the room while they checked on her progress. She'd literally had to force me out with a threat to my fingers because I hadn't taken a bathroom break since we'd shown up. I hadn't wanted her to go through this alone.

Marco had stayed in the waiting room as things progressed, doing what Marco did best, watching everything and everyone silently. But I had a suspicion he was slightly rattled—something unusual for Marco. I'd seen him pace across the doorway a few times, and I wondered if it was the hospital, the act of birthing, or the silent way Cass had been dealing with the pain in the SUV on the way to the hospital that had unnerved him.

Now, he was standing up against a wall, arms crossed, watching the TV, and eyeing the bodies as they drifted by. I sent Mom and Dad another update, even though they wouldn't be able to respond to this one. I'd been sending them updates all the way until they'd boarded the flight from Dublin to Albany. They'd been two weeks away from coming home for spring break, and Mom was a wreck that she wasn't going to be here in the room while her baby had a baby.

The ping of the elevator caught my attention, and a nurse and an orderly wheeled a bed out of it. A little girl lay in it, sniffling, a top hat in her hand.

I blinked, trying to make sure I wasn't losing my damn mind.

But no, it was a top hat.

I blinked again when, out of the doors, behind the bed, came *Cari*. She had on a pair of flannel pajama bottoms and another shirt ten times too big for her. Her blonde hair with its mahogany stripes was up in another hastily constructed bun, and her face was coated with worry.

The bed wheeled past me and down the hall to the pediatric ward.

I couldn't help myself. I was drawn to her side and startled her when my fingers grazed her arm. "Are you okay?"

She wrapped her arms around her waist, pulling her body away from mine.

"It's my daughter. She fell down the stairs," she said.

The young girl in the bed was her daughter, which meant there might be a husband lurking about. And even knowing there might have been someone out there who would care about my reaction to his wife, I couldn't help the waves of emotion pouring through me from the slight grazing of our skin. It also didn't stop me from tagging along beside her with Marco following me at a distance.

The orderly wheeled the bed into a room, and the nurse started hooking up the girl to monitors. *Cari* went to the little girl's side, grabbing the hand that wasn't connected to the wires.

"I don't want to stay, Mommy," the child said with big watery eyes full of so much begging that, even when I didn't know her, I was ready to pick her up and carry her out of the room.

"It's just for the night, *Chiquita*, and I'll be right here. They just want to make sure you didn't bonk that sassy head of yours too hard." *Cari*'s tone was soft and sure, but it didn't match the worry that wafted off of her uptight shoulders.

"It doesn't even hurt anymore," the little one said, pulling her hand from her mother's and reaching for her temple where a bandage sat.

She looked like *Cari*. She looked like Elana. She looked oddly familiar, just like her mother had, as if I was trying to pull them from a memory that my brain refused to access.

The orderly had disappeared, and the nurse put a hand on the child's head. "Do you want green or red Jell-O?"

The girl's face turned up into a grimace. "Jell-O is not healthy at all."

The nurse chuckled. "No, I suppose it isn't, but it's considered a clear liquid, and that's all you can have right now."

"Water is a clear liquid," the little girl spoke as if

she were a teenager instead of the four- or five-year-old person she must have been.

"Water it is, then. I'll be right back with it." The nurse left.

The little girl watched her leave, and her eyes landed on me. "Oh. Who are you?"

Cari's eyes were drawn back to me as well, her eyebrows drawing together in confusion as to why I was still there. I didn't know why, but I hadn't been able to do anything but follow my feet and my instincts as they led me down the corridor after her.

"I'm…Cormac." I caught myself just in time. "I knew your grandmother, or I guess your great-grandmother?"

The little girl ran a finger along the edge of her top hat, and a frown appeared on her face that matched her mother's. They looked alike in more than just the frown. They had similar hair and eyes and lips. But the brows on the little girl were more delicate than the strong ones that defined *Cari*'s face.

"That's quite a nice top hat," I told her, stepping toward the bed.

"Mommy almost forgot it," she said with disgust. "And now they won't let me wear it because of the stupid stitches."

"It's just for a few days," *Cari* told her.

"What happened?" I asked them both.

"I got up to get a glass of water and slipped. It was silly." She looked at her mother. "And it was *not* Molly's fault. She did *not* trip me."

"Wow. Assuming someone dislikes you enough to trip you down the stairs is never a good sign. Who is this Molly?" I asked.

The little girl's lips twitched. "Molly is our dog."

I smiled. "Oh, that makes much more sense."

Cari rubbed both her hands up and down her arms. She leaned forward and kissed the little girl's cheek. "I'm going to be right there in the hall for a second, okay?"

Then, she stood and stepped out into the corridor, expecting me to go with her. Which I did. I glanced around and found Marco several doors down.

"What are you doing here?" *Cari* asked.

"My sister is having a baby," I told her, waving a hand down the hall toward the maternity ward.

"Congratulations. Shouldn't you go back to her?"

"I was just heading that way, but you looked upset. I wanted to make sure you were—"

"Holy Moses," the nurse said, dropping the water pitcher in her hand and sending its contents soaring across the linoleum flooring. She was staring at me. I put my hand to my self-chopped hair. I hadn't grabbed my beanie in our rush out the door earlier.

"You're…" Another nurse came out of the next room and stopped at her friend's mess, taking in her shocked face before taking me in. This new nurse let out a little squeal.

"Oh my God, you're Brady O'Neil!"

"Can I have your autograph?" the first nurse asked.

Beside me, I felt *Cari* stiffen as I forced a smile on my face and nodded.

"Wait. Wait. Right there!" The first nurse went scrambling off down the hallway while the second nurse stood there staring.

In two seconds, the first was back, shoving paper and a pen in my direction, and Marco was closing in on us. I shook my head at him as I took the items.

"Who should I make it out to?" I asked her, smiling.

"Theresa. I'm Theresa," she said, grinning back at me.

"Theresa, you must not be from around here originally," I told her as I signed the paper.

"How'd you know?"

I chuckled. "No one in town asks me for my autograph. They know I'm the kid who got caught one too many times in the apple orchard."

She laughed.

"Plus, how could I forget that beautiful face?" I said, and she turned a deep red.

"Can I have one as well?" the second nurse asked, handing over the chart in her hand.

"This anything important?" I asked.

She laughed. "Oh, yes. Here," she said, pulling a brochure on healthy eating from the wall display.

"And you are?"

"Marissa."

I signed the paper and handed it back to her.

Marco closed the distance again. "You okay?" he asked.

The ladies noticed him for the first time, assessing him with wondering eyes before realizing he wasn't famous as much as my bodyguard.

I nodded.

"Shall I help?" I asked, referring to the pitcher that had spilled.

Theresa turned a deeper shade of red. "No. No. I've got it."

She took off again, presumably to get items to clean up with. The call button in the room behind the second nurse went off, and she sighed before going back into the room.

I turned my face to *Cari*'s to find her squinting so hard I thought it would leave permanent marks. "Cormac. You told me your name was Cormac!"

She was pissed, or embarrassed, or maybe a mixture of both. I was just sad that the cat was out of the bag. I couldn't put it back. I couldn't be the person her grandmother had liked enough to leave something in her will.

"Cormac is my name. My given name," I told her.

"I can't believe I didn't recognize you. I can't believe my grandmother! That stupid mischievous look in her eyes. One last secret for her to spring on me." *Cari* turned and headed back toward her daughter's room.

"Why are you mad?" I asked.

"I'm not mad…" she said, and it felt like it was the truth, but she was still upset. "Why didn't you tell me?"

I shrugged, eyes going to the nurse who came out of the room with the paper I'd signed clutched to her chest and a smile still on her lips. Realization seemed to dawn on her, and she was about to say something when her eyes hit on something behind me.

A woman was hurrying down the hallway in yoga pants and a T-shirt. Her wrapped hair accentuated the high cheekbones that lingered on her dark skin. I recognized her from Elana's store at Christmas. It would have been hard to forget someone so stunning.

"Stacy," *Cari* said, hugging the woman.

"How's she doing?" the woman named Stacy asked.

"More upset about not being able to wear her top hat than the stitches."

Stacy looked over *Cari*'s shoulder to me and then said in a hushed tone, "Why is Brady O'Neil here?"

Cari gave out an exasperated breath. "His sister is having a baby." Then she looked at me with wide eyes. "Wait, is your sister Cassidy O'Neil?"

I nodded. Everyone in this town knew each other, so it didn't surprise me that she knew Cassidy. It was odder that she hadn't put together my name with my family's earlier today than the fact that she knew Cassidy.

"Cassidy is an angel," Stacy said before asking *Cari*, "Is this how you know Brady?"

"No, my grandmother knew him."

"Your grandmother taught me how to play four instruments," I said, and both women turned wide eyes on me.

"Thanks for checking on me," *Cari* said, but her tone was dismissive as if she needed me gone as much as I needed to stay.

"Before I head out, can I ask what your real name is?" I asked.

Stacy was watching us, wide-eyed. *Cari* looked uncomfortable. "It's Tristan. Only Grams called me *Cariño*."

"An endearment." My voice was clogged with a sudden rush of emotion that came from nowhere.

Elana had loved this woman. As a teen, I'd been jealous of how much she'd loved her granddaughter.

How much she'd looked forward to the weeks *Cari* spent in Grand Orchard while I'd been away at camp. If I hadn't loved music camp as much as I had, I would have refused to go just so I could see the infamous *Cariño* in person. Tristan. Her name was Tristan.

Saying her name in my brain had all the pieces suddenly falling together.

She was friends with Dani and Nash. I had vague recollections of them talking about her as if she lived somewhere in Delaware, though. They'd met her through Dani's brother, Mac, and his friendship with Nash when Nash was still a SEAL. Tristan was Nash's friend's widow.

She was a widow.

Layers of emotions filled me. She'd lost more than her grandmother. She'd lost a husband. A SEAL. A hero.

"You're friends with Dani and Nash," I said.

"Yes." It was a pained acknowledgment.

I understood her embarrassment a little more. It wasn't just that I was some random celebrity she hadn't recognized. Her friends were close to me. They were my friends. We'd likely seen each other at their wedding. We'd likely seen each other at other events Mac and Dani's family had thrown over the years. How had I seen her and not been drawn to her before?

All I knew was I needed a piano in front of me so I could put down the *arpeggio* of fiery notes that were filling me. Notes that changed from fast and smooth to slow and choppy. Ones that twisted together, *stringendo*, tightening at the bottom of a vortex where everything suddenly came together…like us. Our universes smashing on top of each other, never to be the same again.

Chapter Eight

Tristan

JUST A FOOL

Performed by Christina Aguilera w/ Blake Shelton

Brady O'Neil was staring at me as if I were some strange creature he'd never encountered before. It was equal parts thrilling and terrifying. I didn't want to be thrilled by him. I certainly didn't want the energy that coursed through my body when his fingers had touched mine. A famous musician. A celebrity who would flit through town and be gone. Why would my body respond to his when it hadn't responded to a single soul since my husband had died? His was a body I couldn't have even if I was in a place to want one.

From the look on his face, he thought I was mad, and I was, but not so much at him as at myself for not realizing who he was sooner. But over the top of the aggravation of discovering who he was, I was worried about my girl.

That thought had me turning away, leaving him and Stacy in the corridor, unsure what to say to him, unsure if there was anything I could say.

I went to Hannah's side. She had her eyes closed, and my heart lurched with panic just as it had when I'd found her at the bottom of the stairs.

The noise of her falling had jolted me from my restless sleep. Seeing her crumpled on the floor had almost broken me apart. I didn't even remember rushing down the stairs to her. I barely remembered pushing Molly off as she'd licked Hannah's face and the blood gushing from her head wound. When I'd called Hannah's name, she'd opened her eyes and groaned before saying, "I'm sorry I woke you."

Those words had stabbed relief and guilt into my soul.

The nurse, Theresa, came in with a fresh pitcher of water, a glass of ice, and a straw. Stacy was right behind her, but thankfully, there was no sign of Brady O'Neil. My body was already too shaken up. I wasn't sure I could have withstood the continued onslaught if he'd stayed any longer.

"Is it okay for her to be sleeping?" I asked the nurse quietly.

Theresa nodded. "Yes, we'll wake her every hour just to make sure, but rest is good."

After Theresa left, Stacy dragged a chair from the other side of the room, placing it next to mine. She took my hand and squeezed. "She's going to be okay."

"I can't get the image of her at the bottom of the stairs out of my head," I said, voice shaking. The terror I'd felt filled me again.

"I can't even imagine," she said.

"I'm sorry I woke you and Jin. You didn't need to come."

"I'm glad you called me. I'm glad I'm here,"

Stacy said. "Now, spill the beans about holy hotness in the hallway."

I shrugged. "Grams left him some things. When he came to get them today, he had that dark beard and a beanie pulled down over his eyebrows. He looked more like a hoodlum than a famous country singer."

"A hoodlum?"

"Ha ha. I'm tired. You're lucky I'm able to converse in complete sentences," I said with a weak smile she returned.

"So, you've never met him before?"

I sighed. "I've never met him up close and personal in the store as "Cormac," the student that no other student could compare to, no."

"What does that mean, up close and personal?"

"He was at Dani and Nash's wedding. He even sang them a song. I'm pretty sure I remember him being at Mac's wedding, too, but that was barely a year after… and that time is still a little fuzzy," I said quietly.

"And let me guess, you never went up to him and said, 'Hello, Mr. Hottie, can I borrow your bones for the night just to relieve the sexual frustration that has been building for almost four long years?'"

I bumped her shoulder. "No. Are you kidding? I barely made it to those events. Everyone there knew…"

I shuddered. Everyone at those events knew about my loss. They knew about the Darren-sized hole in the universe that walked around next to me. I hadn't been looking for anyone to fill my bed—even for a night. And if I had, I wouldn't have gone searching amongst my friends, people who I'd have to see again.

The one thing Stacy didn't seem to understand was that my sexual appetite had shriveled up when I'd buried my husband. Those urges had disappeared with Darren. At least, they had until my entire body had sparked back into being when Cormac—Brady—had touched me this afternoon.

Stacy was eyeballing me with that look she'd started to give me lately. The look that said it had been long enough. That I needed to start searching out a partner, even if it was just for sex. Darren and I had gotten up to some pretty serious hijinks in our day. He'd been so damn strong. He'd been able to hold me, and all my curves, with ease anywhere he wanted me. My body slowly burned at the thought of him, his arms, and the way he'd devoured me. How could anything…anyone… ever make me feel that way again?

It seemed impossible. I wanted it to be impossible.

And that was the problem. Regardless of the fact that I was only in my early thirties, I didn't want another love. I still wanted my one love back.

♫ ♫ ♫

The late-afternoon light was fading as the gray clouds continued to hang over Grand Orchard. It made the light in the studio above *La Musica de Ensueños* shift into shadows and brought me out of the brush strokes I'd been making.

My phone buzzed.

MOM: How's Hannah?

I turned to the futon in the corner where Hannah

slept.

She'd done a lot of sleeping today. My worry over her head wound was slowly easing its painful hold on my heart and lungs, but every time I looked over to see her eyes closed, I still froze until I could see the gentle rise and fall of her chest.

She had the cookbook tucked next to her, and I remembered my promise to make the chocolate cake and the ingredients we'd bought the day before. With the light fading, it meant painting was done for the day. We'd go home and spend the rest of the afternoon making a cake.

ME: Resting, but better.

MOM: How are you?

ME: Starting to breathe again.

MOM: Kids are resilient. Remember when you almost drowned?

I'd been fifteen, and Darren had saved me. It was how we'd met. He'd been new to town the summer before his senior year, and my friends and I had been watching him play volleyball on the beach with the other high school boys. The fact that I'd grown up in the water and still been knocked over by a wave had been embarrassing until he'd pulled me from the water with a naked muscled chest. I'd been a goner. Lost forever in his golden glow.

The bell on the store's front door jingled, so I texted my mom that I had to go and headed down the stairs before the noise woke Hannah. Without Grams here to teach the music lessons, the store was pretty much drying up. The income coming in was nonexistent. If the music festival, or my art, didn't bring in some cash soon, I was going to be in a world of financial hurt.

When I got to the bottom of the stairs, there was a tall, handsome man in a suit waiting there. His dark eyes and black hair were silky and smooth against his pale skin. I recognized him vaguely from attending church on Sundays with Grams.

"Miss Morgan, I'm William Chan," he said, coming forward with his hand outstretched.

I shook it. "You went to church with my grandmother."

He smiled, and it was warm but cautious. "I attend a lot of churches."

I wasn't sure how to respond to that truth. "You do?"

His smile grew. "It's a great way to build rapport with the members of the community."

"Oh," I said, still unsure how he expected me to react.

"I left you a message yesterday," he told me.

I recalled the voicemail. "Yes."

"Is now a bad time to talk about it?"

"You're welcome to talk, but I'm afraid I'm not in a place to make any decisions," I told him honestly.

He slid his hand over his tie and then put both hands in his pants pockets, leaning on the counter. There was a forced casualness to him, as if it was a cover he wore on the outside while, on the inside, he was a tiger ready to leap.

"I understand. It's a difficult time, losing someone you love. But it's also the time when you have to make decisions about their property. About this property." He looked around the dust-filled room.

"It's hard for me to believe Grams would even consider selling you the store. It was her life. She's been right here in the center of town for sixty-plus years."

He gave a curt nod. "That's exactly it. She's the center of Main Street. A street the city council and I are trying very hard to bring into the twenty-first century. This space could be used much more effectively going forward. Antiques and ancient music stores are the way of the past. We need trendy, farm-to-market restaurants for the tourists and coffee shops with poets' nights for the college kids. We need to secure the economic future of our downtown area."

I frowned, remembering a discussion with Grams after she'd attended a council meeting. The new mayor was all about remaking Grand Orchard, but the shop owners who'd been there for decades, if not centuries, were fighting the action plan.

"You're working with Mayor Sanchez?"

He nodded. "I'm one of the city council members. Regan and I have a vision for Grand Orchard that will ensure its continued success. She's the most driven, responsible mayor we've seen in decades."

The tone of respect in his voice did nothing for the increasing wave of irritation growing inside me, because this man had told me Grams was considering selling, and now I knew it to be a lie.

"My grandmother wasn't considering selling to you. So why did you tell me that?"

He hesitated. "It's true she'd turned me down. But we were still trying to negotiate. I knew she was having a hard time. She hadn't paid the property taxes in over a year. She'd missed a loan payment. She'd needed an out."

"How could you know that?" I asked, the burning sensation in my chest only growing.

"As I said on the phone, I'm president of Platinum Bank and Trust. My family owns the bank and her loan."

Grams had paid off the original mortgage on the space years ago, but she'd taken out a small loan to redo the roof at the same time she'd added the skylight to my studio. Looking at the loan over the last few days, I could see she'd used it to pay some small credit card debt and outstanding bills from her suppliers as well. Not to mention the instruments she'd bought for the high school.

I hated to admit that my mother was probably right. Grams had been losing some of her marbles and should have had someone partnering with her on her business and financial decisions over the last few years. I felt like I'd failed her because I'd been caught up in my own recovery.

"The music festival is going to take care of all of that. I'm moving forward with her plans," I told him. I hadn't been sure until that moment, but there was no way I was going to just let this man buy and sell Grams' store when I knew she wouldn't have wanted that. We'd figure it out the way Grams had been for years. We'd use the proceeds from the festival to hold us over. Maybe I could make it an annual event instead of a bi-annual one.

William grimaced softly. "So, you haven't heard then?"

"Heard what?"

"The council didn't approve your permits for the

festival." He sounded sorry, but his body didn't seem it at all. He was still leaning casually on the counter as if he was talking about which album he was going to buy. Anger flitted through me at how nonchalant William Chan was when he knew the festival was going to make or break not only the music store, but many of the other shops on the street.

"Why on earth would they deny the permits for something that's been going on for half a century? What did *you* do?" I demanded.

"Not me." He stood up, hand to his chest, acting shocked. "Not me at all. The police department was concerned about how fast things got out of hand last time, and they can't afford to support it on their decreased budget. The economic situation in the city is affecting everyone. It's the reason we need to improve the draw of the downtown's businesses so we can fund the city."

"The festival can pay for the extra police," I said.

He chuckled. "With what money, Miss Morgan?"

"From the proceeds. Plus, we already have the bands lined up. Tickets have been sold, and businesses have paid for the booths. You know they count on the festival to shore up their revenues. Canceling the festival will hurt everyone," I said between gritted teeth.

He pretended to consider this. "I can see your point. There may be some middle ground we could reach."

"What? Like I agree to sell the store, and you make the permits happen?" I said it sarcastically, not truly believing it, but his slow smile had me clenching my fists before I reached out and slapped him.

"I might be able to convince them. Might even

offer a small donation toward some private security for the festival. I could probably even guarantee the festival continued for the next decade. Your grandmother's legacy doesn't have to die with her."

"Get out," I said, stepping toward him.

He eyed me up and down, my body shaking with fury. With frustration. With a sense of overwhelming loss that shook me to my core. I wouldn't let Grams' legacy fade away.

"I'm sorry I upset you. I truly have the entire town's best interest at heart. So does Mayor Sanchez. Think about it before you react, Miss Morgan," he said as he walked toward the door.

He glanced back at me one more time, gave another curt nod, and then left with the door jangling behind him. The silence of the room became even more pronounced. No customers. No money. Nothing to pull us out of the dark abyss.

I stormed back up the steps.

The mural I'd spent six months creating would have to be finished and sold. It was going to have to fill the bank account so I could fight this from a spot in the black instead of the red.

Chapter Nine

Brady

TAKE YOUR TIME
Performed by Sam Hunt

I woke with more strands of notes filtering through my brain, some *staccato*, some *glissando*. Piano and guitar and saxophone all mixed together. No trumpets yet, but it was on the edges of my brain still, not fully shaped.

It had been a week full of more inspiration than I'd had in months. Emotions of loss from Elana, frustration with my family, waves of attraction from my brief encounters with Tristan, and the enormous amounts of love I'd seen and felt surrounding Cass's baby. The look on my sister's face as she watched her son had been life-changing. All of the songs I'd created were rough and out of shape but were filled with more soul than either of my last two albums.

Ava would help smooth out the wrinkles that remained in no time. I was grateful to have her on this journey with me.

As soon as I sent Ava the newest music, she responded.

*AVA: You're going to have a long list
of songs to choose from by the time you
get back in the studio. What's going on
with you?*

ME: Babies and love and heartache.

*AVA: Someday, Brady O'Neil, you're
going to get your heart broken back.*

Her words brought me back to Tristan, the woman who'd moved my heart just by standing next to me.

ME: Who says it hasn't been already?

AVA: Har har.

I didn't know what was harder: that my friend thought I broke too many hearts or the thought that I couldn't have mine broken.

I headed for the house to check in with Cassidy and make sure Mom wasn't sending her over the edge. My parents had arrived in Grand Orchard frazzled and worried hours after Cass had given birth to Chevelle, and Mom had been hovering ever since. Cassidy had taken it with more patience than I would have been able to do. Mom was constantly correcting things Cass was supposedly doing wrong and warning her to get her balance as she stood before moving with the baby.

As if Cass had suddenly forgotten she didn't have the balance of the average person. As if having a baby had somehow addled her brain and made her forget the things she'd struggled with her entire life.

Dad seemed adrift with the amount of baby stuff, as well as the emotions filling the house. He'd spent the week sneaking off to the college.

When I let myself into the house, Cassidy was sitting in the rocker-recliner in the family room with her eyes closed. I stared at her. She was stronger in so many ways than I was. Stronger in her silence. Stronger in her patience. Stronger in what she'd overcome. Things I'd never understand.

I knew she wasn't sleeping, because the chair was in slow motion. Back and forth. Her taupe hair was tumbling about her face, her long body not quite returned to its former leanness but closer to the sister I'd known over the last few years. The baby was wrapped up in a blanket so tight that the only piece of skin you could see was his face. Wrinkled and red and gorgeous.

I dropped a hand on Cass's hair and then went to touch the baby, but she swatted my hand away. "He's just drifted off. Leave him be."

"How can you even stand to hold him and not touch him?" I said with a smile as I sank onto the couch next to her.

"Because I *am* touching him by holding him, you big goof. And because I'm so tired I feel like I'm going to stumble into a wall if I don't sleep while he does."

"Shall I let you rest, then?" I asked, going to get up.

She shook her head, swallowed, and then said, "I need to talk to you."

I settled back.

"I have to tell you something, but you can't tell Mom and Dad," she said.

I nodded, my light mood slowly meandering

away.

"The clinic had to let me go. The real reason I was working up until the baby came was because it was my last month," she said quietly.

"What? Why?"

"The city had to cut its funding. Grand Orchard has been struggling economically, and the council had to make hard choices, which meant the clinic had to make even harder ones. What were they going to do? Let go of a doctor or a nurse? No, the nutritionist is usually the first job on the chopping block."

"That sucks, Cass. But you know I've got you, right?"

"I have money saved. Living here, I should be okay, but I don't want Mom to find out and use it as another excuse not to go back to Ireland."

"I'm not going anywhere, Cass. I'll make sure Mom knows it. We'll get her back on the plane if I have to have Marco hog-tie her to the seat."

Cass laughed. "That's an image I'll never be able to get out of my head now."

Cassidy struggled her way out of the chair and swayed. I was up, catching her arm before she could fall over. She didn't acknowledge it, but I could tell it aggravated her. Not my hands but the imbalance.

"I'm going to go sleep while Chevelle does," she said.

"Sounds like a plan," I told her.

She eased her way down the hall to her bedroom.

After she left, I went into the kitchen, looked at the menu for the week that Cassidy had posted on the old whiteboard stuck to the ancient refrigerator, and started to pull out ingredients to make shepherd's pie.

It was an old comfort food from our childhood that Cassidy had made healthier by replacing the meat with soy products and enhancing the vegetables until they almost overran the sauce, but it was a recipe I could follow.

It was a lot of steps, but it kept my mind off the fact that Cass had lost her job and would still refuse any money I offered to toss her way. It was exasperating to not be able to help my family in ways I helped others. They were so damn stubborn.

The back door slamming shut brought my head up from the pan I was layering with mashed potatoes. Mom came in with a bag of baby supplies I wasn't sure Cassidy even needed.

"What are you doing?" Mom asked.

"Cooking dinner. Why?"

"Do you even know how to cook?"

"Contrary to what you'd like to believe, neither Cass nor I are little kids anymore. We're adults who know how to take care of ourselves."

She snorted, and I couldn't help the flare of irritation that flamed into existence at her derision.

"What exactly makes you think we can't?"

Mom looked surprised that I'd call her out on it. "Cassidy got herself knocked up, and you don't do anything for yourself. You have a team that caters to your every whim."

"Cassidy had sex with a man, Mom. Did you expect her to be a virgin forever? These things happen, even when precautions are taken. They both—"

"You know who it is! You know and haven't told me?" Her face squinted with anger.

"Please! You're the last person who should be holding the you-didn't-tell-me card over my head."

"What exactly does that mean?"

"It means you knew Elana had died and wrote it on a goddamn sticky note instead of picking up the phone to tell me." The words were bitter, anger and hurt layered in each of them.

She looked momentarily taken aback before defending herself. "You were filming the live episodes of *Fighting for the Stars*."

"Jesus, Mom. Do you really think that would have stopped me from coming?"

"No. Of course not! You've always shirked off your responsibilities for that woman."

God. We always came back to this same topic. The times I'd lost myself in my piano or guitar. The times I'd been late getting back from Elana's. The times that the music driving me had made me forget my family responsibilities. But I'd been a kid. A teenage, hormone-driven, dreams-in-the-eyes kid.

"I missed her funeral, Mom. Her funeral! I didn't get to say goodbye to the person who taught me how to be the person I am. She's the reason I made it into Juilliard. She's the reason for every success I've had."

My words hurt her. A flash of pain coursed across her face before being replaced by nothing. I couldn't help the fact that what I'd said was true. Elana had molded and shaped me as a musician and as a human being. In that moment, I realized Mom was jealous of Elana. Jealous even though she hadn't had the time for me. She'd been too absorbed in all things Cassidy.

"I did what I thought was best," she said quietly.

"That's the problem, isn't it? You think you know

what's best for all of us, but really, it's always been about what's best for you."

She went rigid. Arms crossed. Face and body rock-solid.

"Because what would become of you if Cass didn't need you anymore?" I continued pushing when I knew I should have backed off. But I was hurt and angry, too, and it drove me to say cruel things.

She slapped me.

I stared at her, dazed. My parents had never believed in physical punishment. Never. I'd been grounded, had my instruments taken away, and had been given extra chores, but they'd never resorted to violence to prove their point. Mom looked as stunned as I was that she'd done it.

I stepped away, trying to remember the love that I knew existed between us instead of the harsh words.

"I'm going to go before I say something I'll regret."

I grabbed my coat and beanie from the hooks by the door and stepped out into the rainy, gray evening. The weather had been this way all week, hovering over us like Mom was hovering over Cassidy. Dark like the words Mom and I never usually said to each other. Like the hurt we hid behind the love. Both of which had come tumbling out of me in the wrong way.

I needed a drink. I needed music. I needed noise and chaos.

Marco was going to kill me for going without him, but I'd be gone and back before he knew it. No one in this town really cared about the sensation Brady O'Neil. I wasn't going to cause a riot or be chased down the street by fans wanting to tear my clothes off. The worst that could happen was I'd be recognized, asked for an autograph and some pictures, and I'd have to come back to the apartment. If I stayed here, dwelling on everything that had gone wrong with my relationship with my family, it was going to eat at me until I lost my way.

I looked up at the apartment one more time before walking away. I didn't stop until the neon lights of Mickey's hit me, the glimmer of them reflecting in a blur on the wet pavement. There was a small line waiting to get in, which wasn't always the case. I went to the employee's entrance. Mick had allowed me into the bar that way since my first single had hit number one on the country charts.

In the kitchen, a few people glanced up, but no one stopped me. When I reached the kitchen door, Sheila, the head chef, finally spoke. "Long time no see, Cormac!"

My real name was a sarcastic twist on her lips, and I just gave her a wave as I went through the swinging doors into the heart of the bar. The music was loud, and I realized as soon as I heard the croak onstage that it was karaoke night. I groaned inwardly because it meant the place would be busier than it would have been otherwise.

I hit Mick on the shoulder as he filled a pint at the taps. "Hey, man."

"Brady!" His old, weathered face turned into a smile you could barely see below the wrinkles. He was a man who'd lived his years hard and fast. "Didn't know you were in town."

"Cass had her baby," I explained as I made my way to the spot at the bar that was always mine when I came in and was, thankfully, vacant. The position of the barstool shielded me some from the front door and the tables.

"Did she now? What did she have?" Mick asked.

"A baby boy named Chevelle."

"Chevelle?"

"Yep. That way, no matter what gender he discovers he is growing up, he doesn't have to change his name if he doesn't want to."

The thin red cocktail straw that Mick had hanging out of his mouth, as his way of replacing the chewing tobacco of his youth, stilled. Then, he shook his head. "That Cassidy. She's always a thinker."

I laughed.

Mick sloshed tequila and margarita mix and a dash of a secret ingredient into a salted glass and handed it to me. Mick knew I wasn't any more of a beer drinker than I was a driver. Couldn't really stand either.

There was a pause in the music as the next set of karaoke aficionados worked with the DJ to get the song up and running. I was paying more attention to my drink than the crowd until the first few notes of "Scrabble Tiles" hit the sound system. I groaned internally at my first hit song being played.

Mick grinned at me over the pint glasses, and I tugged my beanie down lower over my eyebrows. The beard was still a good cover. It was so much darker than the hair on my head that it threw people off the scent pretty easily. Making sure I wasn't in my "Brady costume" helped as well. I was in a long-sleeve T-shirt instead of a flannel and there were no cowboy boots or hat anywhere in sight.

The two female voices that took up the song had me looking up in a heartbeat. Tristan and her dark-haired friend from the hospital. Her friend was in a yellow dress and knee-high stiletto boots that made her look like a model, but it wasn't her who had me staring, not in the least. It was Tristan who had my eyes frozen to the stage.

She wore a sexy wrap dress that clung to her curves instead of hiding them like every other outfit I'd seen her in. Curves that made me ache. On her feet was a pair of cowboy boots that looked worn and comfortable. Her hair was down, hanging straight without a lick of curls and allowing the dyed mahogany strips to stand out against the pale hue of honey that was the same color as her daughter's. Even from where I sat farther back in the dim lights, I could tell she had makeup on, because her lashes stood out as if they were a mile long. Dark. Glittery. Eyes calling to me as she sang Ava's words about finding and losing someone.

Tristan didn't have a singer's voice. It wasn't any good at all. Would have been laughed out of Juilliard on day one of voice class, but it still enthralled me. I listened, eyes trained on the stage, while she and Stacy moved around, singing up against each other almost like Ava and I had, once upon a time, on a stage in a salon in New York City.

When the song was over, the DJ said, "Thank you for that remarkable performance, ladies. Let's give Stacy and Tristan a round of applause." The crowd clapped loudly, appreciation for Stacy and Tristan's enthusiasm and stage show rather than their voices.

The two women were laughing as they climbed off the stage, and I stood up so I could get a better look at where they were seated. They were at a booth in the corner, which meant they'd been there early enough to get it. They were sitting with the black-haired man

I'd seen with Stacy at Elana's, arguing over the validity of Fleetwood Mac at Christmas. He put an arm around Stacy, kissing her cheek and claiming her for the world.

There was no other body in the booth, which likely meant Tristan wasn't there with a date. That knowledge sent relief skittering over my skin. But at the same time, the thought of Tristan being a third wheel made my gut twist in objection. I'd been that way with many of my closest friends as they'd found true love and marriage and baby carriages. It was hard being the odd man out.

Before I could think it through, I was walking toward the table with Mick's eyes on my back. Normally, I never left my stool. I drank, shot the bull with him, his staff, and whomever happened to be with me that night, but I never really mingled.

When I got to the table, I said, "Well, that was the best version of "Scrabble Tiles" I've heard in a long time."

Tristan was the one to react first, her long-lashed eyes turning in surprise. Her whole demeanor turned from relaxed to on guard.

"Don't patronize us. It was fun." She flung her words at me.

"I didn't say you were going to win any vocal awards," I teased, lips quirking at her annoyance.

"Brady, would you like to join us?" her friend asked and then winced as Tristan must have kicked her under the table. It only made me want to join them more.

"Sure." I sat down, and my body forced Tristan to move farther in. Our hands briefly touched as they glided along the booth. The scent of her wafted over me—the smell of the music store mixed in with something else I couldn't quite define.

"Brady, this is my husband, Jin," Stacy informed me.

I shook his hand.

"We're celebrating," he said, with an alcohol-induced slur to his words.

"What are you celebrating?" I asked.

"Stacy's charter school was approved," Tristan said, beaming for her friend.

"Wow. Congratulations. That's quite the achievement," I said.

Stacy smiled, wide and happy. "Thanks."

"It also sounds like way more work than I could ever do," I told her. "Like eighty-hours-a-week kind of work."

Stacy and Jin nodded. "Sure, but the payoff is the kids who get the education they deserve."

"You act like you don't ever work eighty hours or more a week," Tristan said.

I laughed.

"It never really feels like work. It feels like a gift," I answered truthfully.

They all stared at me as if I'd said something incredibly profound. I drank down my margarita and flagged the waitress down. She was new to Mick's, or at least I hadn't ever seen her around before.

"'Nother round?" she asked.

Tristan and her friends nodded, and I said, "Can I have another margarita on the rocks as well? This round is on me. Just tell Mick, will you?"

The woman took me in with narrowed eyes as if

I was going to skip off without tipping her.

"Don't worry, he's good for it. He's Br—"

I put my hand over Tristan's lips. Her eyes widened, and my fingers about burst into flame when they landed on those pillows of softness. I turned to the waitress and said, "I'm an old friend. Mick knows I'll pay."

She eyed me again, taking in the beanie and the dark beard before shrugging her way to the counter.

Tristan shoved my hand away from her mouth with the scowl reappearing between her eyebrows. "Why would you do that?"

"Look, most of the locals don't give two shakes of a rat's ass who I am, but the college kids and the tourists can go a little over the top. I'm kind of enjoying my anonymity at the moment."

"Next up, Jin-Kang and Stacy," the DJ announced.

Stacy all but pushed Jin out of the booth. He swayed, and she caught him by the hand with a laugh before leading him toward the stage.

"You've all been here a while," I said to Tristan, looking down at the empty plates of appetizers and the stack of shot glasses littering the table.

"We have. It's the only way to get a booth on karaoke night."

The waitress came back with our drinks, but now she was all smiles with her tank top hanging about two inches lower than it had been when she'd taken our order. She put all the dirty glasses and plates on her tray, shot a glance toward the bar, and then shoved a cocktail napkin at me.

"Will you sign this for me? To Cheyenne."

I wanted to groan but didn't. I forced my smile. "Sure, babe."

I grimaced at the babe. Where was Dani when I needed her?

I signed the napkin. Cheyenne shoved it in her bra and then slid another one toward me before placing my drink on it. "There. Now you have a nice place to land whenever you want."

She walked away, exaggeratedly swaying her hips.

It was so cliché, but I was also used to it. When I turned to Tristan, her eyes were wide.

"Wow."

"Wow, what?"

"Her. Fawning all over you and giving you her phone number." She flicked her eyes down to the napkin that had the woman's name and number on it. I turned the napkin upside down. "I just wasn't sure that stuff really happened."

"It's just part of the gig."

She didn't seem impressed. I couldn't blame her. I changed the subject.

"How's your little girl?" I asked.

Her frown disappeared into a smile. "Hannah's fine. She had a whole load of questions about your music. Then, she Googled you, listened to a bunch of your songs, and promptly decided Grams must have been losing her touch if she'd liked you so much."

I put a hand on my chest. "I'm terribly wounded. Did you tell her I've won a bunch of awards?"

"She wouldn't care. You're not Fleetwood Mac, Zeppelin, or ABBA, so you don't stand a chance."

"That's some pretty specific musical taste for a five-year-old."

She smiled. "She's not quite five yet, but she will be soon. And you can thank Grams for the musical taste. You know how she felt about classic rock."

I nodded. "That I do."

We sat in silence for a moment before I grinned and said, "I feel doubly honored you'd even know one of my songs well enough to sing it, then."

"Don't get too excited. I like country music, and you're on the radio a lot. Can't seem to escape you," she said, and her eyes darkened. Had she meant the double entendre, or were the words merely a slip of her tongue?

Jin and Stacy came back to the table in a giddy mix of kisses and laughter that seemed years younger than their mid-thirties. They broke their kiss to look at us. Stacy smiled and said, "Sorry, we don't get many nights out without the kiddos in tow."

"Please don't stop on my account." I smiled at them.

Stacy wagged a finger. "You're one of those, are you?"

"One of those what?" I asked.

"Like to watch," she said.

I almost choked on my margarita.

"No, no. I'm much more of a participate kind of guy," I said.

"Sorry, no three-ways. That's been the staying power of our marriage," Jin said seriously.

This time Tristan choked.

"Um, I don't think that's what he meant, Jin."

Stacy laughed as if all of our discomfort was the best thing she'd seen in weeks.

"Okay, folks, it's time for one last song. As you know, we always choose a crowd favorite to come back up and close us down. This request is for…" He opened a paper in his hand and read. "Brady O'Neil?" He looked into the crowd with his hand over his eyes.

I groaned. The little witch of a waitress had ratted me out. Mick never would. The crush of people was whispering as they tried to find me. I pulled at the beanie again while Mick stalked from behind the bar to the stage. He took the mic from the DJ and said, "Karaoke is closed for the night, folks. But get ready to shake your booties because Dancing Dan is going to have the tunes up and running until we close. Enjoy."

As he walked by my table, he mouthed, "Sorry."

But the damage had been done. I'd been identified.

Another male body appeared in Mick's place. A man in an expensive suit that looked out of place in the relaxed atmosphere of the bar.

"Miss Morgan, it's a pleasure to see you again. I had no idea you knew my old friend, Brady," the man said.

I took him in, trying to place him. He was tall with a lean, muscular frame. Attractive. Almost sexy with his black hair slicked back, accenting his dark eyes and the five o'clock shadow that coasted over his pale skin. Finally, it dawned on me who he was.

"Well, I'll be damned. Is that you, William Chan?"

He smiled at me, sticking his hand out. I shook it, assessing the man who'd been my childhood best friend.

"I hardly recognized you in the suit," I told him.

He chuckled, drew an unused chair from a nearby table without asking if he could, and sat on it the wrong way—an old habit he'd had when we were growing up. A strange power move, as if using the chair the wrong way made him cooler than anyone else. He'd already been the coolest kid in town because of his dynamic confidence and the power tied to his last name.

"You two know each other?" Tristan asked, and there was an edge to her voice that I didn't quite follow. It was different than her irritation at me. It was almost violent.

"Brady and I grew up together. Chased girls together. Graduated together," William said with a wide smile.

"Then he went off to Princeton, and I went off to Juilliard, and we haven't seen each other since. I didn't realize you were back in Grand Orchard." I didn't like how he was making it sound as if we were still friends. It came with the job, the people who crawled out of the woodwork once you became famous, but after years of Lee helping me practice, I was damn quick to put those people in their place. If you didn't, it led to a whole string of bad requests and bad feelings.

"Been back for a while now. I'm on the city council and charged with fixing the town before it falls completely apart. Right, Miss Morgan?" he said, sending Tristan a coded message that my entire body reacted to. It was like some masochistic anomaly took over me as I puffed out my chest and slid an arm behind Tristan's head along the back of the booth.

"We're going to go dance," Stacy said, giving Jin a shoulder shove. He got out of the booth, and Stacy glanced back at Tristan. "You coming?"

Tristan looked like she wanted to leap across the table and tear William's throat out. Jin caught the drift of whatever I was missing, took Stacy's hand, and said, "Yeah, come with us, Tris."

I looked at William and smiled. "Seems you joined us at a bad time. We're being asked to hit the floor."

I pulled Tristan's hand into mine and tugged her from the booth. She hesitated only until she saw William drag his eyes down to where our bodies were joined. Then she curled her fingers over mine. When I looked down, I was surprised to see there weren't sparks of cartoon-like light shooting off of our hands, because that was what it felt like. Like the Fourth of July had come early. Like sparklers were burning and singeing over our skin.

The song was moody and slow, the best kind of getting-to-know-you song. One that spoke of illicit kisses and hiding in dark corners while the flame of desire flew through you.

I pulled her up close, and she wrapped her hands around my neck.

The smell of her hit me again, and I realized that, mixed in with the music store scents, she also smelled like chocolate. Not the overt, sugary sweetness of milk chocolate, but the bittersweet taste that hit the corners of your mouth with a tang. Between this unexpected perfume and the way her body felt under her thin dress, my body was coming alive.

Parts of me that weren't used to responding this quickly to anyone ached for me to run my hands over the slope of her waist and bury my fingertips into the small but fleshy curves of her hips. I'd become more flirt than action after having enough sex in college and my first year on the road to last me a lifetime. These days, I didn't need the rush of sexual frenzy to shore me up as I once had, but the mere colliding of Tristan's skin with mine had me craving her.

When I looked down into her face, her eyes seemed to absorb me, as if she could read every thought and feeling going through my head. I wanted her to know them. I wanted her, period. Staying in Grand Orchard until the summer became even more of an imperative. The need was no longer just about helping Cassidy. It was also about helping me.

Chapter Ten

Tristan

MEANT TO BE
Performed by Bebe Rexha w/ Florida Georgia Line

My body was reeling from the physical contact of the male body up tight against mine. Not just a male body, but a male body that had already been calling to me like a ghost in the dark. Memories of touches whispering over me.

I forced my mind away from the echoes of dancing with another man and back to the table where William Chan was watching Brady and I move together to the sultry song. My brain raced with the words he'd thrown at me as a reminder of the disaster that was the music shop and the music festival. The bribe. The threat.

Since he'd shown up at the store, I'd contacted city hall about the permits and been informed that they had, in fact, been denied. I'd left messages for the mayor and each of the other council members, and I'd gotten myself on the agenda for the next city council meeting.

Then, I'd started reaching out to the acts Grams

had scheduled, hoping some of them would send letters of support. I sent emails to the businesses who had the prime booth locations each year, asking them to show up at the council meeting. It had kept my mind occupied as Tuesday flew into Friday.

I moved my eyes from William to the rest of the crowd and saw, with a shock, that almost every pair of eyes in the place was directed at us. There were even some phones raised as people took pictures.

It hit me. I was dancing with Brady O'Neil. Superstar. Country-rock legend.

I turned my gaze to Brady's face to find his eyes trained on me. I blinked, trying to get the warm amber color of his pupils out of my head. But I had a feeling the color would be appearing in a painting before too long. It was already etched in my brain, spread out along burlap instead of regular canvas.

"We're making a scene," I said, finding my words.

"What?"

"Everyone is staring at us. Because of who you are."

"There's hardly anyone here who will care," he said nonchalantly.

"I beg to differ," I responded dryly. "I think people are actually taking pictures. This is awful."

He ignored my words and, instead, went for the ones which sent needles into my burdened heart. "What did William mean by all that?"

"He had the permits for the festival denied," I told him. It wasn't a secret, and it would be even less of one when I showed up to fight it next week.

Brady stumbled slightly as if my words had hit

him as hard as they'd hit me the first time William Chan had uttered them.

"Elana's festival?" he said, disbelievingly.

I could only nod.

"Why would he do that?"

"Because he wants me broke enough that I'll sell the store to him."

"No fucking way," he said. "What would William want with the music store? He could barely stand going in there when we were teens."

My brain stalled on the thought of Brady O'Neil working in my grandmother's shop. It seemed surreal. Unbelievable. Strange. I said, "I keep forgetting that."

"What?" he asked.

"The fact that you had worked for Grams. That you…had a life she was part of." My words choked on the emotions, but I refused to cry in the middle of a bar with the arms of a famous country singer around me.

He swallowed hard enough that I could see his Adam's apple bob up and down at my mention of her, or maybe it was at the emotions he sensed in me. His eyes glittered as if he was holding back tears as well, and that hit my heart in a different way, rubbing at the pinpricks like a salve. Somebody else missed her.

We danced in silence for a moment as we both tried to get control of ourselves.

Finally, he asked, "Why does William want the music store?"

"I don't think he wants it for himself. He just wants the space to be used for something better. He wants to revitalize the downtown. Make it hip and trendy. Grand Orchard 2.0 or something."

"But *La Musica de Ensueños* has been part of our community for an eternity," he replied. "It *is* the heart of downtown."

"Maybe a decade ago. Now, hardly anyone comes there except for lessons that I can't teach."

"You need money, then?" he asked.

I stared at him, trying to read the comment that was more question than statement. Was he was offering money? There was no way he would give money to someone he didn't even know, even if it was to save the shop he'd spent hours of his childhood in, right? Regardless of whether he was offering or not, there was no way I could take it.

"I don't want money from you," I said vehemently.

"There's got to be something I can do to help."

The song ended, and I looked back at the table, grateful to see that William was no longer there. I stepped away from Brady, and the heat of him wandered away from me. It had felt soothing. The warmth. The body. The concern. But I couldn't fall into that, or I might never crawl out.

Brady looked like he was going to grab my hand again, and I crossed my arms over my chest, holding my elbows. "Thanks for the dance."

I moved toward the table, and he followed me. I didn't have to look to know it. My body would have felt it even if the eyes around the room hadn't given it away.

Stacy and Jin got there just as we did.

"I think I'm going to call it a night," I told them. Stacy smiled a knowing smile as she glanced at Brady and then back at me. As if one dance would suddenly mean I was ready to sleep with the singer. As if one dance could obliterate another man from the silent memories embedded into my brain and skin.

"You going to be okay to walk home alone?" she asked.

She wasn't ready to give up her night of celebration, and I couldn't blame her. She and Jin worked extremely hard at their day jobs, and they'd worked even harder on the proposals and grants needed for the charter school. They'd earned this night out more than anyone I knew.

"I'll be fine. It's, like, three blocks."

"I'll walk you home," Brady said, his warm timbre coasting along my skin.

"What? No. I'm definitely not walking out of this bar with you," I told him, dashing my eyes around the room to the staring crowd.

Brady seemed to take in the same sight, and his shoulders stiffened a little.

"You're right, but I'm still walking you home. You go out the front, I'll go out the back, and I'll meet you on the corner of Tenth and Main."

"I don't need anyone walking me home."

"I'm not sending a lady out into the night by herself," he replied with a stubborn set of his jaw.

"I'll walk you home and then come back," Jin said, standing up with a bit of a stumble.

I laughed. "If you walk me home, I wouldn't trust you to make it back here without falling into the gutter."

It was either ruin Jin and Stacy's night or agree to the offer from the man making my veins dance. I turned to Brady. "I accept. Thank you."

His face broke into a huge grin. The one he was famous for. The one posted in advertisements all over the world. The one I wasn't sure I'd be able to resist if he kept it winging my way. I might be tempted to kiss it. I'd be as bad as the waitress who'd given her his number on the napkin. I mean, not that it was bad. She'd seen what she wanted and taken the risk. Really, of the two of us, I was the bad one. I was the person who was too lost to take a jump. To dare.

I grabbed my coat and purse, hugged my friend, and then headed for the front door. I felt the eyes on me, as if one dance and a drink at a table with Brady O'Neil had suddenly rubbed some of his "famous" off on me. Brady didn't leave with me. He waited before heading toward the bar and the door to the kitchen, drawing the eyes back to him as I escaped the room.

The line waiting to get in was small, but the voices of the people there and the music of the bar followed me into the night. The storm had turned into a hazy cloud of fog that my breath added to as I walked down the street toward home. When I hit the corner, Brady materialized out of the mist and shadows, and it would have scared the bejesus out of me if I hadn't known he was going to be there.

As we walked, the noise fell behind us, and the dark, silent businesses took over. Even the restaurants were closed. Only Mick's was left open. The hush mixed in with the fog made the world feel mysterious, as if I was on the brink of something new. Like the feeling I got when I started a new painting. Expectations of grandeur that may never come true.

"Thanks again for walking me. I didn't really need it, but I didn't want to break up Stacy and Jin's celebration."

"I'm heading this way anyway."

"Do you live near downtown?" I asked and then grimaced. "No, don't tell me. I'm not asking so I can stalk you or anything."

He laughed, the ripples going through the mist and the night.

"I knew you didn't mean it like that. My parents' house is actually across from the college. When I'm in town, I live in the apartment above their garage."

This struck me as funny, and I couldn't help the giggle that escaped.

"Why is that funny?" he asked.

"Well… You must be worth a lot of money, but you're living with your parents—above a garage."

He laughed again, and it sent shivers down my spine that had nothing to do with the cool air. It was like joy sprinkling over me. One of those moments that were supposed to be lived and felt and remembered—impossible as it may seem for me to be having it with the superstar.

"It does sound funny when you put it that way," he said, and even though I couldn't really see his smile in the shadows, I could feel it.

We got to my corner, and I stopped. "I'm just down there. You don't need to come."

"You're living at Elana's?" he asked.

"Yes."

"I should have guessed that, I suppose." His voice was choked. "I'll walk you the rest of the way."

I let him, but his joy had disappeared, and I felt sadness wash over me as well. At his sorrow. At the loss of my grandmother. Self-pity that I hated to wallow in filled me.

"You weren't at her funeral," I said. There was no accusation in my statement, just curiosity. He seemed to care about my grandmother and yet hadn't come to say goodbye.

"I didn't know."

"You didn't? I mean, you came for the box."

"My mom left a note about it in a stack of messages," he said, a bitterness etched through the words that surprised me because he didn't seem like the kind of person to let sour thoughts color his world.

We got to my porch. The lights were on, and the TV was flickering through the window, but no childish screams reached us, which meant Jay had likely gotten all three kids to sleep. Stacy and Jin's littles were staying with me so they could prolong their celebration.

"I'd like to help somehow," he said, and the acrid tone was gone, as if I'd just imagined it. "With the festival. The shop. Anything. Something…for her."

"I'm presenting at the city council meeting on Thursday night to try and fight for the permits." The words slipped out of me, but they felt right. Grams would have appreciated the help. She would have loved to have Brady there.

"I'll be there. Anything else?"

"I've had one of the acts back out since she died. Have you ever performed at Apple Jam before?" I asked.

"Yes, a lot when I was growing up and then again the year my first record released, but the next time it came around, I was on tour in Japan." His voice was sad again. "I thought I'd be able to do it this time, so it hadn't felt like that big of a deal, but then she didn't ask…"

His voice trailed away.

"That was probably my fault. When Grams asked me to contact the bands, I just took the list from the last festival and started with them."

He didn't say anything.

"It's the weekend before Memorial Day. If you have an opening in your schedule, and we can get the council to approve the permits, would you like to fill the slot? That's stupid. I'm sorry. You probably have a calendar that's filled years in advance."

"No, I'd love to do it. For Elana. I've had my team clear my schedule for the next few months. I'm sticking around to help Cassidy with her new baby."

His words settled in over me with surprise and a tug that I didn't quite understand. The sweetness of him staying to help his sister. It seemed so…not something a famous musician would do.

"Oh. Well. That's pretty amazing of you," I said softly.

Brady laughed again, and this time, the sourness was back as if he didn't believe it.

He stared into my face for a long time. I knew I should go in. I knew there was nothing that could come of the physical attraction brewing between us, but I also knew he felt like comfort. Or he needed comfort. Maybe both.

I wrapped my arms around myself and swayed slightly. A sway I'd picked up from when Hannah was a baby. A soothing motion that had stuck long past the time when she'd needed it to a time when I needed it more.

"You have her eyes," he said quietly.

I knew immediately who he meant.

"I look more like her than my mom. It's like the genes skipped a generation or something."

His hand moved, causing my body to still as he touched my cheek.

"You're beautiful."

I choked on the emotion his words caused. Words said to me for the first time in years from a man who wasn't my family. A man who spoke from a place of need and want and desire. I gulped and stepped back.

Chicken.

No risk in me.

No dare.

The waitress had way more gumption than I did.

"Thank you for walking me home," I said before turning and almost running up the steps to the door that I unlocked with shaking fingers. I never looked back, but I was sure he waited until the door shut behind me, because I could feel his gaze. I leaned against the wood, closing my eyes and breathing in deeply.

When I opened my eyes again, it was to find Jay watching me with a grin on his face. His floppy brown waves were longer than he'd ever worn them before, but they made his slate-gray eyes stand out. I had a feeling his new girlfriend was the reason for the new look.

"Wow," he said. "That was a dreamy look."

"Dreamy? Nah. More like a lucky escape." I hung my coat on the hooks by the door, removed my cowboy boots, and pulled some money from my purse.

"How'd it go?" I asked.

He smiled. "They're all tucked away in your

bed."

"Yeah, but when did you actually succeed in getting them there?" I chuckled.

"Right at eight o'clock," he said solemnly.

"You lie," I laughed.

"Okay, you're right. We had a dance party on your bed until they all fell into an exhausted slumber around nine-thirty. But look at it this way, you'll get to sleep in longer tomorrow."

I laughed. "You know it never works that way. Their body clocks are embedded like carvings in rock. They'll all be up at six thirty, waiting for me to feed them breakfast."

He pulled some books from the coffee table and shoved them in his backpack, sliding into his tennis shoes before meeting me at the door.

"Thanks for watching them for us," I said, handing him the cash.

"It almost seems wrong taking the money from you," he said. "I love being around them."

"We would never take advantage of you that way."

He smiled, said goodnight, and headed out.

I locked the door, went up the stairs, and peeked in on the three faces asleep in my bed. Four, if you counted Molly, who hadn't even budged enough to come greet me. Her tail thumped, but she didn't move. They must have worn her out as much as they had themselves.

I patted her head, grabbed my pajamas, and then headed to the bathroom. I washed the thick coat of makeup off and stared at my thirty-four-year-old face. I felt older and younger all at the same time, small lines starting to appear at the corners of my eyes and my mouth, a deeper crease between my brows from a frown I wore too often.

There was a reason Hannah was so serious. It was because of me. Because I'd buried my laughter at the same time as I'd buried a casket. I didn't want that for her. I didn't want it for me. I wanted us both laughing and singing and finding joy. Finding those simple, beautiful moments you felt and lived.

I just had to figure a way out of this mess Grams had left, and then I swore to myself we would laugh more. It was going to happen.

Chapter Eleven

Brady

LOOK WHAT GOD GAVE HER
Performed by Thomas Rhett

"*I'll foot the bill,*" *I said* to William as I glowered at him across from his pretentious, gold-gilded desk in the president's office of Platinum Bank and Trust. His family had founded the bank decades ago, and somehow, at the young age of thirty, he was now in charge of its daily business. Between this job and his role on the city council, my one-time friend was on a power trip blocks wide.

Instead of being pleased with the idea of my forking out lots of money to help out, he frowned, and that made all my senses go on high alert.

"It isn't just the additional police and security that's needed," William said.

"You just told me the reason the city council withheld the permits for the festival was because of the cost to the police force."

"The entire town pays the price. There's garbage left everywhere, and the damn porta-potties cost a fortune, and they still don't keep the crowds from trying to use the restaurants' and shops' facilities."

"Doesn't the festival pay for the porta-potties?" I asked, and his face turned shadowy, not liking the way I was challenging him. "I don't see the real drawback here if it's going to bring money into the town. All the hotels, restaurants, and stores benefit. Hell, the city probably even makes money off of traffic violations and parking tickets in addition to the sales tax revenue."

"We're trying to reinvent ourselves here. To bring sustainable, year-round income, not spotty, seasonal, or even bi-annual revenue."

The reality hit me. He wasn't after the festival. It was just a means to an end.

"Got it," I said. "So, this comes down to you wanting to buy the store."

He pulled on his cuffs. "No. I don't want to buy the store. I want someone else to buy the store and have the space used more effectively."

"What do you envision going in there?" I asked.

"A farm-to-market restaurant. A place that serves breakfast and brings people to downtown in the mornings. We don't have a great breakfast place. We just have an ancient bakery. Even Sweet Lips won't last forever. I mean, Helen's ancient."

"The music store isn't big enough for a restaurant. Doesn't have a kitchen. The reno costs themselves would make it prohibitive."

"Kincaid's drugstore on the other side has a kitchen from back in the fifties when they had a soda fountain inside."

"Kincaid's has been closed for a decade."

"Exactly."

"You want to merge the two spaces and then sell it?"

He nodded.

"Let me guess, your sister sells the property, and the bank gets to finance it, so the Chan family makes out like the duck that's laid a golden egg."

"It's a goose."

"What?"

"It was a goose that laid a golden egg, not a duck."

I shook my head, trying not to laugh. I stood.

"Whatever happens with the buildings and downtown will have to be decided on the backs of something besides Elana's festival. She was a great woman who loved this town as much as she loved music. I'm not going to see something she created wiped away for something as stupid as money."

I walked out before he could respond.

This I could do.

Elana would want me to help. She'd expect it. I wasn't going to let her down on top of my family.

Marco joined me outside the bank. Silent as usual.

I texted Lee.

> *ME: I'm going to be flinging some cash around. Don't panic when you see some chunks missing from my accounts.*

> *GHOST TEAM LEADER: My panic radar just went up a thousand percent. Explain chunks and cash and why.*

ME: Not that I have to defend myself to you, but I'm going to be funding a local music festival.

GHOST TEAM LEADER: Will your name be tied to it?

ME: No.

GHOST TEAM LEADER: Why not?

ME: This isn't about me. This is about someone important to me who died, and now I'm helping them from their grave.

GHOST TEAM LEADER: What? Who died?

This was the problem with living two separate lives. My Brady O'Neil life had relatively little to do with my Cormac O'Neil life. They hadn't had to merge. I hadn't hidden one from the other, but there'd been no reason for them to be joined. Lee knew about Elana in the sense that he knew my biography. He knew how I'd learned to play and who my teachers had been. He didn't know what she meant to me.

ME: Elana Johnson. The woman who taught me everything I know about music.

GHOST TEAM LEADER: I'll be sure to tell the Juilliard regents that you spent four years there learning nothing.

ME: Don't make me eye-roll emoji you.

GHOST TEAM LEADER: Let me know what I can do to help from here.

ME: Are you narrowing down the list of PR candidates?

GHOST TEAM LEADER: I should have a few folks for you to interview soon.

ME: I might need their help with some of this.

GHOST TEAM LEADER: Dani will help in a pinch.

ME: She has her hands full with her new foundation. She doesn't need to be bothered with me.

GHOST TEAM LEADER: You're not a bother, Brady.

I put the phone back in my pocket and stopped outside of the boarded-up Kincaid's building. The sign inside the window gave the number to call if interested in the space: William's sister's real estate business. I pulled at my leather bands on my wrist. My brain was trying to fit something together, but it was alluding me. It would get there. I just wasn't sure when.

I'd spent the better portion of the week trying to convince my mother she could get back on the plane to Ireland because I would be there for Cass. I'd barely left the house in order to prove my point, jumping up whenever Cass needed something, giving her a break from Chevelle when she needed that, too. It hadn't been a burden. Chevelle was the cutest damn thing I'd ever seen, and his tiny cry had wound its way into my heart.

But in sticking so close to home, I'd frustrated Cassidy. She'd finally growled at me this morning to stop being our mother and to get the hell out of the house before she burned me alive. I couldn't make them both happy at the same time.

I'd turned from my difficulties with them to the difficulties facing Tristan and the Apple Jam Music Fest. Which was the reason I'd shown up at the bank and requested to see William. He was probably regretting the decision to let me in without an appointment now because it meant we were on opposite sides of the field. My former best friend might have been a tough adversary, but I had one thing on my side: the love this town had for Elana.

My eyes shifted from Kincaid's to the music store. I was drawn to it, as I had been for the majority of my life—since I was eight years old and had heard Elana playing the piano and asked her to teach me. The overwhelming sense of loss that spread through my stomach at the thought of her being gone was hard to contain. I'd never walk in and hear her voice calling me again, and that was too hard to fathom. A *doloroso diminuendo* reverberated through my brain, accentuating the feelings with notes I'd never played.

The sadness turned to a dazed kind of longing the moment my eyes landed on Tristan through the windows. She was sitting on the steps in an outfit much like the day I'd met her a week ago. Paint-spotted Chucks, jeans, and a T-shirt that seemed four sizes too big that hid everything instead of showing off the body she'd rocked in the wrap dress on Friday night.

She was talking to a young boy with black hair and skin so dark it was like the depths of the ocean. He had a guitar case flung over his shoulder that was almost as tall as him. Standing behind him was someone whom I assumed was the boy's mother because her black hair and dark skin matched his. Plus, she was wringing her hands in a distraught, motherly kind of way as the boy seemed to sniffle.

When I walked into the store, the boy's voice rang out full of disappointment.

"She told me she was going to teach me 'Fire and Rain' next."

"James Taylor," I said. "Those are some pretty righteous chords."

All three pairs of eyes turned toward me.

The boy nodded and then puffed with pride. "Yeah. But I'm ready for it."

Tristan slowly drew her eyes from me and back to the boy. "I'm sorry," she said, and you could tell that every part of her being ached to make it right. Or maybe she just ached to have her grandmother back. The throbbing sorrow in the room was too much for me. Not when I could ease it even the slightest.

"I can do it," I said spontaneously.

"What?" Tristan breathed out.

"I can teach him the song." I nodded. I stuck my hand out to the boy. "I'm Brady, by the way."

The mom's mouth dropped open. "Wait. You're Brady O'Neil!"

I smiled at her and winked. "Every time I look in the mirror, it surprises me too."

She flushed.

The boy stuck his hand out and shook mine. "I'm Sheldon."

"Nice to meet you. You go up, get unpacked, and start warming up. I'll be right there."

Sheldon didn't even stop to see if the two women agreed with me. He shot past Tristan, making the rickety steps bounce as he ran.

"Brady, I—"

"I want to," I said, cutting Tristan off. "Please, let me."

"I can't pay you." She was shaking her head.

"I'll pay him. The normal rate," the mother said, digging into her purse.

"I don't want anyone's money," I said to both of them but then turned to Sheldon's mom. "But if you could pay Tristan the normal rate to cover the cost of the space, that would be great."

"Brady!" Tristan stood up.

"Deal."

The mom pulled her wallet out, and I eased my way past her as the sounds of a guitar being plucked carried their way toward me.

"We're not done talking about this," Tristan called up after me.

I just waved and went into the practice room where the young boy was already doing scales. I listened, corrected, and then watched some more before we dove into the sheet music he already had for the classic James Taylor song.

Forty-five minutes later, we'd worked our way through it a couple of times, and I'd been able to correct his hand positions and the force of his fingers on the strings. I wasn't a natural teacher, and it wasn't something I thought I'd ever be good at if required to do it for a living, but it worked in a pinch.

When Sheldon's mom reappeared at the practice room doorway, he packed up, thanked me shyly, and then left. She beamed at me. "I don't know how to say thank you enough."

"If you could do me a favor, and not tell the entire world about it, that would be thank you enough."

She looked surprised. "Oh. Sure. Of course."

I wondered if it was already all over her social media that her son was being taught a lesson by Brady O'Neil. I hoped it wasn't. I didn't want that kind of attention. Not while I was here for Cassidy and Chevelle. Not while I was here trying to fix things for Elana and Tristan. Although having word spread that I was teaching classes at *La Musica de Ensueños* would probably bring a crowd to Tristan's door that would only help with sales, it was also something I couldn't sustain in the long haul. I wouldn't want to get anyone's hopes up.

As if my thoughts had conjured her, I heard Tristan's voice in the old storeroom space that had now been converted into her studio. It was strange to see it filled with art supplies instead of boxes and instruments.

As Sheldon and his mom disappeared down the stairs, I looked over to see Tristan on a futon in the corner with Hannah on her lap. The little girl was crying with her top hat askew on her head and arms swallowed up in a shawl that would have made Stevie

Nicks jealous.

I didn't know if I should walk away or stay. But the pain radiating from them both had me freezing to my spot. It was more palpable than Sheldon's had been downstairs. I had the strangest urge to wrap them both in my arms and hug them until the grief and tears went away.

Tristan's eyes met mine. "She heard Sheldon in the practice room and thought…"

She thought her great-grandmother was back teaching lessons. I grimaced.

"I…I…just want to play again," Hannah sobbed.

I tilted my head, eyebrows creasing together, surprise registering in my voice. "Does she play guitar?"

Tristan shook her head. "Piano."

I eased toward them, sinking onto the floor so my face was practically in Hannah's. "Piano, huh? That's what I started on. But I was quite a bit older than you."

"Y-you did?" she asked.

I nodded. "Yep. I use my guitar most often these days because it's easy to take with me, but the piano will always be my first love."

"What's your favorite song?"

"That is quite the question. If I'm playing classical music, I definitely like Claude Debussy's 'La Cathédral Engloutie,' and if I'm playing contemporary music, 'Bohemian Rhapsody' by Queen is up there."

"Grams was only teaching me classic rock songs. That's all I ever want to play," Hannah said with tears in her eyes.

I tried not to laugh as the little girl obviously took

her music very seriously.

"Would you like to play one for me?" I asked.

Tristan's breath caught in a shallow gasp, and I felt like an ass again, as if I'd intruded and broken some unwritten rule, but Hannah's eyes turned wide, and a smile lit up her face.

"Can I?" she asked as she turned back to her mom.

"Are you sure you want to, *Chiquita*?"

She nodded, pushed off her mom, straightened her hat, grabbed my hand, and pulled me toward the practice room with a piano in it older than I was. The one I'd learned on myself. Old and scratched with keys so worn it was as if they were melting away.

She pulled a folder from one of the cubbies where Elana's students had always kept their music and laid out the sheets on the piano. She sat down and patted the bench next to her. I looked at Tristan for approval before making my way to her.

"I can't reach the pedals, so Grams said I shouldn't worry about it yet."

I nodded at this sage advice.

Then, she started into "Let It Be" by The Beatles. Not only did she play, but she also started singing with a strength and confidence that startled me so much I had to put a hand to my chest to make sure my heart was actually still working. Her sweet voice turned the song into something different than its original intention. Something haunting in a brand-new way. She made mistakes on the keys and in her pitch, but it was done smoothly and with a flourish that only Elana could have taught her.

My eyes filled, and when I looked up at Tristan

in the doorway, tears were rolling down her cheeks unchecked. A beautiful song. Two beautiful females. One unforgettable loss. But I could feel Elana in every inch of the room as if she were with us. The missing person. She was there in the keys and the wood and the walls. She was in the skin and the fingers of the little girl playing the classic rock song. She was in the eyes and the face of the woman watching her daughter's fingers move.

When Hannah reached the end, she looked up at me, a huge smile breaking over her little face.

"I messed up, huh?"

I nodded. "You did. Do you know where?"

She pointed to the sheet music at the exact place she'd first made a mistake.

"What would Elana have you do if you messed up?" I already knew the answer, but I wasn't sure if she'd changed her teaching style for her great-granddaughter.

"She'd make me play that part twenty-five times."

I grinned. "She used to make me do the same thing."

"She did?"

"Yep."

"Did you do it, or did you try and cheat?"

I laughed, the sound filling the room and echoing back at me. "Sometimes I did it, and sometimes I tried to cheat, but she always caught me."

"Cheating is wrong," Hannah said with a frown.

I tried to twist my lips back into a serious line, but I failed. "You're absolutely right. So, why don't you do those twenty-five times while I talk with your mom."

I eased off the bench as she set her hands back on the keys and started over at the first mistake.

Tristan wiped her face with her hands and then wrapped her arms around herself as I joined her at the doorway. She was swaying again like she had Friday night when I'd walked her home.

"She's very talented," I said honestly.

Tristan nodded.

"You said she's only five, right?" I had to double-check because her age definitely didn't fit with what I'd just heard.

"She's just turning five this month."

"That's pretty incredible. Like savant-type incredible."

Tristan chuckled. "No, but she takes it seriously right now."

"Elana was teaching her. She was teaching a lot of kids, right?"

She nodded.

"Can I help by taking over some of the lessons? Until you figure things out?"

"What? With Sheldon and Hannah?"

"With as many as I can. I mean, I only know four instruments myself, but I think I could figure out enough to at least help the others get by. How many did she have on the books right now?"

"Twenty."

I tried not to groan. Had I just signed myself up to help twenty kids learn to play an instrument? In the middle of a not-quite musical crisis of my own? In the middle of helping my sister and fighting an attraction to a woman who didn't seem to want anything to do with me?

I cleared my throat. "Twenty, huh?"

"You can't do them," she said. My surprise registered on my face, and she added on, "Like I said earlier, I can't pay you."

"I don't want your money. I just want to help."

"Why?" she asked, the sadness back in her voice.

"Because Elana would want me to."

"Did she ask you to do this?" she asked quietly.

"What do you mean?"

"In the things she left you. Did she ask you to do this? Because if she did, she shouldn't have, and I refuse to hold you to it," she said, frustration rolling through her.

In truth, I'd forgotten about the antique trunk Elana had left me. Maybe not so much as forgot, but purposefully put it out of my brain because I wasn't ready to see what she'd put inside for me.

"I haven't even opened the box," I said with a small shrug.

She stared at me with disbelief.

"So, this is out of some sense of guilt?" she demanded.

"Not guilt. Not even obligation. Just a sense that this is what should happen." I looked down into her eyes the color of the sun as it fell over the lake, and I knew she could feel it too—I belonged there.

Chapter Twelve

Tristan

LET IT BE

Performed by The Beatles

My heart was ramming itself against my rib cage like a baby bird trying to escape the nest for the first time. Seeing Brady on the bench next to Hannah while she played "Let It Be" had hit me with love and sadness, and joy and trepidation all at once. Hannah's sweet singing brought Grams' voice back to me as if she had been there in the room. Her energy vibrated around us, and I could almost hear her correcting Hannah's mistakes while she encouraged my daughter's love of classic rock.

The loss was almost unbearable.

But mixed in with the pain was a tender amazement at the blond man sitting next to Hannah. He'd not only taken the time to teach Sheldon but was now bringing music back to my daughter's world after it had been silent for weeks.

It was my fault. I hadn't pushed her. I hadn't asked her once if she wanted to play because I knew, selfishly, that it would hurt. It would hurt us both, and

I didn't know how to fix it. I didn't know how to heal the wound inside my daughter when I couldn't heal my own. So, I hadn't asked her to play. And now, all I could do was stand there, watching, listening, crying… Tears for my grandmother. Tears for Hannah. Tears for myself.

Now, Brady was offering to take Grams' place temporarily.

And I couldn't allow him to do that.

No way.

For so many reasons, the smallest of them being his wicked smile that made my stomach melt.

I also wouldn't let Grams guilt him into it from the grave.

I shook my head at his offer to teach the lessons, just as Hannah turned to me with a glorious smile on her face that hadn't been there in days and said, "Mom, I think Grams would like Brady teaching me to play, don't you?"

Shit. Honesty from the mouths of babes.

Brady grinned that exact wicked smile I'd just been thinking about, and it not only melted my stomach, it sent swirls of need and longing through my chest and down to my nether regions. I wanted to hate it. I wanted to hate him for making me feel things I'd sworn I'd never feel again.

Staring at both their beautiful smiles, I gave up. I couldn't resist when there was an immense sense of happiness beaming from them stronger than the rays of the sun. Burning me with the intensity of their hope.

"I'll give you Grams' schedule, but I don't expect you to be able to do them all. We can work out some modified version," I said quietly, and his grin got even bigger, stretching so it caused his eyes to crinkle at the corners, the brown pupils sparkling with happiness. Complete, one-hundred-percent, wickedness.

Brady turned back to Hannah. "You haven't finished twenty-five. Can you even count to twenty-five?"

My daughter gave him the biggest eye-roll in the world.

"Duh. I can count to one hundred and twenty-five."

"Should I make you do it a hundred times then?" he asked with a casual tease.

"Please don't, we'll never get out of here for dinner, and I need fuel before I show up at the city council meeting tonight," I said with a smile. A genuine smile which caused his eyes to drop to my lips, lingering there before traveling back to meet my gaze.

"I think I've made some headway on that topic." Brady turned serious.

"On what topic?" My heartbeat was increasing slowly and steadily to a pace that promised to have it bursting through my skin at any moment if the sexy country singer continued to look at my lips as if they were strawberry pie, especially after every sweet thing he'd just done.

"I spoke with William Chan earlier. I'm hoping it shed a different light on the topic of the festival for him."

I just stared at him.

"What?" he asked.

"You can't just swoop in and take over everything without even bothering to ask if people want your help," I said. I wanted to be mad, but it was hard to bring it to the surface after the tenderness I'd just witnessed. The care and attention he'd given others.

He played with the leather at his wrists while taking me in. "You're right. I just… Elana wasn't just my teacher. She was more a mom than my mom was on many days, and the thought of William—of anyone—dismantling something that was hers…it just eats at me."

There was a twist of knife-like pain to his words that made me wonder why he'd needed my grandmother. Why his mother hadn't been there for him when she seemed very much there for Cassidy. My confusion must have registered on his face because he looked back at Hannah and then at me.

"I need to help…need it like I need air to breathe. I'd never forgive myself for not doing everything in my power to fix this for you. For Elana," he powered on.

I gulped and then choked out. "I… I want to insist that I don't require your help. I want to be stubborn and just say I can do it on my own, but I'm not sure it's true."

I closed my eyes briefly after letting the admission break free. He moved, leaning so that his arm was over my head on the doorframe, bringing us closer together and making my body tingle with awareness as if it was coming back to life after a long sleep. When I opened my eyes back up, I got sucked into his gaze. He stared for so long I thought maybe we would both turn to dust.

"We all need help sometimes," he said quietly.

I couldn't look away. I was trapped. I felt like my

life was one huge wave of need. I owed so many people for so many things. For a lifetime of helping me pick up the pieces. It was all I could do to keep my chin in the air and accept one more round of assistance.

Brady's phone buzzed, and he was the one to break our trance, a frown burrowing his eyebrows together.

"I gotta run, but I'll definitely see you tonight," he said, turning back to Hannah. "Don't be a cheater like me, and I'll teach you a new song next time."

Hannah's face lit up. Pure happiness.

It should have filled me with joy, but instead, it filled me with worry because if she got attached to this man…a new teacher…and then he left her, it would tear more holes into her little soul already filled with them. It would tear holes in both of us.

Brady brandished that roguish smile one more time and left, taking some of the sunshine out of the room with him.

♫ ♫ ♫

The town hall was packed and ringing with feverish talk as we waited for the council meeting to start. The old building with its brick walls and wooden pews had once served as a courtroom before all the town's cases had been shuffled off to the county. Now, the building served primarily as a meeting room, and I wasn't sure it had seen this number of people gathered inside its walls in a very long time.

I'd asked for the support of the downtown businesses, and they'd shown up in force. Not only the owners from Main Street, but also the hotels and strip malls that took up the edges of Grand Orchard. Everyone who counted on the revenue the festival normally brought them.

Mayor Regan Sanchez's dark eyes absorbed the crowd with wariness while William Chan whispered in her ear. I wasn't one to hate very often. There were very few who'd ever made it on my list: an asshole at the Pentagon who'd approved a black op that should never have been approved, and now this man. He was trying to destroy something my grandmother had built, and his reason for doing it was simply money. Greed. The same reason which had caused Petty Officer White to push the mission that had taken my husband's life.

The other council members, some of whom had been in and out of Grams' shop and who greeted her with smiles at the bakery or church, were flipping through their agendas. Hardy, Witt, and Castro had all been on the women's shelter's board with Grams. I had no idea what they'd been thinking when they'd let the mayor and Chan talk them into denying the permits to begin with, but I was hoping I could sway them my way tonight.

The mayor hammered a gavel onto the wooden U-shaped table at the front of the room where the entire city council sat. The room went silent. She went through the formalities of opening the meeting, motioning to skip the reading of the last minutes, and then announced the first topic on the agenda. "We'll start with Mrs. Tristan Morgan who requested we revisit the topic of the Apple Jam Music Fest's permits."

I stood, trying not to let the shiver of anxiety flying through me show to the room. I'd never in my life been a person who was comfortable in the limelight. When I was in school, I'd hated giving speeches in a classroom with a mere thirty bodies in it. The fact that I needed to talk in front of all of these people made me want to lose the dinner I'd foolishly eaten thinking it would fuel me.

I fought the wave of nausea, reminding myself that this was for Grams.

I steeled my back, stepping toward the podium. I'd changed from my normal, paint-splattered apparel to a green T-shirt dress partnered with a jean jacket. I didn't have business clothes in my wardrobe. I didn't have much of anything anymore because I'd barely replaced the necessities in the last four years. I'd concentrated on what Hannah needed and not myself. I looked like the last person anyone should take seriously when it came to talk of economics and business.

At the podium, I took out the notes I'd made from the pocket of my jacket with shaky hands. I smoothed the wrinkles from the paper, adjusted the mic, and then looked up at the men and women who made up the city council.

"Thank you for letting me speak today." My voice quivered, and even though he didn't roll his eyes, I knew William Chan was doing it on the inside. I was a ghost of a woman, trying to make a stand against him. Anger and frustration rolled through me again, shoring me up. "I'm grateful to be allowed to speak on the festival's behalf, especially since I wasn't aware the council had met and ruled on the permits already."

It was a slight reprimand I couldn't help but give. I should have been informed. They knew it, too, because some of them had the grace to look down and away. Not William Chan. He almost smirked.

"As most of you know, my grandmother, Elana Johnson, was a member of this community for almost sixty years. My grandparents opened their store in 1965, bringing music to generations of people not only through the albums they sold but through the lessons they taught. Their love of music was what brought them together, and it was what filled Grams' whole world until she finally left it…left us…" I breathed in, trying not to let my voice wobble again, this time with tears.

"My grandparents loved music so much they wanted to share it with the community they also loved, and after the success of Woodstock, they saw a way to bring that joy to Grand Orchard. Every other year since its inception in 1971, the Apple Jam Music Fest has brought this community not only the leading artists of the time, but a wide range of cultural and ethnic groups whom you may never have heard of otherwise."

I paused, and Mayor Sanchez jumped into the space I'd left open.

"We understand the history of the festival, Mrs. Morgan. But, as you know, the world is not the same as it was in 1971. The costs of such events on their communities have skyrocketed. Laws and regulations have changed, requiring a whole list of items your grandparents never had to consider when they first started."

I nodded. "I understand. And we've been increasing the fees in order to cover those costs."

The mayor flipped through a stack of papers and asked, "So, you can cover the five hundred thousand dollar security estimate? Can you also cover the fifty thousand dollar city cleaning fee and the ten thousand dollar insurance rider that we'd have to put in place to cover any lawsuits the city might encounter?"

I sat stunned. There was no way I could come up with five hundred and sixty-five thousand dollars. Not after paying for the bands and the normal outlay of the festival. We had fifty thousand dollars budgeted for security, and her quote was ten times that. We had our own insurance, but it had cost a mere three thousand dollars.

"That's ridiculous!" Helen from Sweet Lips huffed behind me.

I felt a body approaching mine at the podium well before it materialized in my peripheral vision. Brady. He hadn't changed. He was in the same Chucks, T-shirt, torn jeans, and beanie that he'd been in earlier today. He appeared casual, but there was an energy rippling from him that almost made him glow.

A white knight.

I'd already had a white knight in my life. One I'd lost.

I swallowed hard.

"Mayor Sanchez," Brady spoke, his voice traveling through the room without the use of the microphone. Lyrical. Smooth. "I'm sure Councilman Chan has already informed you that I spoke with him earlier today and explained I would cover any additional costs the festival might incur this year."

I gasped at his comment the same way the rest of the room did, a buzz going around as the audience murmured while the council members started turning to discuss this offer with each other.

He'd told me earlier that he'd talked to William Chan, but he somehow forgot to mention the dollars they'd discussed. I put my hand over the mic, turning to him. "Brady, you're talking about a half a million dollars. There's no way the festival can afford that. There's no way I could ever pay you back."

He looked me over, lowered his voice to a whisper, and said, "This isn't about you, though, is it? This is about Elana, the town, and a tradition that shouldn't be spit on because one asshole has a burr up his butt."

I shook my head.

"It's too much. She wouldn't want you to do this." And I believed that in my soul. My grandmother wouldn't want Brady forking out that kind of cash.

"It isn't going to cost anywhere near that. They just want it on retainer. They're just doing this to scare you off. The actual costs will probably be closer to whatever you've been paying in the past. Next time around, you can plan for the increase. This time, I want to help."

He was so certain, so assured that this was all going to work out and that there would actually be a next time. I'd wondered, at times, over the course of the last week, if I was doing this for all the wrong reasons, and now his assertion gave my wavering confidence a much-needed boost. I wouldn't run scared. I couldn't. This was too important. Brady was right. This was about our entire town as much as it was about Grams.

I looked up at William Chan to see his face flushed red with frustration pouring through his veins as he talked heatedly with the mayor. He had his fists clenched tight on the top of the table, and she was waving at him as she talked with her hands, clearly unhappy.

"I motion the permits be granted as long as we have the money in a holding account by the end of the week," Councilwoman Castro motioned.

"We haven't discussed this," William Chan snarled.

"What is there exactly to discuss, William? The businesses and our tax revenues need the boost, and if Mr. O'Neil is willing to foot the bill for any costs that the city might incur, there's really no reason to deny it. Is there? Not unless you have some additional reason for denying it?" Castro said, and I knew right then she was aware of Chan's attempts to redo the downtown. To refurbish it by pushing out businesses that had been on that street for half a century, some even since the town's inception.

I wanted to cheer, my heart lightening as I realized we were going to do this. Succeed. Get the permits.

"I second the motion," Councilman Hardy spoke up.

"I call for a vote," Councilman Witt agreed.

And just like that, my grandmother's festival was approved. I couldn't contain the feelings of gratitude and relief that filled me. I may not end up with any of the income from the festival after I was done giving it all to Brady, but it was going to happen. Relief filled me. I could at least finish this one thing for her. I didn't know what it meant for future festivals, for the store, or for me, but I would at least be able to complete this one thing Grams and I had started together. We'd just shoved a pie in William Chan's face.

I turned to Brady, and he was smiling that same sexy smile he'd been grinning earlier in the day when

I'd agreed to let him help me at the store with the music lessons. Before I knew it, I was hugging him, putting my arms around his shoulders and squeezing him like I rarely did anyone but my daughter. Tight. Hard. With real affection.

It took him a second to respond, but then he was hugging me back. His hands landed on my hips just below the hem of my jacket and seeped warmth into me, scalding me as if he really did hold all the sun's rays like I'd imagined earlier at the store.

Brady's eyes met mine, his brown ones shimmering at me, calling to me, asking me something I didn't know the answer to. He reached up and pushed a strand of hair that had escaped my bun behind my ear, his fingertips a trail of red-hot brands on my skin.

I pulled away slowly, and he let me go.

Before I knew it, we were being surrounded by my grandmother's friends as well as mine. Stacy and Jin. Helen, Irma, and Floyd. The Romeros from the biggest apple farm in town. Business owners from up and down Main Street. Even Mick from the bar.

"This calls for a celebration!" Mick shouted. "First round is on the house!"

Cheers erupted as Mayor Sanchez tried to call the meeting back to order.

Stacy put her arm through mine and drew me from the hall. As we left, the majority of the city's business owners followed in our wake. It was a momentary triumph. A momentary reprieve that I couldn't deny. I couldn't bury it in the well of grief and stress I'd been absorbed in since losing Grams and trying to unwind the mess of her bills. It was a new moment that was supposed to be lived and felt and held tight. A new wall of memories was assembling itself in front of the tumbled bricks that Darren and Grams had left behind.

"Don't," Stacy said as the cool air hit us. Winter was finally starting to let go of its stranglehold on the weather, and an early spring breeze was aloft in the air rather than the bitter cold from a week ago. It was as if Mother Nature agreed with our celebration, letting the ice thaw and allowing the buds to start to form on the trees. New life.

"Don't what?" I asked.

"Don't think about not coming to the bar. Don't think about all the things that need to get done. Just revel in your small victory. Did you see William Chan's face?" She smiled gleefully as if reliving it in her head.

I returned the smile. I was glad that Chan hadn't won this battle in our war.

Jay was at Stacy's house with the kids, and we'd already made plans for Hannah to spend the night there so I wouldn't have to move her after bedtime. There was no reason not to share a drink with the people of this town who'd loved my grandmother almost as much as me. Who'd shown up for her tonight.

I squeezed my friend's hand. "Shots. We need shots."

Her smile grew, hugging me to her.

When we got to the bar, Mick stood on the counter and lifted a pint glass.

"To Elana! May her tenacity and grace forever rock this town," he hollered.

Tears bit at my eyes as the room broke into a

wave of cheers.

Then, Mick shifted the glass in my direction. "To Tristan for not giving up on us or Elana's festival, and to Brady O'Neil for coming in to pinch hit."

More cheers and "Hear, hears" filled the room. I turned to find Brady and his bodyguard standing right behind us. He shifted uncomfortably at Mick's little speech as if he was unaccustomed to getting praise when that was obviously not the case. I was pretty sure he'd won enough awards to fill a wall of whatever place he called home.

Stacy and I made it to the bar, and Mick asked us what our poison was. When we requested shots of something fun, he winked and fussed with a shaker before coming back to pour us something purple. Stacy turned to Brady, handing him one of the glasses.

"Thanks for saving my friend's ass. She doesn't let many people do it very often."

He flashed that naughty grin as his eyes trailed down to my ass clearly outlined by the thin material of the dress. When he returned to my face, there was desire there. My stomach curled. It had been years since I'd had that much longing and lust directed toward me. Sorrow. Pity. Sympathy. Regret. Those were emotions I was used to seeing in other people's eyes.

"I'd happily save her ass any day," he said, and the smoky texture of his voice that made his songs gritty and bluesy flowed over me, reigniting those flames from earlier.

Stacy almost choked on the drink. She coughed and then said, "I'm going to go talk to Helen. I'll be back."

She left me unattended with the one man I wasn't

sure I should be next to.

"To Elana," he said softly, raising the glass Stacy had handed him.

I tapped his glass with mine, and we slammed them back. The drink was sweet and fruity and went down way too easily.

Brady waved at Mick. "Another round, my friend."

"Anything for my hero," Mick said back with a flirtatious wink.

I sat down on the stool so I wouldn't fall over, but Brady didn't. He stood, causing my knees to tangle with his and my shoulder to touch his arm. Awareness continued to overwhelm my senses almost as much as the alcohol. I just let myself savor it rather than pushing to recall the feelings my husband had once evoked in me.

I didn't have a husband.

He was dead.

But I wasn't. And I knew with all my heart that Darren would hate it if I spent the rest of my life only loving my daughter. I could almost feel him there, reassuring me. Rubbing my back like he often had when he knew I was upset. Shoving me forward rather than holding me back.

I wasn't sure how far I could step out from behind the black veil of widowhood I'd been living in, but for tonight—this one night—I was going to let myself just be a woman attracted to a man. Nothing else would come from it, anyway. Brady O'Neil was a superstar. He was in Grand Orchard simply because his family was there, and he would be gone as quickly as he'd shown up. I didn't want anything more from him. Not even sex. I just wanted to know I was desirable. To let this flirt of a man, this Pan-like creature, spread some of his charm my way. To pretend for a few minutes that someone might want me—ugly scars, baggage, and all.

Chapter Thirteen

Brady

SOMEBODY LIKE YOU
Performed by Keith Urban

Tristan was clueless to the fact that she was taking my breath away. I had a feeling she didn't see herself as someone who could stop men in their tracks even when she'd stopped me in mine. It wasn't just her blonde hair and soft curves. It wasn't just the glow of the setting sunlight that seemed to surround her. It was the steel warrior's soul at her core, full of grit and resolve.

She was stunning.

Now, with a handful of shots in her, she'd shed a portion of the barrier normally keeping her from the rest of the world. I'd only seen the barrier ever disappear when she was talking with Hannah or Stacy. With everyone else, it was always there, a thin sheet of chainmail hanging over her body.

"Can I ask you something?" Her voice was light, without the anguish that trailed inside it as often as her armor.

I nodded.

"Why haven't you opened the box from Grams?"

I spun the empty shot glass several times.

"Never mind," she said, and I heard the wall coming back up, and I wanted to kick myself around the room and back for letting it happen.

"No. It's okay," I said, meeting her gaze, curiosity and trepidation—hers and mine—mingling together. "I suppose it's because once I do, I won't hear from her ever again. Whatever's inside…whatever she put…it's like one last conversation. One last teachable moment."

She looked down and then back up. "Sorry. I always seem to ruin the mood."

"What are you talking about?" I said, waving the empty glass at Mick. He smiled a knowing smile and started throwing more alcohol in a shaker for us.

"Well, I'm not exactly a bubble of happiness on most occasions. It's one of the things I admire about your sister…" she said, a breathy intake as she added on, "about you."

"Cass is pretty incredible," I told her honestly.

My gaze traveled to those full pink lips. The gloss that had been on them earlier was gone. Now, they would taste like the purple concoction we'd both been drinking, but I wondered what other flavors would linger there. What was the essence of her that would always lie underneath the scent of what she'd just consumed? Would it be the bitter chocolate I'd sensed on Friday?

A line dance song came on, and Stacy hollered out from across the room, "Tristan, bring that man out on the dance floor with us!"

Stacy's husband was already leading her into the throng of dancers.

Mick set down the entire shaker. A little pitcher of shots.

I poured one for each of us and held it up to her. She clinked her glass with mine, we downed it, and then I pulled her from the stool toward bodies moving to the rhythm. Our fingers pulsed with energy, those sparkles of light that seemed to surround us every time we touched never once receding.

I felt Marco's eyes on me from where he'd taken up a position near the door. He knew I didn't do this sort of thing anymore—dance in a crowded room with a woman. I rarely did anything this personal out in the open, and I was worried for a moment that joining the crowd would mean a wave of people approaching me. But, as usual when I was in Grand Orchard, the town folk ignored me. No one asked for my autograph. No one asked to take a picture. The bar full of people who'd known me my whole life didn't care that I had three platinum albums out in the world. They didn't care that I'd sung onstage and in videos with John Legend and Thomas Rhett. They just saw Cormac, the kid who'd worked at Elana's and would forget his right hand if he was playing his guitar.

I could barely take my eyes off Tristan as she danced. She was smiling tonight. Wide. A light that was always inside her, but was often dimmed, was blooming into full glory, no longer hiding behind a blackout blanket. Tonight, it had broken free. She was radiant as she kicked her boots and shimmied and shook. She made me want to lose myself in her.

We danced to three songs in a row, two line dances before the last one required us to merge our figures together. The slow swell matching the pace of my hand as it grazed her hip, her waist, her side. Our bodies were talking to each other. Speaking a language as ancient as the skies. Attraction. Lust. But something deeper as well.

More.

When the sultry song ended, I led her through the crowd filling the place to bursting back to the barstool where our drinks waited for us. I wasn't sure who'd kept the seats empty and waiting, Mick or Marco, but I was grateful to have a spot at the end of the counter, the place I normally hid out from the crowd.

I poured us another shot, and we downed them.

"Brady O'Neil!" The screech to my left caught me off guard after the long minutes I'd remained almost human instead of a superstar. I turned to the woman, barely more than a girl, hardly old enough to be in the bar. Her face was lit up, happiness bubbling through her.

"Can you sign this for me?" She shoved her arm out at me, angling her wrist, pointing at the tender spot where her pulse would beat, and holding out a permanent marker.

I turned my real smile into my Brady-facing-the-world smile as I took the pen from her. "Sure, darlin'. What do you want me to write?"

"Oh. Well. What do you want to write?" It turned flirtatious in two seconds, even though I'd clearly been drinking with someone else. The fan wasn't being mean or spiteful. She truly just didn't see Tristan. Dani was the one to point it out to me a few years ago—how everyone around me faded away in the intense focus my fans gave me.

I wrote *Spread love into the world, xoxo Brady*

O'Neil. She giggled while I wrote along her wrist.

"That's beautiful," she said.

I handed her back the pen.

"Have a fun night," I said and then turned back to Tristan, who'd watched the entire exchange. The layer of chainmail had started to slide back down between us, and it was the last thing I wanted.

"Take a walk with me?" I asked.

She hesitated. "Let me just tell Stacy I'm taking off."

She weaved through the crowd toward the dance floor where Jin and Stacy were still moving together. It wasn't every day you saw a man who was as happy to spend his time moving and grooving as his wife was. Maybe he just did it for her, but it didn't look like it was much of a sacrifice. He looked happy to have his body pushed up against hers.

I waved my head at Marco toward the kitchen, the way I normally escaped, and he joined me there.

"I'm going to take a walk with Tristan. Why don't you head back to the apartment?"

He looked around at the crowd.

"Let me get you both out and away from the stampede first," he said.

I nodded.

Tristan returned, and I put my hand on her elbow, guiding her through the kitchen, out the back door, through the alley, and to the street that ran parallel to Main. No one was around, and the noise from the clanking of the kitchen and the music of the bar immediately was muffled.

"Call me if you need me," Marco said, and he disappeared into the darkness, his black apparel blending into the shadows.

As if we'd spoken and agreed to it, Tristan and I turned and stepped in the direction of her house. Of Elana's house. A repeat of just a few nights ago, but this time, the weather was at least thirty degrees warmer. As if we'd seen the last of the winter storms. New life. New beginnings.

"Does that ever get…weird?" she asked.

"Which part?"

"Well… The random person asking for your autograph must be odd, too, but I meant your bodyguard hanging around all the time."

I shrugged.

"It probably would be if Marco and I didn't get along so well. He and Trevor are the ones who babysit me the most."

She gave a soft laugh. "Babysit?"

"Well, it's pretty much what it is. Make sure I don't get into any trouble. Keep me safe."

She frowned. "I forgot about that whole Fiona stalker thing. It was what brought Dani and Nash together."

I nodded. It was the only good that had come out of what I always called the Fiona Fiasco. But like Tristan had said, it had brought Dani and Nash together, so I couldn't completely regret it. Their love had survived life and death in an epic fashion.

"I keep forgetting you're friends with them," I said. "It's strange we both revolved around the same people but never really met."

Our elbows bumped together as we walked, allowing more waves of awareness to coast over me.

"Oh, I saw you. You just didn't see me," Tristan

said with laughter in her voice.

I shook my head. "I'm not sure how that's possible. You're bright and shiny and impossible to ignore."

She caught her breath, steps faltering before she continued.

I stopped, pulling her arm so we were facing each other. "Like right now, it's dark as sin. There's no moon, and yet, I feel like I've got my flashlight on. A beam of pure radiance is shimmering around me…from you."

Her eyes were shadowed in the darkness, and while I couldn't see their golden color, her whole face did seem to glow. That light from within.

"You've got pretty smooth moves, but you forget you're the real *estrella*," Tristan said. The real star.

I took a chance, running a hand along her face. The shimmer of light that exuded from her was matched by the smooth texture of her skin. Soft. Warm. Silky. Something I could imagine wrapping myself in.

She didn't push me away, but she did stiffen as if the tender touch was something she was unaccustomed to. It made me wonder how long it had been since she'd been touched by someone who only wanted her.

I inched my body closer so we were touching as we had while we danced with one hand at the soft bend just above her hip and her full breasts pushed up against my chest. The buttons of her jean jacket pressed into me, only increasing the awareness of every single spot where we met. A deep ache filled me. I ached to join our mouths like I'd never kissed a woman before, as if this was my very first time in high school, my body vibrating with unforgettable pleasure and yet hesitant.

The uncertainty lingered, holding me back when I would normally have driven forward. The appropriateness of crossing this line with her was hanging in the air around me. She'd been hurt and lost so much. She needed someone to stay when I only had a track record of leaving. Of forgetting the ones I was supposed to be watching over.

But the desire to taste her was so much stronger than the doubts that I found myself breathing out, "Can I kiss you?"

She searched my face, and I wasn't sure what she expected to find there except the longing that I felt. My body throbbing with the knowledge that it would eventually wither away if I was unable to savor her. Unable to sample those pink lips.

She responded by putting her hands on my waist. They shook. I could feel them through my T-shirt. I wasn't sure if it was from desire or trepidation. She tilted her chin up, mouth parting ever so slightly.

"Yes." She said it so quietly it was almost not a word. A breath of fairy dust, enticing me.

I lowered my mouth and touched hers gently. The soft plushness of our two parts merged into a mixed entity, and holy fires of hell, she was sweet. The berry flavor of the Chambord lingering, barely covering a deeper, hidden flavor. Cream soda and bitter chocolate. Such incredible sweetness that it forced a groan from the back of my throat. I instinctively pulled her tighter while my tongue pushed at the seam of her lips, demanding more of the caramelized sugar and hints of berry lingering there.

She opened for me, face tilting in my hand, as I

slowly licked the inside of her mouth. Touching and exploring. She returned the movements. Soft and gentle, causing a wave of lust to hit me, causing my body to burst into showers of spun sugar.

We stood for what might have been an eternity with our lips and tongues writing a tender path on each other. Our bodies mingled but holding back so just our mouths made this initial step. A first kiss that rewrote the meaning of first kisses. As if there'd never been a more melodic and yet hotter attempt at a beginning.

It was just that. A beginning.

She crushed that thought when she pulled away, closed her eyes, and groaned. It was full of regret. When I tried to put my hand back on her arm, she stepped even farther away.

Her chocolate and spun-sugar-scented lips escaped me as she said, "I'm sorry."

It took the *more* I was dreaming of and shoved it back at me.

Chapter Fourteen

Tristan

I WONDER WHAT YOU KISS LIKE
Performed by Natalie Pearson & Brooks Chivell

The feel of his gentle exploration as he kissed me almost broke me. The slow and steady pull on my sleepy nerve endings was tearing my veins apart. A kiss tasting like berries and wine and picnics in the filtered sunlight between shady tree branches. A kiss that caused a burst of lust to spread through me because of its tenderness. A simple kiss with just lips and tongues joining and no hands or bodies, as if he knew how painful the experience would be for me and was trying to soften the blow.

A simple kiss that was anything but simple.

It felt so damn good it was hard to imagine stopping. It felt perfect.

Which sent a wave of ice down my back.

Perfect.

How could it be perfect?

I stepped away, regret filling me. Regret because I was being cruel, and I didn't like to be cruel. I'd let him kiss me, knowing it could only be a kiss and nothing more. Knowing I couldn't give him what he deserved to be given when he touched someone like that. When he kissed someone so wholeheartedly, so openly, so devotedly.

He deserved a beginning. He deserved someone giving all of themself.

And I didn't have that to give anymore.

I'd already given it away.

I saw the moment it hit him. My regret. The dark night unable to keep the longing and the sting of rejection from his face.

"I'm sorry," I told him, meaning it.

He covered his emotions in a way I was also accomplished at doing, grinning at me.

"Why the hell are you sorry?"

"I shouldn't have kissed you." I turned, unable to look at him as I continued down the street with a mix of emotions tagging along. Hunger. Hurt. Hatred. Hope.

"Why? It was goddamn beautiful," he said, keeping pace with me but not touching me, as if he knew I couldn't handle it.

It had been a beautiful kiss.

I shook my head, my thoughts warring with my emotions.

"Brady…I just…it's not fair to you."

"How can the best kiss I've ever had not be fair?"

I grunted. "Don't even say that. You haven't been a liar. Don't start now."

"I'm not lying, *Cariño*," he said with so much emotion that it almost exploded inside me. The nickname. The words. I pushed it aside.

"Do you even know how many women you've kissed?" I asked, turning the tables on him because I couldn't handle my own turmoil.

He chuckled. "Men and women."

I stopped and looked at him, the wicked smile, the tantalizing pull of his full red lips. I shook myself out of the reverie and kept going, heading to Grams' house. My home. My safe haven.

"It never mattered to me," he said, keeping up with me. "I know there's been lots of talk in the tabloids about it. I like to flirt, and sometimes flirting leads to kissing." The humor in his voice was tossed about easily, like his smiles.

"Well, this kiss… This flirting… It can't happen again," I told him as I tried to process everything he was telling me. Trying to remember if I'd ever heard him talk about being bi or pan or any part of the LGBTQ+ community.

We'd reached the house, and relief filled me because I was almost in the clear.

I mounted two steps before turning back to look at him. He was standing there, hands in his jeans pockets, eyes glimmering in the porchlight.

"I meant it," he said. "I've never enjoyed a kiss like I did that one." He was serious. No flirt. No tease. No infectious grin. "Can you at least tell me why you think it shouldn't happen again?"

I looked down at my right hand that now held my wedding ring instead of my left. I'd moved it there the day of Darren's funeral—a brutal, daily reminder that I'd had something beautiful and lost it, but a promise not to forget it.

He saw the glance, saw me as I fidgeted with the ring.

"I have no idea what that must be like," he said softly.

I looked up at him, fear skittering over my chest. A fear I couldn't put behind me like the fear at the podium tonight. Straightened shoulders and a steady voice weren't going to rid me of this. When I didn't speak, he continued.

"To have something you love with all your heart. To have a future that is twined with someone else's, only to have it ripped away."

I closed my eyes, refusing to cry.

"Some days, you feel like death will be the only reprieve," I said honestly.

He nodded slowly, thoughtfully.

"But you're not dead. You've got that incredibly gifted little girl. You've got friends. You've got family. You still have love flowing through you. I can't imagine he'd want you to keep it bottled up," he said quietly.

"How could you possibly know?"

"Because it's what I'd want for the woman I loved. I'd want them to be caressed and touched and held. I'd want them to be filled with happiness and joy. I'd want them to feel the overwhelming power of love all over again. From the very first beads of new love to the slow, syrupy drops of years spent together. All of it. A full life, not just a shell of one."

He was right in so many ways. His words were an echo of something Nash had said to me years ago. It had pissed me off at the time, but now I knew Darren would want this for me. I'd felt the push of it against me at the bar. I'd want the same for him if he'd been the one left behind. I'd want him to show Hannah what a loving relationship looked like. I'd want him to bring someone into her life who wouldn't replace me, but who could sort of fill some of the gaps and holes my absence had created.

I just didn't know how to do that.

What was left of me to even give to someone else?

Darren had taken it all with him.

But a little voice inside me objected. It was a quiet scream somewhere deep inside of me saying I was the only liar around tonight. Brady hadn't lied once.

He stepped back, edging toward the street, and the quiet voice inside was throwing up its hands and hollering at me to stop him. To not let him walk away without letting him know the kiss had been beautiful. Heart rendering…but beautiful.

So much so that I could see it spread out in color on a black canvas.

"I'll see you at *La Musica de Ensueños* tomorrow. Goodnight, *Cari*," he said.

Then, he disappeared in the night, leaving me with so many different feelings I wasn't sure I'd ever be able to sift through them, neither one at a time nor in heaps. They were going to be stuck in a pile that would have to remain just that for a while. An unfixable knot of emotions.

♫ ♫ ♫

The sound of laughter burst through me. The musical chimes of my daughter's giggles followed by the scrape of Molly's nails on the wood floors as she chased Hannah. I opened my crust-covered lids, glancing in the direction of the clock. It was almost eight in the morning.

I hadn't fallen asleep until well after four because of the tears and thoughts haunting me. I heard Stacy's voice and the loud chatter of her son and daughter as if Kiran and Jalissa were arguing.

I dragged myself out of bed, pulling on a sweatshirt and a pair of leggings over the T-shirt and underwear I normally slept in. The chilly air settled over me with winter still fighting against the sunshine of spring.

When I got downstairs, Hannah had placed her top hat on the counter next to the stove while she stood on the stool, mixing something in a saucepan. I was 99.9% sure it was oatmeal.

"Sorry, did we wake you?" Stacy asked.

I shook my head, smiling. I pulled Hannah into my arms, kissing her neck and making her giggle as she fought against me. "I missed you, *Chiquita*."

"I missed you too, Mommy," she said.

I swung her around before setting her back on the step.

"If you are going to eat oatmeal again, I'm insisting you add something fun to it," I told her.

She frowned at me. "What do you mean?"

"Your choice. Chocolate syrup, caramel syrup, or strawberry jam," I told her.

"None of that is healthy. Cassidy would agree with me," she said.

I exchanged a look with my best friend. "But Cassidy also told you that you had to have fun with your food even if it meant something unhealthy. At least once a day, remember," I told her.

"Fun, huh?" Stacy said with a smile. "Did someone else have fun last night?"

I ignored her as I opened the fridge and held out the three containers for my daughter to choose from. One thing had come out of my sweet kiss with Brady and the hours of reflection last night: I was determined my daughter would find her way back to the joy she'd had before Grams had died. I was determined to have her shed her fear of health issues and start playing the piano more. She was not going to be a fifty-year-old five-year-old. Not on my watch. Darren would hate that more than he'd hate me kissing another man.

I swallowed hard.

"Pick," I told her.

I knew which one she was going to choose before she did because, in her mind, the strawberry jam was at least fruit-based. She pointed at the red jar with a finger.

"Can I have chocolate in mine?" Kiran asked.

"Me too!" Jalissa shouted. The girl had one volume. Loud.

I put the containers on the kitchen table while I dug out bowls and spoons for them. Stacy moved to the coffee machine, making a whole pot as if she knew from just seeing me that I was going to need it to get through the day.

"Where's the rest of the herd?" I asked, referring to the little group of kids Stacy was homeschooling and the fact that it was only Friday.

"Did someone get their brain cells kissed out of them? It's officially spring break," she said.

My hand paused, not just her words about kissing stalling me, but also the realization we were already at spring break. How had that happened? It meant Easter and Hannah's birthday were both only a week away. We'd been making plans for the party that included bunnies and eggs and a scavenger hunt. But I had a boatload to do before the day arrived. I needed to kick my butt into gear.

Stacy and I helped the kids with their sugar-coated oatmeal and then sent them out into the backyard to play while we cleaned up the mess. We left the screen door open so we could see and hear them. Inside the house, it was quiet. Comfortable. Something I was used to with Stacy, reminding me of how lucky I was to have her.

"So. What's next on the school reno?" I asked.

"Don't you dare," she said, waving the pan she was drying at me. "You need to spill the beans. What is happening with you and the country-rock star?"

"Nothing. What could possibly be happening?" I said, but I didn't meet her eyes.

"He just forked out a half a million dollars for the festival," she pushed.

"For Grams," I said, stalling, even if it was true.

We took our coffees and made our way to the back porch.

The kids were climbing all over the giant play structure Grams had bought and installed for Hannah. It had swings, slides, monkey bars, and a turret with a playroom at the top of it. Hannah had her head out the window, her top hat held with one hand and the beads of her shawl swaying as she told Kiran something. He was on the ground, looking up at her with a goofy smile. I wanted to paint it. To put it down in color and form. The joy so clearly spreading through both of them.

"Hannah said she played the piano for him," Stacy said quietly.

I nodded. "It was… overwhelming. He's overwhelming."

She didn't say anything, waiting for me to process things just like she was good at waiting for the kids to process what she taught them at school. She never answered her own questions, even if they stalled. She let them muddle through until something hit them, right or wrong.

"Do you believe in an afterlife?" I asked her.

I'd gone to church with Grams, but it had been more for her than me. Growing up, we hadn't been a Sunday-service kind of family. Jin had told me once that he and Stacy believed in pieces of many different religions, coming from their own interracial families and now raising interracial children.

"If you're talking about the white-cloud, sit-around-playing-harps kind of heaven, then no," she said. "But I believe our energy doesn't just disappear the moment we die. I believe there is a place for them. Why?"

"And soul mates. Do you believe Jin and you were meant to be together? Fated. Destiny…whatever?" I asked.

Stacy's sharp gaze met mine. "I see where this is going."

"You do?" I asked, surprised, because I'd spent half the night trying to figure it out myself—my reluctance at dating someone else.

"If you loved Darren, if he was your soul mate, then you must be destined to spend eternity in the afterlife together as well, right? So how could you possibly consider the idea of loving someone else?" she said gently.

"It's stupid," I said, frustrated with myself.

"It's not stupid, Tris," she tried to reassure me.

"I mean… Who knows if there is even something out there? Maybe this is all we have. Maybe this is heaven, hell, and reality. But I can't keep from thinking of him…of what will happen when I die and he's suddenly there with me, but right next to him is some other person I chose to love as well… How could I choose?"

Just the thought of not choosing Darren made my entire insides splinter apart even as brown eyes and pink lips that tasted like sweet holidays also filled my vision.

"Who says you'd have to choose?" she asked.

"Wouldn't that be unfair? Wouldn't they want to know who I loved more?"

"You can love people differently without it being more or less. What you had with Darren you'll never ever feel again. But that doesn't mean what you feel for someone else won't be equally as strong," she told me.

I wasn't convinced, and as much as I loved my friend, she hadn't had Jin die on her. She hadn't had to choose between staying faithful and moving on.

"Look. Like you said, we have no idea what's waiting for us after these bodies die. For all we know, it's a huge mix of electrical waves where there is no defined unit. No me. No you. Maybe we're all one entity. Maybe we come right back to earth and live again. Maybe there's nothing. But you're thirty-four years old. You'll likely have another sixty years on this planet if Elana is any judge of the life expectancy of the women in your family. You shouldn't have to give up human touch…intimacy…affection…love for all those years."

"Grams did," I said.

It was true. Grams had lived a solitary life after she'd lost my grandfather. She'd lost him when I was younger than Hannah. I barely recalled anything of him that wasn't a picture or a story.

"But she was, like, what, sixty at the time? That's really different, Tris. I mean, I still think she should have gotten her rocks off with old Alejandro Romero. I think he loved her more than he loved his apple trees."

I giggled at the thought of Grams with the seventy-five-year-old grandfather of three. He'd spent a lot of time with Grams, routinely bringing her flowers from the farm he managed with his children.

"Who knows," I said with a smile. "Maybe she wasn't always alone. Maybe she did have fun with him, and that's why he brought her all those bouquets."

I waggled my eyebrows up and down.

Stacy's laughter joined my own. "I wouldn't put it past your grandmother to be a hot cougar like that."

Hannah came running toward me, one hand holding her top hat, the other holding onto her purple-and-pink shawl. "Mommy!"

"Yes, *Chiquita*?"

"I forgot. I have to get to the store."

I smiled. "What did we forget there?"

"Brady!"

Stacy choked and then started laughing while I gave her a dirty look.

"He said he'd teach me a new song," Hannah continued over the top of Stacy's chuckle. "Grams always taught me new songs on Fridays."

She was right. The schedule I'd given Brady had included time with Hannah on Fridays. My days were completely askew right now—too many things I was trying to keep afloat. I looked at my phone to check the time. We had an hour at least.

"We're not late, but why don't we go downtown, and you can tell Helen what flavor you want your cake to be before going to the store."

"Do you think she can make a zucchini cake?" Hannah asked.

"No. We're having a full-on, worst-kind-of-treat-for-you cake. It's what all your family and friends are going to want to celebrate your day with you," I told her.

"But I want them to be healthy, too!"

"I want a chocolate cake with s'more filling for my birthday," Kiran said, joining us on the deck. Jalissa followed them, her stuffed panda dragging behind her on the ground with her black hair and dark eyes shimmering in the sunlight.

"I don't think there's such a thing as s'more filling," Stacy said.

Kiran shook his head. "Helen said she'd make it just for me." He looked down at Hannah. "I bet if you tell her you want it, she'll make it for both of us."

Kiran would share just about anything with those he loved.

"You like s'mores, remember?" I said to Hannah. "Grams made them with you right over there at the firepit on Halloween."

I waved toward the circle of stones at the back of the yard, far away from the play structure.

Hannah's chin wobbled. She flung herself into

my arms. "I miss her, Mommy."

I hugged my daughter tight, knowing nothing I could say would take away the ache inside of her. I whispered into her hair, "Me too."

Chapter Fifteen

Brady

LAST HABIT

Performed by Matt Stell

My phone rang as I went up the steps to the second floor of the old Kincaid's drug store. The realtor, Elsa Chan, was walking ahead of me as she tried not to touch any of the dusty rails or walls with her bright-yellow suit.

Her perfectly cut black bob swung around her face like strands from a willow tree, wispy and gentle. She'd been two years younger than William and me in school, and I barely remembered her, even though I'd bet she left a mark on anyone she'd been in a relationship with. She wasn't the kind of person you forgot. Smart. Sexy. Dynamic.

But she didn't interest me in the least.

I still had the taste of caramelized sugar, dark chocolate, and hints of berries burned into every single one of my senses.

My phone stopped ringing and then restarted. I looked down and saw Mom's face on the screen.

"Hey, Mom, what's up?"

"Where are you?" she asked snappily.

"I had some business to take care of," I told her with a sigh.

The night before, I'd come home from a blissful kiss to find all the lights in the house blazing and Mom on a rampage. I'd been gone for most of the day, and even though it had been at Cassidy's insistence, Mom didn't see it that way. The argument between the three of us had gotten heated, with Cassidy insisting she wasn't going to be treated like an invalid and Mom threatening not to return to Ireland.

It had been Dad who'd brought peace to the household by reminding Mom Cassidy was not only an adult but was also now a mom herself. It hadn't ended well. Mom had stormed off, and Dad had slept on the couch for the first time in what felt like a decade—since the argument they'd had about me and Juilliard.

"Cassidy and Chevelle aren't here!" Panic rang through her voice as I turned to take in my sister. She was dressed in a button-down top and a flowy skirt with ballet slippers on her feet. Her hair was up in a ponytail, and she had Chevelle tied to her chest in some sort of sling.

"They're with me, Mom," I said.

Cassidy had been going stir crazy this morning. We both had, and I'd wanted to check out the space William was trying to find a buyer for next to Elana's. His desire to merge the two stores and his plans to finance the remaking of Grand Orchard were still bugging the hell out of me. Seeing Kincaid's had been the perfect excuse to get out.

"Out? Chevelle isn't supposed to be around other people yet," she said loud enough that both Elsa and

Cass could hear the words.

Cass rolled her eyes and grabbed the phone from me. "Mom, I'm not staying trapped in the house. I'll be fine. Chevelle will be fine. I'm not exposing him to anything dangerous. If you don't stop this nonsense, I'm moving to San Francisco with Megan."

It was the first time I'd heard Cass threaten our mom since Christmas when she'd threatened to get her own apartment. Moving clear across the country to be with her best friend was not something I could imagine Cassidy doing, no matter what happened with her and Mom. But it must have scared Mom enough for her to backpedal because I could no longer hear her screech.

Elsa was pretending not to listen, but she was clearly hanging on every word. I wasn't sure if it meant the conversation would be blasted all over social media or if it would only be repeated verbatim to her brother.

"So, what do you think?" Elsa asked as Cass took my phone and headed down the stairs.

I watched my sister as she went, holding the rail, being extra cautious. I understood my mother's fear when Cass was moving with the baby in her arms, but we also had to trust that Cassidy knew her limitations better than anyone else. Her priority was clearly the baby.

I returned my eyes to the space. It was at least twice as big as the upstairs at Elana's, but it had also been used exclusively for storage. It was one big room with unfinished walls and a wood floor so old I was worried it might have been rotted.

"I think it needs a lot of work," I told Elsa honestly.

"It really does, and it's pretty tight the way it is. As a restaurant, it wouldn't hold a huge crowd. But if you could merge it with one of the spaces next door, it would be plenty big."

I met her dark-brown eyes with my own. We both knew she was talking about *La Musica de Ensueños*. Elana's store. Anger flew through me at both the Chan siblings being so set on destroying the place that had been my sanctuary growing up. There was no way Elsa was talking about merging with the exclusive hair salon that shared the opposite wall with Kincaid's.

The thought of the hair salon did serve to remind me that I needed Patty to fix the mess I'd made of my hair since I'd hacked at it in frustration.

We headed back down just as Cass said, "Mom, I can't discuss this right now."

She hung up and passed me my phone before walking toward the kitchen we'd already been in once. I followed her.

"You know, this place has a lot of potential," she said.

"It does?" I was surprised.

"Sure. If you pushed out this wall until it hit the stairs, the kitchen would be plenty big enough for a restaurant."

"I was thinking of renovating it into a recording studio," I told her truthfully. Then, I grinned and added on, "Because I have to have some kind of backup for when my good looks stop winning me awards."

Elsa scoffed, and Cass flicked my ear.

"I thought you were going to be older than Tim

McGraw while still making albums with your Faith Hill look-alike wife," Cass teased.

I laughed. I had wanted to be like Tim McGraw and Faith Hill with a couple of kids just like them. I was young still, not even thirty yet—not for a few more months, at least. But I couldn't help the image from appearing of Tristan at my side with a baby in her arms while I had a little girl wearing a top hat on my shoulders. A family. The longing for that hit me so hard in the gut it was hard to breathe.

"Well, I could record here and rent out the space when I wasn't," I told her.

I needed somewhere to spend my money and time. My family certainly didn't let me spend it on them. Even Dani had set a limit on how much she'd let me give to From the Ashes as she'd set up the foundation. It was ridiculous the money I had floating around without a real use for it.

Elsa's phone rang, and she stepped out of the kitchen to answer it, leaving Cass and me alone.

"What would you do with the kitchen space then?" she asked.

I shrugged. The point of buying the space had started as a way to keep the Chans' greedy hands off *La Musica*. But I did like the idea of having my own studio in Grand Orchard. It would allow me to be home more.

Elsa returned. "I'm sorry, I have to head out to show a warehouse outside of town. Is there anything else I can do for you today?"

I shook my head. "No, I'll be in touch, though."

She beamed at me as we left the store. She locked up and then headed down the sidewalk to her luxury sedan, the sway of her hips drawing attention from at least two sets of college guys.

"That was for you, you know?" Cass said dryly.

I was almost oblivious to it on most days—the lure that got thrown out to test the waters, to see if I'd take a bite. But after the sensations from the night before, I couldn't imagine biting anyone else but the blonde-eyed sensation who was walking into Sweet Lips across the street. I pulled on the leather bands at my wrist.

"Feel like a cupcake?" I asked my sister.

She smiled. "Maybe."

We made our way in just as Hannah was telling Helen she'd cleared it with someone named Kiran to use his s'more filling idea for her chocolate cake.

"S'more filling, huh?" I asked, and Hannah tipped her eyes up to me. Her entire face burst into a smile, unlike her mother, who actually frowned.

"My best friend, Kiran, said I could have it even though it was supposed to be for his birthday."

"Are you celebrating a birthday?" I asked her.

"Next Saturday. That's not tomorrow. That's another seven days. I'll be five," she told me seriously.

"Wow. That's pretty old. You sure you're going to be able to keep playing rock and roll songs with those ancient fingers of yours?" I asked.

She actually giggled. "I'm not old. Grams was way older, and she could play anything I asked her to."

She was right. Elana could play almost anything. By ear. She'd had a natural talent, and I'd been lucky to be able to learn from her.

Hannah saw my sister Cass and the baby. She

flung her arms around Cassidy's legs, causing Cass to wobble with the force of it. I stuck out a hand to balance her.

"Cassidy!" Hannah cried. "You had your baby!"

Cassidy smiled. "Yep, would you like to meet Chevelle?"

She bent so Hannah could look into the little sling she had wrapped about her. Hannah smiled at the sleeping baby.

"He's all smooshed," Hannah said.

"Yep, but babies like to be snuggled tight."

"I mean, his face is all smooshed."

I couldn't help the laugh that escaped me. When I turned back to Tristan, her face was a flare of red from her daughter's words, but Cassidy was chuckling, too.

"He does look a little smooshed, doesn't he?" Cass said, looking with adoration at her son's face. His nose was pushed up a little and his cheeks were sort of wrinkly. Like he hadn't quite grown into his tiny body yet.

Hannah's smile wavered as she asked Cassidy, "Is it okay to order the chocolate cake with the s'more filling? Mommy said we could."

Cass pretended to think about it and then loud-whispered, "Just don't eat the whole cake in one sitting."

Hannah rolled her eyes, her top hat wiggling on her head. "I'm not going to eat the whole thing, silly. Just a piece."

"Well then, I think it's perfectly acceptable. Maybe even a slice for breakfast the next morning."

Hannah looked at my sister like she had four

heads. "No. No. No. Oatmeal is the healthiest breakfast!" She leaned in and said quietly, "Mom made me put jam on it this morning, but I ate around it."

I was definitely missing something. I looked over at Tristan again and saw worry etched across her face as she watched her daughter and Cass. It took my heart and squeezed tightly. It made me want to fix this for her like I'd tried to fix the issues with the festival.

"What are you two up to this morning?" Tristan asked us, changing the subject.

"Just needed a breath of fresh air," I said.

Cassidy looked at me funny, but I ignored it. I knew from painful experience that I couldn't talk in the open about any plans I might have. If I did, it would be all over the Internet in the blink of an eye. People would be gossiping for days about why I would be buying a business in my hometown. I didn't need that kind of attention right now. Plus, I wasn't even sure if I was going to buy it.

"You haven't forgotten my lesson, right?" Hannah asked, and my heart about wrenched from my chest at the expression on her face. Loss. Fear. Hope. All tangled in a face too young for any of it.

"No way. I have plans for those feisty little fingers of yours," I told her, and I did. It was the first thing that had been on my mind this morning. "I just have to drop Cass off at the house, and then I'll be back."

Cassidy huffed. "I don't need you walking me home!"

"If you show up at the house without me, I'll never hear the end of it. She's already furious you're out with the baby."

It was Tristan's turn to look confused, because why on earth would my sister need an escort to go a couple of blocks in the middle of the day in Grand Orchard? It seemed ridiculous, but the little wobble she'd had from Hannah's small frame hitting her made me realize Cass needed more help than she'd ever let on. She thought she'd outgrown a lot of it, but she hadn't.

Tristan and Hannah hugged Cass goodbye and headed over to the music store while we ordered our cupcakes. I took the box and my sister's arm, and we made our way down the street back home.

"You like her," Cass said.

I didn't need to know who she was asking about. The truth was, I liked Tristan a whole lot. I also liked her genius of a daughter, but I wasn't sure it could ever be anything more than the kiss we'd exchanged. Not only because of the things Tristan had said—and not said—after the beautiful kiss, but because they needed something more than I was good at. They needed someone to stay. To stick to them and their lives in a way my musician lifestyle wasn't exactly good at.

"She's been through a lot," I said.

Cass nodded. "Yeah. So, don't screw it up."

I chuckled. "I'm not sure there's anything there to screw up, Cass. I'm not sure there should be."

"Well, then you better figure it out before you continue to wiggle your way into their lives. It isn't fair to them otherwise."

It wasn't anything I didn't know.

At the steps of the house, I halted. I didn't think I could face my mom and her frustrating helicopter reactions to Cass and me. I didn't want to hear, yet again, all the things I was doing wrong instead of right.

Instead, I wanted to hurry back to the music shop just like I'd always done when other things in my life weren't working. But instead of Elana waiting for me, Tristan and Hannah would be. And even though I knew it shouldn't, even though I'd just told my sister and myself that I wasn't sure we could be anything, my heart bloomed at the idea of them being there when I arrived.

I opened the back door, set the cupcake box on the counter, ruffled Cassidy's hair, kissed Chevelle's head, and then turned to run away—or rather, run to something I truly wanted.

♫ ♫ ♫

Two hours later, my ears were ringing with "I Have a Dream" as Hannah's hands slid over the keys. I was stunned all over again by the talent in her little fingers. The talent of her brain that allowed her to read, filter, and then play the complex notes at such a young age. It was wild. Like something from a movie. I'd heard stories about child savants like this before. It wasn't unheard of, but I'd just never experienced it. There had been a couple of teenagers enrolled at Juilliard when I was there, but I hadn't really thought about what it must have been like for them when they were younger.

I hadn't even started playing until I was eight years old. I'd fallen in love with it because it felt like something that flowed through me naturally. Like my soul leaking out onto the keys. It felt like something that could be mine while my parents were absorbed in the issues with Cassidy.

I stood up from the piano bench, patting the top

of Hannah's hat.

"Ten more times from start to finish."

"'K," she said.

I stepped out of the practice room and into the art studio. Tristan had her back to me, a paintbrush in one hand as she stared at a canvas taller than her. Maybe seven feet by three feet. Narrow but still enormous.

The picture was stunning. It was as if the observer had their eye to a keyhole, the black outline of it visible around the edges. And through the keyhole was a kaleidoscope of color. A lake at sunrise, the sky awash with pinks and purples and grays that were reflected across the rippling water. The edges of the apple orchards to one side, bursting with flowers, the soft whites and pinks shaded by the colors streaming from the sky.

"It's incredible," I told her, and she jumped, the paintbrush coming dangerously close to the canvas, but she pulled back at the last moment. "Sorry. I didn't mean to startle you."

She smiled and put the paintbrush on the palette sitting nearby with several colors spread across it. "I kind of lose track of myself sometimes. It's why I rarely do it when it's just Hannah and me, because everything in the world disappears while I'm working."

Her words echoed every thought I'd ever had about my music.

I was nodding at her.

"For a long time, I thought it made me a bad mom. Like the fact that I could actually tune out my child while I was painting…" She swallowed hard. "But then I realized the only thing that would have made me a bad parent was if I knew and did it anyway without making sure she had someone else watching over her."

"I lost Cassidy a couple of times when I was supposed to be watching her." I told her the truth so she wouldn't hold it against herself. "The first time it happened was the day I brought my guitar home. I was lost, making music, playing chords that weren't anywhere except in my head. I didn't even know she was gone until my mom touched my shoulder. One look at her panicked face and I knew I'd screwed up."

"Where did she go?"

"She took our dog for a walk, going three streets over. She didn't know how to get back. Then she fell, twisted her ankle, and just sat on the curb, crying, until Dad picked her up and carried her home."

"Oh no!"

"Yep. My parents were furious with me. Rightfully so. She was only six, barely older than Hannah."

"What did they do?"

"Took the guitar. Wouldn't give it back for three months."

She grimaced. "Ouch."

I nodded. "Yeah, and you'd think I would have learned my lesson, but it repeated itself several more times before I realized I couldn't even pick up an instrument if I was supposed to be looking after her."

"You're quite a few years older than her?"

"Six. Which isn't really all that much now, but when you're a kid, it's like being in a different area code."

I inched over to her painting, staring at the brush strokes that were so smooth they were almost invisible, as if you were looking at a photograph instead of a painting.

"You're as talented as your daughter," I told her.

She flushed, looking away.

"What do you do with the pieces?" I asked.

"Dani set up a website and some social media accounts for me. I sell a lot of it through there."

"Have you ever had a gallery showing?" I asked.

She shook her head. "No. I haven't even tried to go that route, to be honest."

"Why not?"

"It's just a commitment I couldn't really ever keep. Most galleries would want more pieces than I ever have at one time." I read between the lines that she'd been busy losing a husband, taking care of a little girl, and helping Elana.

"What are you doing with this piece?" I asked.

"Nothing. It's ridiculous because I have six of them. They're a mural, really," she said, referring to a cloth-draped stack on the far wall. From the hidden shape, I could tell they were all as tall as the canvas in front of her.

"May I?" I asked.

She shrugged.

I took off the covering to find myself looking through that same keyhole but in the dead of winter. The lake on display, the apple trees bare, a bright-red cardinal soaring by the opening with its wings spread out across the snowy, gray background. The one behind it was the same keyhole again but a night view. Stars sparkling as if they'd actually pulse against my hand if I touched them. Another was the same scene but with the fiery display of fall leaves. One was the bright greens and blues of a summer you could almost smell and feel with the leaves rustling in an unseen breeze. The final one was the view during a thunderstorm. Lightning crackling, the electricity emerging from the painting to dance in the air. They were each and every one of them gorgeous.

"They're really beautiful. What's the meaning of the keyhole?" I asked.

"Our limited view obscures us from seeing the full picture. We only see a snapshot of what's in front of us. No matter how much the scene changes, we still don't get it all," she said, emotion flowing from her.

"Elana," I breathed out.

She jerked her eyes to me. "What?"

"She was so many things to so many people, but we all only saw her for what she was to us. We didn't see the whole picture."

Her eyes filled with tears as she moved to the paintbrush and the palette, fiddling with the colors there, mixing and blending them. "She had all these lives… Did you know she started as a *cantaora,* like her father?"

"She liked to rub it in whenever I got in a rut. She was like, 'If I can sing *cante*, jazz, and rock and roll, you can sing more than country music,'" I said with a smile, remembering her fury at me limiting myself to one style.

Tristan's face lit up, going from sad reflection to a warm memory. "She was a little opinionated."

I laughed. "Just a little?"

She chuckled too.

The bell on the door downstairs jingled, followed by Stacy's voice, "Hello!"

Feet pounded on the stairs, and two little bodies burst into the studio. A boy—a year or two older than Hannah, if I had to guess—who was a perfect, eclectic mix of his parents. Black hair, dark eyes with graceful curved edges surrounded in dark lashes, and skin the color of sand as the waves pulled away. He was holding the hand of a little girl who looked exactly like Stacy. A riot of curls spiraled gracefully around a fine-boned face with bright-pink lips and dark eyes that sparkled from the depths of skin brushed dark like the blending of trunks in a forest sheltered from the sun.

They both stopped at the top of the stairs. "We're going to the farm," the boy said.

Stacy emerged behind them.

"Hey—oh, I didn't know you had company."

Hannah emerged from the practice room at the sound of the voices.

"Han, guess what? Emerick posted videos of the chicks hatching!" the boy said, excitement pouring from him.

"They did? Can we go see them, Mommy?" Hannah looked over at us.

"Chicks at the farm. Now that brings back memories," I said warmly.

"Are you trying to finish your piece?" Stacy asked Tristan. "I can take Hannah with us, and you can stay."

Her eyes slid from Tristan to me and then back again as she tried to keep her lips straight. As if something was going on between Tristan and me. I wondered what Tristan had told her friend, if anything, about the heart-throbbing kiss we'd shared the night before. The scents and tastes had lingered with me, pouring out of me in an *accelerando* of notes when I'd finally gotten back to the apartment.

"Please, Mommy! I want to see the baby chicks." Hannah was jumping up and down.

"Are you Brady O'Neil?" the little boy's voice cut in. He'd been staring at me, trying to put it together.

I nodded, moving forward to stick my hand out. "Yep. One and the same. And you are?"

"Kiran," he introduced himself. "My mom says you're going to be the person to break Tristan's slump." Both women gasped. Humor, joy, and trepidation washed over me at his words. Cass was right. I couldn't screw this up.

Stacy slid a hand over the boy's mouth. "What have we said about conversations at home staying at home?"

"I can't believe you said that!" Tristan growled.

"It wasn't exactly put like that." Stacy was laughing now. "I think there were the words *I wish* and *hope* in there somewhere."

"I's Jalissa," the little girl beside Kiran announced.

I bent down, trying to ease the awkward moment amongst the grown-ups. "Hey, darlin'. Aren't you just too cute for words? Are you going to see the baby chicks as well?"

"I want one. Mommy says no."

"We absolutely cannot have chickens at the house. I draw the line," Stacy said. "But I'm happy to take you out to the Romeros' as much as you want to see them."

The Romeros' farm was one of the largest apple

orchards in the county. It also was known for its barrage of farm animals. They hosted field trips and apple pickings and cider contests throughout the season. Lidia and Emerick Romero were running it now, while Emerick's grandfather oversaw it. He'd come from Nicaragua and built the farm from scratch into the bustling enterprise it was today.

"I have to wait for this layer to dry anyway, so I'll just come with you," Tristan said.

"Are you sure?"

She nodded, and I felt oddly disappointed, as if she were doing it to escape me.

"Do you want to come and see the chicks with us, Brady?" Hannah asked.

Even though they didn't gasp this time, I felt the inhaled breath of both women again.

I smiled. "I'd love to come, but only if your mom is okay with it."

I looked at Tristan, our gazes locking before her eyes slid to my lips and back. The smell of cream soda filled my nostrils. Cream soda, and dark chocolate, and a deep desire to taste them again. A desire so strong I was willing to forget the argument waiting for me at the house with Mom about her return to Ireland. I was willing to forget about anything. Just like when I was lost in my music.

Chapter Sixteen

Tristan

I HAVE A DREAM
Performed by ABBA

I was trying not to show the wave of embarrassment I'd felt at Kiran's remark. I'd already been fighting off the waves of awareness and longing filling me since seeing Brady in the bakery, and since he'd shown up with a stack of his old sheet music from when Grams had taught him so he could teach Hannah the same songs.

The fact he'd seen in my paintings what no one else had seen—Grams—and that he understood losing himself in his art so completely… It only added to the ridiculous allure he held over me.

But what I'd said to Stacy this morning was the truth. I didn't know how to reconcile my attraction to him with my reality. I didn't know how to share the space in my heart I'd believed was my soul mate's with someone else.

"I'm sure you have a lot to do," I said as a way of letting Brady off the hook when Hannah asked if he could join us. I was half hoping he'd say he did have work to do.

"Nope. Absolutely nothing," he said with his wicked grin and flirty tone.

Stacy choked back a laugh at his easy retort, and Brady's smile widened more. He'd been voted one of the sexiest men alive last year, so how was a simple, mortal, single woman like me supposed to resist his charm?

Before I knew it, we were all bundled into Stacy's giant SUV, the girls in their car seats in the far back row, Kiran in his in the middle with Brady at his side, and Stacy and I were in the front. I had to shake my head at it—the country-rock star tucked into a middle seat, discussing *Yobi, the Five-Tailed Fox* with a seven-year-old.

"Have you even watched Korean anime?" I asked Brady.

"My road manager's girlfriend is half-Korean, and they've introduced me to some. But I'm honestly not up to snuff for any in-depth discussions. Kiran here is definitely educating me," Brady said.

Kiran smiled smugly at teaching an adult.

"You sure you don't want to drive yourself? You may be ready to leave before we are," Stacy said.

Brady shuddered. "Drive? Me? I hate driving. With a passion. I barely have a license."

I couldn't help laughing. "I guess you probably don't have to drive, right? I mean, you probably have a whole host of cars and drivers at your beck and call."

He actually looked a little embarrassed. "Well. Yeah. It's one of the perks."

When we got to the farm, the kids went running for the barn where the chicken eggs had been incubating. Emerick and Alejandro emerged from large wooden doors just as the children were scampering in. Alejandro turned around and followed the kids, while Emerick greeted us.

"Thanks for letting us come," Stacy said to him.

He shoved his cowboy hat back on his dark hair and smiled. "We've been inundated with visitors today. As soon as Lidia posted the video, the calls started."

Squeals of joy came from inside the barn. Stacy and I headed toward it while Emerick turned toward Brady.

"Brady! Surprised to see you here. How you been?" Emerick said.

"I'm good. Once I heard about your fuzzy little creatures, I couldn't resist coming to see them myself."

I didn't listen to the rest of the conversation as my eyes adjusted to the depths of the barn after the bright spring sunshine. The sound of cheeping filled the air, and I found my daughter with a chick clutched to her chest as Alejandro handed another one to Kiran.

Jalissa was jumping up and down, screaming, "Me, me!" Stacy moved over to help her hold the chick without crushing it.

What I didn't expect was the host of other bodies in the room. The dean of Wilson-Jacobs was there with her grandson, who attended Stacy's pre-school, and behind them was another little boy who I recognized as Pastore. He'd been at Stacy's school the year before and was on Kiran's soccer team. He was well-liked with our kids. What I didn't expect was to find William Chan with him, because he wasn't the boy's father.

Stacy and I greeted the dean and the kids, but we both refused to acknowledge William. His eyes settled on me anyway, looking me up and down in a way that made me too self-conscious of my paint-splattered jeans and Darren's old T-shirt, even when they were more appropriate than his expensive suit in the dust and dirt of the barnyard.

"Mommy! Come hold one," Hannah said. I eased over to where my daughter had sat down with the chick. Her top hat hid her face as she stared down at the baby bird who was almost lost in the soft fabric of Hannah's shawl. I sat down on the straw-covered barn floor with her, trying to ignore William's gaze, which I could feel still hovering over me.

The three boys were in deep discussion about the chicks: how long it had taken them to hatch and what they would look like as they grew, which drew my eyes back to the boys. William was standing over them with his hands shoved into his dress pants pockets, looking like the one thing that didn't fit in the picture.

I held back a laugh.

He moved away from them toward Hannah and me.

"I'm glad to see you," William said to me. "I was going to stop by the store later, but now I don't have to."

My blood pulsed and pounded, wanting him to go away, wanting him to stop talking before he said something I didn't want anyone to hear. I didn't have that kind of luck.

"I wanted to let you know we're starting foreclosure proceedings," he said, not even trying to be subtle.

"Excuse me?" I asked, glaring at him.

"You're in default," he said.

Anger filled me at more than just the fact that he would dare to try and take my grandmother's store from me. Anger that he thought nothing of broaching it in front of my daughter, my friend, and others. That he would say it in the middle of this moment that was supposed to be sweet and happy.

"Grams missed one payment before—" I glanced at my daughter and couldn't say the words. "And I missed one after, while I got the paperwork and estate sorted. We're hardly in default."

"You can take care of it by paying the loan in full," he said with a casual shrug as his eyes were drawn to something behind him. Brady and Emerick entered the barn, laughing. "Maybe your hero can save the day once more, but then again, maybe he has his own ideas for tearing down the place after meeting with my sister about Kincaid's."

My veins tingled with awareness as Brady drew closer, but the entire suggestion that Brady was somehow swooping in to save me only fanned the flames of my fury and disgust. The knowledge that Brady had looked at Kincaid's added fuel to the fire in my belly.

Before I could respond, Brady stepped in.

"William, surprised you're here. Don't you hate everything related to dirt?" he asked, eyeing William and me. I knew my face reflected my irritation. It was impossible to hide, even if I was trying to keep it in check so Hannah and Stacy's kids wouldn't be sucked into a grownup rampage.

Wesley joined Hannah and me on the ground with his own chick while William ignored Brady's jibe with a glower. Brady turned to the dean with a wide smile. "Dean! It's really nice to see you." He hugged her. "What are you doing here?"

"My grandson, Wesley, wanted to see the chicks, of course," she responded with a smile at the boy with Hannah.

"That cannot be Wesley! Didn't Dolores just have him?" Brady joked, looking at the child with a bold and beautiful Afro. When they were together, Wesley and Hannah looked like a *That 70's Show* rerun. It usually brought a smile to my face, but today I was having a hard time coming up with one.

The dean laughed. "Time flies when you're having fun, it seems."

Pastore looked up at William from the bird in his hand. "Uncle William, do you think we can buy one of the chicks and bring him home?"

"Chickens belong on farms, Pastore, not in a house," William responded with a clipped tone.

"We could build a coop for him."

"No, we couldn't. We don't live like—"

"Like what?" Emerick cut William off.

William frowned. "Animals belong on a farm, not in the middle of town."

"When did you become such a dick?" Brady asked William.

"Excuse me?" William stiffened.

"Gentlemen, can I suggest you take this entire discussion and your passive-aggressive male testosterone somewhere else," Stacy said, glancing at all the kids before settling back on William and Brady.

"Pastore, we have to leave. Give the chicken back," William said, voice tight.

"Aw. I don't want to leave yet."

"Don't argue with me." He took the chick from the boy's hands, put it with the others in the little cage, and brushed his hands furiously. Then, he turned and walked out, barely waiting to ensure the boy followed him. Pastore's head was low, eyes darting back to us and the chicks we were holding, before leaving the building completely. My anger at the uncle disintegrated into sadness for the child.

"What an utter ass-tank," Brady said before looking around at the kids and adding, "Sorry."

"I believe your father would use the word, *bastardis*," the dean said in Latin, causing us all to chuckle.

"Can't believe you used to be his best friend," Emerick said.

I looked up in surprise again. Even though I'd heard the same thing before, it still constantly came as a shock to me that Brady had grown up in this town. In Gram's town. It felt like he should be a recent addition, like me, but he had more history with these people than I did.

"He was always full of himself, but never quite a…jerk," Brady said.

Brady took a chick from the cage and sat down on the floor with the rest of us, spreading his legs wide. Hannah's chick escaped her hands and walked in between Brady's legs to join its sibling.

"He upset you," Brady said quietly, and I met his eyes over the top of Hannah's hat.

"I can't talk about it. Not right now," I said, looking toward my daughter.

He nodded curtly, jaw clenching and unclenching

as if he was truly distressed because William Chan had angered me.

"Can I take one home, Mommy?" Hannah asked.

"I'm not sure Molly would love the addition of a chick in the house," I told her, wanting to say yes just so that I would be doing the opposite of William Chan.

The kids played with the chicks for a while, disheartened that none of them were coming home with us. We promised we'd be back soon and made our way outside with the dean and her grandson following us.

Before we got into Stacy's car, the dean called out to me. I turned back to her with a smile.

"There are only a few days left on the art contest the college is holding for a centerpiece to go in the theater. I was surprised to hear you hadn't submitted one of yours," she said.

My heart thumped. "I didn't know anything about it."

"We'd love the winner to be someone local, but it's open to anyone in the state," she said. "The information is on the school's website. I hope you check it out."

"I will. Thank you for telling me," I said.

"There'll be prize money awarded to the finalists as well as the winner," she said.

I flushed in embarrassment, knowing she'd heard the conversation with William. I didn't want my art to be chosen as some sort of charity case any more than I wanted the town to know the bank was foreclosing on the store.

As if she could read my mind, she said, "I'm not on the selection committee. I have no sway in the votes because I'm entirely unqualified to judge art. Give me an economic forecast to tear apart, and I have no problems, but ask me if it's a Matisse or a Derain and I'm lost."

The fact that she knew Matisse and Derain belied her words, but I was grateful she was trying to put my unease to rest. She was as good at reading people as she was at running the college.

We said goodbye, and I turned back to the others who were waiting for me in the SUV. My brain was whirling with thoughts, and the mood was solemn as we headed back into town.

"Where should I drop you?" Stacy asked Brady, looking at him in the rearview mirror.

"Just drop me with Tristan. I want to talk to her about the as—*bastardis*," Brady said. Stacy shot a glance at me, and I shrugged. There wasn't anything to say. I certainly wasn't going to be going into all my grandmother's personal business with him. It was bad enough that the dean had heard.

At Grams', the three of us got out of Stacy's car, and it hit me hard—the little family we might look like to an outsider. A mom and dad and their daughter walking up the steps to their front door. I'd never gotten to have that with Darren. He'd been there for Hannah's birth and then was back out on a mission. He'd barely been home again before he'd left on the one that had taken his life.

But God, he'd loved his daughter.

The image of him, bare-chested with our baby lying on him, little fingers twisted about his pinky, with that gorgeous smile on his face hit me hard in the gut. What would he think of her now? What would she think of him if he'd lived? A dad who was in and out of her life for months at a time. The thoughts hurt, stabbing at me.

I unlocked the door, and we removed our muck-encrusted shoes. Molly was whining at the door of the laundry room. Hannah rushed toward the door and the dog she loved.

"Wash your hands before you let her out," I said, and she changed directions to the little half bath downstairs.

I turned to find Brady removing his shoes as well.

It felt…personal…familiar.

We made our way to the kitchen as Hannah stepped out of the bathroom.

"May I?" Brady asked with a head wave toward the restroom.

"Of course," I said.

He disappeared inside, and I headed to the kitchen to wash my hands. Hannah let Molly out, and the dog danced on two legs around my daughter, following her into the kitchen. Molly sniffed and licked and tugged at the beads on Hannah's shawl.

Hannah giggled.

"She must smell the chicks on you. Do you want to change?" I asked.

"'Kay," she said and skipped toward the stairs, holding her hat and her shawl, with Molly chasing her and making her laugh more. It drew a small smile to my lips as well. The sound eased the tension filling me since William Chan had said the word "foreclosure."

Brady entered the kitchen with a grin as he watched my daughter and dog disappear. When he smiled, he went from downright handsome to some godlike level of gorgeousness. His eyes and hair were a deeper color than Darren's had been, but he was still blond and muscled like my husband. His muscles weren't the hefty SEAL ones Darren had sported. Brady's were leaner, and yet still visible with the cuts and lines on display in the short-sleeved T-shirt hugging his frame.

I'd loved Darren the moment he'd saved me from the waves, and that love wasn't going anywhere. But the man in front of me had woken parts of me I hadn't been sure existed anymore. Parts of me I hadn't been sure would survive the loneliness when Darren was gone for months at a time. The loneliness which had become a permanent fixture now that he was gone forever.

I turned away from Brady and my mixed bag of thoughts over both men to the refrigerator. "Can I get you a drink? We don't have any soda, but we have water, almond milk, or juice."

"I'd love a water," he said.

I handed him a bottle, and when he took it, our fingers brushed, sending a rush of desire cascading through me.

"Thanks," he said, leaning up against the counter before opening it and drinking half of it in one go. I watched his casual stance, the way his throat bobbed up and down as he drank. He was dynamic and beautiful.

I suddenly itched to paint him, my previous image of him on burlap twisting and changing so that he was now surrounded by fireflies or maybe Chinese lanterns. Him and them rising from a river in the moonlight.

The sound of music filled the air. Hannah was

practicing the song he'd taught her earlier on the keyboard in her room—without the sheet music. This was all from her memory and her heart.

Brady's eyes widened. "Wow…"

My smile widened. My daughter was wow-worthy. Smart and bright and way too sensitive, but full of goodness and light and music.

"The first time Grams sat her at a piano, it was like some part of her soul reached out and touched it. Or maybe the other way around…it touched her soul?"

"She's got a huge future ahead of her if she wants it."

"She's barely five. I think she has plenty of time to make those kinds of decisions."

If Hannah decided to walk away from music at some point, I'd absolutely support it as much as I'd support it if she wanted to become the next Bach or—as was much more likely—the next Stevie Nicks.

Brady nodded in agreement.

We sat there listening for a few more minutes before Brady brought us back to why he'd gotten out of the car with me to begin with.

"What did William say that upset you?"

I still wasn't ready to have that conversation, so I turned back to the fridge, looking at the chicken I'd planned for dinner. There was no way Hannah would let me cook it now. I was pretty sure my healthy-food-addicted child was going to become a vegetarian on top of it all.

Ignoring his question that still hung in the air, I waved the package at him. "Don't think I'm going to be making this today…maybe never."

I put it in the freezer as he chuckled behind me.

"What's the deal with her and her health foods?" he asked, allowing me to avoid the conversation in a way I appreciated. Brady was good at backing off when he felt me pull away. A dance to our conversations that mimicked the dance of our bodies around topics and emotions difficult for me. I couldn't help but wonder what would happen, though, if one of us pushed past the lines I drew.

I stayed with the easier conversation: talking about Hannah.

"When Grams had her heart attack just after the new year, the doctor put her on a really strict diet. She had us meet with your sister to discuss meal plans, and I guess Hannah saw it as her way of saving my grandmother."

Brady watched me as I flitted around the cupboards, trying to figure out what I was going to make for dinner that Hannah would actually eat.

"That must have been hard for her. For you." His voice was deep with sympathy.

"Cassidy has been trying to teach Hannah balance and that it's okay to have treats in moderation. But Hannah overheard Grams' doctor explaining how the damage to her heart had been done over years of unhealthy eating…" I trailed off.

"So, Hannah thinks she has to protect you, too. After all, you're all she has left," he said quietly.

He was so perceptive it was almost impossible. Maybe it was the artist in him. Maybe he was attuned to watching others so he could display in rhythm and chords what they were feeling, but I was unused to the depth of it in my life.

Brady grabbed my arm as I went to go by him,

stilling me. I looked up into his face and saw a mix of my own emotions reflected back at me. Trepidation. Longing. The essence of him—gritty and deep like his voice—wafted over me. I couldn't move. I could barely think.

"Why don't you want to tell me what William said?" he asked as his finger coasted over my skin, and my body temperature seemed to double.

"There's no point in discussing it," I said, unsure of why I was holding out. Maybe because I was afraid of the exact words that came out of his mouth.

"Maybe I can help," he said.

Once upon a time, Nash had felt like I was his obligation. That he needed to look out for me because he hadn't been able to save Darren, and Darren had made him promise to do just that: watch over me. It was like my life was on repeat. This time, it was Brady feeling like he had to look out for me because of his relationship with my grandmother.

I didn't want to be an obligation. I most certainly didn't want to be this man's. What I wanted from him was what I'd felt the night before. Longing. Lust. Desire. Sex. It stunned me—the thoughts of wanting him—when I'd convinced myself I wanted nothing.

But it was the truth. I craved his hands on me. Longed to be touched. To feel alive. To feel like I was really only thirty-four and not seventy-four. I wasn't sure I could handle much more than a casual flirtation. A few kisses. Some stolen moments. I certainly wasn't ready to unravel the questions surrounding eternity that I'd wrestled with Stacy that morning.

I pushed up on my tiptoes and placed my lips on his. A soft question. A probe at what we'd felt the night before to see if it remained. And the simple touch crushed my senses. The taste of mulberry wine and the soft feel of morning sun rays on your skin.

He groaned, hands going to my waist, pulling me so I was pressed tight against his body leaning so casually against the counter. My hands on his muscled torso could feel his heart pounding at the same pace as mine.

He deepened the kiss, pushing against my lips with his tongue.

I let him.

I not only let him, I pushed back, exploring him and the touch that had been absent for years in my life. My hands went to the back of his neck, fingers tugging into the blond chunks that curled there. Shaggy. Long. Hair I'd never been able to twine into with Darren because he'd had a military crew cut from the moment I'd met him.

I pushed Darren aside, instead focusing on the sound of Brady's breath. Heavy, deep. Focused on the sound of my breath, panting and shallow. Throbbing. Craving. The need twisting in with the ache of absence.

Molly's nails sliding across the wood floor burst into my head along with the silence—Hannah's keyboard no longer making a sound. I pulled back just as my daughter came bounding into the room.

"I'm hungry," she announced.

Brady and I were still staring at each other. Apart and yet still joined in that moment of tangled mouths. He reached out across the space and put a finger on my lips, running along the bottom one as a smile took over his face again. Full and beautiful and so tormentingly sexy.

"Have you ever had sushi?" Brady asked with a

glance toward Hannah.

She wrinkled her nose. "I'm not sure. What's in it?"

"Fish and rice and seaweed."

"Seaweed!" Hannah all but screamed.

Brady laughed. "You can't even taste it, really. It's like eating lettuce."

"Hmm. How is it cooked? Do they fry it? Because I'm not eating fried anything." She put her hands on her hips. She didn't have her top hat on, but she did have a new shawl—a blue and white striped one spattered with butterflies.

"Some of it can be fried, but for the most part, it's raw."

"Wait. Raw fish?" she asked, doubt filling her voice.

"I'll order a bunch of different things, and you can try what you want. I am ordering the gyozas, though, and they're steamed and fried. You'll be missing out on them if you don't at least try one, because they are like eating little pillows of heaven," Brady said as he moved away from me and pulled out his phone from his pocket.

"You don't need to order us food," I finally managed to speak. My voice had held on to the deep longing that had filled me with our kiss. The need. The want. He heard it, and his fingers slowed on the screen, glancing over at me, lingering on my lips that were still parted. Hungry in a different way.

"We haven't finished our…conversation, but I'm as hungry as Hannah. So why don't we eat and then finish where we left off."

The words were bold and full of double

meanings. A push. I could have refused, but I didn't want to. When I didn't stop him, he placed a call to the only Japanese restaurant in town, ordering so many things I wasn't sure we'd ever be able to eat it all.

Hannah took the stool she used when cooking with Grams and moved it to a spot on the counter below the canister that held Molly's treats. She took one out and then turned to Molly who was already sitting and wagging her tail.

"Roll over," Hannah said, and Molly laid down, her tail thwacking on the floor so loudly that it could wake the earthworms buried in the ground below.

She repeated the command. Molly sat back up.

Brady laughed.

"How long you been workin' on that?" he asked.

"She used to do it for Grams all the time, right, Mommy?"

I nodded. She had. But since my grandma had passed away, no one had kept up with it. My throat clogged with a different emotion than the desire that had heated my body.

"Mind if I try?" Brady asked, sticking his hand out for the treat.

Hannah gave it willingly. Brady got down on his haunches, and Molly tried to take the snack from him. He laughed and pushed on her chest. "Sit," he said. And she did. "Down." She hit the floor. "Over," he said while making a turning motion with his hand. Molly completely complied with every command. And then sat back up.

Simple. Commanding. And God did it make me want to hear him command me. Make me roll over. It wasn't something I'd ever wanted before. To be told what to do. To let someone else do all the thinking so all I had to do was feel.

"Good dog," Brady said and gave her the treat.

"Holy tadpoles, you did it!" Hannah said, jumping up and down on the stepstool.

The stool tipped, Hannah went flying, and Brady caught her.

It all happened so fast my heart barely had time to register it was happening before Hannah was in his arms with wide eyes.

"Whoa, little lady, you better be careful on that thing," he said. Hannah's chin wobbled as if she was fighting tears, and he saw it. "I got you. Don't worry. I got you."

My heart splintered into a million little pieces I wasn't sure I'd ever get back.

Chapter Seventeen

Brady

PRAYED FOR YOU
Performed by Matt Stell

The sushi had been a hit with Hannah. I wasn't sure it would be, because—in my limited experience—kids could be temperamental when it came to trying new things. But Hannah had loved all the flavors. I'd even gotten her to try a gyoza, which she grudgingly admitted to liking but said she couldn't have more than one because it was fried, and she even glowered at me a little when I put away the rest of the dozen I'd ordered.

The entire meal had been lighthearted. Laughter. Smiles.

A mood so different than the heaviness that had settled over Tristan right before she'd kissed me. A mood very different than the craving desire that had consumed me when she'd pressed those sweet lips against mine. The kisses had wound their way deep inside me, making me doubt my reasons for not sleeping with her, even when I knew I was everything she didn't need.

After dinner, Hannah asked me to read with her, and I obliged not only because it was impossible to resist her, but also because I wasn't ready to leave. Tristan hadn't spilled the beans about what was going on with William, and I found myself feeling as protective of her as I normally did of Cassidy. Maybe more… But I also wasn't ready to leave because I needed another taste. More of her lips and her hands and her body pressed up against mine.

As I sat on the couch with Hannah's little frame leaning against my shoulder while I read, my heart flipped and swirled in a very different way. Elana's sweet, smart, talented granddaughter was struggling with so much loss it made me hurt for her. I wanted to fix everything for her when it wasn't my place to do so.

When the clock on the mantel chimed seven-thirty, Tristan called a stop to the reading. "It's time for bed, *Chiquita*."

Hannah sighed, slid off the couch, and stuck out her hand to me.

"You want to see my room?"

I looked up at Tristan. Her face was tight, jaw working, as she fought off a wave of emotions. "Maybe another night, *Chiquita*. Brady's already given us enough of his time today. You go up and start getting ready. I'll be there in a second."

Hannah threw herself into my arms, and I hugged her tightly.

"Thanks for the sushi. Thanks for teaching me 'I Have a Dream.'"

Then, she rushed away, going up the stairs while I stared, my heart—like the dog—chasing after her.

"Thank you for dinner," Tristan said, and she

walked to the door, making it clear my stay was done. That she wanted me to leave.

I stood and joined her, standing close enough that I could smell the sugary scent of her again.

"Saying goodnight to me now will not stop us from having the conversation we need to have," I said quietly.

She raised her chin defiantly. Was it directed at me or herself?

"There's nothing to talk about, Brady."

"Keep telling yourself that, *Cariño*."

She inhaled sharply at the nickname. Just like she had the night before. But it fit her. Sweetheart. Dear one. I could see why Elana called her it. She was sweet. But also sexy. Gorgeous. Heart-stopping. My body called to her. Or she called to me. Like she'd said about Hannah and the piano. It was the same. This mingling of souls talking in a way I was unused to.

I pulled on my shoes that were caked with farm muck before turning back to her. I took a risk and grabbed her hand, intermingling our fingers and tugging her gently toward me. She resisted, but only half-heartedly. When she was close enough to me that I could kiss her, I stared down at her pink lips and then just bent and placed a kiss on her forehead.

"I'll see you tomorrow at the store."

Then, I left before I did more. Before I couldn't walk away without touching every single part of her body. Before she and Hannah marked me in a way that wasn't recoverable. I wasn't sure it hadn't already happened.

I walked home, plotting and planning. Thinking of the two females. Thinking of *La Musica de*

Ensueños. Thinking of Kincaid's and Cassidy's words from earlier.

That was where my head was at when I walked in the back door of the house.

"Where have you been?" Mom demanded.

I spun around. She was sitting at the kitchen table, papers spread out around her, the way I'd seen her so many times growing up that it was embedded in my memories of who my mother was—especially if she was waiting up for me. I fought off the sheepish feeling of being caught sneaking in past curfew. It was way too early for curfew even if I wasn't a grown man with no curfew and no reason to feel guilty.

"Romeros' chicks hatched. We went to see them."

"We?" Mom looked up, red pen poised in the air like a wand.

"Tristan and Hannah and their friends."

Mom frowned. "Is that Elana's granddaughter?"

I nodded, and Mom's face shuttered.

"So, Elana's family is now more important than your sister and Chevelle?"

"Jesus Christ, Mom!"

"Don't talk to your mom that way," Dad said, coming in, reaching for two beers and handing one off to me as if it were a peace offering. Then, he said, "Have a seat."

I did. Like I was sixteen all over again and had been caught playing my guitar out back while Cassidy had slipped in the kitchen on a tiny droplet of water.

"Your mom and I need to leave on Wednesday for Ireland."

I just stared, trying to keep back the "Thank God" threatening to come out of my lips.

"You promised you'd be here for Cassidy while we finished up the term," Dad continued the conversation, but I knew it was really Mom speaking through him. They'd probably had an entire conversation about who was going to have "the talk" with me, easily concluding I'd react better to Dad than Mom.

"And I am. I'm here," I said, tugging at the leather straps around my wrist. The ones I'd first given myself as a promise to go after my dreams no matter what. The ones I'd worn since leaving for Juilliard on the bus because Mom and Dad hadn't been able to take me. They'd gone with Cassidy to a specialist appointment while I'd headed off to college on my own.

"But you're not really here," Mom said.

"Arlene," Dad said her name in warning. She huffed, and Dad turned back to me. "Cassidy's body has been through a lot. She's already fallen three times since getting out of the hospital. We need to know you're going to be here the moment she needs you."

They were good at making me feel guilty, even when I knew Cassidy would hate everything about this conversation. She didn't want them, or me, hovering over her like she was still eight years old. She wanted to be treated like the grown-up she was. She was taking precautions. She was making sure her hypotonia didn't result in harm to the baby. She was as protective of Chevelle as they were of her.

"You were both here today. She didn't need me on top of the two of you. I'll be here when she needs me," I told them, meaning every word of it.

They both looked at me doubtfully. I'd earned the doubt from years of my head being in my music. Long before I'd left to go to school, music had been my life, just like I'd told Tristan earlier in the studio. I got what she said about the art causing everything else to disappear.

"Until you get a call from—" Mom started, only to have Dad cut her off again.

"Brady's right. He didn't need to be here today. And he's promised to stay while we're gone."

The argument from the night before that had left Dad sleeping on the couch was still warring with them. I hated the lack of trust between Mom and I was now causing a rift between them. But it also made me wonder if she'd even trust Dad to take care of Cass. Was there anyone who could do it as well as her?

I stood up from the table, leaving the beer behind. "Go to Ireland. Everything will be fine."

I wanted to let the screen door slam behind me like I had as a teen, but I didn't. I shut it softly, and Mom's voice trailed after me even though she'd lowered it.

"She needs us…him…more than she'll ever admit."

"Sometimes we're so focused on Cassidy we forget he needs us too."

The words hit me hard, stalling my feet as they started to walk away from the house.

Mom snorted, and my heart tightened right back up.

"We didn't even know what country he was in last, Arlene. Jesus. What kind of parents don't even know where their kids are at?"

He must have walked away, because Mom called after him, her voice fading as she followed him until I couldn't hear her anymore, "Don't you dare toss that at me, Petri, and walk…"

I swallowed hard. Uncomfortable with all of it. The demands. The regrets. The fact I was causing division in a relationship that I'd always seen as unbreakable. My parents had been there for each other every single step of the way with Cassidy and with their careers. I stormed up the stairs and into my apartment, causing Marco to stand in a rush of movements from the sofa.

When he realized it was just me, in a bad mood, he relaxed.

"Lee and Garner are going to fire me if you keep running off without telling me where you're going and then don't answer anyone's calls," he said.

I brushed a hand through the hair that still needed to be fixed. More people I'd let down today. I pulled out my phone to see that it was dead. When I'd used it hours ago to call for Japanese food, the battery had been low, but I hadn't thought much about it. I'd seen the texts from both Lee and Marco but had ignored them while I allowed myself to linger in the bubble I'd built around Tristan and Hannah.

The bubble that had lasted until it had been burst by a sharp hook from my mother.

"I don't need you here, Marco," I told him, which was the truth but was also driven by irritation at having to explain to everyone what I was doing. I was a grown man, for God's sake. I wasn't a teen with a curfew. "No one in Grand Orchard is going to attack me. Go home. Take a vacation. Do something that isn't me."

"Is that really what you want?" he asked, easily reading how frustrated I was.

"Yes."

He looked me over, waiting to see if I was going to tell him what was really bothering me, but when I didn't say more, he just nodded. "I'll run it by Lee and Garner and talk with Waterton to make sure they'll have someone on-call for you here locally. Then, I'll head out."

"Thanks, Marco."

"You're sure you're going to be okay? With Cassidy and Chevelle, I mean?" His face was emotionless, but I could have sworn there was doubt in his voice, too.

"God, not you, as well. Yes. I'm going to be fine. They're going to be fine. I think I can handle looking after my sister and a baby for a few weeks."

Marco chuckled at my childish tantrum. "Are you sure? I mean…it is you!"

I flipped him off but smiled to take away the bite before heading for the bedroom.

I threw my all but ruined Chucks in the closet and pulled off my T-shirt just as my eyes landed on the antique chest that Elana had left me. I balled the shirt up and tossed it in the hamper before grabbing the box and the key and bringing them to the bed with me.

I ran my fingers along the gold inlay etchings. It was beautiful. Old. I unlocked it and lifted the heavy wooden lid. The smell of vinyl hit me. Old records. A whole collection of them. I started sifting through them. Some were worth a chunk of change now. Classics, in good condition. Forty-fives and LPs. An eclectic mix of genres, including a flamenco album by one Manolo Morente.

My throat closed in on itself.

All of the albums, except the Morente one, were albums Elana and I had listened to, discussed, and torn apart. They were songs we'd hated and songs we'd loved, but they all had meaning to her. To me.

Below the records was a letter in Elana's perfect handwriting. Almost as if it was a script font, the height of each letter hitting the exact same spot it should, as if she'd written it on the lined paper used when learning cursive in school.

Dear Cormac,

I put together this little collection for you a while back when I was cleaning out the storage for mi cariño. *My father's record is a self-serving gift. I want someone to continue to appreciate him as much as I did. I had a heart attack recently, and suddenly, I've been presented with the fact that I just might die. That I might die and not get the opportunity to have the last word with you on several topics.*

Like the validity of Charles Parker as the best jazz musician. He was. End of story.

I laughed, the heavy gloom that had settled over me lightening some.

"You're still wrong," I said to no one and wondering if she could hear me.

I apologize because I have a few requests to make of you. I promised myself I would never demand of you the things your mother demanded. That I would never make you feel like you owed me anything. And you still don't. These requests...I'm hoping they are as much

FOR you as they are OF you.

I hope by now you've met my granddaughter and my little Hannah. I wish it was under better circumstances. I wish it was at a time when you could see all the ways you and Tristan are alike. Your love of me being only one of them. ;-)

The first of my requests has to do with my girls. Please look out for my little Chiquita, *my Hannah. If you could help* Cari *find a music teacher who will not force Hannah to play only classical music, I'd be forever grateful. I don't want anyone to dim the love that girl has for the piano. She is all classic rock, just like she should be, and if she is forced to play Bach for the rest of her life, she'll walk away from it.*

Next, if it hasn't already happened yet, can you please make sure Tristan has help with the Music Fest? She'll try to do it all on her own, and I know how impossible that is. I know now that I should have asked for help but was too stubborn to do so. Tristan is as stubborn as I was, so good luck. Maybe this should be the last festival. All good traditions come to an end at some point.

"Over my dead body, Elana," I growled.

I know your childhood, your memories, and your heart are tied to La Musica de Ensueños *just as I know Tristan's heart and memories of me will now be tied to it. But please don't let her hold on to the store as a way of holding on to the memories and emotions. It is just a store. A store that should have been closed at least a decade ago. The memories will stay with you regardless of the physical space, and in truth, those memories are not even the most important ones. You both have new memories to make. Ones that will matter more.*

I know the critics have continued to hound you about your last album, the words stale and old thrown around repeatedly, but don't let them dictate your sound or your heart. Whenever YOU feel like you're missing something, perhaps you can listen to some of these albums again, and they will help you discover whatever it is you think you're searching for. Maybe the chords and notes and words can lead you to where you belong.

And one last thing. Life is so short. Even with me in my nineties, it seems to have flown by. It is too short to live with things hanging on you. So forgive. Both yourself and your parents.

I'm proud of you, Brady. Of not only the musician but of the man you've become. The heart you have. The gratitude for your fans and your life. Your loyalty. You deserve to be happy and fulfilled.

Which leaves me with this. Please love. Find someone who needs you as much as you need them. Someone who can be the center of your whole world. Someone who will be your inspiration and motivation. The reason you make notes.

With all the music in my heart, I send you my love now and always.

Elana

Tears escaped and rolled down my face that I swiped at with a fist.

I'd won a lot of music awards, but this was like winning the best of them all. Elana being proud of me.

Of thinking I'd earned the right to be happy. To find love.

They were words I'd ached to hear from my parents for longer than was healthy. I'd given up on ever getting them. Mom wondered why I felt closer to Elana than her… It was because Elana had always seen me. Understood me. Supported and uplifted me.

Mom had seen the worst parts of me and continued to show them to me over and over again, blind to any of the good. I knew she loved me, but the love was twisted with disappointment that neither of us could let go of.

I put everything back in the chest, finished undressing, and then lay, looking at the ceiling with sleep escaping me. There were things I could and couldn't do that Elana had asked. Letting the store or the festival go…it wasn't within my abilities yet. They were still too tied to her. And I was sure Tristan felt the same way. Letting go of those things would be like saying Elana was truly gone. Neither of us could say goodbye to the woman who'd shaped us, guided us.

I was honored she wanted me to be there for Tristan and Hannah. *Cariño* and *Chiquita.* I had wanted to be there for them all on my own, but this made that desire quadruple in size. They needed someone.

I needed someone.

Maybe Elana was right. Maybe we could be there for each other.

Love…

Love was another matter altogether. A topic for another day, maybe another lifetime. But this felt right. Me and them at this moment. Sharing this part of our journeys together.

I just had to make sure this time, for the first time in my life, my focus on what I wanted wouldn't come at the cost of my sister's health and well-being. I had to be there for all of them.

Chapter Eighteen

Tristan

DON'T STOP

Performed by Fleetwood Mac

I was in the process of selling a stack of records to a tourist when Brady came into the store for Hannah's lesson. He had two more sessions after Hannah with children he'd agreed to teach. It made the guilt twist in my stomach again because he was doing so much for us. Even if I knew in his heart it was really for Grams, it was still helping me when I needed it.

After the customer left, I went upstairs and mixed the last layer of paint I needed for the mural. I listened as my daughter's sweet voice talked with Brady about chords and notes. The sound of "I Have a Dream" from yesterday faded into new notes from "Don't Stop." It continued to stun me into silence how talented she was.

When the chimes on the door went off, and Sheldon and his mom appeared at the top of the steps, I went into the practice room to make sure the two at the piano knew what time it was.

Hannah was grinning up at Brady as if he was Stevie Nicks in person, and it caught my heart, holding it captive for a few seconds.

"Hey, you two, Sheldon's here for his turn at the Brady O'Neil experience," I said, bringing two sets of eyes to mine, Hannah's more golden than the deep amber of Brady's, but I was caught again how he blended with her. As if he could belong to us when it was ridiculous to even think it.

Brady smiled. "The Brady O'Neil Experience. I like that."

Hannah jumped down. "Is Stacy here yet?"

I shook my head. "Not quite."

She turned back toward Brady. "Stacy is taking me back to see the chicks and then we are going to the mall to get all the things we need to fill Easter eggs for my party."

"You're having an Easter party?" he asked.

She giggled. "No, for my birthday party. It's the day before Easter. You're coming, right?"

How on earth did my little girl continue to invite this man into our lives when I was having a hard time being in the same room with him? It was sweet and endearing and completely exasperating.

Brady acknowledged the invitation with a glance at me before responding, "Well, I haven't exactly been invited."

She flung her shawl over one shoulder with drama and passion. "We didn't know you when we sent out the invitations. But it's next Saturday at eleven o'clock at our house. You can R-S-V-P to Mommy," Hannah said before putting all her sheet music in her cubby and then coming toward me. I picked her up and hugged her.

"You're getting pretty good with those rock anthems, *Chiquita*," I told her. I turned toward Sheldon and his mom. "Why don't you set up in room two. Brady will be there in a second."

They disappeared into the next practice room as the doorbell jangled again. "Tris? Hannah?" Stacy's voice called out from below.

My friend was really too good to be true sometimes. She'd been looking out for Hannah much more than she'd ever done since Grams had passed away. My struggle to keep the store open had me working so many hours I wondered how my ninety-year-old grandmother had done it. Of course, she hadn't had a little girl at home waiting for her. For many years, her house had been empty unless I was staying for the summer. I was sure the store had kept her from being lonely.

"We're here," I called.

"Can you just send Hannah down? I'm double-parked."

I hugged my daughter tightly. "I love you. Be good. Have fun. Listen to Stacy," I told her. I didn't need to say any of it. Hannah was already too good and too old and too wise for her years. I put her down, and she raced down the stairs with barely a backward glance.

"Bye, Mommy. Bye, Brady. See you later."

I followed her down the steps far enough to see her stick her hand in Stacy's and called out. "I'll pick her up around five. Thanks for getting the party supplies."

"No problem. See you tonight."

And they were gone.

The silence was broken by the sound of Sheldon warming up on his guitar. I turned to find Brady watching me. I ran a hand over my ponytail just as he stepped closer, tucking an escaped curl behind my ear and causing my entire body to go still.

"I'd like to RSVP now," he said, eyes traveling to my lips and back up.

"You don't have to come," I said.

"Can I bring Cassidy and Chevelle? My parents leave on Wednesday, and I don't want to leave her at the house alone for too long."

"Of course. We'd love to have Cassidy there..." I trailed off.

"But?"

"It's just. She's not exactly twelve. She doesn't need a babysitter."

Brady's smile slipped away. "I know. But her body's been through a lot, and she falls easily. If something happened because I was gone all day..."

This was obviously not the time or place for this discussion. I had a feeling that the strong, independent woman I knew as Cassidy O'Neil could handle anything her body was doing, but Brady and his family seemed to see her as if she were encased in fragile crystal.

"Consider yourself RSVP'd for three. Now, go teach Sheldon before he explodes with excitement."

"The Brady O'Neil Experience coming to him," he said slowly.

I'd had my own Brady O'Neil Experience the day before, and it had haunted my dreams last night. I flushed at the memory. He saw the flush and winked at me before turning and sauntering into the practice room.

♫ ♫ ♫

Two hours later, Brady joined me downstairs at the register after taunting, teasing, and flirting harmlessly with his last student and her father as they'd left the store. It had been one of the busiest mornings the store had seen in months.

The spring weather had brought out the locals and the tourists alike. The apple blossoms starting to bloom always did it. People journeying to take pictures and mosey down the town's quaint Main Street. I hadn't appreciated it when I'd started spending a few weeks each summer with Grams, the enchantment of the town, but now I felt like I was living in a postcard sometimes.

Brady sat on the stool behind the counter. Grams had used it a lot after the heart attack unless Hannah was perched on it. It seemed odd to have him there, and yet, he also seemed to fit. Every time I was around him, it was a peculiar dichotomy of emotions, memories, and thoughts that didn't belong together.

"You've avoided the conversation for an entire day. What's up with William Chan and you? Is it still the festival?"

I shook my head. I'd allowed myself to put the entire conversation out of my brain for twenty-four hours. Looking through the bank accounts wasn't going to change anything. I couldn't pay off the loan. Even if I used the house as collateral, I had no way of proving that the store—or my art—would bring in enough money to continue to make the payments.

I went to move out from behind the register, but

Brady blocked me, putting his knees up against the counter. "Tell me."

It was that tone that was not quite a demand again. I wanted to talk to someone about it. Someone who'd understand Grams and could maybe help me unravel how she'd let this happen. I couldn't tell my mom, not with her and Bailey still stung by what had happened with the will.

I sighed. "His bank owns the loan my grandmother made when we remodeled last year."

"Okay?" Brady said.

"Grams missed a payment, and I missed a second one after she passed before I got my arms around everything," I said quietly. "So, he's foreclosing."

"That's bullshit!" Brady's voice echoed around the empty store. It was. Grams had died. You'd think the bank would have granted me some leniency. Anger flickered across his face and he said, "I can loan you the money."

I stared at him, mouth dropping open. I was already shaking my head and trying to push on his legs to get out of the small space that he'd enclosed me in, trying to put distance between me and him and the emotions that swelled in me. He didn't budge. His hand came up and wrapped around my wrist.

Sensations of longing mixed with belonging curled through me.

"That's ridiculous," I said. "Stop throwing money around like it's water, trying to rescue me." I was unable to meet his eyes, looking instead at the long fingers surrounding my wrist. Staring at the leather bands that he wore. The words *aspire, dream,* and *gratitude* on metal tied to the leather.

"What's the use of having all the damn money I

have if no one, not my family or anyone I care about, will let me help them?" he asked, frustration flowing through him.

"You're helping by teaching Grams' students for me. Sounds like you're helping your sister by being here. Those things mean more than the money," I said.

"I know they do, but if I have money to burn, why not take that, too?" he asked as if he truly didn't see the reason why I, or anyone, would turn it down. His fingers rubbed softly on my inner wrist.

"Brady, did you see that transaction that I just made?"

He nodded.

"That was the largest sale I've had in a month. I have no way of teaching the lessons going forward. I have no way of keeping the store afloat in the long run. Even if I sell my—" I stopped myself, afraid that if I said more, he'd try to throw money at that as well.

He put his other hand on my chin, drawing my eyes to meet his. "Sell your what?"

I pulled myself away from him, backing into the counter and barely putting a couple of inches between us.

"Nothing."

"Sell what, Tristan?"

I blew out a frustrated sigh. "Even if I sell the mural, it won't be enough to cover more than a few months."

It took him a moment to catch up to the six panels he'd looked at the day before. The art I'd been painting for months, but which had increased to a frantic pace since Grams' had died. I'd needed to put the emotions and loss somewhere so Hannah didn't feel it threatening to explode from my body. She was too sensitive. Too serious. She didn't need me falling apart on her as well.

He stood up, still blocking me, taking in my face and the emotions I was unable to hide from him for some reason when I was an expert at hiding them from everyone else.

"Let me help," he said, and now the demand in his voice was replaced with a beg.

"You do not owe it to my grandmother to help me out of this mess."

"I do. But that isn't why I'm asking you to let me help you. I'm asking because it's tearing a hole inside my chest to see you suffering."

I looked away, unable to watch my pain reflected back in his eyes.

"I think we both need to face the fact that William Chan is right: the store isn't sustainable," I said.

I was taken by surprise when he surrounded me in his arms, hugging me tightly. My head was forced to his chest. The scent of him flooding me. The ache returning that was there whenever we touched. The ache for more than sex. For a partnership. For a friend you showed your soul to. I had Stacy and Nash, but they rarely saw all of me. Like the painting upstairs in the studio at Grams', I only showed pieces of myself to them.

The doorbell jangled again, and I went to pull away, but Brady wouldn't let me. He whispered, "We're going to figure this out."

The thought of not having to shoulder it all alone was a beautiful one. It wasn't one I could allow to make a reality, but it was still lovely in the moment while it lasted.

"Well. Hello," Cassidy's voice traveled over us, humor and intrigue wrapped in the tone.

Brady didn't let me go, but he shifted so he could take in his sister. She had the baby strapped to her body like she had the day before in a sling that looked almost as elaborate as Hannah's shawls. I realized, after his comment earlier about her falling easily, that this was a way for Cassidy to allow her hands to be free if she needed to balance herself and the baby. In many ways, it would be close to mimicking the weight of the baby when she'd been pregnant. Maybe even better because the weight was higher up along her center of gravity.

"What's up, Cass? Is Mom with you?" Brady asked, finally relinquishing his hold but still not backing away enough for me to leave without literally pushing him out of the space.

"No, Mom's packing, which is what allowed me to make my escape," she said. "Which also means you should expect a phone call any moment when she panics again."

"Thanks," Brady said dryly.

"I can't handle it anymore. I may not live until Wednesday if she continues with the over-the-top helicoptering," Cassidy said. "Plus, I wanted to talk to you about something without her interrupting us. But I can catch you later if this is a bad time."

She looked between us with a knowing smile that I wasn't sure I could diffuse but also didn't want to encourage. So, I tried to explain off his presence by blurting out, "Brady's been teaching some of Elana's classes for me. It's been a godsend."

"Really!" Cassidy smirked.

"What's up, Cass?" Brady repeated.

"Well, it's about Kincaid's."

I wasn't sure I wanted or needed to hear this discussion. The thought of the store next door had my stomach falling, returning to the thoughts William Chan had for it and Grams' place while I was still trying to wrap my head around the fact that I wasn't going to be able to save *La Musica*.

Cassidy looked from me to Brady again. She didn't want to do this with me standing there. I pushed against him, and he reluctantly let me past him.

"I'm going to go see if I can get some time in on the mural before I have to go get Hannah," I told them.

"Want me to man the register for you?" Brady asked.

"Are you sure you remember how? I mean, your fingers might be a little unaccustomed to the manual work," I teased.

His chuckle filled the air, and my insides swooshed along with the sound. It was ridiculous. Inconceivable. But his happiness meant something to me. I wanted to hear him like this often. Laughing. Excited. Energized.

I added it to my growing list of wants and desires when it came to this country-rock star. Things that should be impossible, but maybe weren't. If I was ready to just let go. To take a chance. To risk something that I hadn't risked in way too long.

My heart.

But I was terrified of risking Hannah's along with it. Of causing my daughter more loss and pain. I couldn't do that to her. My smile faded away at the thought. I was a mom first and foremost. Protecting her was what mattered more than anything else.

"My fingers are quite versatile," he said, eyes lingering on my lips again, and my whole body ignited at that thought—nimble musician fingers touching me. God, it had been too long. Too long since my body had been awake. Too long since I'd wanted to have it touched.

Was there any way I could keep things with him casual? A round of relief for a tortured body without making it into something I'd regret because of the impact to Hannah or me? I wasn't sure. I didn't know, but I did know that thoughts of him weren't going to leave me anytime soon, not as long as he was here, and it seemed like he planned on staying for months.

Chapter Nineteen

Brady

WHAT IFS

Performed by Kane Brown with Lauren Alaina

Tristan had been full of laughter and happiness before something changed. The shift was obvious as the smile slowly left her face at my flirtation. It was the exact opposite of what I'd wanted. I'd wanted her face to light up because of the innuendos I put behind the innocent words.

"Go, I've got this for a little while," I said, shooing her up the stairs.

She hesitated, looked at Cass one more time, and then disappeared.

Cassidy joined me at the register.

"Have you figured that out yet?" she said, waving her head in the direction Tristan had disappeared.

"Figured out that she tastes like cream soda and that Hannah has already claimed a portion of my heart? Yeah. Figured out how to insert myself into the life of a widow with a child who lost her dad? Not at all."

Cass frowned. "It can't be one of your casual

flirtations, or everyone will get hurt."

"Why does everyone assume that's all I want or that it's all I can ever have?" It stabbed at me a little. Pinpricks into my heart and soul. I wanted *more*.

My sister took in the seriousness of my face as she rocked with Chevelle, the swaying movement mimicking the one I saw Tristan do when she was nervous. I suddenly realized it was some leftover of when Hannah had been a baby and Tristan had soothed her.

"You have a huge heart, brother o' mine. No one questions it. You just haven't chosen to settle down, so I guess everyone assumed that wasn't the lifestyle you wanted."

"Anyone stop to consider that I just hadn't found the person I wanted to keep enough to ask them to put up with all the bullshit that comes with me being a celebrity?"

"Whoa. A celebrity. Be careful that ego doesn't jump out and bite you in the butt," she teased, reaching for my ear to flick. I protected it with my shoulder.

"What did you want to say about Kincaid's?" I asked, stepping away from her.

She looked down, gulped, and then back up. "Well, I know you were talking about using it as studio space, but I was thinking it really is a great restaurant location."

I frowned. "I have no desire to own a restaurant."

She met my eyes, and they were nervous. "I was…I was thinking I might love it."

The surprise hit me so hard I didn't have time to hide it, and Cass grimaced at my expression.

"You don't have to say it. I already know I don't know anything about managing a restaurant. But I know I love to cook, and I'd love to show everyone that healthy options don't have to be tasteless or dry. I think a great farm-to-market, vegetarian place could do well not only with the town, but the college crowd."

She was probably right. College kids ate that kind of crap up like it was free beer at a frat party. Before I could respond, Cass continued.

"I have some money saved up that I was planning on using to buy a house. But if I stay at home a while longer, I could invest it in the business. It just wouldn't be enough. I'd need help… I hate to even ask…but maybe you'd be interested in backing it? A silent-partner kind of thing."

My heart was already jumping with joy, the words I'd said minutes before with Tristan ringing through my ears again. I wanted my money to help the people I loved. The thought of helping Cass build something she wanted, helping her with a livelihood that would support her and Chevelle…I was all in.

"Let's call Elsa and put an offer in on the place," I told her with a grin.

"Really?" she breathed out.

"Yeah." I nodded. "I know shit about any of it either, but I'm sure Lee could help us find some connections who'd be willing to advise us."

"Should we wait to put in the offer until we have a business plan in place? Make sure it is viable? I mean, we should at least do a marketing study, right?"

"Look. I want the place regardless of what goes into it. It could sit empty for another ten years, and I wouldn't care. I want it so that William Chan puts aside his idea of selling it to someone who will merge the space with this store."

"He's *your* friend," Cass said with a laugh.

"He *was* my friend. Now he's just some jerk who thinks he knows best for everyone," I said and cringed because my mom also thought she knew best for everyone. "Let's not tell Mom until they're gone, though."

Cass was nodding. "Yeah, I agree. She doesn't need to know right now."

I hit Elsa Chan's phone number and left a message with a full price, cash offer for Kincaid's, asking her to call me back.

Cass came up, placed a kiss on my cheek, and then flicked my earlobe that I'd left undefended. "Thank you. I promise I'll pay you back. I promise you won't regret it."

I pulled her into a side hug so we didn't squish Chevelle. "Cass, I don't want you to pay me back. I have more money than I'll ever be able to spend in my lifetime or my children's lifetimes. I want to be there to help my family. I want to help you."

She rested her head on my shoulder. "I know, but I also know it won't ever feel like it's mine if I don't at least try to pay you back."

I understood where she was coming from. It was why every single person had turned down the cash I'd tried to throw their way. Self-respect. A desire to do it on their own. Independence. But I also knew we had a long way to go before we had to cross that road. I might not know anything about the food service industry, but I knew enough to know it was a long haul from creation to profitability. I hoped Cass got there, but even if it lost money every single year, I'd still be there supporting her.

Chevelle started to fuss, his tiny voice barely a whisper of a sound.

"Okay, I'm going to go nurse my baby, get some rest, and then start working on plans," she said, a glorious smile appearing on her face that made my sister far more than pretty—it made her gorgeous. "I feel like, for the first time in a while, I have something besides Chevelle to look forward to. Something for me. I'm really, really grateful."

"Stop. It's my first command as a silent partner. No more thanking me. Let's just get it going so Mom can see how you really can stand on your own two feet."

Cass smiled even wider, and then left, patting and soothing my nephew as she went. The role of mother fit her. Just like it fit the woman upstairs in the art studio. Just like it had fit my mother, regardless of the fact that she'd taken it to the extreme. Powerful women with hearts and smarts and ingenuity.

Buying Kincaid's and turning it into a restaurant wouldn't keep William from foreclosing on *La Musica de Ensuenos*, though. I had to let my brain stew on that one for a little longer. There was an answer to this problem as well. I was sure of it.

My phone rang, and I looked down to see Elsa's number.

"Hey," I said.

"Hey yourself," she said, a tone I recognized from using it myself many times: flirtation covering the letdown.

"So, you heard my offer?"

"I'm sorry to tell you it won't be accepted."

"Why the hell not? It's been empty for years. It's cash on the table. Why would the Kincaids turn it down?"

"The Kincaids haven't owned the space since it shut, Brady. The bank foreclosed on them years ago," Elsa responded.

Fucking William Chan. Why would he care if I bought the place? It was exactly what he wanted—a smart restaurant going in.

"So, your brother would turn down cash for a property that's done nothing but cost him money, why? To get back at me? To prove a point?" I growled into the phone.

Elsa sighed. "Look, William's been waiting for years to merge the two spaces. He thought Elana would…"

"What? That she'd die years ago? That she'd just sell something she'd built with her own two hands? Something she loved?"

"He has the town's best interest at heart. He really does. But he only sees it the way he wants it, if you know what I mean," she said.

Fire lit me up, not desire like Tristan had been filling me with, but anger at everyone in my life who seemed to think they knew better than me these days. The critics. Mom. William Chan. I was tired of it. I may just be a country-rock singer, but I wasn't stupid.

"I'll pay another fifty thousand over asking price," I told her.

Silence as she took it in. "I'll talk to him, but I'm pretty sure it'll still be a no."

As soon as we hung up, I was hitting the call button again, this time to Lee. "What's wrong?" Lee asked.

"Why does something have to be wrong for me to call you?"

Lee laughed, and I could see in my head, him pushing his square glasses up his long nose. "You would just text otherwise."

It was probably true. "I need for us to do something we've never done."

"Which is?"

"Use my name to help make things happen. There's this guy in town causing hell for the people I care about, and I don't want to be quiet about it. I want it out there. Do we have a lead on Dani's replacement yet?"

"I've narrowed it down to two who have music PR experience. You could come interview them this week."

I sighed. "I can't do it until after Wednesday. If Mom knows I'm leaving Cass, even for a day, she'll never get back on the plane to Ireland."

"I'll set it up for Thursday then. Tell me some more about this guy and what's going on."

I spent the next thirty minutes catching Lee up, and by the time I was done, he was growling into the phone himself. "Okay. Let me find some resources for you for the restaurant idea. I'm not sure I can help you with the music store, but maybe bringing in enough money from the festival will help keep the foreclosure from happening. I'll ask Alice if she can come out and help with it, maybe give us some ideas on how to make it a bigger event than is already planned. There's got to be some way to eke some more cash out of it."

I flicked my leather bands. "Thanks, Lee. I mean

it."

"You've never asked for us to go to bat for you like this, Brady. None of us. And we'd all do it in a heartbeat. We see what you do for everyone else. If we can help, let us."

It choked me up, emotion sitting in my throat, squeezing against the walls so that I could barely breathe. I couldn't respond, and when I didn't, Lee filled in the void.

"We're on it. I'll get back to you in a little while."

And he hung up.

I was damn lucky. Lucky to be surrounded by a team who believed in me. Who supported me every step of the way, no matter how off the beaten path I seemed to stray. If only my parents could see around my past screwups enough to trust me as well. To see that I wasn't going to repeat them.

I manned the counter for the rest of the day, but very few people came into the store, which was probably a good thing in hindsight. I hadn't even considered what it would look like if someone walked in with Brady O'Neil working the counter.

As the light started to fade, Tristan came down the stairs with her purse thrown over her shoulder. I watched every move she made until she got to the bottom step.

I didn't know what it was about her, but she drew me every time she entered a room. As if my body couldn't stand to have even a few feet between us. As if the call of her was stronger than any call the night had on nocturnal creatures. So, it wasn't a surprise when I met her at the foot of the stairs. It didn't even seem to surprise her.

I took her in as if it had been days instead of a few

hours since she'd gone up to work on the mural. She had a splash of maroon paint on her cheek. I moved my finger to rub it off, and the softness of her skin stilled my hand on her cheek.

"Brady…I…" She trailed off, swallowing hard. "About this."

I didn't need to ask what "this" she meant. She meant us. The two perfect kisses. The stolen moments. The attraction pulling at us so beautifully and painfully.

"About us," I said, my voice going down to a level that I barely used in my songs.

She closed her eyes. "I just…I'm not sure…"

"You're not sure you're ready," I said. It wasn't a question because I knew it was true.

Her eyes opened, the golden flecks sparkling in the antique lights. "I know, to most people, four and half years seems like long enough."

I was already shaking my head. "I can't imagine any number of years being enough."

She inhaled sharply at my words, and I felt nothing but regret for causing her pain when I'd meant to ease it.

"I'd like to be brave," she said. "Like the waitress who left you her name on the cocktail napkin. I'd like to just say, 'come home with me.' But I can't just do a fling. I can't, because even if I tried to keep whatever this is from Hannah, you're already in her life, and I couldn't have another person leave her when you and I were over. It's bad enough she's going to miss you when you aren't teaching her anymore."

"Who says I'm going to stop teaching her?" I asked.

She laughed as if I'd said the funniest thing in the world, and when I didn't join her, she frowned. "Brady, you don't really live here. Where *do* you even live? Plus, you'll be back doing your whole country-rock-star thing when summer hits."

It had been my plan: stay until Mom and Dad were home, then go back and record my fourth album, release it, and go on tour again. But now, I was buying a restaurant and building a relationship with my sister. I didn't know that I wanted to leave anytime soon. I didn't know that I wanted to go back to my loft in New York where I was alone except for the people who came in and out to help me. Cooks. Cleaners. Personal shoppers.

It was no wonder my music had become stale.

Visiting with Lee a few hours a day, or any of my team, wasn't the same as having your entire world shared with someone else.

"I'm not asking for a fling, *Cari*," I told her, and the nickname made her eyes flicker with longing. Longing for the things I also hungered for. I could feel it in her—the need to be someone's *more* again.

Could I be that for her? I wanted it. Tristan made me want to stop flirting altogether, and I'd never experienced that before. I didn't want to just flirt with her because I didn't want the feelings to be a temporary flash in the dark. I wanted them to last much longer. I wanted it not just for me, but for her. I knew if she shoved me out of her life right now, I'd never get any of those feelings back.

"I want to get to know you. To know Hannah. I don't want to kiss you and disappear. I'd really like the chance to be a part of your lives," I said it and meant it with every single particle of my being.

She was swaying again, soothing and thinking.

"But what if…"

I trailed a finger from her cheek to her lips, halting her words, hiding the negative thought that I knew was going to come spinning out of them.

I replaced them with my own. "But what if it works?"

Chapter Twenty

Tristan

GOD WHISPERED YOUR NAME
Performed by Keith Urban

Brady's fingers on my cheek and my lips were leaving marks I wasn't sure I would ever escape. When he was with me, it was hard to see the famous country-rock star. I felt like I saw Cormac, the boy my grandmother bragged on much more than some far off celebrity.

Maybe that really was what I was seeing. Maybe he was showing me the personal side of him the rest of the world didn't get. He was taking a risk. A risk on me. And God, I ached to do the same back.

Hannah was holding me back. Nash would accuse me of using her as a shield again. A way to keep the world at bay as I had so often when she was first born. Back then, when I was holding her, she drew people's eyes. She was what they would talk about and not Darren, or his loss, or how I was holding up.

I couldn't do that to her or me for the rest of our lives. It wasn't fair—to either of us. But she'd just experienced a huge loss. My grandmother. Her teacher and her friend. If I took this step with Brady, moving us past casual acquaintances joined by a shared love for Grams to an attempt at some sort of actual relationship—dating—and it didn't work out, what would happen to my little girl?

He asked what if I took the risk and it worked, and that made my hope zing through me. What if we became something real? Something permanent. It hurt to think of that almost as much as the thought of it not working out. But when I'd sent him home the night before and he'd kissed me on the forehead instead of the lips, I'd felt disappointed.

Putting someone in my life and in my bed that wasn't Darren seemed…heartbreaking. But for the first time since he'd passed, I wanted it for myself. I wanted to feel loved. Even more, I wanted to love someone back. To share someone's world with them. I wanted Hannah to see that love so she knew what she deserved someday.

I took a deep breath. "We're filling plastic Easter eggs tonight. Would you like to join us?"

His face broke into the huge Brady O'Neil smile that graced magazines and billboards and album covers. I'd just invited this world-famous celebrity to fill Easter eggs. I wanted to bonk myself in the head at the mundaneness of it all. Then, I steeled myself, throwing my shoulders straight. This was my world. It was mundane, and if he wanted to be a part of it, he'd have to see it for what it was. There were no flashy cocktail parties or famous actresses or record deals in the making. It was little kids shouting, a dog that begged, and pure messiness.

"I'd really, truly love to. I just need to make sure I check in at home, and then I can come by. Shall I bring dinner?"

It was strange the way he checked in with his parents like he was a teenager. It called out more warning signs just as I was trying to bury them all. But who was I to question family relationships these days? I wasn't. My family was having a hard time with everything that had happened since Grams' death. Maybe before. Maybe they were upset I'd let my grandma pull me from my grief instead of them.

"You don't need to bring dinner. I already have vegetarian tacos planned if that is something you think you can stomach," I answered.

He nodded with a sigh. "I'm being forced into vegetarianism from all sides these days."

I smiled. His thumb caressed my bottom lip, causing my body to tremble.

"'Kay. I'm leaving," he said, but he didn't budge. Not an inch.

I couldn't help the soft laugh that escaped me as I pulled his hand from my face. "I have to go get Hannah, so if you don't leave, I'll be leaving you."

As I went to let his hand go, his fingers merged with mine, and he squeezed as if reassuring me that this was going to be okay. We walked to the door. I set the alarm, and we left. It seemed impossible that not even two weeks had passed since the first time we'd left the store together when I'd thought his name was Cormac.

He kissed my knuckles, squeezed my hand one more time, and then headed off in the direction of his parents' house. I watched for a moment. He turned his head, a smile radiating off him over the distance as he winked at me. God, he really was gorgeous. Dynamic. Things I'd once had and lost and now were trying to reenter my life.

I turned away and headed toward Stacy's.

When I entered, the house was a burst of noise. I followed it back to the kitchen where Stacy, Jin, their two littles, and Hannah were all sitting at the round table, decorating wooden eggs with paint pens. Stacy's looked like a Faberge egg. Jalissa's was a squiggle of color. Kiran had a fox on his, and Hannah's was full of musical notes.

"Hello, everyone," I said, going to my girl, squishing her from behind and placing a kiss on her cheek.

"Look at my egg, Mommy!" she said, shoving it toward me.

"It's beautiful. I love the notes," I told her.

"It's 'Don't Stop,' and it's for Brady because he taught it to me," she said. My heart twisted, and my breath caught. Fear. I had to push past it. I had to attempt to let someone into our lives. It was so unfair to both of us if I didn't.

"Well, good thing he's coming to dinner. You can give it to him yourself."

"He is?!" Hannah cried out with excitement just as Stacy said the same words with a questioning look.

"Well, this is an interesting twist," Jin said, laughter barely contained in his voice.

"Lee Jin-Kang, don't you dare scare her off!" Stacy scolded before turning to me with a smirk. "Go. Have fun!"

Hannah capped the lid she'd been using and carefully set the egg down before sliding out of her chair to run to the door. As she put her shoes on, she said, "Let's go, Mommy. We don't want to keep him waiting."

"Don't you think you're forgetting something?" I asked with a wave of my head in the direction of Stacy.

She skipped back, flung herself into Stacy's arms, and said, "Thank you for the eggs and taking me to see the chicks and for getting all the stuff for my party."

Then, she grabbed the musical note egg and ran back to the door.

I hugged my friend. "Thank you for everything you've been doing for me. I just want you to know I don't take it for granted."

Stacy's eyes filled with unshed tears, and she pushed at my shoulder with hers. "Stop. It's nothing."

"How much do I owe you for the party supplies?"

"I left the receipt on the counter with the bags at your house. You can Venmo me when you get a chance," she said.

I ruffled Jalissa's and Kiran's hair and started to leave before I said, "I forgot, did you see the school today?"

Stacy smiled wide. "Yep, they tore down most of the walls. It's exciting."

"I can't wait to see it."

"Mommy! Brady's going to miss us."

My heart flipped. Stacy and I exchanged a look before I left to join my daughter at the door. Hannah had her hat on and was jumping from foot to foot in the entryway.

"Goodnight," I hollered and Hannah repeated.

"I expect a rundown later," Stacy shouted back,

and I smiled.

When we got to the house, Brady was already there, leaning against the porch pillar in a pose I was sure many a social influencer would love to have on their site. He was still in the beat-up jeans and blue T-shirt from earlier, but in the evening twilight, he seemed to shimmer like an actual star.

Hannah went running up the steps, one hand on her hat, one hand held out with the egg in it. She tripped as she hit the last one, and Brady caught her before she fell, pulling her into his arms. It was the second time he'd had reflexes faster than mine, saving my daughter as if he had worlds of experience catching people from falling.

I wasn't sure if it would include me as I continued to fall.

"I made this for you," Hannah said, completely comfortable in his embrace as he held her up against his chest, her little legs circling him as they usually did me. A monkey holding on.

"You did? Are you sure you want to give it away? This looks like it took a lot of time," he said as he took the egg and squinted at the mix of notes. "Is this 'Don't Stop'?" She nodded, and his eyes met mine. "That's pretty incredible, Hannah."

She beamed.

From inside the house, Molly barked, desperate to be a part of the action.

I unlocked the door, and we all shed our shoes and coats in the entryway before Hannah zipped to open the laundry door for Molly. The two fell in a bundle of yips and laughter on the floor before Molly realized we had a guest, and then she came bounding over to Brady, jumping at him before sitting down and rolling over.

"Wow. You didn't even have to ask, and she's rolling over for you," I said.

He grinned.

We made our way into the kitchen where shopping bags littered the kitchen table. "Did you buy everything in the store?" I asked my daughter. She giggled.

"Stacy said we needed at least ten eggs per kid, and there will be twenty kids at my party, so that means two hundred eggs."

"That's a lot of eggs," Brady said.

"See what you got yourself into?" I told him. "Last chance to back out."

I met his gaze over the bags, and he didn't look away.

"There's nowhere else I'd rather be."

We continued to stare at each other for a moment. The air heavy. Expectation mixed with the caution I still felt.

"Why don't the two of you get everything opened and sorted while I make dinner?" I suggested.

He nodded and started pulling the party supplies from the bags. Hannah helped him, chatting away about why she'd picked pretzels and Goldfish over candy. I mixed the meat substitute with the taco seasoning. Nothing gourmet from me. I got by with the basics.

We ate dinner, filled plastic eggs, and Hannah and Brady started a debate over ABBA and Journey.

"Have you even seen *Mama Mia*?" Hannah asked with disgust.

Brady laughed. "Of course I have."

"Does Journey have a musical with all of their songs?" she asked, and I wanted to choke back tears and laughter because those were my grandmother's words coming out of her.

Brady let his smile slip away and, with a grave face, said, "I see your point."

She nodded, happy to think she'd convinced him of the greatness that was ABBA.

At seven thirty, I sent Hannah up to get washed up.

"Can Brady come see my room tonight?" she asked.

My eyes found his again. His flashed at me, unspoken words. Not walking away. Not backing out. "Sure."

She jumped up and down, the beads on her shawl banging together and her bangs bouncing as she moved. She skipped toward the stairs with Molly on her heels as always. Brady and I followed her. In her room, she ran to the keyboard first, turning back to the doorway and Brady.

"Mommy bought this for me when I turned four. It doesn't sound as nice as the piano at Grams' store, but I can practice here whenever I want."

"And how often is that?" he asked.

"A lot," I said, lips quirking.

Brady moved to the center of the room, spinning slowly, taking it all in, and I tried to see it through his eyes. Peace signs made with rainbows, maroon velour, and a lava lamp that wasn't turned on. My daughter had been born in the wrong decade.

"Wow," Brady said, eyes twinkling as he smiled

at me and then Hannah. "Did you do all this yourself?"

Hannah turned on the lava lamp. It was one of her most prized possessions. "Don't be silly. I'm way too little. Grams and Mommy did it, but they let me pick most of it out."

"Peace signs. Top hats. Velour. You belong at Woodstock," he teased.

Hannah frowned. "What's Woodstock?"

"It was a festival, like the one Grams puts on, where bands came and played," I told her, and her face broke into a smile.

"I like that. Grams said she asked Stevie Nicks if she'd come, but she couldn't."

"Really?" Brady said, looking to me. I nodded. He snapped his leather bands, and I silently begged him not to promise anything he couldn't make happen. He seemed to read me, or maybe he just knew. Either way, he didn't say anything else about it.

"Okay, *Chiquita,* go brush your teeth, wash your face, and put your pj's on," I said, pulling the pajamas from a drawer and handing them to her.

She grabbed them and stopped at Brady. "You can play my keyboard if you want while you wait."

Then, she headed down the hall to the bathroom.

"You don't have to stay up here. I'll be down in a minute," I told him.

"I'm good," he said.

I couldn't stop my gaze from slipping down to his lips which quirked up at my stare. I turned and headed to the bathroom to help Hannah.

I was in the middle of brushing her hair when the first chords of music hit us. It wasn't a tune I knew. The notes were opposing. Cheerful bells followed by deep sweeps. Strong emotions battling it out. It was everything I was feeling. The two sides of my soul roaring at each other.

Hannah barely let me finish the last stroke before pulling herself away to join Brady at the keyboard. He looked ridiculous scrunched up on the stool made for a five-year-old, knees spread wide because they didn't fit underneath the stand the keyboard was on. Hannah stood next to him, one hand on his shoulder as she reached out her right hand and placed them at the very top of the keys, adding a little trill to his notes. It sounded like dancing fairies.

Brady smiled down at her, the glow of the lava lamp hitting his face and turning it soft and warm as if bathed in candlelight. He and Hannah seemed to speak without words as both of their fingers moved along the keys until they suddenly both stopped. He looked awed by my five-year-old, as if she was made of spun gold. I thought maybe she was.

"Okay," I cleared my throat. "Say goodnight."

She flung her arms around him, my hugger of a daughter holding on with all her might, but his only reaction was to pull her tighter to him. So tight her toes lifted from the ground. He closed his eyes, holding on for a second before setting her back down.

She kissed his cheek, and his fingers traced it.

"Night, Brady," she said before slipping into her bed.

I tucked her in, making a little phyllo roll, and kissed her forehead. "I love you to infinity and back," I told her.

"I love you even more, Mommy."

Molly jumped up between us, and Hannah patted the dog's head before Molly curled up at her feet.

I left the door a little open so I'd remember to turn off the lava lamp and then headed back downstairs with Brady on my heels like Molly normally tagged after Hannah. My heart was in my throat. Ready to escape.

I didn't know what to do when I hit the living room. Invite him to sit? Ask him to leave? I stood awkwardly, arms wrapped around me, swaying.

"What was that song?" I asked.

"Nothing yet," he said casually.

"Wait. You just made that up? Then how did Hannah know what to play?" I asked, stunned.

"I guess she just played what she felt," he answered.

I just stared, the dancing fairy notes echoing in my head. She'd been so serious for weeks now. The laughter gone. No more Hulk tackling me to the ground. And in waltzed Brady O'Neil and drew her back into the light.

It hurt and healed all at once. I wanted her to be rebounding. I wanted her laughter and joy filling the house. I tried not to take it personally or beat myself up over the fact that I hadn't been able to do it for her. Just like Grams had been the one to help me instead of my mom. Sometimes we needed something our parents couldn't see. For Hannah, I was sure that my suffering had been shading the house in blue and black. There was no way I'd been the light.

But Brady was almost pure light. The visions of him on canvas with his whiskey eyes dancing in the brilliance of the Chinese lanterns washed over me again. An image that would be forced out of me before too long. It was calling to me.

Like him.

He stepped toward me, and I didn't back away. He grabbed my arms, pulling them from my waist to surround his while his hand went to the back of my neck, tugging me into him. He stared down into my face, a look we'd been sharing all night. Warnings. Acceptance. Pleas. Answers.

"May I kiss you?" he asked softly.

"Why do you ask first?" I asked, matching the quietness of his tone.

"I can't afford not to ask," he said. The enormity of his life settled over me. His celebrity status. It was sort of sad that his fame made him have to ask if he could kiss someone so they wouldn't use it against him. Sue him. Drag his name through the mud.

It was as sad as my daughter having to ask before she could hug another child.

I moved a hand from his waist to his lips, an echo of the trail his thumb had run along mine back at the store. I said, "If we're trying this...whatever this is...you don't have to ask. If I ever change my mind, I'll tell you."

He didn't smile as I thought he might. He looked deadly serious.

I stood on my toes and placed my lips against his. The sensations that hit me were exactly the same as the first and second time. Sunshine and moonbeams and bursts of light. Sweet cherry wine and happiness. Waves of it surging and receding like the shapes inside Hannah's lava lamp. Heating. Cooling. Mixing.

He groaned against my lips, tongue demanding an entrance that I easily gave. As we searched the tender reaches of each other's mouths, his hands journeyed from the chaste spots they'd stayed both times we'd kissed. This time, he explored more than my mouth.

He began a gentle exploration of my curves. My waist, my side, my breasts which pebbled under his touch.

Touch.

Male hands searching me that only added to the blend of sweet and sour making up my emotions. I wanted this and yet hated myself for wanting it. Wanting and needing more. Never wanting it to stop.

I slid my hands under his T-shirt, touching warm skin, and it turned into a wave of goosebumps under my fingertips. It awed me that I could make this man feel that way. Desire. A man who'd easily had hundreds of people touch him. Caress him. Make love to him. I'd been with one man my whole life. I'd been sixteen the first time Darren and I had made love. A bumbled mix of nerves, rushed moves, and not much more except the love that had filled us.

This dance with Brady was so much slower, agonizingly gorgeous, flaming the yearning inside me. I pushed at him, moving us toward the couch, wanting to feel the weight of him on top of me. Needing it more than I'd needed anything in a really long time.

We collapsed there, a tangle of limbs and tongues and hands. Searching. Guiding. Finding. His T-shirt hit the floor followed by mine, and when I went to join our lips again, he held back, finger dragging along my collarbone, down the middle of my chest to settle between my breasts.

"You're so beautiful," he said quietly, reverently, as if he'd never seen a woman before.

I wasn't embarrassed by my shape. It was not the skin and bones and soft waves of my twenties. I was curves and stretch marks and breasts that had nursed my daughter. None of it was anything to be ashamed of, but I also knew it wasn't the tight frames he was probably used to. Like my life being mundane, I was as well. Normal. Average. Not a size two and not a size fourteen. In the middle.

He'd have to take me as I was if he wanted me. I couldn't change for him, and even if I could, I wouldn't. The scars told me I had lived. The marks a secret treasure of who I was. Once I had doubted their value, their beauty, but I didn't anymore. Now, they were just me.

Brady leaned in, taking my nipple into his mouth through the silk of my bra, and I moaned from deep inside me, a monster coming from the recesses of a cave where it had been hibernating too long, needing the sunshine of the spring that pushed away the winter.

He unhooked the bra, and I let him, forgetting everything but him and me and the feel of our bodies touching. My brain shutting down like it did when I was painting. Lost only in the waves of desire that seeped through us.

Then, his lips were back on my breasts, no layer between them. Sucking. Licking. Heating the core of me and slicing away the icy numbness that had been there for so long. Too many days and weeks and months. Years.

Chapter Twenty-one

Brady

HERE TONIGHT
Performed by Brett Young

She was so intoxicatingly gorgeous. Soft and sensual. A burst of daisies in a field of roses. Light amongst the red. And with every move of our lips and every tingle of our touch, I was making music in my head. *Crescendos* folding into *diminuendos*. Like we were a *legato* of notes blending together in a smooth connection while the chords came alive around us.

Never had I seen music while making love.

Notes and chords were part of my life, but they'd never been part of a sexual experience for me, and now they were. We were partially clothed, only chests bare, and yet my entire being was straining to become merged with hers. To find a tempo and a dynamic that meant us.

I was lost in the music we were making.

And it brought me suddenly back to reality, to the things that happened when I got lost in notes and rhythms, especially when I had others who were counting on me. Instead of pushing my fingers into her leggings and pulling them down her body, I slowed our pace. The tempo, a *larghissimo* of broad strokes. A cooling of the heat.

Tristan resisted at first, hands and tongue trying to pick up the pace. Need filling her as it filled me. I wanted to touch her, to make her come and feel her fall apart against me, but I wouldn't jump from nothing to all in. I wouldn't allow either of us to forget the world like she'd admitted she did as easily as me.

We would be art. We would be paint and chords blended together. But not yet. Not when her little girl was upstairs, and we'd barely agreed to find out what this even was. I hadn't even taken her to dinner. I hadn't shown her she was more than kisses caught between stanzas.

She deserved all of it. She deserved *more*.

I eased away from her, elbows on either side of her, looking down into her face, and I just stared until her eyes fluttered open. A smile curved her full pink lips upward.

"Well, dang. The Brady O'Neil Experience is quite something."

I laughed, and it came from deep inside me. Guttural. The desire still littered across the sounds.

"That wasn't even close to a Brady O'Neil Experience. That wasn't even a half a Brady Experience." I grinned at her.

Her soft laughter joined my own.

I sat up, bringing her with me so she ended up in my lap, head on my shoulder with my arms wrapped around her chest. Peace settled over me. The notes resting. My brain stilling so I was only aware of the heat and scent of her.

She pulled away slightly and picked up our T-shirts from where they had fallen. She pulled hers on, and I barely resisted the urge to tear it back off so I could stare at the perfect skin longer. Pale but with a hint of warmth I was sure made her tan with barely a glance of sunshine.

Bare in the sunshine was a place I couldn't let my imagination go, not when my jeans were already straining to keep my male body parts inside. Not when I wanted to continue the concert we'd started performing.

"Thank you," she said quietly when she'd settled back against me once more.

"For what?"

"For knowing we needed to stop. I got lost there for a second," she said.

I nodded. "Me too. I just don't want it to be like this—on the couch with Hannah upstairs and you regretting it."

"I wouldn't have regretted it," she insisted.

I wasn't sure about that. I thought maybe she would have if we'd found ourselves naked and merged together on the first night we'd agreed to start whatever this was.

"I'm not going anywhere. There isn't a need for us to rush."

"Speak for yourself. I haven't had sex in almost five years," she laughed.

I chuckled. "Well, it's been over a year for me, but I'm still not willing to go full-speed ahead."

She pulled away from my chest to meet my eyes. "Over a year? Really?"

I rested my head on the back of the couch, closing

my eyes. "Yes. Why does everyone seem to think that's so impossible?"

"Because you're famous. You're hot. And you have women and men drooling all over you, calling your name."

I opened my eyes, looking into her golden ones. "That's just it. They're saying my name, but it's not really me they're calling. I learned that pretty fast. I'm not saying I haven't had my fill of experiences—I began those way back at Juilliard—but what I *am* saying is I know the difference between sex and making love."

Her fingers on my chest stopped moving.

"Yeah?"

"Sex is about bodies and desire. Speed and force and tearing each other's clothes off. It fills the ache. It's satisfying. It can be damn beautiful. But making love is finding a part of the other person that will forever belong only to you, whether your relationship last ten minutes or twenty years. It's a raw connection that can't be replaced or forgotten."

"Which was ours?" she asked carefully.

"You already know the answer to that," I told her, my hand soothing her arm. "But just so you know, I'm all for sex at times too. I just want the times of making love to be more."

There was that word again. Haunting me. Following me.

More.

"You realize the ridiculousness of this, right?" she asked, and I couldn't help it from stabbing at the heart I was trying to lay open for her.

"All I feel is the rightness of it," I told her the

truth.

She seemed to take that in for a long moment before nodding, and that eased the worries bouncing around my heart.

"I should go," I told her. I made a promise to Mom and Dad that I'd help them redo my old bedroom for Chevelle first thing in the morning, and I didn't want to be dragging my ass around.

"Why does that sound like you're a teenager with a curfew?" she teased.

I chuckled. "It does, doesn't it? I guess you could say I'm trying to make sure my parents will trust me enough to leave Cassidy with me."

"I don't get it. Why is your family so protective of Cassidy?"

"I don't really like to tell the story because it's Cassidy's to share if she wants to, but she was diagnosed with Triple X when she was little more than a baby. She's gotten a handle over almost all the symptoms, but her muscle tone will never be the same as the average person, so she falls and gets hurt pretty easily." I tried to keep to the facts because, just like I'd said, it wasn't my story to tell.

Tristan took that in, pulling fully away from me and standing up. I joined her, looking into her face. It looked happy. Almost happier than I'd seen it since meeting her. Joy filled my chest, knowing it was partly due to me.

"Will I see you before Tuesday?" she asked. That was the next day she had me scheduled to teach classes. We'd agreed on three days, and even with those days, she'd had to cut everything back to a minimum. I was surprised to find myself enjoying teaching more than I thought I would. Maybe because

Elana had already instilled in all her students a deep love and appreciation for music that I easily returned.

Thoughts of the lessons and helping out at the store brought the issues with it to the forefront of my mind, serving to remind me of William Chan and my anger at him for blocking the sale of Kincaid's to Cass and me.

"I have some things I'm working on for Cass that might take some time, but I'll try to swing by the store if I can." I pulled out my phone. "I need your number."

"Need, huh?" she smiled.

"Need. No doubt about it. One that might make my entire body seize up if it isn't met."

She laughed, put her number in, and then handed the phone back to me.

I walked to the door. I turned back to her and said, "I'd like to take you to dinner. A real date. Do you think we can make that happen?" Ideas of romance flowed through my brain.

"My entire family is arriving on Friday for Hannah's birthday and Easter, so it'll be a little chaotic," she said.

"I'll be in the city on Thursday, interviewing candidates for Dani's replacement," I told her, frustration blooming through me that we might not be able to make a date happen within the next week. But then I reminded myself of what I'd told her. I wasn't in a rush. I wasn't going anywhere. We had time.

I kissed her slow and gentle, the heat hitting me all over again, making me long for the *crescendo* that would come from finding my way into every piece of her, but I pulled back. It would have to wait.

"Goodnight, *Cariño*," I said softly.

"Goodnight, Brady O'Neil," she returned.

I lingered for a second and then opened the door and walked into the night while every single part of me ached to go back. To find that peace that I'd felt sitting on the couch with her in my arms.

♫ ♫ ♫

I spent Sunday cleaning out my old room with my parents, getting rid of things that were so old I'd forgotten about them. We were turning the space into a nursery for Chevelle so he wouldn't have to stay in the bassinet by Cass's bed.

I pulled out a stack of my old songbooks from the closet shelf, and I couldn't resist flipping through them.

Mom came up from behind me and saw what I was looking at. Her face softened. "Do you remember the song you wrote for me?" she asked.

My eyes grew wide. I did. I was surprised she remembered.

"It was awful," I told her. All rhyming words that didn't fall on the correct beats.

She chuckled. "It was, but it was the moment I knew we'd lost you."

"You didn't lose me, Mom. I've always been right here," I said, trying to hold back a wave of emotion.

She patted my face. "You were gone long before you left for Juilliard."

She moved away, taking a stack of books with her.

She was right and wrong. I'd stepped away from

them when I'd found music, but it had saved me from feeling alone when Cass had been the center of their world. Ever since then, there were parts of my life—me—I kept far away from this house and this family, but I was still grounded in it. I still felt the love…mine for them and theirs for me.

Now, all the parts seemed to be colliding together. Tristan's face flashed through my brain because, somehow, she was at the heart of the collision. I took out my phone and sent a simple text.

ME: I miss you.

It took her a few minutes to respond.

CARI: You're not missing much.

ME: What are you doing right this minute?

CARI: We're on the couch, watching Mama Mia *for the hundred millionth time. Trust me, it isn't something you're missing.*

She was wrong. The thought of being with them, cuddled together on the couch…it made me ache. It made me want to walk out of the room and let my parents do their thing, but I couldn't. Not when the trust I was rebuilding was so fragile. Not when Dad was going to bat for me in a way I'd never known him to do before.

ME: That sounds way better than the paint-fumed hard labor I'm putting in.

CARI: You're painting? I love painting.

ME: HAR. Not that kind of painting.

CARI: I love ANY kind of painting. Color layering over color. It changes things.

Change. God, my entire world had been flipped on its lid since coming home. I'd been aching for something since Christmas, but I hadn't expected what I found to make me think the wild thoughts crossing my brain these days, like thoughts of staying in Grand Orchard permanently.

ME: You've changed me.

I texted it before allowing myself to doubt it, but then I immediately worried I'd said too much. Pushed her when she was barely acknowledging what was blooming between us. The dots came and went, but finally, she responded.

CARI: You've changed me too.

Those words filled my entire being with hope and pride and fucking joy. I needed to do something for them. For us. Together. Something more than just practicing music, and eating dinner, and making out like teens on the couch. Although, the making out was pretty damn good.

Dad saw me texting and the goofy smile on my face, and he stopped, taking me in for a second before smiling also.

"You've met someone," he said. "Someone more

than just a passing fling."

More.

"How can you tell?" I asked, shoving my phone in my pocket and turning my attention to the painter's tape and the baseboards.

"That expression. It isn't just…you know…lust."

I wanted to laugh at my dad trying to talk about sex with me. He'd failed completely and horribly when I was twelve, confusing me so much that Mom had to fix the bumbling images he'd created with real ones from a book.

"It is more than lust, and I'm worried I'll screw it up," I told him truthfully. "That I won't be here for them like I haven't always been here for Cass. For you."

Dad stared at me for a long time. "You're a good man, Cormac. Let your heart guide you, and everything else will work out."

Then, he turned away to start mixing the paint.

I stared at the back of his head for a long moment. I'd never had a problem following my heart, but when I was younger, that had been wrapped in teenage selfishness. My heart had always directed me to my music. Now, it seemed to be directing me to people. My family. Tristan. Hannah. Those thoughts were accompanied by a sudden rush of lyrics and a melody, but I pushed it aside so I could be present with the people in the room.

The music could wait.

Dad and I painted the walls while Mom and Cass assembled furniture.

When we were finished, the room was a clash of vibrant colors. Not a pastel in sight. Cass insisted children saw bright, primary colors better and that it strengthened their brains. The intensity of it reminded me, in some ways, of the wild mismatch of colors in Hannah's room.

By the time dinner came, I realized Mom and I hadn't fought or spat at each other once. There'd been laughter in the room instead. It had been a good day. A day we hadn't had with the four of us in a really long time…maybe ever.

When I got a call from Elsa Chan late in the evening, Mom barely squinted when I walked away to talk in private.

"So, I'm sorry, but the bank rejected the offer," Elsa told me, and she actually sounded like she was truly sorry.

"I can't believe the bank's board would agree with William's call," I told her. She was quiet, and I knew I had latched on to something. "Who should I talk to?"

She sighed. "I'm not saying it'll work, or that William's wrong, but if you wanted to talk to someone who might change their mind, you could talk to our Aunt Victoria. She's the Chairman of the Board."

"How do I get a hold of Aunt Victoria?"

"She lives in New York City because she spends most of her days on philanthropic efforts there. I can send you the details for her office."

A quiet settled between us. "Why are you helping me?" I asked.

"I love my brother, but he really needs someone to cut him down a peg or two before he loses any decent part of him that's left," she said.

I laughed. "He's definitely a different William

than the one I used to hang with."

"I kind of wish we could have that William back." Her voice was wistful.

"Well, thanks," I said.

"I can't say it'll help, but good luck."

We hung up, and when I came back into the living room, Cass was alone. I caught her up on the situation with Kincaid's.

"The last thing I want is for you to spend more money than the place is worth," Cass said quietly, her eyes darting to the kitchen where our parents were chatting about whether or not Dad should have the third piece of cake. At least it seemed like the rift between them was healing some, because it was a good-natured ribbing.

"This isn't just about buying Kincaid's for you, Cass. This is also about *La Musica* and Tristan. If I can get someone over William's head to put pressure on him, it could solve everything. I have to be in New York City on Thursday to interview the two candidates Lee has lined up for Dani's job, so I'll see if I can get Victoria Chan to meet with me then."

"Fine, but promise me you won't do something ridiculous and spend more than we can ever get back," she said.

I nodded with a smile. "Promise me you'll find someone to hang out with you so I won't be leaving you unattended."

She rolled her eyes. "I'll figure it out."

"Promise me," I demanded. "Or I won't go. I'll just do all the meetings via video."

She flicked at my earlobe, and I wasn't quick enough to protect it. She smiled at her small success as I winced. "Stop being as ridiculous as she is," she said, sending a look in Mom's direction. "But I promise."

Chapter Twenty-two

Tristan

SOMEBODY LIKE THAT
Performed by Tenille Arts

Hannah and I had spent Sunday on the couch. A lazy day we hadn't had together in a long time. We watched all her favorite musicals, ate popcorn that she actually let me butter, and stayed in our pajamas.

Intermixed with our movie binge, I had texts from Stacy, showing me the work on the school building and asking me my opinion on the wall colors, which reminded me of Brady who was painting walls for Chevelle.

The texts Brady sent came and went in between Stacy's and were achingly sweet. He'd said he missed us, that he wanted to spend more time with us, and it felt right in a way I couldn't shake.

By the time Nash phoned for his weekly video call with Hannah, I was half asleep, relaxed, and hardly paying attention to what she was saying to him.

"NaNa, guess what?"

"I don't know, you tell me, BoPeep," he said with

a smile that he saved for my daughter.

"Brady O'Neil is going to teach me how to play 'Money, Money, Money,'" she said, and my heart skipped a beat because I was pretty sure Nash and Dani didn't even know Brady was in town.

"He is?" The surprise registered all over Nash's face.

"Yep, and he's coming to my party."

"But I'm still going to be your favorite guest, right?" he teased, and I laughed when Hannah had to actually think about it.

They said goodbye, and Hannah handed me the phone. Nash immediately said, "I didn't know you knew Brady."

"I didn't. He showed up on my doorstep to claim a box Grams had left him under his real name. I had no idea the famous Brady O'Neil was Grams' prized student, Cormac."

Nash frowned. "And now he's teaching Hannah? Will he even be there long enough to do that?"

My heart that had been relaxed and at peace tightened back up. The worry of Brady leaving. The worry about what we would do when his celebrity lifestyle and the demands of his music career came back to hit us in the face.

"Tris?" Nash's voice brought me back.

"Honestly, it's just temporary at this point, but he brought music back into her life, and for that, I can only be grateful."

"Don't let him charm the pants off you." It was said with a tease but also a note of caution. Nash was the protective older brother I'd never had. He'd taken Darren's request to watch over me more seriously than I'd almost been able to handle, until Dani had entered his world and brought clarity to his life. Dani had saved my relationship with Nash in many ways.

"When have you known me to be swayed by a pretty smile?" I asked him, and he chuckled. But the truth was, I had been swayed by Brady's smile. It wasn't pretty. It was wicked, and dynamic, and heart-searing.

I was glad Dani and Nash were coming for Hannah's party. I missed them. But I was also nervous because they would be able to tell something was going on between Brady and me. All of my family would, and I wasn't sure I was ready for the rejoicing or the recriminations that might come with it. I was grateful Darren's parents weren't going to be there, because I wasn't sure I could handle their thoughts on the matter. They were in Japan where his dad had been stationed for the last three years. Their military life had never once stopped, not even after losing their only child to it.

All those concerns were pushed aside by a text from Brady, wishing me sweet dreams. For the first time since Grams died, I slept through the night, my alarm being the thing to jar me from my slumber instead of worries or nightmares.

I woke Hannah, and we got ready for our day.

While Stacy would normally watch Hannah for me, even though it was spring break, she and Jin were going to be at their charter school all week. Stacy's parents had taken Kiran and Jalissa for a few days so Jin and Stacy could be on-site, working with the crews on the remodel. I'd debated shutting *La Musica* down so I could help too, but Stacy wouldn't hear of it. Plus, I had Hannah and no one to watch her.

It was frustrating to not be able to help the people who always helped me.

Hannah skipped and sang "Money, Money, Money" as we walked toward the store. When we turned the corner, there was a crowd outside the shop. I stared at the group, wondering what was going on and hoping it had nothing to do with William Chan and the foreclosure notice.

When we got closer, they whipped out cameras. While they were taking pictures, they started shouting questions at me. At us. I could barely filter through them as I picked Hannah up and hugged her tightly to my body. Fear flew through me, not for myself, but for her and the aggressiveness of the crowd. Cameras were flashing, and the volume of their voices increased as I tried to shield her from it all.

Their questions finally started to register.

"Tristan, how did you meet Brady?"

"How long have you been dating?"

"Were you childhood sweethearts?"

My heart was beating at a wild pace. This was about Brady? How did anyone even know we'd started seeing each other? Had he posted something?

I literally had to shoulder and elbow my way through them to the door. Hannah was holding on to her top hat, eyes wide, as I finally got the door unlocked. I slid us in, and as I went to shut it, a man stuck his foot in the door.

I twisted Hannah away from his reach, but he just held a business card out.

"I can give you a half-page in *The Exhibitor* for fifty grand."

My eyes probably looked as big as Hannah's. He

was offering me money to spill my guts about Brady and me? To tell personal information about us? It seemed ludicrous. Wild. Out of this world. I looked pointedly at his foot in the doorway.

"We're not open yet, please leave," I said pointedly.

"No one else is going to offer you more than that," he said.

"If you don't leave, I'm calling the cops."

He slid the business card into my hand and then stepped back. I swung the door shut, locking the bolt, and resetting the alarm before all but running up the stairs to the studio with Hannah still clinging to me.

"Why were those people taking our picture, Mommy?" Hannah asked. She wasn't scared as much as overwhelmed, whereas I was rattled beyond belief.

"Remember, Brady is a famous singer, honey. They just wanted to know about him."

"But why?"

"I… I don't know. Maybe it makes them feel like he's their friend, too," I said, setting her down and throwing the business card into the trash. "Why don't you go practice while I talk to Brady."

"Okey dokey, artichokey," she said, heading toward the practice room with the piano in it.

I took several deep breaths before pulling out my phone and hitting Brady's number.

"Good morning, *Cariño*," his voice greeted me on the other side. It was warm and gritty, and it loosened the tightness of the nerves in my neck and my shoulders slightly.

"The store is surrounded by the press," I told him.

"What?" he growled.

"They were taking our picture and asking questions about us. About you and me. One of the men tried to force himself into the store." My voice shook more than I wanted. I was trying to be strong about this, but I hated confrontation almost as much as I hated the limelight.

"I'm calling Waterton Security right now. I'll have someone there in just a few minutes. I'll call you back," he said and hung up.

The store was filled with the sound of my daughter's voice and the rhythm of the keys. "Let It Be" was one of her favorites. She was using it to warm up before she would move on to practicing the other two songs Brady had taught her. What would the press think if they ever found out about her abilities? Would they hound her like they were hounding Brady?

A shiver went down my spine.

I paced the room while waiting. It was a good fifteen minutes before the phone rang again.

Brady's voice was an attempt at soothing me. Soft. Gentle. "Waterton is sending two men down. They'll be there in just a few minutes, but don't open the door until they get there," Brady said. "Their names are Prabhjot and Josh, and they'll be in black clothes with the Waterton logo on it. They'll show you IDs. I've also talked with Lee and Garner, and Marco and Trevor will be here before the end of the day."

"How did they even find out?" I breathed out.

"There was a post a week ago when you first danced with me at Mick's," he said. "It didn't get picked up anywhere, so I wasn't worried about it. It looked like it was just me with some random. But then we were seen dancing together at Mick's again on Thursday, and that's kind of gone viral. There's a whole video."

"There is?" I sat down on the futon, shocked.

"I didn't know about it 'til I just logged into my Insta account while I was talking to Lee."

I pulled up my phone, opened the app, and put in Brady O'Neil in the search bar. There it was. Brady and me dancing together. We were smiling at each other, but the look on his face was what had my heart pumping extra hard. It was as if there was no one else in the room but me. He was completely focused on my face and on my smile even as the song progressed. When it ended, he caught my hand, and we left the dance floor. The video continued, following us all the way until Marco led us out of the kitchen door.

"Oh my God," I said quietly.

I hadn't even thought about this part of Brady's life when I'd invited him over. I'd been so focused on my mixed-up feelings about dating someone again, about letting someone into our lives, that I hadn't once stopped to think about what it meant to let someone in who was followed around by fans and paparazzi and stalkers. Oh, holy hell. He had stalkers.

Hannah.

I felt like I was going to be sick.

"Tristan. I'm coming down. But I have to wait until security is there," he said. "Otherwise, it'll just be a shitstorm."

"Okay," I said, but it really wasn't okay at all.

Ten minutes later, there was a sharp rap on the glass door of the store, and I sped down the stairs to see two enormous men standing on the other side of the glass, all in black. They had a logo on their shirts, and as I got closer, I could see it was a shield with a name written across it.

The black-haired one had a badge pushed to the glass, and I quickly read his name and the Waterton business logo again before I turned off the alarm and unlocked the door. He squeezed in while the other man remained outside, turning so his back was to me, arms crossed, stance wide.

A stance I recognized. Soldier. Military.

My heart was flipping over and over, making me dizzy.

"I'm Prabhjot." He stuck out his hand, and I shook it.

"Thanks for coming," I said.

He waved his hand at the alarm. "Is this your only alarm?"

I nodded.

"We're going to need access to it and the company you're using. Can you call them? We'll do a full assessment and let you and Mr. O'Neil know what changes we recommend be made." He spoke in a calm voice that was far from how I felt. I was a jitter of nerves.

"It's not hooked up to any company. It's just an alarm," I told him. We'd never needed it. "I think your boss probably installed it a decade ago."

He brushed a hand through his hair and muttered something I didn't catch because I was distracted by a storm of voices shouting outside the store. Prabhjot went back to the glass door. Soon, he was unlocking it to allow Brady and another muscled man to slip in. This man was as dark and intimidating as his counterparts.

The door closed, and Brady rushed over to me,

pulling me into his arms while cameras began flashing through the glass. He turned me away from them so his back was to the windows and pushed me gently toward the stairs.

When we reached the top, the sound of Hannah's voice and the piano keys hit me again. Sweet. Joyful. God, this was awful. She didn't need this. I didn't need this.

Brady pulled me to him again.

"It's going to be okay," he said into my hair.

I pushed away from him, wrapping my arms around my middle. "How can you even say that?"

"It'll die down," he said, flicking his leather bands. "But for now, I have a team going to your house, and we'll have someone here whenever you're here."

"Brady…they were screaming at me. At Hannah," I said, eyes getting watery.

He stilled, eyes drifting toward the practice room and then back to me. "I'm so sorry," his voice was strangled. "I didn't think." He dragged a hand through his hair. "Shit, I'm so sorry. Was she upset?"

I shook my head. "She just wanted to know why they were asking questions about you."

He looked pained. "It *will* die down, but it'll also get worse before it does."

"I don't want her picture all over the media," I said in a half-whisper.

"I've got Lee working on it, and he's calling Dani. I know she'll help out until we have someone on board. I'm hoping to have someone hired and up and running by the end of the week."

I stilled. Dani. Which meant Nash would know

after I'd pretty much blown it off the night before. I was surprised my phone wasn't already roaring with texts and calls from him. What would I say? What could I say?

I sank onto the futon, and Brady joined me.

"If we stop seeing each other, it'll go away sooner," he said calmly, as if he was trying to not care, but I still heard the hurt and hope and longing twisted in his words. He was offering me a way out, but even as he did so, the spin of awareness was flitting between us like fireflies, calling us back together.

Could I walk away?

If I didn't, what would it mean?

"I…" My voice trailed off as I tried to speak. Uncertainty. Fear.

He pulled my hands into his, eyes meeting mine. "It's okay. I get it. This circus isn't for everyone. I understand you wanting out before it gets hotter."

Again, the tone was bland, as if he was hiding every emotion he was really feeling behind a brick wall. I knew the energy it took to do that, hide what was trying to escape from you. I knew the sacrifice he was making to himself and what he wanted by giving me an out.

"I don't know what I want at this moment. I…it's just a lot to take in." It was all true. The emotions flowing through me were saying to throw my arms around him, kiss him, and reassure him that a few little people taking pictures of us wasn't enough to cause me to back away from what we'd started. But my brain was telling me to stop the campaign before it collapsed into a heap of body parts just like the ones that had come home to me in a coffin. Except, these parts would be mine. And Hannah's. Our hearts and our lives strewn about instead of muscle and bone.

I ached in every single part of me.

Suddenly, the music Brady had played on Hannah's keyboard on Saturday night filled the room. The notes he'd said he made up. The discord of soft and loud and slow and fast with Hannah's own little twinkle of fairies dancing over the top of it. Us. The three of us. Mixed together.

It was beautiful.

It held so many possibilities.

Brady's eyes grew wide as he listened. "She's…there are not enough words… I can't believe she remembered it so well."

He had already snuck inside both of our hearts. It was too late for him to leave without causing damage. But he would do his best to leave us whole, because he seemed to look out for everyone in his life but himself. The way he was willing to just walk away if I thought it was the right thing to do when it was the last thing he really wanted was just one example.

I flung my arms around him, kissing him with a passion I'd thought would never be mine again. Passion for someone willing to give up their wants and desires for me. For Hannah.

He hesitated for a moment before his arms surrounded me and his lips pushed back. I could feel the relief coursing through him even when they weren't my emotions—or maybe they were. All I knew was that I'd just tangled us deeper together instead of pulling us apart like I should have done.

There was no backing down now.

Not easily.

Not without tearing deep wounds into all three of

us.

But I couldn't walk away.
Not yet.
Maybe never.

Chapter Twenty-three

Brady

A clearing of a throat pulled me from Tristan's embrace. My blood was pumping with relief and also regret. I'd been sure she'd want out. Who would want to stay with the circus-like shitstorm downstairs following them? Who would want their five-year-old mixed up in that? I'd told her the truth. This was just the beginning, and it would get worse before it died down.

But I couldn't let her go. Not if she was willing to stay.

I wanted her and Hannah in my life.

More than just wanted them. I felt like I'd never be complete again if I didn't have them with me. The perfect peace of Saturday evening would forever allude me if she walked away.

I turned to the giant of a man Waterton had sent, who'd cleared his throat to interrupt our kiss. Prabhjot said, "I've put together a list of suggested changes to the store's security. Waterton said the team at the house is ready to install the alarm system if you can get us the keys."

I turned back to Tristan. "I'm paying for an alarm at the house. I just… regardless of what happens with us, you'll need it. Can you give them a key?"

She looked stunned again. Almost like she'd looked when I'd first walked into the store. She got up, went to her purse, and took a key off a key ring, handing it to Prabhjot.

"We'll get it back to you in a few hours," he said before heading back down the stairs. The sound of his heavy boots ricocheted off the walls in the silence left behind as Hannah stopped playing the song I'd made up and that she'd somehow memorized after hearing it one time.

"I'm going to go check on Hannah," Tristan said, squeezing my hand and then heading off to the practice room just as my phone rang.

Dani's picture filled the screen.

"What the hell, O'Neil?" she said harshly.

My eyes closed.

"What do you want me to say?" I asked.

"I want you to tell me you aren't putting moves on my dear friend who's already lost her soul mate."

I couldn't do that. I'd already tangled us together, but I'd also given her the chance to escape, and she'd stayed. For now. That had to mean something.

Dani didn't like my silence. She rumbled, "Nash and I are coming up on Saturday for Hannah's birthday party. Are we going to have to bury you alive in a grave somewhere?"

"I really like her," I told her quietly. It was a true statement as much as it didn't even begin to break the surface of what I felt.

"She's been through a lot, Brady. Nash is extremely protective of her. I am too."

"Is this why I was never properly introduced? Because you think I'm going to screw with her? Do you know me that little?" I couldn't help the hurt that threaded its way through my voice. I was a good enough guy until it came to thoughts of introducing me to someone they cared about. I wasn't good enough to be trusted with an actual relationship. That's what it felt like everyone thought of me.

Dani sighed. "I know you aren't a love-'em-and-leave-'em kind of guy. But that doesn't mean you can give her what she needs after mourning a husband for four years."

"Four and a half."

"What?" Dani said in surprise.

"Four and a half years. I know how long it's been. I'm also painfully aware it will probably never be enough time. But I can't help it. She's…" I sought for the word I needed. "She's the thing that's been missing my entire life."

It was Dani's turn to remain silent, seconds ticking away before she finally asked, "You're falling in love with her?"

"Falling. Fallen. Who knows? I just know Hannah and her…they need me as much as I need them."

I hadn't really even thought the words before I said them, but they were the truth. The females in the other room did need someone. Needed someone to pull them from the winter into the warmth of spring. I could be that. I wanted to be that with every inch of my soul.

"What should I say in the post?" Dani's voice still held a hint of reprimand, but also a reluctant acceptance.

"I don't want anything about Tristan or Hannah in any post we make," I told her firmly.

"Brady, the post is literally a response to you and Tristan dancing in the bar. How can we not put anything in it about her?"

I sighed. "Our official response is no comment."

Dani snorted. "You know that isn't going to work, right? That will just send the hounds baying after you even harder.

I dragged a hand over my face.

"Just say something about me catching up with old friends in my hometown."

She snorted a second time. "Have you seen the video? There isn't anything friendly about the look on your face."

I had seen the video. Briefly. I'd been filled with panic and an overwhelming sense of need to protect her before I'd made the call to Lee. I'd been careless. I was surprised Marco had let someone film us that long, but from the angle of the filming, someone had been pretty sly about it. It was half under a table or something.

It wasn't Marco's fault. It was mine. I should have known better than to try to prance around my hometown as if no one would care what I was doing. It wasn't ever that simple anymore.

"It's as much as I'm willing to put out there right now, Dani."

She sighed. "Fine. I'll see what I can do. Is she okay?"

As Dani asked the question, Tristan came out of the practice room with Hannah in her arms. The little girl was smiling, top hat slightly askew, shawl wrapped around her. She was the cutest damn mini-me of Stevie Nicks there ever was.

"Dani wants to know if you're okay," I said to Tristan.

Her eyes grew wide. "Tell her I'm fine but that I'll call her or Nash later."

"She said—"

"I heard," Dani cut me off. "I like you a whole lot, Brady. I count you as one of my closest friends, but I'm not going to step between you and my husband if you fuck this up."

"I understand," I told her.

She hung up, and I slid the phone back into my pocket.

"So. Cass was making veggie burgers for lunch with cauliflower fries. Who's up for some?" I asked the two females.

"I've never had cauliflower fries, have I, Mommy?" Hannah asked her mom.

Tristan shook her head. "Not to my knowledge." She looked up at me. "Are you sure it's okay?"

"We can't stay here, we can't go out, and your house is off limits until we have the alarm installed. Our house already has the works."

It was the only damn thing my parents had let me do to the place, and that was only after the entire fucking Fiona fiasco. For a while, we weren't sure where Fiona would look for me or who she'd hurt. Thankfully, she'd never come after my family. The thought of anyone coming after these two made me want to tear my body apart limb by limb and throw it to the wolves.

But goddamn, I didn't want to walk away from them.

Prabhjot and the four hulks who had been sent by Waterton got us out of the store and into an SUV with blackout windows. The press—which looked like it had grown even more—screamed at us before the doors were shut, and we took off.

When I turned to Hannah, her eyes were wide and a little scared.

"They won't hurt you," I told her. I wouldn't let them. Over my dead body.

"They're so loud," she said.

"*Fortissimo*. Wait 'til you hear the crowds when I'm onstage. That's *fortissississimo*," I told her. She gave me a weak smile.

We didn't have a car seat for her. She was wrapped in Tristan's arms. I'd have to fix that. From now on, we'd have a booster seat available whenever I went anywhere. Thank God we were only traveling a couple of blocks.

The crowd of reporters hadn't converged in front of my parents' house yet.

The SUV let us out at the back gate. I held on to Tristan's hand after helping her down, squeezing it, trying to reassure her that everything was going to be okay. When we entered the back door, Mom looked up. Her eyes widened as they traveled from the two females with me, down to our joined hands, and then back up to my face.

"Mom, you know Tristan and Hannah, right?" I asked.

She nodded. "Of course, nice to see you again."

The timer on the oven went off, and Cass came hurrying into the kitchen.

"Oh, hi!" she said as she hit the buzzer.

"Sorry to invade without an invite. Brady told me it would be okay," Tristan said.

"We've kind of got a media shitstorm issue," I said.

Mom's eyes squinted. "What did you do now?"

Cass laughed. "Is this about the video that went viral?"

"What video?" Mom asked.

"Can we not do this right now?" I asked, looking from my family to Hannah and then back again.

"Oh yes, of course. So, you're staying for my world-famous veggie burgers, right?" Cass said with a smile directed at my girls. "Do you want to help me make them?" she asked Hannah.

Hannah beamed and pushed out of Tristan's arms. "Oh yes. I like to cook. Are they like the ones in the *Healthy Eating* cookbook I showed you?"

"Mine are way better," Cass said in a conspiratorial whisper. She pulled one of the kitchen chairs over to the counter. "Come on up, and I'll show you what I've already done."

My family took in the two females with smiles and warmth, and as the day progressed and the fanatic wave of media continued to grow, they cocooned them in a pretend world where we were all just friends and family visiting each other. Outside the safe haven of the house, the press stormed into Grand Orchard as if the possibility of Brady O'Neil finding a new girlfriend was the most important topic facing our planet.

We spent the afternoon and evening playing board and card games I hadn't realized we still owned. Chutes and Ladders, Candyland, Old Maid, and more. Childish and lighthearted. Even my mom smiled more than frowned throughout the day, with her face softening when Hannah danced around the room with her top hat wobbling after she'd gotten to one hundred before anyone else in Chutes and Ladders.

The vision hit me hard. The mix of them all together with smiles on their faces. Family. Belonging. Love.

Marco let himself in the back door as the sun went down, and a rush of relief flew through me. I trusted this man with my life, and I knew he'd do everything in his power to protect Tristan's and Hannah's, just like he did mine and my family's. My parents called out a warm welcome to him. He waited at the door for me, and I joined him, hugging him.

"Thanks for coming," I said. It was my fault he'd left to begin with, and now he'd barely gone home only to have to journey back again.

He gave a curt nod. "Sorry about the video."

"Nothing you could have done about it."

He still felt guilty. I saw it written all over his normally stoic face.

"Waterton's men aren't done at Tristan's house, and the bulk of the media is there now that you've left the store. I don't think they should go home tonight," he said.

The guilt he'd felt took its turn rushing through me. It was my fault. They couldn't go home. Not yet. I met Tristan's gaze through the kitchen arch to the family room. She patted the top of Hannah's hat and then made her way over to me.

"What's up?" she asked.

"They aren't finished installing the security at the house, so I think you and Hannah should stay here tonight. You can take my bed at my place over the garage."

She swallowed. "Is it that bad?"

When I didn't respond, her eyes went to Marco's face. He looked down at the floor. I put a hand on her arm. "I'm sorry."

She took a deep breath, and I had to give her credit. After the momentary breakdown this morning, and the talk we'd had about us, she'd just taken everything else in stride. She wasn't as fazed by it as much as I was when I should have been used to it. She just smiled and shook her head. "It's not your fault."

"It is."

"Stop. Neither of us expected this," she said, meeting my gaze with a sure one.

"Trevor and I will take turns on watch tonight. We've got the security van and the extra detail up and running," Marco said. Then he looked at Tristan. "From what I've experienced, you just need to give it a week, and then things will be back to normal."

Her eyes widened, but he was right. News of celebrity relationships came and went so fast it was hard to keep up with them, even if you wanted to.

Marco left, and I turned to Tristan, pulling her into my arms, holding on tight. Afraid if I let her go, she might change her mind and back down from all the Wild West adventures she'd just been flung into.

"Thank you," I said quietly.

She wrapped her arms around me.

"Why are you thanking me?"

"For seeing all this and still being willing to give me a chance."

She looked up from my chest, eyes locking onto mine. "Darren and the SEALs…" She paused like she did every time she talked about him. "They had a saying: 'All in, all the time,' and I guess it stuck with me. If I put my foot into something, I'm not going to walk away from it without a damn good reason."

I kissed her because it was so beautiful. Her words. Her heart. Her soul. I made my own promise to her. All in. All the time. For as long as she'd let me.

Chatper Twenty-four

Tristan

THE GOOD ONES
Performed by Gabby Barrett

Once I told Hannah we were having a sleepover at Brady's, she giggled and flung herself into his lap. "Where are we going to sleep?" she asked him.

He cleared his throat. "Well, my room is actually over the garage. Would you like to see it?"

She nodded.

We said goodnight to his family, and he led us out the back door to the stairs hidden by a tall fence. The stairs weren't visible from the street, and I realized how perfect this place was for Brady to hide out. I instantly regretted the thoughts I'd had about it seeming juvenile for him to be staying with his parents. It wasn't juvenile at all. It was self-preservation. Survival.

The apartment was pretty bare: a couch, a small kitchenette with two stools at the built-in bar, a ginormous TV, and musical instruments, including a saxophone, a guitar, and a keyboard that Hannah went running to as soon as she was inside.

"This is way bigger than mine," she said.

"Well, I'm way bigger than you, so that seems fair." Brady smiled at her. "Let me get you something to sleep in."

He walked into the bedroom, and I followed. This room was as bare as the other one. A double-sized bed with a plain comforter. A dresser with nothing on it but the trunk my grandmother had given him. I swallowed hard at it.

"Have you opened it?" I asked, trying not to choke on the emotion of the question.

He saw my glance at the box and nodded. "I did."

"Was it like Pandora's box?" I tried to tease.

His hands in the dresser drawer stilled as he turned to take me in. "You know, in some ways, it was."

What had my grandmother put in there? How did it affect me? Because Brady's look left no doubt that it had in some way. I looked away from the gaze, unsure what to feel, because whatever this was between the two of us was already precarious.

He pulled out two T-shirts and a pair of sweats. "Everything will be huge, but it'll at least be more comfortable than jeans."

I agreed. I took the clothes and called Hannah. "Come wash up, *Chiquita*."

She came running into the room, taking it in with a small frown before saying, "Brady, your room needs help."

A deep chuckle broke from inside his chest that I couldn't help joining in.

"It really does," he said. "And now that I'm

planning on being here more than I was before, maybe you can give me some ideas."

"You definitely need a lava lamp!"

He chuckled again. "I'll go start a list."

He left us, and I took Hannah into the small bathroom where she washed her face, and I used Brady's comb to brush her hair. It was strangely personal and impersonal all at the same time.

She changed into a *Ghost* album T-shirt that hit her ankles. She looked adorable in Brady's clothes, but my wearing them brought back painful hints of another man's clothes I'd worn for way too long. But I'd never worn Darren's bottoms, and I had to roll down the waist and roll up the cuffs of Brady's sweats to even make them stay on. It would almost be better to go without them at all.

I tucked Hannah into the bed, phyllo style.

"I'll join you in a little bit," I told her. "But for now, I want you to try and go to sleep. It's been a long day."

"I miss Molly," she said. Brady had assured me the team was taking care of her, but I missed her too. There weren't many times since she'd come into my life that we hadn't all been together. A handful. So rare they could probably be counted on two hands.

"I do too. She'll need extra treats tomorrow when we get home." I kissed her on the top of her head and stood. "I love you to infinity and back."

"Mommy?"

"Yes, *Chiquita*?"

"I think Grams sent us Brady so we wouldn't be so sad. Don't you?"

Her innocent words hit me hard in the chest,

making it difficult to breathe. I glanced over at the box on the dresser, wondering if it was more true than Hannah even meant. Had Grams asked him to look out for us the way Darren had asked Nash? Were we just another obligation?

I shook my head to clear the thought before it could fester.

No. Brady felt something for me. For us. I could read it in his eyes and his touch and his smile. Regardless of whatever Grams had said to him, we weren't that. We weren't an obligation.

"I think you might be right," I said softly.

"I love you, Mommy."

I kissed her on the top of her head one more time and then left, leaving the door open a little so the dim stove light shone into the room slightly. I didn't want her to wake somewhere she didn't know without me, but there was also no way I could sleep yet.

When I turned around, Brady was sitting on the couch, a notebook in his hand. He was scribbling and erasing and scribbling again. He was a stunning mix of golden colors that made me ache in an intense way I was still trying to reconcile with my lost love. In the house earlier, he'd held his nephew, feeding him a bottle while Cassidy cooked, and the view had stalled my heart completely. He'd had this adoring look on his face watching the tiny baby, and I'd realized he looked at Hannah the same way.

It made him almost completely irresistible.

I made my way toward him, and the movement brought his eyes up. He shut the pad and slid it onto the coffee table, eyeing me in his clothes. He patted the seat next to him. I was suddenly nervous again. Like I had been on Saturday after Hannah had gone to bed. Before we'd shed our tops and lost ourselves in nothing but touch, and skin, and emotion.

They'd been heady kisses, and just the recollection of them warmed my body.

I sat down next to him, and he pulled me up tight, tucking me under his arm.

"Can I ask you something?" I spoke, tilting my head so I could see his face.

"Anything."

"Is living the dream worth it?"

He considered my question before replying, "Yes and no."

"What do you mean?"

"Making music and singing to a crowd…it's all I've wanted since my hands first touched the keys. Elana…she insisted I was good enough. If she hadn't pushed me to submit my audition tape to Juilliard, I feel like my life would have been totally different. I wouldn't have met Ava. We wouldn't have played at Georgie's salon, and Blake Abbott wouldn't have found us. None of it would have happened."

"You didn't want to apply to Juilliard?" I asked.

"I did, but when my mom found out, she was furious. She told me it was ridiculous to have such lofty expectations, and it made me think she might be right, that I was reaching for stars that were billions of light-years away instead of settling for the moon."

The thought of his mom putting him down tore at my soul. I could never imagine saying those words to Hannah. To stop her from working toward her dream.

"That must have hurt," I said softly.

Pain flitted across his face before he put it away behind a wry smile. "It did. Elana caught me as I started to destroy the tapes. She made me listen to about a hundred albums after that—first albums and last albums so I could hear the difference in the tone and skill of the artists. She said I might not be as good as I would be someday, but I had as much talent as any of the people we'd just listened to and that not trying would be like thumbing my nose at fate."

Thoughts of Grams normally stabbed at me, but as I sat there wrapped in Brady's arms, all I could think about was how glad I was she'd been there for him.

"What did your mom say when you got accepted?" I asked.

He chuckled. "She said it was a moot point because they didn't have the money to send me there, especially when I could get a free education at Wilson-Jacobs."

"You went anyway?" I couldn't imagine how much courage it must have taken to do that. To step away from everything he knew without the financial security. I hadn't had to do that, ever. Not until now, when I was struggling to fix the mess Grams had left.

"Mom's never quite forgiven me for leaving."

The tension that was there when he talked about his mom made more sense, but it was hard to reconcile the version of her he'd just shared to the laughing woman I'd spent the afternoon with.

"She's not the evil stepmother of my story," he said, and I realized my expression must have revealed my conflicting emotions. "Elana was right when she told me my mom was afraid that if I left the nest, I'd never come back home. And, to be fair, I really haven't. I let her down in a lot of ways."

This filled me with a wave of anger. "How could

you possibly have let her down? Not only are you successful and passionate about what you do, you use it to help others. I've heard from Dani and Nash about the charities you give to, the people you help."

He didn't look like he believed me, and I realized his being there for Cassidy was all tied to this twisted relationship with his mom. I understood how relationships could get so skewed so quickly. Look at what Grams' estate had done to Bailey's and my relationship. Hell, it had even stutter-stepped my relationship with my mom. But in my heart, I knew that the good Brady did outweighed anything he could have done by staying in Grand Orchard.

I swallowed hard. Would he stay now because of me? Would that prevent him from doing even more good in the world?

"If you had one wish, would you change what you've done?" I asked.

He thought for barely a second before he was shaking his head. "The only thing I'd wish was that Ava was singing next to me."

He'd mentioned her before. A memory of a dark-haired woman with a throaty, sexy voice tugged at the edges of my brain. She'd been at Mac and Georgie's wedding, I thought. At Dani and Nash's as well, but I didn't think we'd ever truly been introduced.

"We were at Juilliard together," he explained into my silence. "She was my songwriting partner then as much as she is now. When I got signed, they wanted both of us—a duet—but she chose a different path."

"Wow. Not many people would be able to walk away from something like that," I said. Brady's voice was filled with emotion when he spoke of her, and I wondered if he'd loved her. I wondered if there had ever been anyone in his life whom he'd loved like I'd loved Darren.

"She'd been controlled her whole life and couldn't allow herself back into a situation where she wouldn't be the one determining what happened to her."

I was quiet for a moment. "Did you…do you love her?"

His brown eyes met my lighter ones. "Yes. Like a sister. There was a brief time, when we were first at Juilliard together, that I would have done about anything to be the guy she chose. But I realized early on that we weren't meant to be in that way. Our paths had crossed because of the music and not because of our hearts. But even without loving each other romantically, our souls are still tied together somehow because we get each other. The words. The chords. They always seem to fit."

Like every time Brady drew emotion from me, I was a mix of them. Not quite jealous at the thought of someone else being tied to him in some way, but also joy that he had someone who was that important to him who was helping him in this chaotic business.

It was like the emotions I used to have about Nash and Silver Team. It had been hard to share Darren, but I'd known he needed them. They'd been a part of him in a way I could have never been, but it hadn't changed or dimmed the love we felt for each other.

"Can I ask *you* something?" He twisted my words back at me, and my heart hammered. I nodded.

"Do you ever wonder what would have happened if he hadn't been a SEAL?"

I fidgeted with the wedding ring that was now on my right hand. He saw it, and instead of getting upset about it, as a lot of guys might have been, his fingers joined mine, twisting it for me. I wasn't sure I'd ever be able to remove it, and I somehow got the sense that he wouldn't ask me to.

"Yes," I breathed out. "But it's like the chicken and the egg question, because if he hadn't been a SEAL, he wouldn't have been Darren, and then I probably wouldn't have fallen in love with him."

It felt strange to be talking about Darren with Brady. To be talking about him with a man I wanted to kiss for hours and see naked in a bed next to me. A man who I wanted, in many ways, so I could finally put to rest the images haunting me of my husband. Not replacing them as much as taking over for them. Which wasn't really right either because I didn't expect Brady to be Darren.

I blew out a frustrated breath.

"I'm sorry," he said. "I didn't mean to cause you pain."

I put my hand on his jaw, the beard rough and comforting against my palm.

"You didn't. I just… Sometimes it's hard to explain how I feel, even to myself."

His hand traveled from my ring, up my arm, under the sleeve of his shirt I was wearing, and back down. His other hand found the hem of the T-shirt, sliding underneath it, running over my stomach. Flickering lights surrounded me at his touch, pushing everything aside but him and me and the pulse that quickened the blood flowing through my veins.

"I don't want you to not talk about him around me," he said quietly.

I gulped on the wave of physical and emotional pain that filled me.

"Thank you for saying that."

"I can't be him…" His words slid away before continuing. "I don't want to be him. But I do want to matter to you and Hannah. I want…to be yours."

Hannah's words filled my head—Grams bringing Brady to us to make sure we didn't feel so sad anymore. Maybe my dead husband and grandmother had both conspired to make this happen. Me. Brady. Someone who could understand Hannah and the music inside her. Someone who understood the need to create inside me.

"I think we'd really like that," I said. Then, I lost myself to his kisses and his touch. The kind full of want and need and hope and futures. Ones that made me forget I was once filled with loss. Ones that seemed to increase the size of my heart so I didn't have to carve Darren out of it to fit Brady in, but so I could fit them both.

This was another beautiful moment that needed to be lived fully. Remembered.

I turned in his arms, straddling him, our kisses increasing the pace at which our hearts beat. Our bodies aligning through the clothes in a perfectly glorious way. Our touch flowing over the top and underneath the material like pubescent teens, seeking a relief that wouldn't come from bodies fully clothed.

He groaned, deep and guttural, and I felt it all the way down into the depths of me as my hips skated over his jeans, the sweats doing very little to hide the hardness of him pressing against his zipper.

He slid a hand inside the waistline of the sweats, floating gently over my hips and finding my heat and curling into me. I gasped, eyes opening to meet his brown ones, concern filling them as if he had taken things one step too far, and his hand stilled.

"Don't you dare stop," I said softly, reassuring him and me at the same time.

I could do this. I needed this. I needed him.

He smiled that wide Brady smile, wicked and charming all at once, knocking me out of myself. Knocking me out of my mind that thought too much so I was left with just my artist brain, simply feeling with my soul. Feeling every plunge of his graceful fingers. Feeling every hopeful emotion pouring from him. I came hard, my body quivering and gasping while my heart marched one step closer to his.

♫ ♫ ♫

My phone buzzed on the nightstand by the bed in Brady's room. Hannah was passed out next to me, arms and legs flung in every direction. Lying in his bed only brought back thoughts of his touch and the make-out session on his couch.

I'd tried to return the favor of the orgasm he'd given me only to have him pull me away, saying, "If you touch me, I'm going to be so loud that not only will Hannah hear, but so will every single one of those media hounds outside."

It had sent more thrills of desire over me. The knowledge that he'd be loud while we made love, and that I'd be the one to make him do so. It felt intoxicating and foreign. Doors I'd closed finding their way open again.

The phone vibrated again, and I grabbed it before it could wake Hannah.

STACY: Are you okay? I tried to see

*you, but the security team was all over
your house and said you weren't there.*

Well, hell. What was the right answer to that? We'd talked the day before in the middle of game day with Brady's family, so she knew where we were and what had happened.

ME: I'm at Brady's.

I could imagine the mischievous look in her eye over that fact.

STACY: Well. Um. Wow.

*ME: Get your mind out of the gutter,
lady.*

I responded before she could say anything else.

*ME: They weren't done installing the
alarm. Hannah and I slept in his bed.
He slept on the couch. I'm hoping we'll
be able to go back to the store and our
house today.*

*STACY: The news vans were still
staked out at both places.*

I groaned. A week. Marco had said it would take a week for things to cool down, and Brady had agreed. On the one hand, I didn't think I wanted the store to be closed for that long, but on the other hand, it wasn't like the tiny bit of money I'd bring in over the course of a few days was going to pay off the loan and save *La Musica* from William Chan's grubby hands.

ME: Okay. I'll keep you posted on where we'll be.

STACY: You're always welcome here. You know that, right?

ME: I do. But I don't want to bring this zoo to your house. Plus, you need to just concentrate on the school this week. How'd it go yesterday?

STACY: It looks UH-MAZ-ING! I can't wait for you to see it.

ME: Me either!

I had just set the phone down when it vibrated again. A call, my mother's face appearing on the screen.

I slid out of the bed, creeping out of the room, past Brady who was asleep on his stomach, bare-chested, a pair of sweats riding low at his waist and almost making me forget my mom in the desire to join him there.

The vibration persisted, and I slipped out of the apartment onto the landing, sitting with my feet on the first step. I shivered. It was still cold in the mornings even as we moved closer to spring.

"Morning, Mom. What's up?" I asked.

"Isn't that really my question for you? You're all over the news," she said.

I sighed.

"What's going on, Tristan?" she asked. "Are you dating Brady O'Neil?"

"Did you know that Brady was Cormac?" I asked.

"Cormac? As in the kid who used to work at *La Musica* for your grandmother?" The frown was apparent in her voice.

"Yep, the one and the same."

"Brady O'Neil is Cormac?" she said again, stunned, and I laughed.

"At least I don't feel like I was the last one to find out."

She blew out a sigh. "That woman had more tricks up her sleeve than a full-on magician."

The words made me think of the trunk sitting on Brady's dresser again.

"Yep. Took me totally by surprise."

"Well, you didn't look that surprised in the video of the two of you dancing. You looked…" Mom's voice cracked. "Happy."

Had I? It was hard to avoid the twinges of guilt that still invaded me at the thought of dating someone new. I'd given my life to Darren. For better, for worse… but death had parted us.

When I still didn't say anything, Mom spoke again. "Are you happy? What does Hannah think of all this? Are you dating him?"

"Hannah is overjoyed to have someone to play piano with. Molly has already decided she'll roll over for him when she wouldn't for anyone but Grams. And me… I'm still figuring it all out, but it feels…" I didn't know what to say, so I resorted to a partial truth. "It feels good."

"Dad and I thought we'd come up early if you needed help, but maybe you don't need as much as we thought," she said, teasing. I was glad to hear the tease after the tension that had existed for weeks between

us.

"I'd love to see you whenever you want to come," I told her, meaning it. I'd do just about anything to help heal the divide that Grams' will had left behind in its wake.

She said she'd let me know, and we hung up with "I love yous" in the air.

When I went back in, Brady was sitting up, and Hannah was at the keyboard.

"You look good," Brady said with a smirk that I couldn't help matching. His broad chest almost glowed in the light streaming in through the shutters.

"Right back at you," I said, and his grin widened.

I went over to my daughter, pulled her away from the keyboard, swung her around, and kissed her cheeks. "Morning, *Chiquita*."

"Morning, Mommy. Brady said he'd teach me another song."

Before I could think about it, Brady was at our side, pulling both of us into his arms, placing a kiss on my cheek much as I'd just done to Hannah. Being wrapped up like a family sent warm bliss through my veins. I'd wanted this more than I ever thought…to be a family again. I only hoped that my desire to have this, the three of us as a unit, wouldn't cloud my judgment when it came to the famous country-rock star.

Then, his words from the night before settled over me. *I want to be yours.*

I met his eyes, breath catching at the joy that radiated from them.

This was going to be okay.

Chapter Twenty-five

Brady

IN CASE YOU DIDN'T KNOW
Performed by Brett Young

Holding Tristan and Hannah felt like the best damn thing that had ever happened to me. Better than being on the stage and accepting my first Grammy, which I thought was something that could never be topped. But this… Their smiles… The happiness spinning in the air… It was more satisfying than I'd ever even imagined. It was *more*. It was exactly what I'd been searching for, and I knew it as strongly as I'd known music was my life the first time my hands had touched the piano.

"I absolutely will teach you a new song," I told Hannah, my voice deep with emotions I was pretty sure Tristan could see clearly on my face. "But I can't possibly do it on an empty stomach. How do donuts with extra bacon sound?"

I knew before her little face twisted with disgust that Hannah was going to object.

"Donuts and bacon are very, very bad for you," she told me with a little frown.

Tristan made a sound as if she'd protest, but I spoke before she could. "Cassidy makes donuts about as healthy as you'll ever see them because they're baked instead of fried. And she only lets me eat turkey bacon when I'm home. Let's go see if she'll make them for us today."

Hannah didn't look like she was convinced.

I reluctantly let the two females go in order to drag a T-shirt over my bare chest from where I'd thrown it after Tristan had gone to bed the night before. After I'd kissed and caressed her into a gasping orgasm that had spread an odd sense of pleasure and pride through me. I'd wanted to continue making slow and steady love to her so I could hear that same sound repeatedly, but I couldn't because I knew I'd be loud and throaty as I took her, and there was a little girl a few steps away with the door open. I wouldn't be irresponsible. Not with her. Not with Tristan.

The three of us made our way into my parents' house to find it filled with more people than I'd expected. Lee and Alice sat at the table while Cassidy cooked breakfast at the stove behind her. Mom was rocking Chevelle and laughing at something Lee had said. It felt like a Sunday morning on a Tuesday. It felt like maybe my two separate worlds that were slowly blending together might actually fit somehow.

I hugged Alice. Her hair was black after months of being fuschia, and it made her gray eyes appear almost lilac. She was dressed like me: Chucks and jeans and a T-shirt. Except, her shirt had a rainbow with "black trans lives matter" written across it.

"Thanks for coming, Alice. How bad does Becca hate me for taking you away from her right now?" I asked her.

"She's got her head so deep into research for her next novel, I think she'll only realize I'm not there when no one puts food in front of the computer," she said with a smile and not a single trace of bitterness for the fact her girlfriend would be lost in a made-up world.

Alice looked at Tristan who had Hannah still wrapped in her arms.

She stepped forward and stuck out a hand. "It's nice to meet the first person to make Brady O'Neil stop chasing his tail…or other tails?"

Tristan flushed but took Alice's hand. "Um. Nice to meet you too."

"Hey, Stevie," Alice said to Hannah, and the little girl smiled, her top hat barely hanging on as she rested against Tristan's shoulder.

"I'm Hannah, not Stevie," she said.

"Well, dang, you could be her twin."

I squeezed Lee's shoulder. He was in a suit at eight in the morning, and I was sure he'd traveled a good portion of the night, but you'd never know it. He looked as put together as always, his black hair shining, his smooth, tan skin glowing. Lee was ageless in a way that fascinated me. He was older than me by about fifteen years, and while my face and body had aged considerably in the years since we'd first been brought together, Lee hadn't changed one bit.

He tweaked his glasses before standing and taking a turn at shaking Tristan's hand. "Lee. Should I be apologizing for this nuisance?" he asked, waving his head at me.

I laughed.

"I hardly think she'll need an apology after—"

Tristan's hand on my mouth halted me, and I grinned behind it. I wouldn't have said anything in front of my mother or Hannah that would've been too bad—only a little innuendo to toss back at my manager's words.

She wasn't upset with me, though. Her face was lit up with a brilliant smile.

I turned to Cassidy and the turkey bacon she was draining on a towel-covered plate. She had two pie dishes set on the counter, with quiche in them. It looked like she'd been up for hours.

I stepped up next to her, stealing a piece of the bacon. I lowered my voice and said, "I'm sorry you're doing all this. Can I help?"

She shook her head, smiling up at me and saying quietly, "This is good practice."

She looked happy. No. Not just happy, really excited, and my chest tightened again. So much damn pleasure filled me this morning. I promised myself if I couldn't make things happen with Kincaid's, we'd find somewhere else in town to start her restaurant. Cassidy deserved this chance.

Soon, we were all seated around the dining room table, which hadn't been used in months because we normally ate in the kitchen. The noise was a soft buzz filling me with a strange sense of completeness. The people I cared about most were surrounding it. Marco and Trevor and the gang deserved some food as well, and as if reading my mind, Cassidy said, "I'm going to take some of this out to the security team."

"Let me help," I said, jumping up.

I felt my mom's eyes on me, and when I looked over, she was actually still smiling. I didn't know what to make of it. She'd smiled through the afternoon yesterday as well. Maybe, for once in my damn life, I wasn't going to let her down.

When we got back, Tristan joined us in the kitchen.

"I'd like to go home so Hannah and I can change and see Molly. Is there any way that can happen?" she asked.

"Absolutely. Maybe we can bring Alice and Lee with us? They'd like to look at the plans for the festival and see what we might be able to do to increase the revenue."

Tristan stared at me like I had five heads, and I realized I'd never told her about the conversation with Lee or our idea about Alice. I'd invaded in on something that was essentially hers, no matter if I'd thrown down a bunch of money into an account for the city to use as a retainer.

I flicked my bands. "Sorry. I— Well, I should have asked you first."

Worry crossed her face. "It isn't that I don't appreciate it, Brady. I just…I can't afford it all."

"Alice and Lee work for me, regardless. It isn't like their salaries are going to change because they're taking a look at the festival arrangements. It's just two more heads. Alice is really good at planning events."

Tristan snorted. "I don't have any doubt about it if she plans your tours for you."

I smiled. "She's kind of the backbone of my entire stage presence. She coordinates with the dancers and choreographers and set designers. She's pretty much a rock star all on her own."

Alice came into the room as the last of my words

left my mouth. "Are you talking about me again? You keep blowing up my ego, and I'm going to think I'm worth even more money."

I winced because it was the money Tristan was worried about. Alice saw it and frowned. Our light banter had never been uncomfortable for either of us, but she held her tongue.

Alice's phone rang, and she stepped away to answer it.

I turned back to Tristan and smiled. "I pushed. I'm pushy. But it's usually when I'm at my best…wouldn't you say?"

The innuendo made Tristan flush a little, and I couldn't help myself from bending to kiss her lightly on the lips. Her mouth parted, and the innocent kiss went up a thousand degrees in a nanosecond. My dad's loud laugh burst through the air, bringing us back to the crowded house.

Tristan stepped back with her lips curling up at the corners and her eyes crinkling as joy radiated from her. "Don't think that wicked smile will always give you a free pass, but I'll let it slide today."

My smile widened. "Wicked, huh? I could get used to being called wicked."

My voice was deep and throaty, and if the house were empty, I probably would have thrown her down on the kitchen floor and finished what we'd started the night before.

Instead, Mom came into the kitchen, carrying a bunch of empty plates. Tristan took them from her, insisting on doing the dishes. I joined her so my family wouldn't be stuck cleaning up after my mess.

When the kitchen was put back to normal, Lee and Alice joined the three of us as we headed to the

SUVs. The cameras and voices broke into a cacophony of light and sound as soon as they saw us. Marco, Trevor, and the team shielded us from the waiting hyenas. I was used to it, but I felt Tristan tremble under my touch, and I saw Hannah's eyes grow wide, which left me feeling like a schmuck for bringing this to their doorstep.

I'd blown into their world without much thought, and it had backfired. I'd focused on what I wanted instead of what was good for everyone, and the guilt hit me. Especially when the crowd at Tristan's was even bigger than the crowd at my house. Marco had to get out and move people from the entrance to the tiny driveway along the side of the house. We all disembarked and headed toward the front door. Waterton's men were there, and they let us in with the lead agent, Prabhjot, handing Tristan back her key.

"Let us get settled, and then you can walk us through the systems you installed, okay?" I said to him. He nodded.

"I'll be out here when you're ready," he said, taking up a post outside the door.

Inside, Molly bounded over to us. She and Hannah were a mix of beads, fringe, and fur as the dog yipped and barked in excitement at seeing her females back with her.

"Go up and wash up, and I'll be right there," Tristan said to Hannah, who took off for the stairs with the dog on her heels like always. Tristan turned to Lee and Alice. "Come on in. Let me get you the festival files. Grams has a lot of it in hard form. I've slowly been transitioning the majority of it online, but it'll give you an idea of what's planned, the schedule, and the vendors we've got coming."

She disappeared into a room off the entryway that I realized for the first time was a home office of sorts. Bookshelves and a desk. I'd never spent much time at Elana's growing up. Our time together had revolved around the music store. Tristan came out with a plastic file box and set it on the dining room table next to a laptop that was already there. She took the lid off the box and started unloading manila folders while she waited for the computer to boot up.

"These are the files going back for the last ten years. The older stuff is in storage at the store, but this will give you the most relevant details." She logged into a website on the computer. "And this is the website for the festival. I can give you numbers when I come back down."

Alice and Lee started diving into the files, and I followed Tristan up the stairs.

We stopped outside the bathroom where we could hear Hannah singing "I Have a Dream." I smiled at the sound. She really was a musical savant.

"Is this really okay?" I asked Tristan as we both listened at the door. "Me…the team?"

"Honestly, the festival has overwhelmed me from the get-go. If they're willing to help with ideas to keep me from screwing it up, I'll forever be grateful. I just don't know how I'll ever be able to repay it."

I pulled her into me, hand going to her cheek, and her eyes fluttered closed.

"Not everything needs to be repaid, *Cari.* Sometimes, we just need to accept help as the gift it is. No strings. No expectation of a return. Sometimes people just do good things because they want to."

"I feel like ever since Darren, that's all I've done. Take. Take. Take." She said it with a tortured regret in her voice that I hated.

"I'm pretty sure Elana didn't see you as taking from her."

"I did. She let me live here rent-free. She got the damn loan just so she could renovate the second floor of the store into my studio…" Her voice broke completely. I put a hand to her neck and pulled her into my chest, crushing her with my arms.

"We're going to figure it out, *Cariño*. I promise," I said.

She nodded, pushing away from me and turning toward the bathroom where her daughter waited. I realized I had a lot of work to do if I was going to be the man at Tristan's side. Work to help her see her worth. Work to help her see the gift she was to others.

♫ ♫ ♫

My team and I spent the majority of the day working with Tristan on the festival. Alice came up with the brilliant idea of adding an online version of the event where people could pay a reduced price to have an all-access pass to the performances via the Internet. We had to clear it with the bands who were already scheduled, but she dove into action-mode to make it happen.

I was hopeful those tickets alone would help offset any real increased costs Tristan saw from the city, and I saw the hope reflected in her eyes at the idea. My chest pressed with happiness. If we could somehow hold this together for her and Elana, anything was worth it. I took Alice to the side later and told her to offer my collaboration with any of the bands who hesitated at signing off if she thought it would sway them.

"Are you sure?" she asked, and I nodded. I was.

While Alice made calls to bands, Lee worked on getting me time with Victoria Chan. She finally agreed to a meeting on Thursday before the interviews Lee had set up with potential new PR managers. While I hated the thought of leaving Tristan and Hannah, heading out of Grand Orchard for a day or so might help smooth out the media circus, which was growing instead of decreasing.

Lee and Alice left after a vegan spaghetti dinner Tristan made them, and I left with them because I wanted to make sure my mom didn't have a reason or a chance to not get on the plane the next day. Kissing Tristan goodbye and trusting her in the hands of men I didn't know very well made my heart pound, so I asked Marco to stay with them.

He didn't look happy about it, but he agreed.

My sacrifice in not staying with Tristan proved itself needed as I was confronted with my mom pacing through the living room with Chevelle, worry written on her face. I was itching to pick up my guitar and write some of the lyrics and chords that had been filling my head since my skin had touched Tristan's the night before, but just like I hadn't stayed with Tristan herself, I didn't dare leave the house. Instead, I stayed until everyone yawned and went off to bed.

Then, I allowed myself to get lost in the *adagio* of loud and soft notes filling me to my core. The depths of my being poured out onto the strings. It wasn't country. It wasn't blues. It was just emotion I could finally share after living so long without it. It was early in the morning before I finally put the guitar down, sending a slew of videos to Ava to filter through when she woke.

Because I'd stayed up so late, I was a twisted mix of exhaustion and pent-up energy when I helped my parents stow their bags in the back of the SUV Trevor was driving them to the airport in. My worlds were weaving themselves together, and instead of feeling uncomfortable, it felt right.

I hugged Mom. "I'm sorry about the media circus."

She returned the hug, and as I stepped away from her, she put a hand to my cheek. "Take care of them all, *mo leanbh*. Not only Cassidy and Chevelle, but these other two females you've dragged into your wild life. They could all be hurt so easily."

My chest tightened at her words. I'd thought she was happy. I thought she'd seen it all as a way for me to look out for everyone, but instead, she made it sound like my team…me…we were all a danger to them. Doubt replaced the calm that had filled me, pulling at the strings and trying to unravel the weave that I just thought I'd started to tie together.

Mom was good at making me doubt myself, and there was no Elana around anymore to unravel the worries Mom embedded in me. I hid the hurt as I turned to hug Dad while Mom got into the SUV.

He placed a hand on my shoulder and said quietly, "You have damn good people working for you, son. I'm not worried about it like your mother is."

Even though it helped to know he didn't feel the same way as Mom, it also wasn't the relief that it should have been. When I didn't respond, he added on, "You're not responsible for Cassidy's hypotonia or her body or even her baby. Your mother needs to realize Cassidy is a grown adult who can and will handle whatever comes her way without you or your mom intervening. Us going back to Ireland…it's a good thing. It will allow me to work on unwinding her some more."

I snorted at the innuendo that was so unexpected from my dad.

He went to get into the vehicle and then turned back with a wink that looked like mine. "Don't you dare tell her I said that."

I laughed, the weight in my chest lightening a little.

Chapter Twenty-six

Tristan

DREAMS

Performed by The Cranberries

Wednesday morning, I woke from another full night of sleep with a twist of hope in my belly that hadn't been there in weeks—maybe not since Grams' passing—and I knew the majority of it was due to Brady O'Neil.

Not only because of the way he made me feel when he was standing next to me, not only for the way my daughter was half in love with him and him with her, but also because his team had taken on the festival and started turning it from an old-school event into a true technological, worldwide phenomenon. Grams would have been beside herself.

If we could get the final okays from the last few bands to show the event live online, I was confident I wouldn't need to use any of Brady's money. The event would take care of itself. Not only that, it might actually be something I could repeat in the future and keep Grams' vision alive when I'd thought it was going to die with her.

My insides flipped with happiness.

If only I could find a way to keep the store from going under as well, I would feel like I'd done everything Grams had needed me to do. In order to do that, I needed more money. And the only way I knew how to make money was from my art.

I hadn't made a killing off of it, but I'd made chunks here and there. Enough to keep my bank account positive. In the media circus of the last few days, I'd completely forgotten the Wilson-Jacobs art competition the dean had mentioned.

I pulled up the college website until I found the page with the contest and sat back stunned. The grand prize was a hundred thousand dollars! The artist selected would have their piece hanging on the huge marble wall in the lobby of the new theater. From the images on the website of the space, I knew exactly what should go there. If the keyhole mural won, it would be hanging in a theater where my vision of Grams would forever be tied to the music she loved. The concerts they'd hold there would be a sort of tribute to the painting and vice versa.

In addition to the grand prize, they were offering two smaller prizes for second and third place, and I certainly wouldn't turn up my nose at any of the cash prizes, the smallest being ten thousand dollars. The deadline for applying was Friday. My heart hammered at the thought that I'd almost missed it even after the dean had told me about it.

While Hannah watched Korean anime and practiced her piano pieces, I spent the morning loading pictures I'd taken of the mural into the application and filling out the questions about the piece and why it was important to me to have it hanging in the theater.

I'd just finished when the doorbell rang.

A peek through the door showed Brady standing there with an enormous smile on his face and a bouquet in his hands. When was the last time a man had brought me flowers? My heart leaped.

I opened the door, and he'd barely gotten inside before he was crushing me in a hug I felt through every single fiber of my being. When I lifted my face to him, he kissed me tenderly, stealing my breath.

"Well. Good morning," I said with a smile, stepping back.

His grin widened. Wicked and charming and all Brady. "It is definitely a good one now."

He handed me the flowers.

"They're beautiful, Brady. Thank you," I said, turning to the kitchen to find a vase for them. He followed along.

"Where's Hannah?" he asked.

"Upstairs. If you wait two more seconds—" I didn't need to finish my sentence as Hannah's music filled the air, and he smiled.

He rocked, hands in his pockets, seeming impossibly nervous for a famous musician.

"So, I was thinking," he started. "How would you and Hannah like to escape Grand Orchard for a few hours?"

"What do you have in mind?" I asked, a bit of doubt flickering through me.

"There just so happens to be a concert in Albany tonight that Hannah might enjoy."

"Yeah?" I said, hands pausing on the bouquet to

look at him.

"But it means you'll be out pretty late, and I'll have to leave from there to go to New York while Trevor brings you back here."

"Who's playing?" I asked.

"ABBA."

He said it as if it wasn't a big deal when we both knew it was. Hannah was going to lose her mind. She was going to jump out of her skin with excitement, and I was going to jump out of my skin with joy because he'd done something so wonderful for her.

"And you were able to get tickets at the last minute?" I said breathlessly, my heart pounding so loud I was sure he could hear it.

His grin was slow and happy, but his shrug was humble. "Well… It's a perk."

"A perk." I was well aware I was talking like an imbecile.

"Kind of a scratch-each-other's-back kind of thing. They can't join the festival schedule because of a prior commitment, but when I found out they were in Albany—"

I kissed him. Lips and tongue and heart all his. Giving him more than I thought I could stand to give and hoping it would be safe at least for a few days or months or years.

The stairs rocked with the sound of Hannah and Molly's feet. We'd just pulled away when they bounced into the kitchen.

"Brady!" she hollered and threw herself at him. He picked her up and hugged her, and my heart was all but lost.

"Guess what? Your mom said I could take the

two of you somewhere special today."

"Where? Where?"

"Wanna go see ABBA live in person?"

Hannah stared at him, mouth hanging open, and then said quietly, reverently, "ABBA? I could actually see them…"

He was nodding, and she tightened her grip around his neck and kissed his cheek. "You are the best friend I ever had. Kiran is going to be mad you're taking his place, but he's never taken me to see ABBA!"

♫ ♫ ♫

Hannah fell asleep on the way to Albany, which I could only think was a good thing. It was going to be a late night. We were in one SUV while Trevor followed us in a second that would take Hannah and me home later while Marco and Brady went to New York City.

I was squished between Brady and Hannah's booster seat. I'd tried to protest that he didn't have to sit in the back with me, but he'd completely ignored me. Now, his hand was holding mine, fingers running along the palm, a soothing motion that I wasn't sure I'd ever felt before.

"She's going to be talking about this for days," I said, giving him a smile he returned with an almost bashful one.

"I don't think I ever remember being that excited about anything when I was her age," he said quietly. "I only remember feeling that kind of joy after music was brought into my life."

I squeezed his hand because I didn't know what

to say to that admission.

"Did you always want to be an artist?" he asked.

I shook my head. "No. I didn't even really do much more than doodle until my freshman year when my art teacher put a paintbrush in my hand, and then everything clicked."

His eyes widened. "You'd never painted before then?"

"Nope. My family is the real outdoorsy type. We surfed, hiked, camped, and basically lived in nature. Bailey, my sister…she hated it from the get-go and begged Mom to enroll her in dance classes. So, she had an entire life filled with dance competitions and cheerleading, while I just continued to do whatever my parents wanted to do. Don't get me wrong. I had friends, and we hung out, but a lot of times, they'd actually come with my parents and me."

"I can't even see you doing any of that," he said honestly.

"I didn't hate it. I liked being around my parents. I was never one of those kids to revolt."

He nodded. "You were a good girl."

The smirk that accompanied his words had me shoving my shoulder into his.

"Not that good."

He growled softly, pulling me into him and nibbling at my ear.

I flung a look in Marco's direction, but the man seemed to be completely oblivious to anything happening behind him. Or at least, he was trained to ignore it. I wondered if he'd had to ignore more than just an ear nibble. Then, I squashed that thought. I already knew there was a long line of people who'd come before me. It didn't matter. It only mattered what happened from here forward.

"So where does Bailey live now?" he asked.

"She lives in Florida, takes care of her triplets, and throws elaborate get-togethers for her husband's architectural firm."

"Holy hell, triplets? Does that run in your family?" He looked shellshocked, and I chuckled.

"No. She did in vitro when they couldn't conceive."

"Are you two close?"

It hurt, the ache that I'd somehow lost my sister in addition to my grandmother. "We were fairly close, but we've never had a shared interest that really brought us together. Still, we talked a couple of times a week before January."

"What happened?"

"She's still angry Grams left me everything and her pretty much nothing."

"I'm sorry," he said.

His hand rubbed along my palm before twirling my wedding band with his fingers. It had me swallowing hard. The tenderness toward the symbol of my love for another man. It caused tears to hit my eyes that I refused to let loose on a day filled with goodness.

"If she knew what a mess Grams had left everything, she probably wouldn't be jealous," I said sarcastically.

"Why haven't you told them? Your family?" he asked.

"It felt wrong…to be like all, 'Hey, you know all this stuff Grams left me? Guess what? I need your help with it all now.'"

He was quiet for a moment. "Do you really think they'd feel that way?"

I liked that he challenged me. That he wasn't just accepting what I'd said at face value, and it did make me wonder. Maybe I wasn't giving my family enough credit. Maybe they would dive in and help, like Brady and his team had. But then it would just be one more thing I'd had to be dug out from under.

"Maybe not, but I wanted to be able to do this on my own. It's ridiculous, because I'm not. You've been the one saving the day every step of the way."

"Throwing money around is easy to do when you have it."

"But it hasn't just been money. You've been teaching Grams' students, and I know you showing up at the city council meeting went a long way to them approving the permits, money or not. You do more than throw money at things, Brady. You're here helping Cassidy. That's not money. That's you and your time."

"I had the best of intentions to be here just for her."

I frowned. "What do you mean? You are here for her."

"But I'm no longer here *just* for her." His eyes bored into mine. "Being in Grand Orchard is doing something for me I never expected. You're doing something for me. You're filling in all these gaps in my soul I could never see before but always felt. Emptiness. When I'm with you, all the holes go away, and all I feel is complete."

I was speechless, throat clogging with words and emotions I didn't know how to speak. Feelings I normally would pour out onto a canvas in order to release them. Instead, I leaned in and devoured his lips, ignoring the fact that we weren't alone. Ignoring the fact that Hannah might wake and see us. I didn't know how else to explain to him that he was doing the same for me. Filling in the voids that had been there for years. Even before Darren had died, his continual absences had littered the fabric of our marriage with cuts. And now, it was a sweet relief to find them finally disappearing.

♫ ♫ ♫

When we got to Albany, we ate dinner at a sushi restaurant in a private back room so we weren't besieged by fans. Brady got Hannah to eat three of the gyozas, and my soul continued to rejoice at how he was mending us with his persistence…with other emotions I was afraid to name.

After, Marco took us to the theater, leading us in the back door. The theater had been built in the 1930s and still held the golden glitz and glamour of that age. Art on the ceilings and walls. Red velvet curtains. Intricate railings and décor.

The colors and textures made my fingers itch for a canvas. It also made me feel underdressed in my T-shirt dress, jean jacket, and boots. Hannah looked slightly more appropriate with her top hat and intricately patterned maroon-and-gold shawl she had on over a pink dress.

Brady wasn't any more dressed up than I was, though, and that had me relaxing. He did appear more like the famous Brady O'Neil tonight with his plaid shirt, a pair of expensive cowboy boots, and even a black cowboy hat. It was like he'd donned his musician role for the purposes of the concert. Maybe because he'd gotten the tickets by being Brady and not Cormac.

His attitude toward Hannah and me was the same. Caring. Smiling. Kind.

Hannah took in the stage with wide eyes, and Brady smiled down at her with tenderness.

"Have you ever played here?" Hannah asked him, turning from the railing we were seated up against to look at him.

He shook his head. "Nope. Maybe you'll beat me to it."

"Me?" Hannah looked surprised. "What do you mean?"

"Well, you keep playing the piano the way you do, and I can imagine a whole host of people who would want to come and see you perform."

I frowned a little. Brady saw my frown, and his smile stalled slightly. He added on, "Of course, you could decide by the age of ten that music isn't your thing anymore, and that would totally be okay, too."

Hannah sat on my lap as she considered what he said with a serious expression before replying, "I think I'll play for a few more years at least."

I couldn't help the small laugh that escaped me, and Brady chuckled along.

The lights went down, ABBA came on, and I lost my daughter. She stared and smiled and sang and danced. She tuned the entire world out except the band and the stage. Brady and I could have disappeared in a cloud of smoke, and it wouldn't have mattered. And I knew then that she would never walk away from music, just like I could never walk away from painting. Our art might have been different, but it was written into our DNA.

I leaned in and kissed Brady's cheek. "Thank you," I said, having to shout to be heard. He rubbed a finger along my face.

"I'd do anything for the two of you," he said back. I wasn't sure I could take it, the pure pleasure and joy rolling through me.

After the concert ended, we waited for it to clear out, and then Marco led us through the back again. Instead of heading out, we went toward the sound of voices and laughter coming from the green rooms.

We approached a small crowd with Agnetha Fältskog, Björn Ulvaeus, Benny Andersson, and Anni-Frid Lyngstad in the middle. Brady lifted Hannah into his arms so she could see better. We waited as the crowd around them chatted and got autographs. Hannah watched with a smile that grew and grew the closer we got to them.

By the time it was our turn, she looked like she'd seen a unicorn her smile was so glorious.

"Why if it isn't Stevie Nicks in the flesh," Agnetha said, grinning at my daughter.

Hannah giggled. "I'm Hannah, but Stevie is my all-time favorite singer ever."

"I'm wounded," Benny said with a hand to his heart.

"Thanks for getting us in," Brady said, stretching out a hand to Benny who shook it.

"Anytime."

The band handed Hannah a CD they'd all signed, ooh'd and ahh'd over her top hat, and then moved on to the next group. We made our way out of the theater to the waiting vehicles with Hannah clutching the CD to her chest like it was a magical lamp.

Hannah hugged Brady tightly, put her hands on both sides of his face so the CD was smooshed up against one of his cheeks, and said, "Thank you for the bestest night in my entire life."

He chuckled. "I'm going to remind you of that someday."

She giggled. "Are you going to teach me how to play 'Dancing Queen'?"

"If that's what you want, then absolutely."

She hugged him before letting me tuck her into the car seat. I shut the door and turned to Brady. Trevor was already in the driver's seat. Marco was getting into the second SUV, ready to take Brady to New York. They had a longer drive ahead of them than we did. He'd done something special for us, but it was going to make his day that much longer.

"I don't even know how to say thank you enough. Not just for today…" I said as tears hit my eyes.

Brady pulled me into him, kissed the side of my head, and whispered, "I want this to work, Tristan. I want us. I want to give you both all the stars."

"We don't need the stars, but I kind of think we might need you." My voice was clogged with emotions.

He adjusted our bodies so he could look down into my face before kissing me tenderly on the lips like he had that morning and on the drive to Albany. Some kind of reverent promise I hoped we both could fulfill. Me. Him. Family.

"I'll call you. It may not be 'til after the meeting with Victoria Chan, but you'll hear from me. I promise," he said and meant it. I could tell.

I'd been surprised when he'd told me he was trying to buy Kincaid's for Cassidy. Not because he wanted to do something for his sister, but because I knew it was about *La Musica* as well. If Cassidy put in a restaurant next to the music store, at least I wouldn't have to worry about William Chan trying to sell off the store to merge it with something bigger. In one move, Brady was trying to change everything for Cassidy and me. A checkmate William wouldn't be able to come back from.

Brady ran his thumb along my jaw before groaning and stepping back.

"It's really hard to walk away from you," he said.

My heart tore a little. I was used to the man I cared about leaving me. I was so used to it that I hadn't really even given it a thought. Darren had left me for months at a time. The fact that I'd see Brady again in a day or so was much easier than the six months at a time I'd lived without Darren.

Brady winked at me, accompanied by his wicked grin, and then got into the SUV with Marco. I clutched my stomach and went around to the other side of the Escalade to climb into the back seat next to Hannah. Her eyes were drooping again, even though she'd slept on the way there. It was after eleven. She normally was asleep for hours by now.

As we drove back to Albany, my brain whirled. Brady had just finished a world tour, but he was set to record a new album soon, which would mean another tour. Weeks and months on the road. My stomach clenched. Was I so predictable that I kept choosing men in my life who were destined to leave me? Brady might not be out on a mission with guns directed at him, but he'd still be gone.

His words of *I want to be yours* were a return volley to my doubts. The fact that he had this enormous life outside of Grand Orchard scared me, but I couldn't let it stop me. Not when he hadn't given me a reason to doubt he wanted it as much as me.

Still, it sobered me. It took the beautiful day we'd spent together and wrapped a gray cloud around it. I didn't want the gray. I wanted the sun to break through with a rainbow coming to life like the first day I'd met him. When the shimmer of rain and sunshine had waved a colored wand over him standing under the *La Musica de Ensueños* sign. I wanted that. I wanted to feel the unicorn moment like my daughter had earlier, but I was clutched with this awful foreboding that the rain was going to hit us and take away the bright colors.

I pushed at the thought. I was just tired. I was letting my internal worries manifest into bigger things. All that mattered right now was Hannah and me caring about Brady and him caring about us. I didn't need to jump to months or years from now. To things that may never happen for more reasons than him being a famous country-rock star.

Chapter Twenty-seven

Brady

GOT WHAT I GOT
Performed by Jason Aldean

When I arrived back in New York City in the wee hours, my loft felt cold. It was full of things that were mine, and yet it still felt empty. The reason was clear.

I'd left Tristan and Hannah.

Our day together had been this magical mix of joy and pleasure. The look on Hannah's face as she'd watched ABBA onstage was irreplaceable. The look of adoration on Tristan's face had struck me dumb.

I missed them when I'd barely said goodbye, but it wasn't just Tristan and Hannah I missed. It was my sister with her vibrant smile and quiet determination and Chevelle with his soft cheeks and tiny cry. When I'd left Cassidy that afternoon, she'd been in the kitchen with ingredients spread about her as she tried different combinations for the restaurant menu. Chevelle had been watching with wide eyes as he happily rocked in the infant chair she'd strapped him into. I wouldn't have left at all if she hadn't said Helen was coming over to work with her. They were planning ways to bring some of the bakery's items into the restaurant so Cass wouldn't have to make everything herself, while still having everything made from scratch.

I realized that Grand Orchard was full of people who brought joy to my life. Even my parents. The apartment felt like a place where I'd never had anything. It felt like a life I'd shed and didn't want to go back to.

When I dragged my ass out of bed the next morning, I had a new determination. My appointment with Victoria Chan was even more important. As I sat in her office, waiting for her to see me, I debated calling Tristan. But it was still fairly early, and I didn't want to wake her if she was still asleep after our late night. I almost jumped when my phone rang just as I was putting it away. I looked down to see Dani's face.

"Hey," I said warily, wondering if she was going to chew me out over Tristan all over again.

"Hey back," she said before diving into business like Dani was so good at doing. "So, I was thinking about the interviews today."

"Yeah?"

"Maybe you should ask them how they'd handle the whole Tristan thing."

"I don't want anyone to say anything about her," I growled. "She shouldn't have to deal with this, Dani."

"It's too late for that," she said. "If you care about her as much as you profess, you have to do something to send the hounds home."

The reality was, I more than cared about Tristan.

More… There was that damn word again. Hannah and Tristan had both written themselves on the pink edges of my heart like a tattoo. One I didn't want to remove.

"I think I've found my Faith," I told her honestly.

"What? Religion? You?" Dani scoffed.

I chuckled. "No, my Faith Hill. When I was younger, I used to say I wanted to be Tim McGraw with my own Faith Hill, and we'd have two kids named Tennessee and Londyn."

"If you name your kid Tennessee, I will personally send Nash to murder you in your sleep."

"You like tossing around his murder capabilities a lot," I teased back.

"He likes being threatening and broody," she said. "But focus, Brady. Back to Tristan. If you give the press nothing, it's just going to get worse. They'll think you have something to hide, and as much as you all look alike, and as interested as Hannah is in music, they might just draw the conclusion she's your love child."

I groaned. We did look alike in some ways with our dirty-blond hair and eyes differing shades of brown. But we didn't look alike enough for me to be Hannah's dad. My heart lurched at that thought. Being there for her for the rest of her life. Being front and center at her first concert. Taking pictures while she got ready to leave for prom. Walking her down the aisle when she got married.

"I'll talk to Tristan," I told her gruffly.

"Denying them isn't going to protect them," she repeated her point, pounding it home. "So, find out what these PR hopefuls might say, and it'll give you a good idea about how much you can trust them with your personal life."

She was right. Dani was always right. I wished to hell she wasn't leaving me, but I also understood the good she was doing with From the Ashes. Her foundation was giving people—whole families—the new beginnings they needed.

Just like I wanted to give Tristan and Hannah the new beginning they deserved.

The male assistant outside Victoria's office kept shooting me looks under his lashes. He was tall and muscular with a sexy, nerdy vibe. When he finally rose and said, "Victoria will see you now," there was an undeniable innuendo to the words.

He held the door open for me, and I winked at him as I went by. The guy flushed about twenty shades of red before asking, "Can I get you anything to drink?"

"No, but thanks," I said, continuing my smile.

The guy stood there until the woman behind the desk finally waved her hand. "Shoo, Demir."

The assistant closed the door, and I turned to meet Victoria Chan for the first time. She had high cheekbones and eyes so dark they appeared black. The depths of them were accentuated with curled black liner. Her silky black hair was up in a do from the forties or fifties. She reminded me of a Chinese Audrey Hepburn who'd aged with more grace than seemed humanly possible.

I stuck out my hand. "Brady O'Neil. Thanks for meeting with me."

She didn't take the hand, and I dropped it, sitting in the chair on the other side of her desk. She was as intimidating as hell. If she couldn't make William do her bidding, I wasn't sure anyone would be able to sway him.

"I'm not sure I can help you, Mr. O'Neil. I may be on the board of the bank, but I leave all the day-to-day business to William. He's proven himself more than capable."

Hardball. I was going to have to play hardball. "I offered him a full fifty thousand dollars over the asking price for one of the properties the bank owns. Cash. And he rejected it. That doesn't seem like the smartest move for the bank's stockholders."

"It's not just about the stockholders, though, is it? William cares a great deal about Grand Orchard. Our entire family does. Where would we be without the support of the community, after all? If William doesn't want to sell the place to you, it's likely he doesn't believe you're in the best interest of the town."

My insides tightened, and I held back the anger I felt at her words.

"I'd just be a silent partner, so it really should have nothing to do with me. My sister, Cassidy—who is well-loved in the community—intends to open a restaurant. Vegan. Farm-to-market. Exactly the kind of place William was talking about. He just doesn't want us to buy Kincaid's because he wants to merge it with the music store next door, and I don't intend on letting him do that."

She eyed me, and I tried not to squirm. It felt like I was under a microscope. One I hadn't been under for a long time. Probably since my Juilliard days and the open mic nights Ava and I had played.

She steepled her fingers together in thought.

"I'm still not sure why I would care," she said.

I looked behind her to the plaques and pictures on the wall. Victoria was with a whole slew of celebrities at different charity events, and there were several charity-of-the-year awards. Her life was about the image she portrayed. The donations she gave at those prestigious events were much more for her than for the cause itself.

"I can donate another fifty thousand toward your charity of choice," I told her.

Her eyes narrowed, and then she chuckled.

"This is exactly why I love dealing with people with money. They'll throw it around like water to get what they want."

It irked me not only because I hated having to buy my way through this. But I wasn't going to let William win any more than I was going to let him take away Cassidy's new dream or Elana's old one. I would be there to help all the women in my life, no matter what it cost. Even if it cost me everything.

"I'll have a talk with William. You can write a check to the Quiet Escape Women's Shelter and leave it with Demir at the desk," she said, turning to her computer, dismissing me in a way very few people did these days.

"I'll have my manager wire the money over. I don't actually carry checks on me. I'm not sure anyone does anymore," I said, and her eyes narrowed at me and my sarcasm while watching me leave. "It'll happen once I get a call from Elsa that the deal is moving forward."

I shut the door behind me and headed out.

"Have a nice day," Demir croaked at me as I got to the office door. I just waved when, normally, I would have at least asked if he wanted a picture. I wasn't in the mood.

Marco was waiting outside the office for me, and

we made our way down to the garage and out into the heavy New York City traffic. The noise and chaos had once felt exciting—inspiring—to me. I'd spent many hours on these streets when I'd been at Juilliard, letting the city fill me with chords. Now, the music inside me was springing from a different well. One that felt stronger and more authentic. Maybe just different.

Maybe just *more*.

When we arrived at Lee's office, the first candidate was already waiting for me. She was a smartly dressed redhead with curves, freckles, and ivory skin. I greeted her with a smile and a handshake before standing behind Lee's desk, leaning up against the wall.

We spent a few minutes on normal job-like things. Her background and her goals. Then, I asked her, "So, I'm sure you've been following the shitstorm up in Grand Orchard. What would you suggest Tristan and I do about it?"

She considered me with a tilt of her head.

"Are you serious about her, or is this just another passing fling?" she asked, and I cringed because I hated that the world would even think it. Dani was right. We needed to say something, and yet I still loathed to talk about Tristan with anyone. I didn't even want to talk about her with Lee. It somehow felt like a sacrilege of the "us" we were building.

"Serious," I said, and her eyes widened in surprise.

"Give *Rolling Stone* an exclusive then," she said. "The whole love story. How you met, who pursued who, the whole shebang."

I hated it, the idea of opening myself up that much

to anyone and letting them see what I felt for her. Sure, Tim and Faith had interviews. They talked about their marriage as well as the ups and downs of it. His alcoholism and partying. Her calling him out on it. They talked about their love, their daughters, their family. But this, with Tristan and I, was new and fragile. The emotions were unnamed even though they felt permanent.

Lee asked her a few more questions before we thanked her, and she left.

He turned to me, adjusting his glasses, and then said, "Well?"

I flicked my leather bands and rubbed a hand over my face. "I don't know, Lee. She seems…impersonal."

"You and Dani had a friendship. Nothing is going to feel the same."

"I'm friends with all of you. Alice. Marco. My band. I don't want anyone in my life who doesn't treat me that way. I don't want to be just a job. That's what happened with Fiona. She only cared about what I could give her at the end of the day."

Lee sighed. "Being professional and not your buddy doesn't mean it's going to end the way Fiona did."

I nodded. "I get that. I do, but I also know friendship breeds a loyalty I won't ever have from people who see me as their paycheck."

He didn't disagree with me but buzzed his assistant to let in the next candidate.

Assad was a skinny young guy with skin so dark I thought he might blend into the leather seat. The black curls on top of his head led to a perfect drop fade which meant time, money, and care. But it wasn't his attractive looks that struck me the most. It was his knee bouncing with an energy and nervousness the rest of his persona seemed to hide.

While we repeated the same round of introductions we had with the redhead, his leg never stopped moving—until I dropped the same question to him as I had to her, and his knee crashed to a halt while he thought. Then, it bounced back to life as he talked.

"Look. Your private life—especially your love life—should be your own. But you *are* a celebrity, and people crave knowledge about you because they see you as a friend—as ridiculous as that sounds. So, instead of asking me what I suggest, I have a question for you. What do you tell your friends? What would you tell *me* if *I* was your friend?"

I sat there for a moment, assessing him and my thoughts before I responded. "I care about her. It's new, so we're keeping it to ourselves while we figure out exactly what it is. Not only for us, but also for her daughter, and I hope everyone will give us the space and privacy to do just that, figure it out."

He was nodding as I spoke. "Yep. That."

I smiled. I liked him. Lee knew it, too. Lee's phone jingled an alert that we both knew by heart by now. He looked down and softly swore.

"What?" I asked, my heart jumping into my throat.

I bent over his shoulder in time to see Cassidy and Tristan on the steps of my parents' house. Tristan looked pale and shaky like she'd just heard the worst news, and Cass was waving her finger in a scolding fashion right before she went skidding off the step, folding like a chair, and hitting the sidewalk with her face.

My entire being cried out. The only thing that would have been worse was if Chevelle and Hannah had been in the picture, which thankfully, they weren't.

My phone was already ringing. Mom's picture. How the hell had she seen it so fast? I sent it to voicemail, failure ringing through me, panic trying to take over.

I hit call on Tristan's name in my phone.

"Brady?" she asked.

"Cassidy," I croaked. "What happened?"

"She's okay. We're at the hospital. They say she needs a couple of stitches, and she's going to need some work on a tooth." Tristan's voice was shaking even as she spoke.

"I'm on my way," I choked out, hanging up and turning to Assad. "You want to prove you can do this job?"

He nodded.

"You're up. You can come with me to Grand Orchard. I'm leaving as soon as Lee can get me on a helicopter."

"What?" Lee exclaimed.

"I need to be there—now. If we could teleport, I'd be willing to pay to do that. Find me a way there, Lee."

♫ ♫ ♫

A little over an hour and a half later, Marco, Assad, and I were climbing out of the helicopter Lee had hired to land us on the hospital's landing pad. We kept low, skirting the blades, and headed for the hospital's doors.

The press was at the hospital, making my stomach clench even tighter. They must have followed Cass and Tristan, and that made me want to send Nash after a few hundred people. We headed directly to Cass's room where Trevor was standing guard with a grim look on his face.

I didn't even acknowledge him as I went inside, but I was pissed at me more than him. It wasn't his fault the press wouldn't stay away. Assad waited outside the room with Marco and Trevor to give me privacy, and I appreciated the fact I hadn't had to tell him I needed it.

Tristan was sitting on the foot of Cassidy's bed, and when she saw me, her eyes filled with tears she blinked away. I wanted to know what had happened. None of the footage we could find online had any sound. Or at least nothing we could hear.

I turned to Cass and wanted to cry myself. The entire right side of her face was scraped, her lip swollen and busted, and she had a bandage over her eyebrow where I assumed the stitches were that Tristan had mentioned. She looked like she'd been assaulted.

"Shit. Cass," I said, remorse and sadness in my voice.

"I'm fine. I don't look fine, but I'm fine. Nothing that will last. Well, maybe a scar," she said, touching the portion of her eyebrow still showing.

Her tone was light, blowing it off as she'd blown off all her falls over the years. No big deal—except this one was. When she talked, I could see her front tooth was chipped. My beautiful sister marred. Guilt rode over me like water over sand, leaving its mark.

"What do the doctors say? Do you have a concussion?"

"They don't think so." She fingered her hairline. "They just want to observe me for a few hours."

"Where's Chevelle?"

"He's with Stacy," Tristan spoke, standing up from the bed, crossing her arms over her middle, and starting to sway in that way I'd come to know so well. "We left the kids with her while I helped Cassidy with some of the business license paperwork, in case you had good news for her today."

I shoved my hand through my hair. "I'm so sorry I wasn't here," I said with remorse.

Cassidy shook her head and winced. "Stop. This is *not* your fault. And if you'd been at my side, nothing would have changed."

"I could have caught you," I said.

"God! No, you couldn't have! It happened too fast," she said, angry. I wasn't sure if it was at me, or herself, or the world.

"What did happen?" I asked.

My phone rang—Mom. I'd avoided her calls as long as I could because I'd needed to know Cass was okay for myself before I answered them.

"Mom," I said, and Cassidy rolled her eyes, provoking another wince.

"Where *were* you?" The accusation and disappointment leaked through the phone.

"She's okay, Mom. Stitches. A chipped tooth. No concussion."

"You promised, *mo leanbh*." The term of

endearment felt like a cuss word.

"I know. I had to go to the city," I told her.

"This is exactly why I said I couldn't leave. We can never count on you to stay." Mom was crying, which only tore my gut up even more. Another goddamn failure I'd never be forgiven for.

The phone was ripped out of my hands. Cassidy had stood and grabbed it before I could even think about it. She wobbled, and I reached out to stabilize her.

"Mom. I'm fine," she said. And I could hear Mom's fraught tone on the other side before Cassidy cut her off. "Listen to me, Mom. Brady was in New York for *me*. Do you understand that? He went for *me*. He's trying to make my dream of owning a restaurant come true. He's been putting himself out for me over and over again, and I don't want you to make him feel bad about it. I'm a grown woman. I have muscle tone issues. I'm going to fall. I'm going to get hurt. No one can prevent that. Not you. Not him. Not being wrapped in bubble wrap."

She took a deep breath.

"You have to stop blaming Brady for my body and my decisions."

The room was silent. The call was silent. Then, Mom must have asked about the restaurant, because Cassidy's lips quirked. "I asked him not to tell you. We're trying to buy Kincaid's, and I didn't want you all up in arms until we knew it could happen."

My sister listened, rolled her eyes, winced, and handed me back my phone.

"She wants to talk to you."

I grabbed the phone.

"Yeah?" I asked.

"I'm upset," Mom said. I didn't know how to respond to that. I was upset as well, but at least she wasn't cursing at me in Gaelic. We both sat there, silent, keeping our thoughts to ourselves.

I heard my dad's voice in the background, the tone encouraging but the words unrecognizable. He'd said Ireland was the space he needed to help Mom work on things, but I was sure this had just put a huge dent in those efforts.

"I'm trying to be here," I said, wanting her to know how much it mattered to me and feeling so much like that twelve-year-old kid who'd lost his sister again. I was almost thirty fucking years old. There was no reason to feel this way, but family easily did it to me. Guilt and regret mixed in with the love.

She sighed. "I know. I just don't think it will ever be enough."

The knife she could wield so easily cut through me, scoring my veins.

"I gotta go," I said. I hung up, turning away from the two women as I tried to fight for control. I wouldn't throw the phone. I wouldn't scream. I wouldn't curse.

I finally breathed in and out deeply. A shudder went through me, and then I turned back. Cass was watching me carefully. Tristan was looking out the window.

"What happened?" I asked.

Cassidy shot Tristan a look, causing the panic I'd first felt on seeing the damn video to invade my body all over again.

"Tristan?" I asked quietly. She looked back at me,

and the tears were no longer in check. They were rolling down her cheeks. I stepped toward her, and she backed away.

It hurt worse than Mom's words. The fact that she stepped away from me. That she wouldn't let me comfort her. I hadn't been able to shield her from shit. Nothing. Staying quiet certainly hadn't helped. The security detail hadn't helped. I'd let them all down.

Chapter Twenty-eight

Tristan

CHIQUITITA
Performed by ABBA

I stared at Brady and was agonized by the hurt on his face as much as the pain rippling through my gut. Hurt and sorrow. Shame and remorse. And seeing him, feeling the way my body responded to his as soon as he'd walked into the room…it didn't help me with any of the emotions I'd felt since the first moment the reporter had flung his words at me.

I was a cheater.

I was the worst kind of low.

I took a breath and told him the truth. "One of the reporters asked about Darren."

The surprise registered in the way his eyes widened before his mouth tightened. The gorgeous, happy smile he was famous for was nowhere in sight. More regrets rushed into me, but I just continued to plow through all of it, knowing I couldn't hide what I felt.

"He asked how I could dishonor the memory of him by dating you when Darren was barely in his grave. When he'd died fighting for our country…"

"Four and a half years," Brady said, voice choked.

It only made the tears come harder that he knew exactly how long it had been. That he knew because he cared about me. But in actuality, it didn't matter if it had been one or two or ten years. The reporter was right. I'd let Darren slip from me in order to feel good. In order to have an orgasm and a few laughs.

I was an awful human being.

"*Cariño*." Brady's voice was deep, and the nickname only brought more tears. I shook my head.

"Don't call me that," I said. "I'm glad you're here. I didn't want to leave Cass alone, but when Stacy brings the baby, I'm going home with her."

"Please don't go," he said, voice cracking, pain showing through.

"I'm going to wait out in the lobby."

And I left. I knew I was running. I knew it with every part of me, but I also couldn't stay. The pain was just too much. I was grateful Stacy came into the hospital carrying Chevelle in his car seat just as I made it downstairs. She gave me a look that said she was ready to knock me over the head, hugged me, and then said she'd be right back after taking the baby to Cassidy.

She didn't say a word to me as we drove back to her house with Trevor following us in the Escalade.

When I walked into Stacy's, Hannah ran and tackled me, pulling me to the ground like she hadn't done in months. "I'm the She-Hulk, Mommy! I got you!"

I laughed over the tears and pain, hugging her

tightly.

"You certainly did, *Chiquita*."

"Is Brady back yet? Did you bring him with you? I want to play the song I made for him."

I sat on the floor, with her tangled about me, as my heart stammered to a stop before it crashed back into a pattern of beats that felt like stutter steps. She'd made him a song? "He's with Cassidy, but I'm sure he'd love to hear it when he gets a chance."

Stacy's eyes met mine over the top of my daughter's hatless head. We'd lost the top hat in our battle with gravity and Hulk-ness.

"Hey, Han, why don't you go make sure Jin doesn't sneak any chocolate chips into the granola bars we're making while I talk to your mom."

"We can have a few chocolate chips, but not too many," Hannah said and then took off at her normal scamper for the kitchen.

My heart tried to lift with the realization that Hannah was allowing herself to have a few unhealthy things mixed in with the strict diet she'd been observing. But because my heart was already so low, the lift barely made a dent. Instead of getting up off the floor where we'd landed next to the sofa, I just pulled myself into a cross-legged position and rested my head against the cushions.

Stacy joined me, our knees and shoulders touching.

"What happened?"

I couldn't repeat it again. It was just too harsh and painful.

"Reality," I said.

"You looked so upset in the video," she said.

"What did they say?"

"Nothing that wasn't true," I told her.

"Tristan. Talk to me," she said.

"I can't right now. I just…need some time to process it."

She hugged me tightly. The very best kind of friend. Knowing when to be there and when to back off, and knowing I'd tell her when I was ready. I was lucky. More than lucky, I was truly blessed. The universe had brought a whole group of beautiful people into my life. People I wasn't sure I'd ever deserved.

I just wanted, for once, to not be the one they were having to pick up off the ground. Not that I wished anything bad on them, I just wanted to be the person providing the shoulder instead of the one taking it.

♫ ♫ ♫

I didn't sleep Thursday night after several nights in a row of deep rest. Instead, I spent the night scrolling mercilessly through social media about Brady. Waiting for the shoe to drop. Waiting for someone to talk about Darren and me, and how I was the shittiest person ever to exist for moving on so quickly after he'd barely been buried.

But nothing ever showed up.

I didn't know if that was because something had changed, and the man had decided not to post it, or if I just wasn't looking in the right places.

I gave up on sleep and social media at about four in the morning. I made a cup of coffee and gave Molly way too many treats. Then, I sat down at the table and started writing names on the metal bunny baskets

Hannah had picked out to give to her friends at her party.

Hannah joined me at around six thirty, her favorite shawl of Grams wrapped around her. I hugged her tightly, breathing in the scent of her, allowing my focus to switch back to the most important thing in my life. My daughter.

She was turning five tomorrow. In so many ways, it seemed impossible while also like it had flown by in a blink of an eye. I was afraid if I blinked again, she'd be graduating high school, and with another blink, she'd be out of college, and then another, she'd have a family of her own.

We'd just finished the baskets and moved on to prepping party platters when my mom and dad arrived. My mom looked so little like me it was sometimes surprising to people that we were related. She was short and dark-haired and curvy. My dad was tall and broad-shouldered and once had hair as blond as mine but now was just a barely-there shade of gray.

"Papa! Grammie!" Hannah cried out with a smile and hugged them. She was such a good hugger. Her enthusiasm was contagious, and I found my smile finding its way back to my face.

My mom turned from her hug of Hannah to me, wrapping me in her arms and holding on. No matter the tension that had sprung between us since the funeral, I knew they loved me. That their first concern was always going to be the well-being of their daughters and their grandchildren.

"Are you okay?" she asked.

Tears hit my eyes because every time I was asked that damn question I couldn't say yes. I wanted so badly just to scream to the world that I was happy and good and fulfilled. I didn't want to be whiny and sad and hurt. So, I forced the smile to stay in place and gave my mother a lie. "I am."

"You looked really upset in that video," she said, pulling back to search my face. I was surprised she'd seen the clip as much as I'd been surprised she'd seen the one of Brady and me dancing, because my mom wasn't one to spend hours trolling social media.

"It's been a little overwhelming, but it's all okay," I said.

She didn't believe me much more than Stacy had the day before. But I was determined not to need more of their shoulders to cry on.

We spent the day getting ready for the party, and I was grateful for the help. It had morphed into a much bigger gathering than I'd originally planned, but I was thrilled Hannah was excited about it. That she was looking forward to something.

Midday, my phone buzzed.

> *THE BRADY O'NEIL: Can I come see you?*

> *ME: My parents are here, so probably not a great idea.*

> *THE BRADY O'NEIL: We need to talk.*

> *ME: There's nothing really to say.*

> *THE BRADY O'NEIL: We both know that isn't true.*

I didn't respond. I couldn't. He tried a few more times during the day, and I couldn't bring myself to respond any of the times. I didn't know what to say to him. The guilt I felt was so harsh and overpowering it was hard to see past it. How quickly and easily I'd let my guard down for him was something I couldn't quite forgive myself for. It wasn't his fault. It was mine.

Nash called, and I let it go to voicemail as well. When I checked later, it was just to let me know what time he and Dani were arriving for the party. But there was a tone in it that said he was in his Nash-the-man-who-has-to-save-me mode. The one he'd been in when Darren had died. The one he'd stayed in until I'd kicked him out of my house and he'd found somebody else to protect—the woman he loved more than life itself.

It stabbed at me. Love. The love I'd had for Darren was like that. All-consuming, overwhelming. My entire world. I'd forgotten that in order to feel something for Brady. Another overwhelming, all-consuming kind of man.

Mom helped Hannah get ready for bed as Dad and I finished hanging the last set of balloons on the porch, and when we came back inside, music from Hannah's keyboard was filling the air. I went upstairs to check on them and make sure she actually made it into bed.

My mom was sitting on the mattress, watching as my daughter's fingers flew along the keyboard. When the song was over, Hannah turned around, a worried frown on her face. "Do you think he'll like it, Grammie?"

My mom had her hand on her chest. "If you'd made it for me, I'd say it was the best thing anyone had given me, so I can't imagine him not liking it."

Hannah sighed, relief coasting over her face, and my gut swirled as I realized the song was the one Hannah had said she'd made up for Brady. The notes had been full of happiness, like Brady himself often was. Joy and smiles and flirtation. It had been full of the dancing fairy notes she'd added at the end of the song he'd made up. My daughter had found a missing piece in him just like I'd thought I had.

"Time for bed! We don't want the birthday girl to be falling asleep in her cake," I said over the emotions.

I tucked my girl in with my normal words of infinity, kissed her on the cheek, and then we left with the lava lamp glowing and the door cracked. It all felt so normal, but also different because Brady had changed things for both of us.

"I can't believe she made that song up," Mom said as we headed downstairs. "Your grandmother was right. She's much more than just talented."

My throat closed at the mention of Grams. I could only nod.

"How are things going with you and Brady?" Mom asked.

My heart twisted painfully, screaming at me for blocking him out and sending him away. For ending it. This was a death, too. One I was forcing. And that knowledge stabbed more holes into me. Holes I'd thought were being filled but had really left behind even more gaps and spaces.

"Honestly, Mom, I don't think it's going to work," I finally said.

"Why not?" She looked concerned.

"For many reasons, but mostly because his life is way bigger than this." I waved my hand around the house but meant my world.

"Tristan—"

"I love you, and I love that you're concerned about me, but I don't want to focus on Brady right now. I want to focus on Hannah, and the festival, and the store."

"You're turning into her. She lived alone after Dad died, and she didn't need to," Mom said, and that made me pause. The fact that Mom had seen the solitary life Grams had lived. Grams had been in her sixties when Gramps had died, and she'd never talked about her time *without* him. She'd only ever talked about their life together. She'd shown me, without words, how she understood my grief, but we'd never really talked about what came after the grief. Maybe neither of us had ever believed there was supposed to be something after it.

Or maybe it was only what I wanted to see because there had certainly been something between Grams and Alejandro. But not enough for her to make a life with him. Maybe that was all that I could have, too. A fling here and there.

It wasn't what my mom wanted to hear from me.

"I'm not saying I'm never going to move on, but I'm also not sure I'm ready for anything serious right now. It isn't fair to Brady or Hannah if I let them assume we're going to be closer than we are," I said, the words tearing at me. *Liar*, my heart screamed.

But I wasn't sure I was lying. If I felt so completely and utterly unfaithful to Darren with the mere mention of his name, it had to mean it was too soon to move on. Didn't it?

Brady

SOMEONE YOU LOVED

Performed by Mitchell Tenpenny

I was nervous when Cassidy, Chevelle, and I arrived at Tristan's house on Saturday. I had my present tied in paper with red velvet paisley swirled on it that reminded me of Hannah's favorite shawl. I was nervous about whether she would even like it. It was such a simple gift. But even more than the nerves over the present, I was anxious about seeing Tristan.

She turned down my request to talk and then hadn't returned any more of my texts or calls on Friday. I didn't know how she'd feel about me showing up, but I couldn't *not* show up for Hannah's birthday. It meant too much to her, and the little girl meant too much to me.

There was security checking IDs against a guest list before letting people through the door, and the guilt hit me all over. Hannah's birthday was being scrutinized by every media outlet on the planet. Because of me.

Cassidy squeezed my arm as cameras took our

pictures.

"It's going to be okay, Brady."

I looked down at my beautiful sister in a flowered skirt and lace top with the baby strapped to her chest, and my heart sagged. Her face was a series of scabs and bruises, the stitches knitted into her eyebrows. I couldn't help but feel it was my fault as much as anything else.

Cassidy had been trying to defend Tristan when she'd fallen. She'd been chewing out the asshat who'd thrown Darren in Tristan's face and lost her balance. I learned that from Trevor, who'd been there for the whole thing. My new PR manager, Assad, had proven his worth by hunting down the man and threatening him with a libel lawsuit if anything like what he'd been insinuating hit the streets, and so far, nothing had, but it didn't make me feel any better.

"Do you think she'll forgive me?" I asked my sister, running a hand over my beardless face and then trying to drag my hand through my hair, realizing there was hardly any of it left to do so. The sides were shaved with the top a mere millimeter of stubble. It was the only way Patty had been able to fix my bad self-chop job. The cut was a completely different look for me, but I didn't hate it. Plus, it served me right for acting in frustration and anger. Things Elana would have berated me for. I wondered if she'd berate me for what I was putting Tristan through as well.

"It's not your fault. There's nothing to forgive," Cass took a turn at defending me.

But it was my fault. I was the one who'd chosen to become a celebrity, not my family. Not the woman who made my heart pound and blood throb at just the thought of her. I was the reason she'd been accused of being unfaithful to the memory of a man she'd loved with all of her. The father of her child. I'd thought maybe I could be enough to make her happy again, but it had backfired. I'd brought her more pain instead.

When we entered the house, the noise was almost louder than the chorus of voices outside asking me for an interview.

The first person I saw was Dani, dark hair up in a twist, clad in yellow and royal blue—both colors she adored because of their meaning which I'd long since forgotten. I hugged her.

"Hey! It's really good to see you," I said.

My ex-PR manager hit me on the shoulder—hard—and I winced.

"That's for dragging Tristan and Hannah into all this." Remorse washed over me again, but before I could respond, she was already turning to the baby in Cassidy's arms as she exclaimed, "Oh, Cassidy, he's gorgeous!"

Dani put her hand on Chevelle's dark hair and smiled down into my sleeping nephew's face. He was pretty fricking adorable. Cassidy's eyes lit up as she looked down at her son. Love. It was bursting from her.

"Brady!" Hannah's voice called out, and I turned to see the little girl skipping toward me, the awkward steps of a little kid who barely knew the motion. My heart soared with pleasure. My name and the smile on her lips. I wanted this girl to be happy.

My arms went around her automatically, lifting her off the ground, swinging her around, and squeezing so tight she groaned and giggled. "Happy birthday, *Chiquita*!" I said, the nickname Tristan called her slipping from me for the first time, but she didn't even register it.

"You cut your hair!" she said, staring at me as her eyes caught onto my present. "What did you get me?"

I laughed. "You'll just have to wait 'til you open your presents to see."

I put her down, but she didn't let go of my hand. "Come meet my papa and grammie," she said as she dragged me from the entryway with Dani and Cass watching us go.

"Whoa," Dani said behind me, a stunned look on her face, and Cass laughed.

"Yeah. You haven't seen anything yet."

When I got to the backyard, it was full of people. Tristan's family, Stacy, her husband and their kids, more kids from the daycare with their parents. The only good thing about the crowd was that very few of them would care that Brady O'Neil had shown up.

"Grammie… Grammie, look, here's my friend Brady," Hannah said, pulling me to a woman who looked nothing like Tristan. She had much deeper brown hair, was short, rounded in a way that spoke of middle age, and exuded an air of cheerful charm. But when she looked at me, there was a wariness to her expression I couldn't quite blame her for.

Her widowed daughter was being courted by a man the entire world had labeled as a flirt and a philanderer. It didn't seem like I was someone who would settle down and protect her daughter's or her granddaughter's hearts. And seeing her doubts was like seeing my mom's all over again. People who didn't believe I could be counted on.

This wasn't a fling. I didn't need to ruin Tristan's life in order to have sex. I could get that anytime I wanted. But it was my fault that all people could see in me was the man who slept around. It was what I'd shown the world for a long time. I wore the flirty, casual image like I wore my plaid shirt and my cowboy boots. Not quite an act, but the version of me I chose to give as Brady O'Neil.

"It's a pleasure to meet you, Mrs. Conrad," I told her with a wide smile, hoping she could see past it to the real me.

"It's Crystal, please. It's good to meet you, too," she said. "Boy, that smile is quite something in person."

"Han, come play. We need someone to be the queen," Kiran said, and Hannah left me without even a glance, joining her friends in the backyard.

Before the air between Crystal and I could get awkward, another voice cut in, deep, saying my name like it meant death. "Brady."

Nash was tall, dark, and the epitome of broody. Since retiring from the military and going to work permanently for his family's flower farm, he hadn't lost an ounce of his muscle or build. He still looked one-hundred-percent badass.

"Nash," I said, our eyes meeting, neither of us backing down. I couldn't help the way I felt about Tristan, and I knew he wanted to protect her like he'd been doing for years. I wanted to tell him that if all I was going to do was bring her pain, I'd back down myself. But I had to figure out if that was true before I walked away. None of those words would come, so we just stared instead.

Dani joined her husband, arm going through his, and asked, "What do you think? Do we need to have everyone help us bury him in the back of the yard?"

Nash chuckled.

Tristan walked out of the house carrying a stack of baskets, and my entire body froze as the world came to a complete stop around her. She was in a maroon, flowered dress I'd never seen on her before, the heart-shaped neckline accentuating the slope of her breasts I'd barely had the pleasure to know and wasn't ready to give up. The skirt hit her hips and flared out, hiding the swell of her curves I wanted to pull tight up against mine. The dress's color brought out the mahogany highlights in her hair, the streaks standing out against the lighter blonde. The mix of color so much like Tristan herself. So many dichotomies of personalities and emotions.

She was breathtaking.

Like the apple trees bursting into bloom in the orchards surrounding our town, I'd seen her start to come to life again. At my touch. At my smiles. At the love I'd freely given. My chest ached at the thought. Love. Goddamn, I did love her. The *more* I felt with her was because of the love.

She thought she was doomed to a sad, lonely life, and all I saw when I looked at her was the vibrant woman she was destined to be. A mix of motherhood and art and heart. She had so much love to give, and selfishly, I wanted it to be mine.

When she saw me, she stopped so quickly it caused the baskets in her hands to topple and fall to the ground. I was at her side in an instant, helping to pick them up.

"I wasn't sure you'd come," she said quietly.

"I wanted to be here for you both," I told her.

We stood up and stared at each other, and it felt like the entire yard paused momentarily to take us in, a ridiculous display of curiosity and judgment circling

us.

An annoyed voice calling out, "Pastore, wait!" dragged our eyes from each other to the back door where William Chan stood, squinting with frustration at his nephew. Pastore blew past us to the enormous, turreted play structure in the yard where Hannah and her friends were running amok.

I couldn't blame him for wanting to escape.

William's eyes landed on Tristan and me, and he straightened his suit, moving toward us. I felt her stiffen next to me, and it took everything I had not to wrap her in my arms to shield her from him.

William eyed me for a minute before saying dryly, "You had to go see Aunt Victoria."

"I figured there had to be at least one person in your family who could still talk sense into you. The question is, did it work?" I grunted out.

He tucked his hands into his pockets. "Elsa is writing the paperwork up as we speak. Cash only."

I shrugged, trying to hide what I really felt. I wanted to dance around the yard, stand on the play structure, and shake my arm to the sky like Rocky, but I didn't. This was only round one, and my joy over it bled away just as quickly as it had come when he smiled smugly and said, "I'm still foreclosing on *La Musica de Ensueños*, though."

Tristan inhaled sharply, and I growled, "This isn't the time or place."

"Tristan, I'm so glad Wesley dragged me with him here today, because I wanted to talk to you in person," a voice said at my shoulder.

I turned to find the dean of Wilson-Jacobs College at my side. I wasn't sure how long she'd been standing there or how much she'd heard, and I could tell Tristan wasn't either because she flushed with embarrassment.

Regardless of what she'd heard, the dean was smart enough to smell the tension wafting between the three of us.

"Dean Torkelson," William acknowledged her.

"Badgering the locals again, William?" she asked.

I held back a laugh.

"Dean, it's so nice to see you again," I said, hugging her.

"Beverly," she insisted, and I couldn't help the grin that took over my face because she hadn't told William to call her by her first name.

"Can I go play, Grandma?" Wesley asked.

"Of course, sweetie," Beverly said, and the boy took off running.

"Elsa will be by to pick Pastore up later," William said, heading for the door.

The dean didn't acknowledge him, but her eyes flitted in his direction as she loud-whispered to Tristan, "I'm not supposed to say a peep, because the formal announcement isn't until tomorrow, but congratulations, the board chose your mural for the theater lobby."

William's feet stalled, and Tristan's mouth fell open. "What?"

Beverly chuckled. "You won the grand prize, my dear. The mural is absolutely stunning."

I had no idea what she was talking about, but if they were talking about the same mural as I suspected, I knew what it meant to Tristan. She wouldn't just give it away when it was her memories of her grandmother.

Beverly was still talking to us, but her eyes were on William again. "Whatever are you going to do with the hundred thousand dollars you won?"

Then, she walked away, following her grandson toward the play structure and the laughing children and leaving a stunned silence in her wake.

My urge for Rocky cheers was coming back. I wouldn't have held back at all if I'd had Tristan's assurance that she wasn't giving up on us. It would have made the wins of the day complete.

William, however, was not of the same mindset. He stood exactly as Beverly had left him, and a quiet rage took over his face. He looked back at Tristan. "Good luck with the store. I have a feeling you'll be closed before the year is out. You can't sustain it the way it is. This town doesn't need a music store anymore."

His cold words stabbed me in the heart, and if they did that to me, I knew they were torturing Tristan even more. I stepped between them. "Like I said before, this isn't the time or place."

William looked around at the eyes we were drawing. Not everyone was paying attention to the conversation, but Nash had suddenly become aware of our rigid stances and was stalking over.

William saw it as well, turned sharply, and left.

I breathed out a sigh, giving Nash my best *Everything's fine* look so he'd stay away and I could talk to Tristan again.

"Are you okay?" I asked quietly, assembling the baskets I'd helped her collect.

She nodded, but I knew her well enough, that the nod was hiding her real mix of emotions.

"You gave away Elana's mural?" I asked. I didn't intend for it to be an accusation as much as deep sorrow that she was giving away the thing that had gotten her through her grief. The art that represented her grandmother in all her forms. On top of that, I was pretty sure it was worth way more than the hundred thousand she was getting for it.

She raised her chin, slightly defiant. "I didn't give it away. I entered it in their contest."

"You didn't have to do it for the money," I said, voice lowering a notch with worry.

"The money was only part of it. This was also about the mural…about Grams."

"We would have found another way."

She glanced around the yard one more time before whispering, "Stop trying to save me."

Then, she grabbed the baskets and walked away, distributing them to the kids so they could search for the eggs she'd hidden. The ones she, Hannah, and I had spent an evening filling. It had been the start of something. I'd felt it in my bones.

I needed to talk to her. I needed to make her see that this thing between us was too big to yield just because of one shitty comment from one shitty human being. But just like the party wasn't the place for William's conversation, it wasn't the place for our conversation either. I'd have to hold on to it until I could get her alone and make her see how much *more* she too deserved out of life. Until I could prove to her that the way we filled the gaps and holes and missing parts of each other was meant to be.

Chapter Thirty

Tristan

WHY WE TRY

Performed by Matthew Mayfield w/ Chelsea Lankes

The party flew by in a blur of people, games, songs, and cake. Hannah was beaming from the start of the day until the very last visitor left. She'd had a good day, and that fact filled me with happiness. I wanted my daughter to have only sunshine kind of days. No more loss. No more heartache. It was ridiculous to assume I could give her that, but for a few more years, I hoped I could at least minimize the sadness.

I placed the musical note pin in tri-colored gold Brady had given her on the dresser. It was to hold her shawls together so she didn't have to grip them while she played. It was beautiful and thoughtful and made my chest hurt in a different way. Not quite sadness but a whirlwind of unknowns.

Seeing Brady at the party today, smiling and joking with people who were not only my friends but his, had made all the feelings I'd been having for him come whooshing back in. I'd tried to bury them behind my wall of memories of Darren, but it seemed that Brady had started his own wall in my heart. He hadn't broken Darren's apart. He hadn't overshadowed it. He'd just started laying a new one, brick by brick, right next to the one already there.

I kissed my girl, rolled her blankets around her tight, and said, "Love you to infinity and back."

Her eyes were already drooping as she said, "I love you more, Mommy."

I walked out of her room and stopped at Grams' door. The mural I'd painted for her was going to be hanging in the college theater. Dean Torkelson had caught me as she was leaving and told me there'd be a plaque under the piece saying it was made in loving memory of Elana Johnson. Just that was worth giving it to them. Like I'd told Brady, the money was secondary, even though it was important, too. It would allow me to keep Grams' store for at least another year.

William's harsh words came back to me. He was right that I wouldn't be able to keep it going forever. I wish she was here to tell me what to do, what she would have wanted me to do with her dreams that were crumbling around me.

I opened her bedroom door with shaky hands, and the smell of peppermint washed over me. The same as the day I'd found her. It hurt so profoundly. The loss of her. The loss of Darren. The loss of Brady. I'd avoided him today because I hadn't known how to tell him goodbye. I hadn't learned how to say the words to someone who was living. I'd only learned how to say them to a grave.

I stood at Grams' dresser, staring down at the dozen or so pictures scattered over the surface. I'd never really paid attention to any of them before, and I realized for the first time there was one of Brady and Grams. He was young, maybe fourteen or fifteen. Skinny and more arms and legs than anything else because he hadn't grown into the man he was yet. They were sitting at the piano in the practice room. They were both smiling, hands on the keys as if they were dueling it out, and Grams had a look of great affection on her face.

She'd loved him as much as she'd loved me.

A touch on my shoulder brought me back with a start. Mom put her arm around my shoulder. "Sometimes I think once I grew up and left Grand Orchard, I forgot who she really was," Mom said sadly. "She was all about the music. Like Hannah. Like you are about your art. I understand now why you felt more comfortable here with her than with us, and I understand why she left you everything. She wanted you to be able to stay if it was what you wanted."

I didn't want to cry, so I choked back the tears and whispered, "Sometimes, I think she knew who I was better than I did myself. For so many years, I was just Darren's wife. The Navy SEAL's wife. Now, I'm Hannah's mom. And here, I'm Grams' *Cari*, a granddaughter she loved. But I'm still not sure who I am or what I want."

Mom shook her head. "You're wrong. You know who you are, Tristan. You're an artist, and a friend, and a woman who loves the people in her life deeply. It's not your fault that either of them died, and you don't owe either of them the rest of your life. Go after what you want because it will be the best way to *honor* them. They'd both want that for you."

The word honor scorched itself through me. I couldn't imagine how my mom had heard about the question the reporter had thrown out at me that had sent me spiraling for two days now. But her emphasis on the word made it clear she had.

"How'd you hear about it?" I asked, still trying to hold the tears at bay.

"That lovely woman, Cassidy, told me."

I didn't know if I was mad or relieved.

Mom picked up the picture I'd been staring at of Brady and Grams. "Do you love him?"

Did I? I felt like we still had so much to learn about each other, but I did love the way he smiled, the way he made me feel, the way he looked after Hannah. The tenderness he gave me and his sister. The way he gave of himself without thought or care to what it meant for him. The possibility of loving him was there like a thought just beyond reach. Lurking. Hovering. Wanting to be known.

"I think I might have blown it with him," I told her, because ghosting him the day before and then all but ignoring him today was not exactly a way to show someone you cared about them.

"If the way he was looking at you during the party is any sign, I would say that is definitely not the case."

I smiled at her weakly. "That's just Brady O'Neil's normal look."

"No, sweetie. He didn't give that look to anyone else in the room but you. It was the look of a man who's found someone he can't live without."

I swallowed hard. There was still so much that might not work with us. He had to know it as well as I did. My life was here, working in a store and painting a few pictures. His life was in New York and all over the globe, making and singing music, filming a TV show. Things that had nothing to do with me or Hannah or this sleepy little town.

"Look. Hannah's asleep. Your dad and I are here for the weekend. Why don't you go talk to him?"

"Now?" I said, looking at the clock that read eight.

"If you feel like you blew it and want to make it up to him, why wait?"

My heart stopped and started. If I went, I wouldn't be able to stop this. I wouldn't be able to walk away unless it fell apart completely. Could I handle it if it did? I'd handled a lot in my life already. Not always well. Not always with my shoulders back and my head held high, but I'd weathered the storms.

What if, in some wild way, we could make it work? God…wouldn't that be worth it? The joy. The love. The feeling that my body belonged tight up against someone else's. Knowledge that every single part of me belonged to him just as every single part of him belonged to me. I'd loved Darren that way—with all of me. Loving someone else besides Darren wasn't dishonoring his memory. Loving someone else didn't require me to choose between whom I loved more. I could love them both differently and equally.

I'd deal with forever and the afterlife when it came time for it.

I looked at myself in the mirror. I was still in the dress I'd bought and worn special for the party. I hadn't purchased anything for me in so long I hadn't even known my size and had to go back twice just to find one that fit the curves of my body. The curves Brady had already seen quite a bit of and hadn't seemed to mind. The ones he'd said would make him too loud to make love to me with Hannah in the room a few feet away.

I gulped and nodded at my reflection, giving myself courage. My mom's face broke into a smile, wide and happy, and I realized it was Grams' smile. I had thought she looked nothing like my grandmother and me, but it was there in our shared smile.

I squeezed her tight before letting her go and heading for the stairs.

Her voice stopped me with my hands on my purse.

"And if you don't come back 'til tomorrow, we won't be worried."

I choked, flushing at the insinuation, and when I looked up, her eyes were twinkling with Grandma's mischief. Another similarity I hadn't seen before.

I left via the back door, keeping to the shadows, and avoiding the few news vans still parked on the street. A lot of them had disappeared for the night, and they were slowly going away altogether. A week, Marco had said, and we were nearing that point. Some other hot celebrity news was sure to make them go scurrying in a different direction soon.

When I got to Brady's street, it was almost empty, as if the media didn't care what he was up to with his family. They only cared if he showed up at my place—the woman with the dead SEAL husband.

Marco saw me coming and smiled. He opened the back gate for me and said as I went by, "He's in the apartment."

He hadn't needed to say it because I could hear the music. The guitar and his gritty voice. I couldn't hear the words, but I could hear the ache in it. It matched the ache in me. Need. Loss. Hope.

I walked up the steps and knocked on the door.

The guitar and his voice went silent, and then I heard his footsteps before he opened it. He was shirtless, in just sweats with his feet bare. My mouth went dry, and my body shook at the thought of his body touching me. Of making me forget everything and anything but him and me and the emotions that pulled around us like a cloak.

"*Cariño*," he said quietly, deeply. The gravel in his voice sent spirals of shivers and goosebumps across me. I'd asked him not to call me it, but I was glad he'd ignored it. I wanted to be his sweetheart.

"I…" I looked down at my toes, the nails painted bright pink in the sandals that were also new. When was the last time I'd painted my toenails before last night? I couldn't even remember. "I was hoping we could talk."

When I looked back up, his eyes were sparkling, and I wasn't sure if it was from unshed tears or if it was just a trick of the light. His lips burst into the wicked smile that had my body thumping…wondering about the full Brady O'Neil Experience.

He stepped back, letting me in, and I put my purse down on the counter before turning back to him. He'd shut the door but hadn't really moved. He was taking me in from the top of my hair down to my painted nails and then back up. A man who wanted a woman. My blood pulsed a reply, but we needed to talk, and I think he knew it as well, because he was ignoring the call of our bodies as much as I was.

I licked my lips, and he groaned quietly.

"I wanted to apologize," I said.

"You don't need to," he insisted, but I was already shaking my head.

"I do. I told you I wanted to try this. Us. I told you I was all in, but then I scrambled away at the first hill that rose before us."

He took two steps closer to me, and I took one step back, bumping into the counter. It halted him, a shadow of doubt coasting over his face, and I didn't want him to doubt me, but I also had to be straight up before I let myself lose myself in his skin.

"I've already been with a man who loved me but couldn't stay by my side. Even if he'd lived…" It didn't hurt quite as much to say it as it used to. "Even if he'd lived, he still would have been gone more than he was home. And you, your lifestyle…it's sort of the same thing."

He smiled and snorted. "I'm not risking my life onstage."

I smiled weakly in return. "Well, no, but it still could risk us."

The grin disappeared from his face, and he moved until he was next to me, grabbing my hand and bringing it to his heart, covering it with his. "I have two things to say to that. First, there is no one on this earth, man or woman or animal"—his lips curled back up—"that could ever make me look twice at them after seeing you. After being with you. You are everything I've ever wanted. You're the *more* I've been looking for since I realized something was missing."

My free hand journeyed to his lips, rubbing a thumb along the bottom one. Full and pink and tempting me. He kissed it, and then pulled it away, joining our hands with the ones already on his chest so that the thump of his heart beat against both our palms. A rhythm. A song I wondered if he would write about.

"Second, when Cass and I first went to look at Kincaid's, it was because I was thinking of building a studio there. Obviously, that's changed, but I'm still hoping to find a place here in Grand Orchard. This way, I don't have to be gone unless I'm on tour. And I can already guarantee you, those tours are going to be much shorter, because just the two nights we've been apart has been enough to make me want to tear out every vein in my body."

I couldn't help the small quirk of my lips at his dramatic words. Music and lyrics. Heart. "I'm not holding you to any of that," I said. "We've hardly gotten to know each other. You might hate everything about me once you really get to know me."

He laughed. "Not possible."

"I'm serious, Brady."

"So am I," he said.

I didn't know how to argue with that. I couldn't argue with his feelings. They were his. Mine felt like I was falling and falling hard, but I didn't want to put the expectation of a lifetime on him.

"There is one thing I ask," I said.

"Anything," he said.

"If we…if we don't work out…" He was shaking his head in disagreement, and I couldn't help how it made my small smile grow into a bigger one. "If we don't work out, you can't forget about Hannah. She's going to count on you, and if you break her heart, I won't be able to forgive you."

He let go of my hands to put them on either side

of my face, moving so our bodies were aligned, touching and curling with longing and desire. "I'd hire Nash to bury me alive if I ever hurt her."

It was a vow. A promise that pulled at the last remaining strings holding my old heart together. It crumbled apart in his hands.

"Can I kiss you now?" he asked, serious. No smile. No tease.

My answer was my lips on his, the sweet sunlight filling the room when our mouths met even though it was night. Everything else disappeared. There was just him. His touch. His tongue. His lips. His voice saying all of my names—*Cari*, *Cariño*, Tristan—like a song he was singing. A beat that was just him and me. A song that was as brand new as the dress I was wearing.

Proving the quote right, the simplest things were really the most beautiful. A kiss. A touch. A word. That was all I ever needed.

Chapter Thirty-one

Brady

DONE

Performed by Chris Janson

She was here in my space, kissing me, and it filled my head with a *rubato* of notes. Random volumes and lengths and tempos, as if there was too much and not enough. I dragged my hand through her colored strands of hair, landing on her neck and trying to pull us closer together when there was already no space between us.

My tongue explored, with a slow circle, the soft recesses of her mouth. The taste of dark chocolate and cream soda overwhelmed me like it had every time we'd kissed. Intoxicatingly sweet and torturously sexy.

Her hands slid across my bare chest. I'd forgotten to put a T-shirt on when I'd gotten out of the shower because I'd had notes filling me that had needed to be played. I'd barely been able to write them down when she'd knocked.

Now, I had more chords flying through me, vibrating at each touch of her hand, at the way she moved slow and steady over my chest. When her fingers curled into the waistband of my sweats, I shuddered in joyous expectation.

I let the hand not tangled in her hair explore the heart-shaped curve of her dress, and her flesh puckered under my touch, her nipples rubbing along the heel of my hand, and I hardened to an almost painful level. Thoughts of her and me with no clothes between us.

I picked her up and set her on the stool, my hand finding the skirt's hem and sliding underneath it, trailing over white silky skin. She pulled her lips away from mine and made her own trail, this one with kisses across my neck and down my chest, licking my hard nipple and making me groan.

My hand skirted the satin of her panties, remembering the beauty of how she'd come, riding my jeans while wearing the sweats I now had on. Remembering the soft gasp, and needing that again, I slipped my fingers underneath, and she moaned again.

"Too many clothes," she panted.

I stopped all my movements, pulling away to look down into her eyes that were no longer honey-colored but darker, stormier. Desire. Lust. For me. I'd seen it in a lot of people's eyes before, but seeing it in hers was almost enough to send me over the edge without having been inside her at all. Without having been the one place I ached to be.

"Are you sure?" I asked.

She was undoing the drawstring on the sweats as a way of answer. I tugged at the zipper on the side of her dress, and before I knew it, we were both naked, taking each other in. We were both artists, and I felt like we were memorizing this moment in unique ways but still ways that would pour out of us. Hers on canvas and mine on keys. Color and song.

I took her hand and led her toward the bedroom where we could explore each other without gravity or counters or chairs getting in our way. Where I could stare at every inch of her and record it in my brain. Where I could be loud and throaty when I came with her wrapped around me.

I kissed her soft, velvety lips again as I laid her down before I stopped touching her to stare at every piece of her once more, burning into my memory every hill and groove. The beauty mark on her rib cage, the gentle stretch marks I was sure were left over from her pregnancy, the way her waist flared in and then curved out with plush skin I couldn't help but squeeze.

"What?" she asked, the longing changing her tone completely. A husky timbre full of a carnality I reacted to with a low moan of my own.

"I want to record every inch of you so I can replay it in my brain whenever you're not with me." The words were wrong because I could see the doubt flash through her after I'd just promised I wasn't leaving for long periods. Not after she'd been left for months on end and then left in the worst way possible. I didn't want to leave her. I wanted her with me every moment.

She journeyed a hand over her stomach as if she might wrap it around herself again, and I pulled it up to my lips, kissing the palm, licking it, and then bending to lick the spot it had touched above her navel. I wanted to leave my own mark on her. A permanent one. I wished it would be as visible as the beauty or stretch marks, but it would have to be written in her veins instead.

I proceeded to touch every ounce of her flesh with fingers and tongue. She tugged at the whisper of my hair that was left, arching into me, and I smiled at my ability to make her breath quicken.

"God… Brady…I need you," she said, gasping as if she were drowning in me.

"I'm not rushing this, *Cariño*," I growled back. "I've been dreaming of it for too many days."

"I'm going to fall apart," she said.

"Good," I said, and I proceeded to make her do just that with my mouth and my hands, a hum of chords bursting from me now and then. Chords without words. Lyrics without a song.

After I'd made her come with my everything but the one part of me straining to be merged with her, I reached for the drawer and the condoms I'd placed there after she'd spent the night in my bed. A hopeful gesture, one my heart sang about coming true.

When I finally settled between her, her face was flushed, eyes glossy, and lips twisted upward. I kissed each corner, and she placed her hands on either side of my face, stroking, reading something inside my eyes. I wondered what she saw. Was it the love I couldn't hide? The deep affection that started somewhere in the pit of my stomach and journeyed outward to every part and extremity. More than ever before.

Fucking *more*…

She inhaled as I entered her, her face bursting into a full smile. The one that lifted her cheeks and crinkled her eyes and shouted out joy. She grabbed my hips and held me still for a second, tightly.

"Are you okay?" I asked.

"The colors. They're spinning so fast," she blew out. Then she began to rock her hips underneath me. "Blue and gold and waves of green."

Our bodies were perfectly joined, hers surrounding us in hues, and mine surrounding us in music. My heart felt like it might explode as much as my body. We moved together in a rhythm I'd never experienced and would want to play every single damn night of my life. I wasn't going anywhere without her. Without this woman who filled me as much as I was filling her.

We moved, a slow *legato* building toward a *crescendo* at the *coda*. A magical piece that was only ours as she purred my name and I growled and shouted out hers in a gritty hue of love and desire as we both came at the top of the piece. A first that would never be able to be repeated. A first that would only turn into a glorious new mix each time we joined again. Slightly different notes but equally as magnificent.

I stilled as the waves broke over us, letting them float through the air like the very last notes in a piece. Then, I twisted so I was on my side, and she was curled up into me, our hearts and bodies trying to return to our quieter state. She rested her head on my shoulder.

"The full Brady O'Neil Experience was quite the wild ride," she said, and I felt the smile that vibrated through her body.

I chuckled. "That still wasn't the full experience, *Cariño*. That was just the opening act."

She laughed. Light. Happy. Fulfilled. It rocked its way into my soul.

"Well, it's a good thing my mom told me to stay as long as I needed. I think I'm going to enjoy the full experience."

I kissed the top of her head. "Give me about ten minutes, and we can start act two."

She was kissing my shoulder and then dipped lower to my chest, and my side, and my waist, before returning to the nipple that she'd tortured earlier, and suddenly I didn't need ten minutes. I didn't even need two.

♫ ♫ ♫

The silence woke me. I'd had my ear pressed to her chest when I'd finally fallen asleep hours after she'd arrived. The beat of her heart had lulled me into a deep slumber, and when I woke, it was gone. No heartbeat. No Tristan.

I ran a hand all the way to the edge of the bed before opening my eyes to confirm the fact that my bed was empty. I sat up, my heart thudding at a pace that was pure anxiety. She'd left. The apartment was way too quiet for her to be in it.

I ran a hand over my short hair, the bristles so unfamiliar to me.

The sun was barely peeking out, and the room was still half in shadows.

Had she left to be home before Hannah woke? My eyes settled on the dresser and the trunk that Elana had left me. I'd come home from the party yesterday and pulled out the albums, looking for the one from Elana's father. There'd been a pattern of notes in one of his songs that I'd suddenly needed to hear again. In doing so, I'd left the letter Elana had written out on the dresser.

I stood and walked over to it. The letter was opened. I'd left it that way. Her words of finding someone for me had hit me all over again when I'd thought I might have lost Tristan. Now, I was worried for a different reason.

Tristan hadn't wanted to be an obligation. Nash had watched over her for so long at Darren's request, and now, this made it seem like I was doing the same—taking care of her for Elana—when it was absolutely not the truth. I loved her. This was a first for me. A first and, hopefully, a last because I wanted to be there for her until we were both too old and gray to move.

I pulled on jeans and a T-shirt and then went to the other room to find my phone. I'd left it on the coffee table while I'd been recording last night. More notes I was still trying to figure out with Ava.

I debated what to send. "I miss you" seemed overly needy and slightly stalkerish after one night tangled together. "Where are you?" seemed demanding and more alpha male than I'd ever been. But both were true. The demand. The aching need.

I settled for, "Are you okay?"

Then, I stared at the phone, willing for her to text back.

She didn't.

Fear started to replace every other emotion. If I hadn't lost her over memories of a dead husband, I certainly wasn't going to lose her over a note from her dead grandmother.

I threw on a pair of shoes, my beanie, and my sunglasses and left. The man on watch outside the gate was one of Waterton's men. Someone I didn't know.

"Hey, the woman who was here…do you know when she left?"

"About twenty minutes ago," he said.

"Which direction did she head?"

He pointed south toward downtown, and I took off in that direction, hoping she'd just gone to get coffee or donuts or just to get fresh air. Hoping she wouldn't think I was ridiculously clingy and needy when I did find her.

Main Street was still shuttered and dark. Sunday meant later starts except for Sweet Lips Bakery. Their warm glow hit the sidewalk with a welcoming light and smell. When I peeked in the window, there was no Tristan, and I moved on before anyone saw me.

Three doors down, the windows of *La Musica* were softly lit. The main lights hadn't been turned on, but the stain-glassed ones over the counter were. When I tried the door, it opened easily. I wanted to curse at Tristan for leaving it that way where anyone could have walked in, but the curse flew out of my lips when I saw her.

She was in the dress from yesterday, arms around her hips, swaying, tears pouring down her cheeks. My heart couldn't stand it. In two steps, I was behind her, enveloping her in my embrace, and I was grateful when she didn't fight me or pull away. She rested her head back against my chest instead, and some of my worries eased.

"*Cariño,*" I breathed out, tortured because she was tortured.

"I'm sorry, I read the note," she said.

My throat tightened, making it hard to swallow the lump that rose immediately at her words. The note.

"I need you to know I'm not with you because of that note." I hoped she heard the sincerity in my words. She turned in my arms, putting her hands on my cheeks.

"I know."

Relief rushed over me.

"Then, why did you leave after reading it?" I asked, puzzled.

"It was the line she wrote. *You both have new memories to make,*" she said. I gulped. Elana hadn't wanted us to hold on to the store, but I couldn't imagine Grand Orchard without it.

I nodded.

"So, it made me wonder…" She turned back to the rows of albums and CDs. "Could we turn this into your studio?"

My heart flew up to my throat, catching on the knot that had already formed there, making it hard to breathe or think or move. Turn the music store into a music studio? I tried to eye the space differently. The size and shape of it. The blocking we'd have to do, the places we'd have to close off, especially if we wanted to rent it out and still give access to the upstairs without impacting the recordings going on.

The practice rooms could be turned into specialized sound booths. Tristan would still have her art studio. I could make music while she painted. A life twined together. Memories built together.

"*La Musica de Ensueños* Studios…" My throat was still clogged and the words coming out stuttered and gritty, but as I said them, my heart leaped and my skin broke out in goosebumps.

She looked up at me, excitement filling her

beautiful eyes. "Really?"

I nodded. It absolutely would work. Our past memories turning into future ones. We could draw clients who needed to work away from the hectic pace of Nashville or New York City. It would cost a lot of money, but I had money to blow. I had money that would be stacked on top of money for decades. I'd bought one residence, the loft in New York. I didn't own a boat or a jet or even a car for that matter. I spent money on my security, my team, and my music, and not much else. My financial advisors had been crawling at me for years to diversify, get some tax write-offs.

The studio would likely lose money, but I didn't care. It wasn't about that. It was about the woman standing in my arms with shining eyes and a heart so big she'd been able to find room in it for me alongside all the people she'd lost.

I kissed her because I didn't have any more words to tell her just how much it meant to me. How deeply I felt it in my bones. Ava was the word part of our duo much more than me. But I could show Tristan what I felt.

Her hands went around my neck, and we lost ourselves in the delightful dancing of our tongues and souls. Our lives had both revolved around a woman who had taught us how to be grown-ups. How to survive life's disappointments as much as the rewards. I wasn't sure if Elana had known that, once Tristan's and my worlds crashed into each other, we wouldn't be able to walk away, but I did think she knew we were both artists lost and needing to be found.

I may have made it to the top of the musical food chain, but I still had been missing something important in my life. The holes had found their way into my music, into my voice and my beats and my rhythms, and I could see them shrinking with every touch and smile and kiss I shared with the gorgeous person in front of me.

A future. A purpose. A goddamn new song to sing that promised to be new and fresh every day.

♫ ♫ ♫

Eight weeks later

The air was hot but not yet heavy like it would be in another few weeks as I stepped out onto the patio with a plate of bean burgers Cass had made. She'd insisted they would hold up to the barbecue, but I wasn't so sure. Not because of how she'd made them, but because I wasn't the kind of guy to grill anything successfully.

The voices in the house followed me out the screen door, and as I looked inside, my heart filled with warmth at what I saw there. It once had been Elana's house, and then it had become Tristan's, and now it was ours. I'd been living with her and Hannah for most of May. Cassidy and Chevelle were fine on their own, but now that my parents were back, there was even less of a reason for me to be at my parents' place.

I watched through the screen door as Cassidy laughed at something Hannah said. The little girl had tied me around not just her pinky, but every single finger she owned, and I loved it just like I loved her. Her top hat was askew, as usual, and the smile on her face was real. I couldn't wait to see how big her smile got at the opening of the festival on Friday. The surprise I had planned for her made me almost as giddy as she looked.

Cassidy came to the screen door. "What are you doing? Are you going to start the burgers or stand there dreaming?"

"Smart-ass," I groused, but it was said with a grin that she matched.

My sister and I were building our dreams next door to each other. It was nothing I'd ever thought possible back when I was a teen. I hadn't ever thought there would be a place where our lives would collide. Maybe because I hadn't known either of our dreams well enough. Or maybe they'd both changed before we'd realized it.

But now, we were in and out of each other's spaces daily. The store. Tristan's. Our parents'. It felt good. It felt right. Without Mom and Dad overshadowing us and our relationship, Cass and I had not only gotten to know each other, but we'd helped each other out as we tore apart and renovated the two spaces standing next to each other on Main Street.

Cass's restaurant was still a few months away from its grand opening, and she still couldn't decide on a name, but the old Kincaid place was slowly turning into a mystical garden. Fountains and ferns and windchimes. So different than the trendy metal and wood of the studio Tristan and I were building in *La Musica,* but also the same because they both had heart in every object and every piece being put into them.

Cass turned, tripped on some unseen object, and steadied herself with her hand on the counter as Mom came by with Chevelle in her arms. Mom's eyes flickered, but she didn't make a big deal of it. Instead, she just patted Cassidy on the shoulder and then came out the door to join me on the patio.

Our parents had barely arrived back in town the weekend before with the school term finally over, and their time in Ireland had come to a close. It meant they'd be in Grand Orchard permanently again. I'd been nervous when they'd shown up at the house this afternoon and been introduced to Tristan's parents for the first time. But so far, everyone had gotten along. Even my mom and me.

I turned back to the grill and placed the burgers on them, jumping back as the flame burst out at me. Mom laughed. "Do I need to ask your dad to come and take over, *mo leanbh*?"

"I got it," I said, watching as the first burger began to ease through the grates. "Maybe."

Mom came a little closer, but not close enough for Chevelle to be caught in the smoke. "You're doing fine."

The rare compliment hit me in the pit of my stomach, and I looked up to find her eyes serious.

"They won't be perfect, but they'll be edible," I said.

"Perfect is often an illusion," Mom responded, and somehow, I knew she was talking about more than bean burgers and the grill. She swallowed, looked down at Chevelle chewing on his fingers, and then back. "I'm sorry."

"What?" I croaked out.

"The last few months, your father and I have had a lot of time to talk…to reflect…me more than him," she said with a wry smile, and I almost couldn't breathe because my mom never admitted weakness. "My frustration at you for not protecting Cassidy was really just a manifestation of my own frustration at myself for not being able to do it either. But the truth is, none of us can ever do enough to protect her. Just like she can't always protect Chevelle, and you won't always be able to protect Hannah."

Hannah's laugh rang out at that exact moment, and my gut tightened. I would do everything and anything in my power to keep her from being hurt, and it made me appreciate my mother more. The way she'd tried so valiantly to look after the daughter who was destined to get hurt repeatedly—at least physically. I couldn't imagine how hard that must have been on my parents.

Long days on her feet as owner and chef of a restaurant weren't going to be easy, and Cassidy had realized she needed to be as strong as her body would ever let her be. So, she'd started a new fitness routine. Once Marco had gotten wind of it, he'd offered to help out. I think it was out of pure boredom, because I rarely seemed to need him these days, especially now that the press had gotten their story and left. It all meant that Cassidy seemed to be getting stronger, even if it was unlikely she would ever hit the average curve for muscle tone.

"I think I understand how you felt more than I ever did," I told her as I watched Molly jump at the treat Hannah was waving above the dog's head.

We were both quiet for a moment as the noise from the house continued to drift over us. Mom took a deep breath and then said, "I'm sorry we didn't share your world with you more, and I am grateful you've found Tristan and are going to be staying in Grand Orchard so we might have a chance to make it up to you."

Tears filled my eyes. "Damn smoke," I said as I

brushed at them, and Mom smiled softly.

I turned back to the grill and flipped the burgers, only destroying the one that had already lost its battle with the grate and the flames.

"You love them a lot," Mom said, looking in at the happy scene in the house.

"I do. I want to marry Tristan. I want the world to know she's mine and I'm hers, but I'm sort of waiting for the right time to ask," I said. "Then, I get afraid it might be too soon, you know?"

Mom didn't get a chance to answer because Hannah was suddenly there, tugging at my sleeve and rocking the plate I was holding precariously.

"Brady, Mom says dinner before cake. Are the burgers ready?" she asked.

I leaned in and said, "How about cake with dinner?"

She grinned back at me. "Maybe."

I liked to think I was responsible for corrupting her health-food-fanatic ways, but I was sure Cassidy had a much bigger influence in that regard. I loaded the burgers onto the plate, and we all went inside. The noise and laughter filled the house in a way Elana would have loved.

"Thanks, lady," I said silently up to the sky.

After dinner, Hannah led the family in singing "Happy Birthday" to me before handing me a small box. When I opened it, it was a custom guitar pic with the three of us on it. A picture we'd taken at the ABBA concert, our faces squished together to fit into the screen. Smiles on all of our faces.

"I love it," I said. "But not as much as I love the real thing."

I scooped both my girls up and kissed their cheeks while our families looked on with rolled eyes and smiles.

Hours later, my family was gone, her parents had retired to the guest room that once had been Tristan's, and I was waiting for her in our room while she tucked in Hannah. I looked about the space that used to be Elana's and that we'd redone. New furniture, new paint, but old and new pictures on the dressers. Elana's, Tristan's, mine, and ours. Old and new memories blending.

When Tristan finally came into the room, it was with a painting turned the wrong way. My heart caught at the look on her face. Her honey eyes were twinkling, her smile wide and full. She'd had paint on her shirt all day because she'd been in the studio before the party, determined to finish something. I understood that drive and hadn't questioned it. I hadn't known she was working on something for me.

"I couldn't wrap it because it was still wet," she said.

She turned it around, and it was a picture of the three of us on burlap. My smile was wide, and my eyes were adoring as I looked down at her and Hannah. We were a wavy reflection in the water, and behind us, in the sky, were hundreds of Chinese lanterns floating away into a dark expanse of midnight blue.

"Happy birthday," she said. I pulled her to me and kissed her long and hard before she pulled her lips away from mine, touching my cheek and saying, "I love you."

It was the first time she'd said it, and it rattled through my veins and deep into my core stronger than the drums that shook my body when I was onstage, the simple three syllables stirring a universe of emotions. I'd said them to her many times since we'd made love the first time. I'd said them in actuality as much as in the songs I'd made and sung to her in the shower or over breakfast or as we walked to the studio hand in hand. And I'd never demanded it back because I knew she was still wrestling with demons of loving another man, and I wouldn't dishonor that—or her—by forcing something I knew she felt by her actions. The words would come in time.

But just like my mom's apology earlier, I hadn't realized how much it actually meant to hear Tristan say it. The tears that had tried to hit earlier filled my eyes all over again, and I pulled her tight up against my chest, emotions flowing through me.

"I love you more than music," I said, and I meant it, looking down at her.

We stood there, staring and reading each other's souls for a long moment before we shed our clothes and did exactly what we were good at together, losing the world. Making love to colors and sounds and beautiful rhythms that had infused every single song I'd chosen to go on my new album. The actual recording might not be for months until the studio was finished, but these moments with her would only embed the emotions into the songs more when they were laid down, the tracks a reflection of us.

Nothing stale or cold or soulless about them.

Love spreading out into the world.

More.

Chapter Thirty-two

Tristan

BUT I DO LOVE YOU
Performed by LeeAnn Rimes

The opening day of the Apple Jam Music Fest had flown by in a beautiful mix of chaos and structure. Brady's team and my family had been working shoulder to shoulder with us as the vendors and bands had filtered into town over the course of the week. The booths had gone up, and the carloads of people had begun arriving. Grand Orchard was a bustle of energy you could feel just by walking down Main Street.

It made me proud to be Grams' granddaughter all over again. That she was responsible for this coming together of people. I was grateful I'd been able to continue it, and I knew for a fact it wouldn't have been possible without the man now performing onstage with his band.

Brady worked the crowd into a frenzy. One I understood because I felt it every single time he was in the same room as me. My veins felt like they were bursting open when he was nearby. And when he touched me, it was like every color of the rainbow blended into us.

Brady was a pretty big artist to open the festival with, but we'd been lucky to have several very high-profile bands sign up since Lee and Alice had come onboard to help us. We had musical legends booked for all three nights, and Sunday we'd be closing the festival with Watery Reflection, who'd just released their thirteenth album only to have it go platinum in record time. I was pretty sure half our ticket sales had been because of Derek Waters and his band, although Brady had brought in his fair share.

I wasn't sure what I'd done to have the worldwide phenomenon known as Brady O'Neil choose me to be at his side. I did know that seeing him like this, onstage, twisting and turning his body, smiling that huge smile at the crowd, was like the tiniest bit of cold water down my back. He was incredible. He could have just about any person in the world that he crooked his finger at, and instead, he'd set his eyes on little ol' me.

Hannah jiggling at my side brought my eyes down to her. She was dressed in a black velvet dress, cowboy boots, Grams' maroon shawl, and her top hat. The fringe of her bangs had been trimmed earlier in the week to match her idol's. As she grew, it seemed she looked more and more like Stevie Nicks. She'd grown almost a half an inch just since her birthday. Two months and our lives had changed completely.

I missed Grams. I missed Darren. But I didn't feel like there were only lonely aches in our lives anymore. Brady had come storming in and filled them.

As Brady finished his song to a round of applause, the stage went dark while he talked to the audience and the stagehands moved the set so that two grand pianos were facing each other. One black. One white. Classic contrasts.

I felt like I was going to throw up at the thought of Hannah walking onto the stage. It was a place she belonged, just like she belonged with Brady and the music they made together, but it was also like opening our doors wide and inviting strangers into our house. Things and people I wouldn't be able to protect her from.

Surprisingly, it was Brady's mom who brought me a shred of comfort. Arlene and Petri had helped more with the festival than I'd ever expected. Not only had they been helping at Cassidy's food booth as a way of promoting her upcoming grand opening, but they'd been running errands for me and smoothing feathers of bands and vendors as needed. Tonight, they'd watched Brady's entire set from the sidelines. Another new thing for them.

"I know you want to keep her safe," Arlene said quietly, eyes going from me to Hannah and then back.

I nodded.

"Brady has her," she told me. "He won't let her fall."

The faith she had in him was new and yet stronger than it had ever been in either of their lifetimes. I hugged her.

"Okay, y'all, for my last song of the night, I have something new I haven't even recorded yet. It's something extra special, and for that, I need to have a little help. Will you please put your hands together for the little lady who has taken over my heart, Hannah Morgan."

I squeezed her hand, kissed her cheek,

straightened her top hat, and said, "I love you to infinity."

"I love you more, Mommy. Gotta go." And she skipped onto the stage as if the thousands of people sitting on the field in lawn chairs and standing and dancing meant nothing to her. As if she'd been in front of thousands of people every time she'd played the piano.

Arlene wrapped her arms around me while my heart thudded with panic, praying to Grams and Darren that they'd watch over her while she opened herself to the world.

The crowd aww'ed when she joined Brady at the front of the stage. She stuck her hand in his.

"Say hello to the world, *Chiquita*," he said, and she waved and did a little curtsey.

The mic taped to her face picked up her little lyrical voice as she said, "Hello, world!"

The crowd burst into laughter and more awws.

"Ready?" he asked her with his heart-stopping Brady smile, and she gave him one back that was as equally heart-stopping.

"Yep."

They moved to the pianos, and he helped her get seated on the white bench, pushing her in closer while the audience ate it up. Then, he covered her mic and whispered something in her ear that made her smile even more before winking. She winked back, and goddamn, my heart wasn't sure it could take much more.

Brady left her to go to the black piano. He ran his fingers over the keys, and Hannah copied him. He grinned at the audience, and Hannah did the same.

They played a little back and forth duel before Brady stopped and said, "Okay, let's hit it."

They broke into the song they'd made up together. It was a song about the things you loved. Rainbows and unicorns. Birthdays and surprises. Baby chicks and ABBA lyrics. It was a happy song, dancing and prancing through the stage and the night air, catchy like "Shake It Off," and would likely be stuck in people's heads for days. My daughter's sweet voice the perfect contrast to his rich, gritty one. Sugar and spice and everything nice.

As they played, the tension in my body eased. She'd not missed a single key. Her voice hadn't cracked. She looked and sounded as if she were playing in the practice room at *La Musica*. As if there were an audience of one instead of being live-streamed to millions.

When the song was over, the crowd went wild, and it was the first time Hannah seemed surprised at all. Her face flushed, and she looked unsure, but Brady was at her side, picking her up, hugging her, holding her for the world to see while she took off her top hat and tipped it at the cameras. The crowd was a storm of claps and stomps and cheers.

"Okay, folks, we have just two more songs for you," Brady said.

"One more," Hannah said with a frown at him that had the crowd chuckling.

From the opposite side stage, a woman emerged. Hannah hadn't seen her yet, but I swore I was going to keel over from the sweet ache of it.

The woman's top hat and shawl shimmered in the stage lights.

"Well, *Chiquita*, I threw in an extra one because

I thought you might want to play with this lovely woman." Brady turned with my daughter in his arms so she could see Stevie Nicks for the first time.

Hannah's face was the epitome of stunned. Wide eyes, mouth hanging open, and she smiled so hard I thought it would break her cheeks. "Whoa…" Hannah said quietly.

Stevie Nicks joined them. Her smile was beautiful. She looked nowhere near her real age, even though she still looked old. "Like that hat, beautiful," Stevie said, and Hannah beamed at her.

"What do you think of our surprise?" Brady asked the audience who roared their approval.

"Thank you for having me," Stevie said. "The band and I were honored to be in attendance at the very first Apple Jam Music Fest, and I'm grateful to be back honoring the person who started it all. Elana Johnson was a beautiful human being and will be missed."

The crowd agreed. Shouts of "We love you, Elana," made my heart clench and tears hit the back of my eyes I wasn't sure I could hold back much longer. But, God, would Grams have eaten it up.

Stevie looked down at Hannah. "I hear you've been learning to play "Has Anyone Ever Written Anything For You," is that correct?"

Hannah nodded.

"Would you like to perform it with me?" Stevie asked.

"Yes, please. Very much," Hannah said, and the crowd was a mush pot of affection for my girl.

Brady took Hannah back to the white piano while Stevie went to the black one. Brady sat next to Hannah on the far side of the bench. My heart and body were a mess while he helped her get situated. I wanted to kiss him for not leaving her on her own after he'd surprised her. I wanted to kiss him, period.

Stevie Nicks and my daughter sang and played together. Deep and sweet. Fitting together almost as well as Brady and she had. My tears could no longer be contained as the words and the beautiful, touching moment Brady had put together for Hannah overcame me.

I knew, somewhere up there, Grams was crying as much as I was.

There was a reason she'd kept Cormac from me. She'd known I didn't need him back then. She'd saved him for the right moment when Hannah and I both needed him the most. When he needed us as well. And we'd collided together into the perfect rainbow of hope and futures.

When they were done, the crowd went wild, stomping and cheering.

Brady took a mic, joining Hannah and Stevie Nicks at the front of the stage, and the crowd got quiet again.

"Okay, y'all, this is the last one of the night, and it's the perfect end to the opening of the Apple Jam Music Fest because it's a song about how we can all be better for each other. It reminds me of the woman who taught me and this little lady"—he tapped Hannah's top hat—"everything we know about music. We're grateful to the incredible Thomas Rhett for letting us sing it here tonight."

The three of them sang "Be a Light," and I wasn't the only one in tears. The entire audience was waving their phones, and water streamed down their faces. It was gorgeous, and so exactly everything Grams would have wanted.

When the song was over, the three of them took a bow, but as Brady turned to walk offstage, Hannah tugged at his hand. He leaned down to hear what she was telling him, and he looked surprised before shooting a look to the side of the stage in my direction.

When the crowd had calmed down a little, Hannah looked my way too and said into the microphone, "Hey, Mommy, Brady wants to know if you'll marry him."

My knees would have given out if Arlene hadn't been there to catch me. She was laughing. And I was a mess. Tears for my daughter. Tears for me. Joy scattered through every pore that used to hold so much grief.

"You better go out there and give him an answer," she said with a little push.

I shook my head. Onstage? In front of thousands in the field and millions online? No way. Then, I looked at Brady and Hannah, their wide smiles and faces full of expectation. How could I ever break their hearts? How could I disappoint them?

I swallowed hard, moving out of the shadows and into the bright lights that made me squint, hoping my dress was on straight and that my hair wasn't too wild. Hoping I didn't look like a ghost because I'd barely put on any makeup as we'd run out the door so we wouldn't be late.

By the time I joined them, Stevie Nicks had disappeared off the other side of the stage. Hannah pulled on my hand, jumping up and down. "Say yes, Mommy. Say yes."

I met Brady's eyes. "Is this what you want?" I

asked quietly, hoping the mic didn't pick it up.

"Do you have doubts?" We stared at each other. "I guess I'll have to fix that."

And he kissed me, swooping me into his arms, bending me over backward, demanding a response from my lips that came easily to me. A response that had my hands going to the back of his neck and my blood pounding in my veins.

The crowd was going wild, and I flushed a color I knew would be picked up on every screen around us. The noise was so loud I was sure it could be heard in the next town over. When he pulled me back upright, I brushed at the lipstick stuck to his lips and smiled.

"Yes. I think I just might need the full Brady O'Neil Experience for the rest of my life."

Then, he was kissing me again and dragging me offstage while Hannah skipped around us, and the crowd roared, and my life seemed to find a new beat. A new rhythm. A new song that would forever be us.

The perfect palette of dreams and rainbows.

♫ ♫ ♫

Not ready to let these characters go? *Read the FREE BONUS EPILOGUE* **checking in on Brady, Tristan, and Hannah a few years later.**

https://www.ljevansbooks.com/freeljbooks

Want to read Cassidy O'Neil's happily ever after story? Check out this excerpt from the next *ANCHOR NOVEL,* <u>***TRIPPED BY LOVE***</u>**.**

He's a broody bodyguard with secrets he can't share. She's a busy single mom with a restaurant

to run. They're just friends until a little white lie changes everything.

"What happened?" I demanded, wanting to know what had left such a huge scar on him. Had left him feeling like there could never be a way back to redemption.

"I don't want to tell you," he said. It was hushed and pained.

"Why?"

"Because you won't see me the same way," he said gently. "And I'm selfish enough to want to keep the stars in your eyes. I want you to look at me like you do right now. As if I'm the hero of the story. The knight who shows up on his steed whether the princess needs him or not. Even if it's just to pick up a sword and swing at her side."

I shook my head. "But the princess doesn't fall in love with the knight because he shows up, Marco," I said with all the confidence I could muster. "She falls in love because when the war is over, he takes off all the armor and bares himself to her. Because they share their dreams and their goals and their hopes and their fears. She might admire him on the battlefield, but she loves him when he's entwined himself into every part of her."

His finger fell to my face, crashing into my lips, running a thumb over the bottom one, and tugging at the top as if they were fascinating pieces of art instead of pieces of a body that everyone had. They were mundane really, but he seemed enthralled by mine.

TRIPPED BY LOVE is FREE in Kindle Unlimited.

https://geni.us/anchorlje

Did you miss the Anchor Novels from the beginning where Brady O'Neil first appears with his songwriting partner, Ava? Check out the completed interconnected series today:

THE ANCHOR NOVELS

Did you know that you can get the 1ˢᵗ **THREE ANCHOR NOVELS** as an eBook box set with a bonus novella? Don't miss any of these **slow-burn, sizzling, military romances** about true friends, real "family", and the dreams we reshape as we go through this wild ride called life. It includes: ***GUARDED DREAMS***, ***FORGED BY SACRIFICE***, ***AVENGED BY LOVE***, and ***THE HURRICANE*** — a bonus novella with the entire gang.

https://geni.us/anchorset

If you want to keep tabs on LJ' stories as she writes them and get exclusive content, giveaways, and more, then you might want to join her weekly newsletter, http://bit.ly/LJEmoGive. You can get all these FREE Flash Fiction stories when you sign up: https://www.ljevansbooks.com/freeljbooks.

Want even more teasers? Want even more chances at giveaways? Join her Facebook Group, **LJ's Music and Stories**, to chat with LJ on a daily basis.

Message from the Author

Thanks again for reading *Branded by a Song*. I hope you loved Brady and Tristan's story of love that I wove for you here. I hope the strength and resiliency of the characters, along with my mix of lyrics and story, burned a memory into your soul that you will think of every time you hear one of the songs from now on.

We talk about music, books, and just what it takes to get us through this wild ride called life a lot in my Facebook reader's group, LJ's Music & Stories. If you do nothing else with the links here, I hope you join that group. I hope that we can help *YOU* through your life in some small way.

Regardless if you join or not, I'd love for you to tell me what you thought of Brady, Tristan, and little Hannah by reaching out to me personally. I'd be honored if you took the time to leave a review on BookBub, Amazon, and / or Goodreads, but even more than that, I hope you enjoyed it enough to tell a friend.

If you still can't get enough (ha!), you could also sign up for my newsletter (http://bit.ly/LJEmoGive) where I write lyric-inspired scenes and share them with you on a regular basis. Plus, you'll get the details on releases and be entered into a giveaway each month for a chance at a signed paperback by yours truly 😊 .

Finally, I just wanted to say that my wish for you is a healthy and happy journey. May you live life resiliently. With hope and love. I truly hope to hear from you!

Thanks for reading my little story.

LJ EVANS

♫ *where music & stories collide* ♫

www.ljevansbooks.com

Facebook Group: LJ's Music & Stories

LJ Evans on BookBub, Amazon, and Goodreads

@ljevansbooks on Facebook, Twitter, Instagram, TikTok, and Pinterest

Acknowledgements

I'm so very grateful for every single person who has helped me on this book journey. If you're reading these words, you **ARE** one of those people. Even if all you did was read my words, it's important to me. I'm grateful to you for reading the stories that I can't help but write.

My child and my husband continue to not only listen for hours and hours about my stories and characters and this complicated book world, but also encourage me to not give up. Thank you for our life together and the love you give me.

My sister and my parents have always been my biggest defenders and fans. Thank you for celebrating with me and lifting me up when things get tough.

I don't know what I'd do without the people who I am lucky enough to have as part of my publishing team. Megan Keith at Designed with Grace, you are much more than my cover designer, you are a true friend and partner. Jenn at Jenn Lockwood Editing Services, I will forever be grateful that you read *Country Album* and then reached out to me in order to make it all it should be. Karen Hdrlicka, thank you for ensuring the final versions of my books are beautiful. To the entire group of beautiful humans in LJ's Music & Stories who love and support me there and throughout the Internet kingdom, I can't say how much I adore each and every one of you.

I've learned so much in this last year on how to START being a better human being for our future generations and about supporting marginalized communities. My growth has been encouraged by a beautiful group of human beings in Culture 101, and I'm so grateful to be able to talk safely and openly in that group. Thank you Korrie Kelley for starting it and making sure I always have the right sensitivity readers. Thank you to Rose at Griot Editing Services and the beautiful Katherine

Hong Kobzeff for helping shape the words in this book so they are accessible to more and a burden to less. Thank you to the inspiring author, Kathryn Nolan, for being my White accountability partner.

To all the bloggers who have shared my stories on your own time and your own dime, I cannot say enough. From my heart, I am full of love for Rachel at NovelMomma, Launa at Energy Rae, Candyce at The Book Dutchesses, Rebecca with Bex Book Revieuxs, Candice at Bibliophilecpt28, Menotah at Canadian Girl Book Blog, Tracy at The Pages In-Between, and the kind and generous Jenn at Jenns Book Vibes. Thank you for helping me accomplish my dreams and making me feel like a rock star.

To the other independent authors who have helped keep me sane, including Hannah Blake, Mika Jolie, Stephanie Rose, Annie Dyer, Kathryn Nolan, Mia Kayla, Amanda Johnson, Maria Luis, Erika Kelly, Jennifer Hanks, Kelsey Kingsley, Stefanie Torrez, and Jonella Brown, I have not enough words. Thank you, and virtual hugs to all of you.

Thank you to Emma Scott, Amy Harmon, and Jessica Park for not only inspiring me with your words but with your kindness and generosity. Every time I read your stories, I'm encouraged to make mine better. Your talent truly blows me away.

To all my ARC readers who have become incredible friends, thank you for encouraging me to continue this book adventure. To Leisa Ann, a great big thank you for naming the Apple Jam Music Fest and for always spreading the love for my books into the universe. To my social media peeps who make me feel like a rock star including Sarah, Judy, Amy, Michelle O., Dana, Michelle F., Zilpha, Lisa, Emily, Misty, Tara, Shonte, Stephanie, and Melissa, thank you for sticking with me through all my writing foibles.

I love you all!

About the Author

Award-winning author, LJ Evans, lives in Northern California with her husband, child, and the three terrors called cats. She's been writing, almost as a compulsion, since she was a little girl and will often pull the car over to write when a song lyric strikes her. A former first-grade teacher, she now spends her free time reading and writing, as well as binge-watching original shows like *Ted Lasso, Wednesday, Veronica Mars,* and *Stranger Things.*

If you ask her the one thing she won't do, it's pretty much anything that involves dirt—sports, gardening, or otherwise. But she loves to write about all of those things, and her first published heroine was pretty much involved with dirt on a daily basis, which is exactly why LJ loves fiction novels—the characters can be everything you're not and still make their way into your heart.

Her novels have won multiple awards including ***CHARMING AND THE CHERRY BLOSSOM,*** which was *Writer's Digest's* Self-Published E-book Romance of the Year in 2021. For more information about LJ, check out any of these sites:

www.ljevansbooks.com

FaceBook Group: LJ's Music & Stories

LJ Evans on Amazon, Bookbub, and Goodreads

@ljevansbooks on Facebook, Instagram, TikTok, and Pinterest

Books by LJ

Standalone

The Last One You Loved

A single-dad, small-town romance

He's a small-town sheriff with a secret that can unravel their worlds. She's an ER resident running from a costly mistake. Coming home will only mean heartache…unless they let forgiveness heal them both.

Charming and the Cherry Blossom

A contemporary romance with hints of magical realism

Today was a fairy tale…I inherited a fortune from a dad I never knew, and a charming guy asked me out. But like all fairy tales, mine has a dark side...and my happily ever after may disappear with the truth.

My Life as an Album Series

My Life as a Country Album — Cam's Story

A boy-next-door, small-town romance

Spirited athlete's Cam's diary-style, coming-of-age story about growing up loving the football hero next door. She vowed to love him forever. But when fate comes calling, will she ever find a heart to call home? Warning: Tears may fall.

My Life as a Pop Album — Mia & Derek

A rock-star, road-trip romance

Bookworm Mia is trying to put behind years of guilt when soulful musician, Derek Waters, strolls into her life and turns it upside down. Once he's seen her, Derek can't walk away unless Mia comes with him. But what will happen when their short time together ends?

My Life as a Rock Album — Seth & PJ

A second-chance, antihero romance

Growly, trash artist Seth Carmen knows he's better off alone. But when he finds and loses the love of his life, he sends her a series of love letters to try and win her back. Can he prove broken is beautiful?

My Life as a Mixtape — Lonnie & Wynn

A single-dad, rock-star romance

Lonnie's always seen relationships as a burden instead of a gift, and picking up the pieces his sister leaves behind is just one of the reasons. When Wynn enters his life just as her world is disintegrating, their mixed-up pasts give way to new beginnings neither saw coming.

My Life as a Holiday Album – 2nd Generation

A small-town romance

Come home for the holidays with this heartwarming, full-length standalone full of hidden secrets, true love, and the real meaning of family. Perfect for lovers of *Love Actually* and Hallmark movies, this sexy story twines the lives of six couples as they find their way to their happily ever after with the help of family and friends.

My Life as an Album Series Box Set

The 1st four Album series books + an exclusive novella

In the exclusive novella, *This Life with Cam*, Blake Abbott writes to Cam about just what it was like to grow up in the shadow of her relationship with Jake and just when he first fell for the little girl with the popsicle-stained lips. Can he show Cam that she isn't broken?

The Anchor Novels

Guarded Dreams — Eli & Ava

A grumpy-sunshine, military romance

Eli's chasing a dream that he's determined to succeed at, no matter the consequences. He isn't looking for love, but when the free-spirited singer, Ava, breezes into his world, he finds himself changing his tune.

Forged by Sacrifice — Mac & Georgie

A roommates-to-lovers, military romance

Mac is determined to change the world. A life in politics is his future. The dream Georgie once gave up is finally in reach—a law degree. When her family's past makes his future an impossibility, they have to decide just how much they're willing to sacrifice for love.

Avenged by Love — Truck & Jersey

A fake-marriage, military romance

Travis's focus is on his Coast Guard career and his brother's future. But once beautiful, comic-loving Jersey crashes into his world in desperate need of medical care, he offers a marriage of convenience to help. But what happens when convenience turns to love?

__Damaged Desires__ — Dani & Nash

A frenemy, military romance

Nash is all about honoring a promise to his dead brother, so accepting a challenge from the long-legged force of nature tempting him isn't in the cards. Not if he wants to keep his only remaining friend and stick to the code he grew up on. Several dares later, he has to decide whether to continue hiding in his past or face a new future.

__Branded by a Song__ — Brady & Tristan

A single-mom, rock-star romance

Brady's come home to help the sister he left behind and find inspiration for a new album. What he doesn't expect is to discover his muse in a woman who's completely off limits and lost in the past. Can he help her find the strength to sing a brand-new love song?

__Tripped by Love__ – Cassidy & Marco

A broody-bodyguard, single-mom romance

Cassidy is juggling her restaurant, a tiny human, and unrequited love. There's no time for her ex to try and derail her. Marco is determined to bury the feelings he has for his boss's sister, but that doesn't mean he's going to let the sniveling father of her child steamroll her. What happens when a little white lie changes everything?

__The Anchor Novels: The Military Bros Box Set__

The 1st three slow-burn romances + an exclusive novella

Guarded Dreams, Forged by Sacrifice, and *Avenged by Love* plus the novella, *The Hurricane*!

The Anchor Suspense Novels

__Unmasked Dreams__ — Violet & Dawson

A second-chance, age-gap romance

Violet and Dawson had a heart-stopping attraction they were compelled to deny. When they're tossed together again, it proves nothing has changed—except the lab she's built in the garage and the secrets he's keeping. When she stumbles into his dark world, Dawson is forced to break old promises to keep her safe. But when the swells subside, will their hearts still be intact?

<u>**Crossed by the Stars**</u> — Jada & Dax

A second-chance, forced-proximity romance

Family secrets meant Dax and Jada's teenaged romance was an impossibility. A decade later, the scars still remain, so neither is willing to give in to their tantalizing chemistry. But when a shadow creeps out of Jada's past, seeking retribution, it's Dax who shows up to protect her. And suddenly, it's hard to see a way out without permanent damage to their bodies and souls.

<u>**Disguised as Love**</u> — Cruz & Raisa

A chemistry-filled, enemies-to-lovers romance

Surly FBI agent, Cruz Malone, is determined to bring down the Leskov clan for good. If that means he has to arrest or bed the sexy blonde scientist of the family, so be it. Too bad Raisa has other ideas. There's no way she's just going to sit back and let the infuriating agent dismantle her world…or her heart.

The Painted Daisies

Interconnected, slow-burn romances with an all-female rock band, the alpha heroes who steal their hearts, and suspense that'll leave you breathless. Each story has its own HEA.

<u>Sweet Memory</u>

An opposite-side-of-the-tracks, second-chance romance.

Trouble—that's what her sister calls him. But she can't resist, not even when his past threatens her world.

<u>Green Jewel</u>

An enemies-to-lovers, single-dad romance.

He did it. She'll prove it. Her body's reaction to him be damned.

<u>Cherry Brandy</u>

An opposites-attract, forbidden romance.

Being on the run with only one bed is no excuse to touch her…until touching is the only choice.

<u>Blue Marguerite</u>

A Hollywood-celebrity, frenemy romance.

She may have to work with him to save her sister, but he'll never have her body or heart again.

Royal Haze

An antihero, secret-society romance.

He was ready to torture, steal, and kill to defend the world he believed in. What he wasn't prepared for…was her.

Free Stories

https://www.ljevansbooks.com/freeljbooks

Perfectly Fine – FREE with newsletter signup

A Hollywood, second-chance romance

He's a charming, A-list actor at the top of his game. She's a determined, small-town screenwriter hoping for a deal. They form an unexpected connection until heartbreak ruins their future.

Rumor – FREE with newsletter signup

A small-town, rock-star romance

There's only one thing rock star Chase Legend needs to ring in the new year, and that's to know what Reyna Rossi tastes like. After ten years, there's no way he's letting her escape the night without their souls touching. Reyna has other plans. After all, she doesn't need the entire town wagging their tongues about her any more than they already do.

Love Ain't – FREE with newsletter signup

A friends-to-lovers, cowboy romance

Reese knows her best friend and rodeo king, Dalton Abbott, is never going to fall in love, get married, and have kids. He's left so many broken hearts behind there's gotta be a museum full of them somewhere. So, when he gives her a look from under the brim of his hat, promising both jagged relief and pain, she isn't giving in.

The Long Con – FREE with newsletter signup

A sexy, antihero romance

Adler is after one thing: the next big payday. Then, Brielle sways into his world with her own game in play, and those aquamarine-colored eyes almost make him forget his number-one rule. But she'll learn…love isn't a con he's interested in.

The Light Princess – FREE with newsletter signup

An old-fashioned fairy tale

A princess who glows with a magical light, a kingdom at war, and a kiss that changes the world.